UNDER GROUND

S. L. Grey is a collaboration between Sarah Lotz and Louis Greenberg. Sarah is a novelist and screenwriter and die-hard zombie fanatic. She writes crime novels and thrillers under her own name, and as Lily Herne she and her daughter Savannah Lotz write the Deadlands series of zombie novels for young adults. Louis is a Johannesburg-based fiction writer and editor. He was a bookseller for several years, and has a Master's degree in vampire fiction and a doctorate on post-religious apocalyptic fiction.

By S. L. Grey

The Mall

The Ward

The New Girl

Under Ground

9030 00004 9204 2

UNDER GROUND

S. L. GREY

PAN BOOKS

First published 2015 by Macmillan

This edition published in paperback 2016 by Pan Books
an imprint of Pan Macmillan
20 New Wharf Road, London N1 9RR
Associated companies throughout the world
www.panmacmillan.com

ISBN 978-1-4472-6645-7

1 3 5 7 9 8 6 4 2

A CIP catalogue record for this book is available from the British Library.

Printed and bound by CPI Group (UK) Ltd, Croydon, CR0 4YY

Visit **www.panmacmillan.com** to read more about all our books
and to buy them. You will also find features, author interviews and
news of any author events, and you can sign up for e-newsletters
so that you're always first to hear about our new releases.

UNDER GROUND

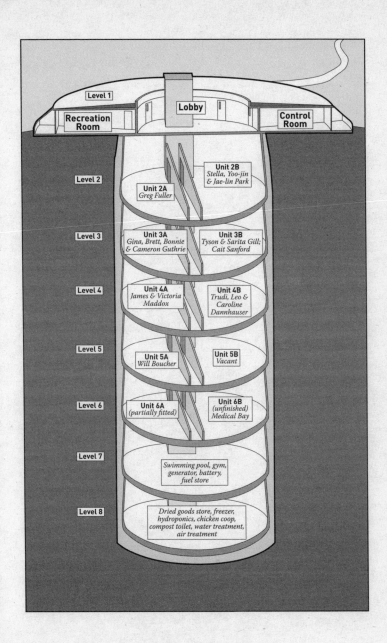

PLAN OF THE SANCTUM

PROLOGUE

Sarita opens her eyes, but still she can't see. She sits up, pats her hand around her pillow for her toys, and finds Strawb, but Simba's not there. She doesn't want to make a noise, wake up Daddy, but she has to find Simba.

When she pulls back the comforter and Simba's still not there, she starts to cry. But softly. She has to work this out, think like a big girl. Daddy will be mad if she wakes him up about this.

Maybe Caity will help her. Sarita glances at the clock: 3:17 a.m. That's too early. Caity says try not to wake her until the first number is 6. But she can if it's an emergency, of course.

Is this an emergency?

Daddy wouldn't think so. It'll turn up, he always says.

She'll think like a big girl. Caity always says, think of where you saw it last. Where did you last have it? It wasn't at story time or bath time or TV time or supper time. It was before that, when Caity took her down to the swimming pool. Simba and Strawb were lying under the plastic palm tree in the swimming pool room. She must be there. She'll go and find Simba herself. Caity and Daddy will be proud of her.

She checks in the top drawer of the bedside table where

she put her photo album, the one with the pictures of Mommy in. That's still there. Sarita slips out of bed and peeks into Caity's room. The kitchen light is on and she can see Caity sprawled in her bed, just a single sheet twisted over her. When she looks into Daddy's room, he's not in his bed. She'd better hurry. She doesn't want him to be mad. It's easy to walk quietly in this apartment because the carpets are thick and the floor is hard and solid, not like the creaky, thumpy wooden floors at home.

She goes out the front door of the apartment and closes it softly behind her. She wants to do this like a big girl. She wants them to be proud. The lights come on in the corridor like magic. She watches the red and black patterns in the carpet as she walks, feeling the softness of it on her bare feet.

There are just wooden boards where the elevator should be, with a broken stripe of yellow tape hanging on one side, so she pushes through the door to the stairwell. The door bangs behind her and she has to jump around and wave her arms to make the lights switch on. The bare floor here feels cold and gritty on her feet, not soft like the carpets. She's careful not to rub her arms on the metal banisters so that she doesn't make her PJs dirty. Her breathing sounds louder in here and her footsteps echo.

'Waa!' she says, not too loud, but so that she can hear the funny ringing sound her voice makes on the stairs. She goes down and down, the magic lights following her like they should.

When she thinks she's on the right level for the pool, she pushes out of the stairwell door and looks around. This floor doesn't look like it did earlier. Unlike the bright pool area, the passage is lit only in dull orange. There's a doorway covered with a plastic sheet, and a flickering light coming from deep inside. She peers through the plastic. Maybe it's Simba, having a dance party. Simba needs to go to bed now, or else he'll be tired. Sarita pushes aside the plastic and tiptoes through.

Now she's remembering some of those scarier stories. The one about the monsters who are really scared of a mouse. The one about the beastie in the dark room whose shining eyes turned out to be nothing: just kittens.

But she doesn't want to think about those stories. Actually she'd rather be back in her bed. She thinks of coming back with Caity in the morning, but the thought of going back upstairs without Simba makes her worried. She'll pick up Simba and come straight back.

Caity says Mommy's always watching over her.

She walks through the cold room, following the flashing light past some shiny metal closets. With a push of will she rounds the next corner to a bathroom. It's a flashlight flickering on the floor. It switches off for a minute, and Sarita wants to run away, but she doesn't know where. She's standing in the doorway, not sure how to move.

When the light comes on again, she sees something crumpled next to the bathtub. It looks like a pile of clothes and boots. She takes two more steps forward. No, it looks more like a person sleeping there. And as she approaches, the flashlight turns on and off again, and she sees it's a man wearing a red-checked jacket. She's relieved that someone else is here. Maybe this man can help her fetch Simba.

But why's he sleeping in this bathroom?

'Hello?' Sarita says.

The man doesn't answer. He doesn't move.

'Are you sleeping? Hi, Mister . . .'

He's still not answering. She comes in the last couple of

steps to where he's lying. There's a mess of dark liquid around his head, paint maybe or ketchup. Something stinks. Like pee. Like raw meat.

'Hello?'

Sarita doesn't know what to do. She feels something sliding under her toes. She looks down. The sticky trickle has reached her feet.

The flashlight flicks off, leaving her in darkness.

Sarita screams, a sound that makes the still air shatter.

1
GINA

All morning I've been cleaning the condo, wiping down every surface with disinfectant, vacuuming the carpets and the upholstery and the purposeless drapes. There're no windows down here, no natural light. Behind the curtains are just screens with moving photos: a forest scene in one frame, a snowy mountain, a tropical beach right next to it. They make me feel nauseous.

And built-in closets everywhere.

Thick, crisp sheets and built-in closets. This condo is so luxurious, I should feel happy, like we're on some sort of dream vacation, but I'm hating it already. I wish we could just go back home. I wish Daddy had never bought this place.

Momma changed when we moved out of town and into the trailer on Mr Harber's farm. I never really understood why we had to go, but I knew it had something to do with Brett being suspended from school again. And Momma was mad when she found out that Daddy had spent her inheritance on this place instead of the family home she'd always dreamed of. 'What's the point of a house we can only use when it's the end of the world?' I remember her saying. She was crying. 'What about now, Cam? What about now?' She hardly ever raised her voice to Daddy, and he didn't take kindly to it. But she knew just as well as Daddy that life couldn't stay the same, and after that she covered up every complaint with prayers.

She looked so tired when we arrived at The Sanctum that I told her I'd clean the place up and she should just rest. 'You sure, hon?' she asked as she lay back and pulled up the coverlet. 'You'll be fine out there with *him*?' I told her I'd be fine. 'You just come to me if you get afraid. Alright?'

'Sure, Momma.'

I finish washing and drying all the dishes – brand-new sets of plates, glasses, mugs, thick steel cookware, shining stainless steel cutlery – and wipe down the cabinets' shelves before I replace them.

'Don't forget the door handles, Gina,' Daddy says. 'We've got to make this place shipshape. Don't want to be living in here with some Mexican builder's cooties, do we?' He says it like that to include me, to make it some sort of joke we can share, and although he's treating me like a kid I appreciate the gesture. We've got to be a team in here, even more than we were up on the lot.

'Sure don't, Daddy.'

But Daddy and Brett don't do anything to help me, just sit drinking coffee and eating sandwiches at the breakfast bar, talking about politics and football.

'You think we're going to be back in time for the season, Dad?' Brett asks. He's jiggling his knee, an M1911 on the counter in front of him, still antsy from when Mr Fuller asked us to hand over our guns. Daddy agreed to let Mr Fuller put them in the safe later when we're settled, but I can't see Brett going along with that without a fight. I stare at him for a moment, willing him to look at me, like I have for the past two years, wishing he'd remember who I am – his twin sister – despite how he's changed, despite what happened two years ago. We used to never be apart, we used to speak in each other's minds. But he doesn't turn his face. 'They were into trials already, but maybe . . .'

Daddy looks at Brett and frowns. He breathes a lot before he says, 'I'm not sure there's gonna be a season, son. It's not going to be the same when we get back – this isn't just some flu. Things are gonna shift. We can expect a breakdown in social order in the next couple of weeks – looting, rioting, destruction. Soon there'll be martial law. There'll be a significant death toll that's going to affect even basic services. We're gonna have to make a new life up there when we're done here.' Daddy's voice grows deeper and louder, like it does when he's talking politics with his friends. 'But we'll sit it out, and be strong and ready to take our place in the new order.' Brett's nodding along. 'Things are gonna get a lot worse before they get better. But they will get better.'

'It's the Chinks' fault,' Brett says. 'They're getting what they deserve.'

'Yeah. But you see how fast the virus is spreading into the US. It's a malicious threat, militarized. It's going to hit, and it's going to hit us big. Worse than there. It was aimed at us.'

'But how come their own people are dying, Daddy?' I venture, as politely as possible so that he knows I'm not debating.

Daddy shrugs. 'Some foul-up? They dropped a vial or something?'

'I bet they experiment on their own,' Brett says. 'Chinks'd do shit like that, Dad.' Like he's an expert on the world situation. I've noticed lately how Brett's taken to calling Daddy *Dad*. And debating with him like he's some friend down at the gun range.

Daddy waits for him to finish. 'Fact remains, it'll be months before there's a cure. This is what we've been waiting for. All this hasn't been for nothing.' He sweeps his hand in the air in front of him.

I want to ask Daddy why he and Brett had to shoot the horses, but I don't. I know he'll yell at me. I know what he'd say anyway. *You want them to starve to death, Gina, or be killed for food while we're gone? You want that to be on your conscience?*

I step up onto the short kitchen ladder to put a clean batch of dinner plates into the cabinet above the stove. I lean on the cabinet door as I step up, just lightly, honestly not more than a touch, and the top hinge comes swinging free. The door cracks me on the head and I jerk away, and the top plate slides off the pile and smashes against the stone counter with an almighty crash. I just about manage to shove the rest of the plates onto the shelf before I stumble off the ladder. I'm immediately down and collecting the pieces before Daddy even starts roaring at me.

'Be careful, girl!' he bellows. He comes around and inspects the cabinet door. 'Look at this now!'

'I'm sorry,' I say, making myself small. I know he was just shocked by the noise. His temper will die down as quick as it flared, but I just need to keep out of range until it does.

Momma comes out of the bedroom, glances at Brett and Daddy before she hurries over to me. 'What have you done?'

I say nothing. *Thanks for your support, Momma.* From my crouch on the floor, I look across at Brett, where he's still sitting calm on his high stool. Not so long ago, he would have helped me out. Now, he looks away.

*

Later, Daddy and Brett have gone up to inspect the perimeter with Mr Fuller. I can tell that Daddy's very proud that we were the first to arrive. He says preparation is half the battle won. Momma's in her room, still napping. Lunch is made and everything's cleaned up. Daddy's fixed the cabinet with a screwdriver. I didn't want to tell him about the rat droppings I saw when I was cleaning the tops of the cabinets. He'd find some way to blame me.

I still can't keep the thought of the horses out of my mind: Reggie's great big eyes, and Dwight's dapple flanks like choc chip ice cream. To distract myself, I flip through the Welcome brochure lying on the breakfast bar again. 'Welcome to The Sanctum! Your own luxury survival condo comes with pure peace of mind!' When we arrived yesterday, Mr Fuller went on about The Sanctum being self-sustaining, told us about the vegetables they grow down here under lights and how there's even a compost toilet in the basement that goes to feed the produce. It sounds filthy to me, but I guess we use cow dung on our plants back home, so . . . There's even a chicken pen down here, and Mr Fuller said I could help take care of them. I haven't asked Daddy yet, but I wonder if he'd let me. That would give me an excuse to get out of the condo. It's not fair that just because Brett's a boy, he can leave any time, go where he likes, and I have to ask permission. Brett did say he'd take me to see the pool later, but why should I wait that long? If Momma wakes up, she can look after herself a minute.

Before I lose my nerve, I open the condo's front door a crack – it doesn't squeak on its hinges like the one in the trailer – and step out into the pure darkness of the hallway. You'd never believe it's lunchtime. It's always night in The

9

Sanctum. As I close the door and the motion sensors pick me up, the lights flip on.

I slide my thumb onto the locking panel outside the door to test it. The door clicks and it gives when I push against it, so at least I know I can get back in if I need to.

A scuffling sound makes me pause. 'Hello?' I whisper.

I hold my breath. Hear nothing but the suck of the air-con. It's colder out here in the corridor than in the condo. Goosebumps rise on my arms – I should have brought a sweater.

Our condo is on level three – the swimming pool and the gym are down on level seven. I can't take the boarded-up elevator so I tiptoe towards the stairwell. The lights flick on as I open the door and step onto the landing. My feet are cold on the bare concrete as I walk down. The floor below us has a doorway identical to the one above. I hurry down to level six, where there's supposed to be another condo and a medical suite, but Mr Fuller says they haven't got to finishing them yet. I hesitate while I wait for the next motion sensor to wash out the blackness below.

I open the level six door a crack and peer out into the corridor. The paint stops halfway to the ceiling and the doors are covered in thick plastic. A clanging sound makes me jump and I step back into the stairwell, letting the door squeak closed. It sounded like it came from behind the plastic sheeting, but that can't be right. Mr Fuller said we were the only ones here.

2
JAE

Time to die, bitch.

Jae ducks behind a pillar, melting into the shadows. The warlock is finally out of defensive cooldowns, and this could be his only chance. He prepares to stun her with a kidney shot, but then the arena flips back to the login page and he finds himself staring stupidly at a 'You have been disconnected from the server' message. *'Shitballs!'*

'Jae!' His mom glares at him from behind the kitchen counter. 'You know how I feel about that gangster language.'

She doesn't usually get on his case like this. 'Sorry, Moms, but this wi-fi is seriously lagging. I thought this place was supposed to be equipped with long-range.' He can't even get a signal in his bedroom; he's been forced to set up on the breakfast bar, right under his folks' feet.

His mom sighs. 'That's no excuse for bad language. You'll damage your eyes if you don't have a break from that game. It's all you've done since we arrived.'

'My eyes are fine, Moms. Twenty-twenty vision and all that.'

'Greg said there are a couple of teenagers here. Why don't you see if you can find them?'

'What if they're dicks?'

'Jae!'

His dad, who's helping Moms unpack the cooler bag, tips him a wink.

'I saw that, Yoo-jin,' his mom tuts, but she's smiling.

Dad takes her hand and kisses it. PDA overload as usual. Jae used to kind of like their constant displays of affection, but back when he was in sixth grade, in the days when Dad would actually leave their apartment more than once a month, he'd caught a senior sniggering at his parents and overheard the bastard saying, 'Check out Moby Dick and Jackie Chan getting it on over there.' His face gets hot whenever he thinks about that.

As he logs back into the game, his stomach hitches. Scruffy is online. *Finally*. He's been building up the courage to ask her if she wants to Skype or chat over Viber, but he can't quite make the jump yet. He taps in a message: **<Where you been, Scruff? You get my message last night?>**

<Hey Jae. Been sleeping. You cool?>

<Define cool>

<Heard it's spread to the States. I've been worried about you>

Jae feels a flush of warmth. **<Thanx. Word is, it could reach the East Coast soon>**

<You seen the pics of the body bags in Asia? Total mindfuck ☹>

<I saw them> This isn't entirely true. Jae only glanced at the images on CNN last night, and he's been avoiding Reddit. He hasn't wanted to look. It's not like he has any relatives left in Korea – Dad's folks died years ago, after the family emigrated to Canada and Dad hooked up with Moms – but the thought of all those people dying over there still makes him hollow inside.

<So . . . what's the bunker place like?>

<It's ok>

<Don't be such a noob! Need more!>

<Imagine a high-end apartment block buried underground. That's basically it>

<MORE DETAILS>

<Okaaaay . . . You can't see anything from outside – just the entrance hatch that looks like a safe door (lame) and a wind turbine. LED screens instead of windows (lame), submarine-style doors (ultra lame), biometric locking system (fairly cool), wannabe high-end decor. Oh yeah, there's a rec room, a gym and a pool, haven't checked that out yet. You should see the control room. Wall-to-wall CCTV screens, real paranoid security shit. Like who's going to bother breaking in here? It's miles from civilization. Middle of Maine. Nothing but forests and fields. Kinda like being in Middle Earth or somewhere LOL> He hesitates, then deletes the LOL. Like a lot of gamers he knows, Scruff is a real grammar Nazi and gets weird about text-speak and bad spelling.

<How deep underground are you?>

<50 feet, something like that>

<Can you send me pics?>

<Yeah sure. Watch this space>

<How long will you have to stay there?>

<No idea. The folks are freaked about it all, although they're trying to pretend we're on vacation>

<Met any other residents?>

<There's only one other family here so far. Greg (guy who runs this place) says more are on the way. Big whoop. They'll all be paranoid survivor types>

<RICH paranoid survivor types>

Like Dad, Jae thinks, with a flush of shame at his disloyalty. When he'd overheard his father tentatively suggesting to Moms that they splurge a million and a half big ones on a luxury survival condo in Maine, Jae assumed he'd been joking. Sure, his dad's anxiety about what he called 'the inexorable breakdown of Western society' had been growing over the last few years, but Jae had thought of it as another one of his dad's quirks and anxieties, like the fact that he rarely left the apartment unless he had to. Or the panic room he'd installed behind the spare room last year, and the store-room filled with canned goods that Jae and Moms jokingly call the 'holocaust shed'. Moms hadn't laughed, though. She hadn't reined his dad in. Lately, Jae's been coming to the conclusion that his parents' relationship isn't entirely healthy. His mom lets Dad's survivor shit slide and he doesn't nag her about her Sara Lee cherry cheesecake habit, despite what it's doing to her health. He changes the subject: **<What's happening your side Scruffs?>**

The wi-fi is lagging again and it's almost twenty seconds before Scruffy's next message appears: **<No cases in the UK yet. But they've started showing these adverts about what to do if you or any of your relatives get sick. Creepy. School might shut for a while, so yay>**

Jae's seen the pics of Scruffy's school on Facebook – some high-end girls-only place just outside London. He knows it's dumb, but he has this dream about visiting her after he finishes his senior year. He'll have to lose a couple of pounds first of course – his profile pic is from last year, before his jowls started to get flabby – but he has this image of driving up to her school gates on some fucking cool motorbike and taking her away with him. They could tour Europe. Explore Paris together maybe. That would be cool.

<Wait. Gotta go>

Scruffy goes offline before he can reply. He calls up his Dropbox journal and scans yesterday's entry. Looking back on what he was thinking or doing the day before is always a bit disturbing. Sometimes he goes into a trance when he's writing – can't even recall what he's put down. Yesterday's is sketchy, basically just two paragraphs discussing Scruffy's Arena rating, nothing about what's going on in real life. He'll update it later; he's not in the mood right now. Besides, he's not sure it's sunk in yet. Sure, he's seen the images on TV, and the prospect of those scenes from Seoul and Tokyo happening here frightens him, but outside, at least while they were driving here, it was just a normal fall day. No dead bodies in the streets. Who knows how serious it will become? It may not even spread this far. Scruffy still hasn't come back online and he doesn't feel like logging into the game only to get disconnected again. What the hell. Maybe he should head to the rec room and see if the signal's better there.

He slides the Lenovo into his backpack. 'Okay, folks, you win. I'm out of here.'

His mom gives him a frayed smile. Her face is blotched and sweaty – the long drive from Boston has wiped her out. For someone in the medical profession, she's pretty lax about her own health; she hasn't looked a hundred per cent for a while now and she must have put on twenty pounds this year.

'Don't get lost,' his dad says as Jae heads out the door. 'It's a big place.' Jae can tell that his dad is hiding his disappointment with The Sanctum. It's nowhere near as slick as the website promised.

The motion sensors kick in and the light blinks on a second after he steps into the hallway. It freaks him out that if the electricity died they'd be in pure, pitch darkness. He digs out his iPhone, scrolls through to an old Azealia Banks track, and mouthing the words to '212', he pads up the stairwell. The place stinks of paint and fresh concrete, which always smells like piss to Jae.

He enters the rec room cautiously, breathing with relief when he sees it's empty. It reminds him of the communal area in a mid-range hotel: interlocking couches, long backlit bar, the image of a waterfall in motion projected onto one wall. According to the brochure, along with the high ceilings, fake LED windows and carefully modulated artificial light, images like this are supposed to help eradicate claustrophobia. All it does for Jae is make him want to pee.

He heads for the TV and entertainment area; the Lenovo's juice is running low and if he's going to do some raiding, he'll need to recharge. Someone's left the TV on. The sound is off, but the Fox News rolling banner blares: 'Several Confirmed AOBA cases in LA, San Francisco and Seattle. WHO Declares AOBA Virus Outbreak Public Health Emergency and Possibly "Beyond Control". Public Urged to Stay at Home.' Images flip onto the screen: men and women wearing white overalls and breathing masks swarming into a plane; a child screaming as he's dragged out of a car.

Jae jumps as he hears a voice behind him. Greg's stepping through the control-room door, barking into a satellite phone. 'You said the parts would be in last week. I was relying . . .' His voice trails away as he catches sight of Jae. 'I'll call you back.'

Greg slaps a grin on his face, but Jae isn't fooled. He was in the middle of a heavy conversation. 'Hey, Jae. Settling in okay?'

'Sure.'

Greg glances at the screen. 'Looks like it's gonna get really bad.' Jae shrugs. All the paranoid prepper nuts – yes, including his dad – have been proven right: the Big Event they've been preparing for has finally happened. 'You've come to the right place, Jae,' Greg continues. 'Got nothing to worry about in here.' A note of insincerity has crept into Greg's voice, as if he doesn't quite believe what he's saying. 'You met the Guthrie kids yet?'

'Nope.'

'Gonna be great for you to hang out with someone your own age. They're good kids, you'll like them.'

'Awesome.'

There's a slightly awkward pause and Jae steels himself for more adult-trying-to-connect-with-a-teenager conversation.

Greg glances at his phone. 'You checked out the pool yet?'

'No.'

'You should check it out.'

'Okay.' He's not really in the mood to slog down eight flights of stairs or whatever – when Greg showed them to their condo, he'd broken the news that the elevator wasn't yet operational – but he can take a hint. Greg gives him a thumbs-up as he heads out the door towards the stairwell.

The air gets colder the lower he goes, and he tries not to think about what would happen if an earthquake hit and all this concrete splatted on top of him.

He pauses to take a pic of a doorway covered in plastic sheeting, types in a message: **<Check it out Scruff. I'm in a RL version of Asylum>**

Shit. No signal. He'll have to send it later.

And just for a moment, alone here in this concrete box, a shard of real panic lodges in him. He picks up his pace and he's slightly out of breath when he reaches level seven. He pushes the door open with his shoulder, slips into an open-plan area, a plunge pool in its centre, a motley collection of gym equipment scattered around it. A pair of kids – a girl with long black hair, and a stocky guy – are hanging out in the small basketball square in the far corner. They stop talking as the door slams behind him. Jae's gut curls tight. He's not socially inept or anything, but meeting new people always makes him anxious. He reckons it's something he's inherited from his dad.

'Hi,' the girl says. She's cute. Slender, couple of inches shorter than he is. She's dressed in the sort of outfit the hipsters at his school would kill for – only Jae's certain she's wearing that Mickey Mouse tee and those mom jeans without any irony. The guy's a different matter. He looks older, crew-cut hair, snub nose, muscles on his muscles.

'Hey,' Jae says.

The guy looks Jae up and down expressionlessly, then grabs a basketball out of the bin.

The girl wipes her hands on her jeans. 'Have you just arrived?'

'Couple of hours ago.'

'Hi. I'm Gina Guthrie. This is my brother, Brett.'

Brett. The guy looks like a Brett. Or a Butch. 'I'm Jae-lin. But you can call me Jae.' The girl nods, scuffs a shoe across the floor. Jae reaches for something to say. 'When did you guys get here?'

'Yesterday.'

'Cool. What do you think about this place?'

Gina fidgets with her hair and shrugs. 'It's okay.'

'Yeah, right. You can't stop talking about how great it is. You think it's like the Howard Johnson,' Brett says.

'I do not!' Gina says. 'It's just so . . . new.'

'Most hotels I've been to have windows. And rooftops,' Jae says, hoping he doesn't sound like a dork.

Brett snorts. 'Where you from, Jae-Jae?'

'Vancouver. But we moved to Boston last year.'

18

Brett begins bouncing the basketball. 'No, I mean where are you from *originally*?'

Jae can't tell if the guy is just yanking his chain or is genuinely ignorant. 'Like I said. Canada.'

'You Chinese?'

Jae makes his face go blank. *Jesus. Is this guy for real?* He's never really experienced any hardcore racism, just the usual shit, some trolling on the *World of Warcraft* boards, but that he can handle. 'My dad was born in Korea.'

The guy throws at the hoop, and Jae smiles inside when it goes wide.

'Lots of people dying over there.'

'I know.' *Time to go.* 'It was cool to meet you. I'd better head back and—'

'Aw, don't be like that, Jae-Jae,' Brett smirks. 'Stick around, shoot some hoops with us.' Brett tries for another shot, misses again.

'I'm cool. Thanks.'

'What, you scared you'll lose?'

Jae hears the door opening behind him, turns to see a man entering the room. 'Gina, it's time for—' The guy stops short when he sees Jae. There's no way he can be anyone except Guthrie Senior. Same hard blue eyes. Same don't-fuck-with-me attitude. Combats. One of those survival knives at his hip as if he thinks he's Walker Texas Ranger or something.

Gina picks at her jeans. 'Daddy, this is Jae. His family arrived today.'

'That so.'

'Nice to meet you,' Jae says.

Guthrie Senior's eyes laser into his. 'What condo you in, son?'

'2B.'

'That one of the three-bedroom units?'

'I guess.' Jae has to will himself not to drop his gaze.

Finally, Guthrie turns back to Gina. 'Gina, go on back to the condo.'

'But, Daddy, you said I could—'

'Go on, now.'

She shoots a shy glance at Jae and blushes. A real blush, pink flooding her cheeks. Guthrie Senior gives Jae a curt nod and follows her out.

The last thing Jae wants is to be left with Psycho Boy, but if he leaves immediately he'll look like a total wimp. They're going to be stuck down here together for who knows how long; he's got to try and connect with him on some level. Maybe Brett's psychoness is just some kind of asshole shtick. 'So, Brett. Where do you—'

'Catch!' Brett suddenly throws the ball at Jae's head with full force. Jae tries to duck but it thwoks off his nose, and he has to scramble to stop his laptop case from hitting the floor. Pain blossoms and he sniffs back blood.

'What did you do that for?'

Brett puts on an innocent expression. 'Hey, I told you to catch it.'

There's no way he can take this guy on physically. Brett has fifty pounds on him. For the first time, Jae regrets giving up his ninjutsu classes (bad enough that he's a gamer, he didn't want to be the total Asian kid cliché). 'Whatever, dude,' Jae mumbles. A dribble of blood trails over his top lip. Head down, he stalks towards the door, Brett's laughter following him out.

This is just the start of it. He just knows it.

3

CAIT

The tailback on the airport approach road tells us some-thing's wrong. Tyson's drumming his fingers on the steering wheel and sighing, just in case I haven't noticed he's pissed off. As if this is my fault.

I was quite happy to take a taxi, but Sarita begged to come to the airport to see me off. So now I'm subjected to more of Tyson's sulking.

The traffic jam inches forward and he launches off, making an ill-tempered game out of narrowly missing the Cadillac ahead of us. The bottle-blond man in front eyes him from his rear-view mirror.

At last we get into the terminal complex and see the electronic signs flashing 'All Flights Delayed'.

'All flights?' I say. 'But I checked this morning. The connection to JFK was still on. They'd only cancelled flights from the West Coast.'

'Damn it!' Tyson says.

Sarita looks up, startled, and I pat her arm, as if that will neutralize his negative energy. But I'm sick inside. I just want to go home.

'F–' Tyson checks himself. He takes a deep breath but that doesn't reduce the colour in his face, and to make matters worse, it's too late to turn around. We're trapped in a one-way jam till we pass the terminal building and get out the other side. As we pass the doors of the terminal, I catch a glimpse of a throng of people in the concourse, the boards a throbbing mess of red like a migraine. I power down my window and hail one of the security guards strolling along the drop-and-go. 'Excuse me. Excuse me.' He turns to the car, locates me in the back seat and raises his chin.

'Is it true? That all flights are grounded?' I ask. 'I had a connection to JFK. It was supposed to be on schedule,' I say, as if a rational explanation will encourage this man to change the facts. Lately they're always doing this, grounding flights at the slightest threat. Surely they can just let me through. I just want to go home. I won't be any trouble to anyone.

He looks away, along the busy entranceway. 'All air traffic, ma'am.' He scans the crowd of bottlenecked cars and passengers, alert, puffed-up.

I try to catch Tyson's eye in the rear-view mirror, but he's busy looking at his phone. The car in front moves forward and Tyson jerks ahead into the gap without looking ahead of him.

'So you're not leaving, Caity?' Sarita says.

'Maybe not today.' I try to smile at her, but a rock has sunk in my chest. Instead of entertaining the growing panic, I focus on getting the airline's number from my crappy phone's browser. Meanwhile, Tyson's clenching his jaw as we crawl behind a goods truck onto Post Road. When I eventually do get through, there's an automated response, a computerized message monotoning, 'Please leave a message, we'll get back to you.' But the beep never comes.

Tyson overtakes on a solid line and heads north to the 95, intoning something under his breath. I manage to get on the airline's site and confirm that the flight from JFK to Johannesburg is also delayed. 'Indefinite'. My skin burns as I allow the flush of panic to hit me. I can't actually believe it. I've missed my flight and now there's some deadly virus coming our way. They always say Africa's full of crime and violence and disease but there's nowhere else I'd feel safer right now than home, and it suddenly seems so bloody far away.

I should have listened to my friends when they laughed at me. '*Au pairing?* Are you serious? Nuh-uh, that's not for you, Cait'. I should have listened, although to my surprise, it did actually suit me better than I thought. But my six months is up now and it's time to get back to my life. Tyson's been difficult to work for – snappy, constantly working, no time for his daughter's needs or even to mourn for his wife – but I've really formed a bond with Sarita. I have felt guilty, like I'll be abandoning her when I go home, but I know Tyson will replace me with someone better qualified to look after her.

'Let's play Ninja Queens,' Sarita says.

'Sure, let's.'

When Tyson carries on past the 195 interchange, I look up. 'You missed the turn-off'. He might be taking us straight to his office, expecting me to entertain Sarita or take her home myself. Is this what it's come to? We've barely spoken since I gave my notice last week, and I've been dealing with his passive aggression ever since. I know he must be bitter that he has to go through the mission of finding another nanny, but I've got my own issues to deal with. 'You're taking us home, right?'

But he only hisses, 'Please, Cait.'

We pass the Dunkin' Donuts Center – I took Sarita to see *Disney on Ice* there, and yeah, we had doughnuts – which means we're not actually heading downtown. 'What are you doing, Tyson? Come on. Take us home.'

But he just carries on straight, stuck in the fast lane, tail-gating a ponytailed guy in a pickup. 'Tyson, please turn the car around. This is ridiculous.' I grab his arm from between the seats.

'Don't,' Tyson snaps.

Sarita's eyes widen and she starts to cry. I take her hand in mine, and it's a real effort to give her a reassuring smile. 'It would be nice if your daddy let us know where we're going, hey?'

'Yeah,' she says, sniffling. 'Let us know, Daddy.'

'We're, uh, going to Gran-Gran's, okay?' he says.

'What? You just decided to do this now?'

He sighs. 'Yeah. Look, they've cancelled the flights for a reason. We'll be safer out of the city.'

'You think it's that bad? You don't think everyone's over-reacting?'

'Haven't you been watching the news, Cait?'

I'd been packing last night, so no. But I'd caught a seg-ment on *Good Morning America* yesterday, and that was all about the outbreak in Asia. Then they cancelled the flights across the Pacific, but I thought that was just supposed to be a precautionary measure. I didn't think there was an imme-diate threat here. 'But how will I catch my flight?'

'You saw for yourself, the planes are grounded.'

'But it might be reinstated.'

'Then I'll bring you back.' He sighs again. 'Look, I know it seems like a snap decision, but I really think it's for the best.' He's softened his voice and I sit back, slightly mollified.

'What about Sarita's clothes?'

'Don't worry about that.'

It's only several miles later, when we're out in the sticks, passing Attleboro and Manchester Pond that he seems to ease up a little more. There's less heavy traffic, and Tyson puts the Lexus on cruise. It was just last month that we took Sarita out here for her fourth birthday, but that summer day feels so far away. The trees are turning and the water reflects a brooding, grey sky.

I put my arm around Sarita and sit back, watching the unfamiliar scenery rushing by, thinking about home. It's always been a call or a flight away but now, driving into this huge countryside, it's starting to feel even more distant. I guess I was selfish, to leave Mom and Megan so soon after Dad died. But I also needed a break and Mom was so great about it. 'You've done everything you could, love. You were here for him and for me. Go, you deserve some time out.' My plan was to spend the summer au pairing then come home ready to go back to university next year. I didn't plan to enjoy the escape so much, or to fall for Sarita quite so hard.

Sarita's finally fallen asleep in her car seat, her head sprawled back at an uncomfortable angle. Tyson glances at the GPS, then takes a left onto a barely visible path that cuts through the forest.

When we stopped for gas and a pee in some tiny village in New Hampshire, Tyson grabbed three-packs of kids' T-shirts and sweatpants from the garage shop's aisle along with an armful of snacks. I got a bad feeling then that hasn't left me. It's been miles since I last saw any signs of habitation – can Sarita's grandmother really live all the way out here? The couple of photos I've seen of her in Sarita's album show a smartly dressed, urbane woman with sad eyes at what looks like Tyson and Rani's wedding. Somehow I can't picture someone like her living way out here. This area is beyond rural. If the airline calls to say that air traffic is back to normal and my flight has been rescheduled, how will we get back in time?

'Is it much further, Tyson?' I ask.

A grunt that could be a 'no', could be a 'yeah'. He's hunched forward in his seat, tapping his fingers on the steering wheel.

'Tyson? Where exactly are we?' He doesn't answer. 'Hello? Tyson?'

'Nearly there,' he says in a flat voice.

That wasn't what I asked.

Tyson slows as a massive chain-link fence comes into view. It's ringed and studded with blossoms of razor wire, and through it, I make out a patchy clearing with some sort of concrete building in the middle. Two trenches with cattle grids have been dug across the road and two black, solid-metal gates are closed across it. One of the CCTV cameras set atop the fence slowly revolves to face us. A sick chill creeps in my gut.

Sarita stirs, disturbed by the sudden quiet.

'What is this place, Tyson?' I ask, a catch in my voice. This institutional security makes me think of some grotesque asylum. Maybe that's it . . . Maybe Rani's not dead like he said, and he's shoved her in here. Or, even worse, maybe this is some sort of orphanage, and he intends to leave Sarita here.

Cut it out. I'm being ridiculous. There has to be a rational explanation.

'Tyson?' I fumble in my bag for my phone – no signal. *Damn it.* 'Tyson, I need to call my mom again. Make sure she got the message about my flight being cancelled.'

'You can do that once we're inside.'

'Inside where? You told me we were going to Sarita's grandparents' place.'

No answer. The back of his neck is sheened with sweat.

The giant gates begin to swing inward to let us through. I should have just grabbed my luggage, leapt out the car and taken my chances at the airport.

There are a couple of grey pickups and a sleek black sedan parked behind the concrete block. We pull in alongside them and when Tyson opens the door, a beautiful scent of pine and freshness blasts in. It's a relief after breathing recycled air for the last four hours.

The concrete square houses an open hatch door, which reminds me of a giant-sized safe door, the sun flashing off its metal shell. A big blond man with a paunch under a farmer's shirt emerges through it and heads towards us. 'Hey, Tyson. Good to see you again.' He shakes Tyson's hand and smiles across at me. 'This must be Mrs Gill.'

'No. No,' Tyson says. 'This is Cait Sanford. She's been looking after my daughter. That's her in the back. Sarita.' Tyson stares into the distance. 'Rani, uh, passed back in May.'

'Heck. I'm sorry,' the guy says, placing a hand on Tyson's shoulder. 'Must've been hard on you.'

I feel like I'm in a bad dream that I can't wake from, or worse, stuck in a Discovery Channel documentary, but I can't stop myself from hoping that the big guy will ask the question that I've been dying to ask ever since I took the job: *What really happened to Rani?*

Tyson nods. 'I see others have come in too,' he says with fake jocularity. He's an expert at changing the subject.

'Yup,' the guy says. 'It's a clear and present danger. Just what we're here for.' He smiles like a salesman, but his eyes look less confident. He comes over to where I'm standing by the back door. 'Good to meet you, Cait. I'm Greg Fuller.' He extends his hand, but I ignore it.

The fear has been eclipsed by anger. 'For the last time, where the *fuck* are we, Tyson?' Tyson winces at the curse word. Good.

Sarita is awake now and groggily surveying her new surroundings. 'Caity? Are we at Gran-Gran's yet?'

Greg looks from me to Tyson and back again. 'You're at New England's premier disaster-proof security establishment, Cait.' He spreads his arms wide. 'Welcome to The Sanctum.'

What the fuck? I round on Tyson, my heart thumping in my chest. 'You've brought us to some sort of . . . *bunker*?'

He holds up his hands. 'Cait, you saw what was going on at the airport.'

'You had no right to just bring me here without my consent, Tyson!'

'Come on, Cait. It wasn't my plan, but your flight was grounded. What choice did I have? Sarita needs you. I need you. Okay?'

'No, it's not' – I bite back another profanity – '*bloody* okay.' But I honestly don't think I could leave Sarita here alone with him. 'How long are you intending to stay here?'

'Ma'am,' Greg breaks in. 'I guarantee this is the safest place you could be right now. That virus is spreading fast. It's all over the news.'

Tyson kept the car radio off, so I have no idea if this is true. 'Is it really getting that bad?'

'Yup,' Greg says, almost cheerfully. 'If it hits us like it did over in Asia, and indications are that it will, you don't want to be anywhere but here.'

'Caity?' Sarita whines. 'Caity, I dropped Strawb.' I move to her side of the car.

'Soon as the flights are open again I guarantee that you'll be on the first one,' Tyson says. I can't tell if he means it or not. I don't really have a choice. I could just drive away, but I have nowhere to go. And if the virus is spreading to the East Coast, I guess I would be safe here.

I hear a thud and a scrape and look to the hatch. A tough-looking kid emerges, followed by an older version of him, both of them florid and meaty and small-eyed, like rugby forwards.

Greg introduces them as the Guthries, but it's clear that Tyson and the older guy – Cam – already know each other.

'Help the lady, Brett,' the older man says.

'Sure, Dad,' the boy drawls. He looks me up and down so shamelessly, I can't breathe for a moment. I can feel the heat from him; smell his odour of stale sweat and manure. His frank stare makes me think of some animal. There's no effort at civility. I'm suddenly burning with self-consciousness. I was dressed fine for the airport this morning. Out here, I feel embarrassed, which makes me furious at myself. I've got to hold it together.

'Help you, ma'am?' he says, staring at me as I go round to Sarita's side, like he has every right in the world to do so.

'No thanks,' I say, tugging my T-shirt over the waistband of my jeans.

Tyson goes to the back of the car and emerges with a tote bag. I end up hefting Sarita on my right hip, slinging my day pack over my shoulder and wheeling my suitcase behind me through the hatch door and into a small space. 'I'm not happy about this, Tyson.'

'We'll talk later,' he says. I carry Sarita and my case into a vestibule between the open hatch and another massive metal door, this one painted in bright green. The space is an air-lock, I realize, just a few metres long, which is way too small as the boy chortles behind me – *huh huh huh*. The low, dark, unintelligent sound makes the hair on my neck stand up. Either that or the cold air that blasts in when Greg opens the green inner door. When we're all through it, he slams it shut and my ears click with the shift in air pressure and I try not to think about all the things they might need an airlock to shut out.

We file down a steep metal stairway dotted with func-tional fluorescent emergency lights. I'm expecting some sort of utilitarian bunker-style space, but we emerge into a plush, high-ceilinged lounge, like something in a twisted holiday club.

I drop my bags and put Sarita down on a couch.

'I'll need to ask for all your weapons here. We'll check them into the safe,' Greg continues.

All your weapons? 'We don't have any—'

But as I'm talking, Tyson reaches into his briefcase and fetches a gun. He fiddles with it then hands it, butt-first, to Greg Fuller. 'Good idea, I guess.'

Cam Guthrie grunts in disapproval. 'I don't think so. I ain't happy about it. But that's the rule for now.'

Greg laughs, as if it's some running joke he shares with the Guthrie men. 'You know it's just us down here, Cam. If a threat emerges from outside, then we'll have the weapons readily available.'

I glare at Tyson. 'You've been carrying a gun with you all the—'

'Come on, Brett,' Cam Guthrie interrupts, and I'm sure it's out of fraternal solidarity, helping rescue Tyson from the woman's nagging. 'Let's let these folks get settled in.' Brett's eyes linger on my chest, but I don't want to let myself be intimidated.

'Look at the waterfall, Caity,' Sarita's saying. 'Can I take Strawb and Simba and go look?'

'Sure, sweetie. But just there. Don't go any further, okay? Stay where I can see you.'

When she's out of earshot and the Guthries are hefting our cases towards a stairwell door, I say, 'How can you bring your daughter to a place like this, Tyson? What were you thinking?' I clench my voice, so that Sarita doesn't pick up the tension.

'I put a lot of money into this safety net,' he says. 'You should count yourself lucky that you're here . . .' I think he's going to complete the sentence . . . *instead of Rani*, but he bites it down.

Lucky? 'I should be at home,' I say to no one in particular, but I look at Sarita, standing enchanted by the fake light.

4
JAMES

'Can't you go any faster?' Vicki says for what has to be the twentieth time.

Deep breath, don't lose it, but, Jesus, how many more fucking times? 'You know I don't want to take any chances, babe.' The car is built for terrain like this, but James sure as fuck isn't. He knows intellectually that the SUV is unlikely to lose traction, but it still feels like he's driving over ice without snow chains, the back wheels skidding whenever they hit a patch of loose gravel. His fingers ache from gripping the steering wheel; his ass is numb.

They were getting ready for work when one of their connections at the Boston Preppers Society called to say he'd heard that they were heading for a city-wide quarantine. Vicki insisted they leave immediately. He hates to drive – they have a contract with a limo company for a reason – but there was no way they could let some random workaday chauffeur know where they were going. And in any case, their bug-out bags were already packed in the SUV they kept in their apartment block's underground parking lot. He can't even have a cigarette to blunt his nerves because she'll flip out if she finds out he's started smoking again. James's shirt is sticking to his underarms; his chest is tight. The car is humming with eau de shih-tzu, and if he doesn't get some fresh air he's worried he'll puke down the front of his Paul Smith jacket. Without taking his eyes from the road, he fumbles for the window button.

'What are you doing?' Vicki snipes.

'I can't breathe in here.'

'There could be anything in the air. Microbes – anything.'

'You're being paranoid. There are no cases in Boston yet and, anyway, you can't catch it like that.'

'How do you know? How do you know for sure, James?' She's accentuating her English accent, which she only does when she's pissed, horny or – as James is discovering – scared shitless.

'If you'd let me listen to the fucking radio I would know, wouldn't I?'

'Keep your voice down. You're upsetting Claudette.'

Bullshit. The dog's tongue is lolling out of its mouth, its vacant button eyes barely visible through its fringe of coiffed hair. James is certain there's a 'no pets' clause in The Sanctum's manifesto. Oh well, if they're stuck in The Sanctum longer than they expect, they can always eat the goddamned thing's food (it's expensive enough), or – worse case scenario – the dog itself. *How do you like your shih-tzu, babe? Braised or lightly grilled?* He snorts.

'Something funny, James?'

'No.'

'The least you can do is concentrate on your driving.'

James angrily mashes his foot on the accelerator and the SUV jumps forward.

Vicki clutches at the dashboard, and James feels a flash of triumph as the dog almost tumbles off her lap. 'Slow down!'

'I thought you wanted me to go faster?'

'I didn't mean—'

There's a thunk, and the car pulls to the right, the paint-work scraping against the scrub at the side of the rutted dirt road. James slams his foot on the brake, and there's a sickening second, just before the ABS kicks in, when the steering wheel feels like jelly in his hands. He eases off the brake and lets the car limp to the side of the road.

He thumps the dash. 'Fuck!'

'What was that? Did we hit something?'

'Think we got a flat.' His hands are shaking. Jesus.

Vicki makes no move to chuck the dog off her lap or unclick her belt. 'Do you know how to change a tyre?'

Does he? It's been years since he had to do something like that. Handbrake on or off? He can't remember. 'Just google it, okay?'

'You want me to google how to change a tyre?'

'Are you deaf?'

'There's no need to get so pissy, James.'

There's every need, you bitch. She's supposed to be the strong one. The bulldog in the boardroom. The senior partner in more ways than one.

She huffily fishes in her bag and fiddles with her phone. 'There's no wi-fi.'

Really? In the middle of buttfuck nowheresville? What a surprise. 'Use your data.'

'No signal.'

Fuck.

He slams out of the car, hoping to Christ that the spare is sound. Why didn't he think to check it before they left? The left front tyre is shredded, fine metal wires glinting through the rubber. There's no way they can drive on that. The SUV should have been equipped with run-flats; he's going to sue the shit out of the dealer who sold them the vehicle when all of this is over.

He hauls open the trunk, has to jump back as a twelve-pack of sparkling Evian topples out, missing his toes by inches. It'll take him ages to shift all the crap that Vicki's piled on top of the wheel bin. 'A little help here?' he shouts.

No answer.

He chucks crate after crate of Claudette's gourmet dog food ('buffalo liver and caviar' or some shit) onto the verge, followed by Vicki's vanity cases and their bug-out bags. And, Jesus, what else has she shoved in here? A magnum of Cristal, two hairdryers, a case of Stoli, and a jar of sun-dried tomatoes. Sun-dried tomatoes, for fuck's sake! So that they won't be deprived of antipasto while the rest of the population's innards turn to soup.

He's really sweating when he finally clears enough space to unclick the wheel bin cover. Thank God – the spare looks sound. He unearths the lug wrench, but where the hell's the jack?

'What's taking so long?' Vicki calls. Still clutching the goddamned dog, she picks her way towards him in her pencil skirt and Louboutins. Her work clothes. She wouldn't even let them pause to change into suitable attire. 'Did you have to throw our things all over the place? They're covered in dust.'

'I can't find the jack.'

'The what?'

'The *jack*. You think you can lower yourself to help me look for it?'

She sighs and pushes her sunglasses to the top of her head. She's really showing her age – the midday sun highlighting every line around her mouth (Botox can only do so much, after all). 'What about Claudette?'

'Leave the goddamned dog in the car.'

Vicki turns on her heel.

'Where the hell are you going?'

'I'm going to wait in the car.'

'Wait for what?'

'For someone to come along.'

He snorts. 'How do you know anyone else is going to come along? We are literally in the middle of fucking nowhere.' According to the GPS, The Sanctum's at least fifteen miles from here. Why didn't they invest in a satellite phone?

'There's only one road to The Sanctum. We can't be the only ones who are en route.'

'Really? You know that for sure, do you?'

'James, your negativity isn't helping anyone.' He glares after her as she self-righteously sashays back to the passenger side. It's typical of her to accuse him of being the hysterical one, conveniently forgetting that she's spent the entire journey losing her shit. He eyes the bug-out bag where he's hidden a carton of menthols and his new Glock 18. He'd bought it on a whim last month, and he still hasn't told Vicki about it yet. It's his. Another one of his little secrets.

Still, he has to admit, if it wasn't for Vicki, they wouldn't have bought into The Sanctum in the first place. Christ knows what they'd be doing right now if they hadn't shelled out for their 'luxury survival condo' – barricading themselves in their apartment, probably, buying surgical masks by the gross, avoiding social contact, checking their vital signs every ten minutes.

She was the first to catch the prepping bug. It began as a joke – a game. She started googling End of the World scenarios after catching a doccie about doomsday preppers on Discovery. *Hey, James, guess how many ways there are to die?* Never mind muggers, car accidents and cancer, what about those Big Events that could just come out of nowhere? Before you knew it, you could be frying in a solar flare, or fighting over a can of beans in the aftermath of economic devastation. She joined internet discussion groups, reading out some of the wackier theories to him in bed so that they could laugh at them. He can't remember exactly when it had stopped being a joke – probably when she suggested it would be a fine idea if they learned how to shoot. They were both surprised at how quickly their excursions to Winston's Gun Range became the highlight of their week. There was something cathartic (and sexual, don't forget sexual) about firing a clip into a cut-out of a criminal after a week spent discussing stock options in sterile glass-and-chrome boardrooms.

Their first Survival and Primitive Training Skills weekend away with the Boston Preppers Society had been a revelation. There was something about sleeping out under the stars and learning how to build a fire that reignited their comatose sex life. Some days, just the thought of Vicki in her designer weekend warrior outfit – Ralph Lauren combats and a bandanna – was enough to make him hard. And the prepping thing had been their secret – who would have imagined that James and Victoria Maddox of Maddox & Maddox, with their Georgia O'Keefe prints, Argentinian wine collection and Jasper Conran furnishings, got their kicks gallivanting off to the boondocks to skin rabbits?

It was good there for a while, before everything turned to shit again. Before Vicki returned to her old ways, sniping at him when he least expected it, guilt-tripping him at every opportunity.

The grumble of an engine jerks him out of his thoughts.

'James!' Vicki shouts. 'A car! Make it stop!' She gets out and hurries to join him.

A green pickup rounds the corner, slows, and pulls in next to their vehicle. The driver's window lowers, revealing a thirtyish man in a John Deere cap and mirrored sunglasses. 'You folks need help?'

'We'd appreciate it,' James says. 'Got a flat. Can't seem to find the jack.'

The man nods, then eases the pickup to the side of the road in front of them.

'Thank goodness for that,' Vicki murmurs.

The guy climbs out, grabs a jack from the truck's bed and moseys towards them, his hand outstretched. 'Will Boucher.'

The last thing he wants to do is shake hands with a stranger, but he smothers his paranoia. 'James Maddox. And this is my wife, Victoria.'

'Good to meet you.' Will's handshake is brief and firm. He's half a head shorter than James, but somehow gives the impression of being taller. Not bad-looking, a wiry physique, dark stubble, scuffed jeans, work boots. James thinks he can detect a slight whiff of booze wafting out of Will's pores, and that accent is pure New England rube. Doesn't look like the sort of person who'd be able to afford a place in The Sanctum, but appearances can be deceptive. Some of their wealthiest clients looked like they shopped exclusively at Goodwill. 'You folks heading for Greg's place?'

'Do you have a condo at The Sanctum, Will?' Vicki asks, mirroring James's thoughts, as usual.

'Nope. Worked on it for a while. Project manager.'

'And I'm assuming you're heading there now.'

'Yep. Greg asked me to help out for a couple of days.'

'So you know all The Sanctum's secrets.'

James glances at her – is Vicki flirting with him?

'Some.'

'Well, thanks for stopping,' Vicki says. 'It's incredibly kind of you.'

'What anyone would do.'

'Not necessarily.'

James has to stop himself from screaming *Cut the chit-chat, there's a virus on the rampage*. But Will isn't acting as if he's in any rush to get to The Sanctum, so maybe he should just chill the fuck out. They texted Greg earlier to tell him they were en route, and he didn't mention anything about going into lockdown at any particular time. And even if he did lock it down, he can't imagine Greg refusing to allow them in. He'd better not – he and Vicki blew two years of savings on The Sanctum. They could have bought a chateau in Provence for the same price.

'Well, best get to it,' Will says. 'Your handbrake on?'

James squirms. 'Um . . .'

Will leans in through the passenger door, hauls it up, then heads straight for the flat.

'I can do it,' James says, feeling prissy and ineffectual in his suit.

'No bother.' Will gets to work popping the hubcap and loosening the wheel nuts, moving with a smooth efficiency, the ropey muscles in his forearms bulging. There's not an ounce of spare flesh on his body. James glances at Will's left hand – there's a single gold band on his ring finger.

'So, where you from, Will?' James asks, gathering the wheel bolts together in an attempt to look useful.

'Got a place just outside Augusta.' Will clears his throat. 'Heard they were setting up roadblocks, closing off the New

Hampshire border. You see anything like that en route?'
James gets the impression he's trying to steer the conversation away from anything too personal.

'No, thank God,' Vicki says. 'But the sooner they set up a countrywide quarantine, the better.' There's a hint of smugness to her tone – and why not? They've had the foresight to be prepared. Millions haven't.

Claudette starts wriggling in Vicki's arms and she places the dog carefully on the ground. 'Go pee pee for Mummy, Claudette.'

James winces, but Will doesn't react to this nauseating display. Claudette snuffles closer to the car, her fur dragging in the dust.

'Watch it doesn't piss on the tyre, Vicki,' he hisses.

'Don't call her *it*.'

James bites his tongue. That fucking dog. It's since Claudette came into their lives that things have slid back to the Old Ways. The pre-prepper ways. They couldn't join the next primitive skills weekend because 'Claudette doesn't like the outdoors.' They couldn't slip off to the gun range because 'She'll get anxious if we leave her in the car and the noise might hurt her ears.' He blames goddamned Claudette for the fact that their sex life has waned and the fights flared up once more. Well, the dog and Vicki's other . . . issues. But he's been careful lately – he's only slipped up once in the last six months – and he'd know by now if she'd found out about that relatively minor aberration. She'd have made him pay for it. She usually does.

'Do you like animals, Will?' Vicki asks.

'I don't mind them. Pets allowed in The Sanctum?'

Vicki stiffens. 'Why not? We don't have any children.'

'Guess you have a point there, ma'am.'

'Vicki, please,' she says, mollified.

Will slides the spare onto the wheel base and tightens the bolts. 'All done.' He places the rotten tyre back in the wheel bin, and starts piling their belongings on top of it. James rushes to help, feeling a flood of shame at how decadent the crates of fucking designer dog food and champagne must look to this man.

Will wipes his mucky hands on his jeans. 'Best if we travel in convoy the rest of the way, in case you run into any more trouble.'

'That would be wonderful,' Vicki gushes.

Will nods, and finally removes his sunglasses. His eyes are slightly bloodshot.

James climbs back into the driver's seat and shrugs off his jacket. Vicki settles Claudette on her lap, then smiles at him. It's a real smile – possibly the first genuine smile he's received from her in months.

James starts the engine, hanging back as Will drives off to avoid the dust.

'So, what did you think of our saviour?' Vicki asks.

James shrugs. 'A man of few words. The Lone Ranger of the byways.'

'Boucher. That's French, isn't it?'

James shrugs. 'I guess.'

'I saw you checking him out, by the way.'

He's instantly on the defensive. 'I was not!'

She laughs and squeezes his thigh. *Thank fuck.* 'You think we're going to run into any of our old friends from that godawful sales weekend Greg organized?'

James forces a chuckle. 'God, I hope not.'

'You know, I can't even remember what possessed us to go there. We'd already paid the deposit.' She checks her make-up in the rear-view. 'What was that chap's name again?'

'What chap?' He somehow manages to keep his voice light.

'You know, the gun-toting Republican. The one who looked like he was always on the verge of asking us if we'd met his best friend Jesus.'

James breathes out. 'Guthrie, I think.'

'Oh yes. Guthrie. Still, I suppose they weren't all bad. I did like that older man, the one with the European accent. There was something . . . charismatic and mysterious about him, don't you agree?'

Relax, she doesn't know anything. 'I guess.'

Claudette whines and Vicki starts babbling to her in baby language. For the first time, he's grateful they brought the dog along.

It'll be fine. He's just being paranoid.

Finally, the edge of the fence comes into view: 'The first line of defence,' according to The Sanctum's website. Chain-link, topped with barbed wire and security cameras. Not much of a defence against a pair of wire-cutters, but who's going to find this place anyway?

'This is it,' Vicki says. 'We're going to be fine, aren't we, James?'

'Sure we are, babe,' James says, feeling the knot of anxiety the drive has caused beginning to loosen. 'We're the lucky ones.'

5

WILL

Will dumps his bag on the breakfast counter and takes a quick look around the condo. He's exhausted – he was up looking after Lana till four a.m. – but he can't help but assess the work: several of the cupboard doors are off-kilter and the paint detailing around the cornices is sloppy. The condo next to his is little more than an empty shell; Greg's scheduling must have gone all to hell. The deadline for finishing the work was three months back.

Will grabs his mobile and dials home without thinking – but there's no cell coverage down here of course. It caused endless trouble during the build; his crew had to rely on cheap walkie-talkies that were notoriously unreliable. He logs on to Skype instead, listens to the dial tone.

The nurse answers on the eighth ring, just as Will's anxiety is building to a whole new level. 'Boucheron residence?' She sounds like she's eating something.

'It's Boucher. This is Will Boucher speaking.'

'Oh hi, Mr Boucher. Your wife's doing fine. Sleeping.'

'You know you have to wake her at seven for her pills?'

'Yeah, I know. It's on the list. Don't worry.' The CNN theme sounds in the background. 'Isn't it just awful what's happening? All medical professionals are on high alert. You think it'll spread to Maine?'

'I doubt it. They're shutting down the borders.'

'I heard that.'

'I'll keep checking in. You have the number for the specialist?'

'Yes, Mr Boucheron. It's on the list.'

He doesn't bother correcting her again. The signal dips, and for a second he thinks he's lost her. 'There's no phone signal where I'm at, but I'll keep checking my email. I'll be back the day after tomorrow.'

'I know. And don't worry, we're fine.'

He hangs up, hoping to God that's true. He's never used this agency before; the one he called in occasionally had no one available at such short notice, and the nurse who showed up looked barely out of her teens. He's got no choice but to trust she's capable. He needs the job.

There's a tap on the door. Will hesitates before he opens it, resisting the pull of the J & B bottle at the bottom of his bag. He knows who it'll be. He and Greg haven't yet had a chance to talk. The Maddoxes took up all of Greg's attention when they arrived, loudly complaining about the elevator not working and griping that the colour scheme in the rec room didn't match the specs in the brochure. James and Vicki were exactly the type of people Will imagined would buy into a place like this. Rich and paranoid. If Greg was pissed they'd brought a dog along, he hid it well.

Greg lumbers in, and claps him on the shoulder. 'It's good to have you back, Will. I'm sorry to ask this of you, buddy. Like I said, I needed someone I could trust.' Greg's tanned face ripples. He's not a man who can hide his emotions. 'I know how hard it must've been for you to leave Lana.'

You really don't. Will's grief, a black, noxious monster that's been hibernating inside his chest for the last six months, flexes its claws. And then there's the guilt, which is somehow harder to bear. The guilt at the relief he's feeling at having a legitimate excuse to get away for a couple of days. 'I've only got the nurse for two days.'

'I know, buddy. Just need some back-up while everyone gets settled in. Case they get antsy, that kinda thing. You're good with people, Will. Look how you handled the dispute with the fella over the filtration system. What was his name?'

'Kenneth Collier.'

'That's it.' Greg wipes a palm over his face. 'Gonna be straight with you, Will, The Sanctum's not as operational as I'd like. The fella I hired after you quit, he wasn't the best, if you want to know the truth. Be good to have you around in case we run into any teething problems. Bonus in it for you.'

Will is well aware that Greg is carrying the full financial weight of this venture on his own shoulders – bankrolling The Sanctum's build with the proceeds of the sale of his security business. And in Will's experience of the building trade, you get what you pay for. From the little he's seen of The Sanctum so far, it's clear Greg has been cutting corners. 'Is everyone here?'

'All but one family. The Dannhausers. Said they were en route, but there's no sign of them yet. Gate lock's engaged, but people are getting nervous and I'm gonna have to lock the place down soon. Everyone's meeting in the rec room for a briefing in fifteen, but I got an errand to do first. I'd appreciate your help.'

Will follows Greg into the stairwell, decides not to mention the sealed-off elevator doors. The shaft itself was an addition to the existing structure, a government facility that was abandoned, half completed, back in the eighties, during the nuclear war hysteria. Greg seemed to think it was intended as a bolthole for the great and the good. Will hadn't been around for the later stages of the build – Lana had needed him – and he assumes the elevator is another casualty of Greg's dwindling resources.

Greg knocks on the door of a unit up on level three. It's opened by a big man with a ruddy face. Not as tall as Greg, but built.

'Hey, Cam,' Greg says. 'This here is Will Boucher, used to be my project manager. Will, this is Cam Guthrie.'

So this is Cam Guthrie. Will recalls Greg talking about him. He was one of the first to buy into The Sanctum, had to sell everything he owned to do so, even with a discount. Guthrie holds out a paw the size of a ham-hock. 'Pleasure, Will. You done a good job with this place.'

'Appreciate you saying that.'

'What can we do for you, Greg?' Cam asks. 'Aren't we going into lockdown soon?'

'Yup. That's what I wanted to talk to you about. Remember we discussed putting those guns of yours in the safe for a few days till everyone gets settled?'

Will's expecting Cam Guthrie to say 'from my cold, dead hands' or something along those lines, but he merely nods. 'Come on inside.'

'Appreciate this, Cam,' Greg says as Guthrie steps back to let them in.

The Guthries' condo is one of the smaller, two-bedroom units. The heat is cranked up high and Will can detect the odour of broiled meat under the new-paint smell. A teenage girl, who's sitting on the couch next to a skinny woman with limp black hair, looks up and smiles nervously when they enter. On the TV a preacher in a white suit mops his brow and holds his hands up to the sky.

'Hey, Gina. Hey, Mrs Guthrie,' Greg rumbles. 'How you doing?'

'Who's this?' The woman looks up and glances suspiciously at Will.

'I'm Will Boucher, ma'am. I'll be helping Greg out while you folks get settled.'

'We're settled already,' she says.

'Bonnie, why don't you and Gina go on into the bedroom? Go do some folding,' Guthrie says before Will can frame a response.

'Come on, Gina.' Bonnie Guthrie gets to her feet, and the girl follows with no resistance. Bonnie pauses at the door and fixes Will with that defensive gaze again. 'We got things under control here. Don't need no help but the Lord's.'

Will hasn't had much use for God since Lana got sick, but he doubts this woman would appreciate hearing that.

'Brett!' Cam calls. A younger version of Cam Guthrie appears at the door to the second bedroom, nods at Greg and looks Will up and down. Will puts him at seventeen or eighteen or so.

'Howdy, Brett,' Greg says. 'This is Will. My right-hand man.'

Brett eyes Will warily. 'Hi, sir.'

'Brett,' Cam says. 'Will and Greg need to put the firearms in the safe.'

'No one's taking my guns,' Brett says flatly.

Greg chuckles. 'Son, I'm only talking about putting them in the safe for a few days.'

The look of hatred on the boy's face almost takes Will's breath away. 'Not going to happen.'

'Now, Brett. There's no threat here,' Cam says.

'First thing you taught me, Dad,' the kid says in that same deadpan manner. 'Never let no one take your guns.'

Cam nods. 'And that's correct. But not in this situation. Now do as I say, boy. That's an order.'

Brett's cheeks flush with blood, but he does as he's told and slopes into the main bedroom. Greg makes awkward small talk while they wait, the preacher on the TV gesticulating silently. Brett returns, lugging two huge tactical drag bags, which he drops at Will's feet. Will bends to pick one of them up, staggering under the weight of it. The boy sneers.

'Is that all of them?' Greg asks.

'You want to sweep the unit, Greg?' Cam asks in a tone of voice that screams *You calling me a liar?*

'Nope,' Greg says, keeping it light. 'Your word is good enough for me, Cam.'

'Good.' Cam shows them out, and Will waits for Greg to comment on what went on in there, but Greg merely chuckles again, adjusts the strap of his tactical bag and says, 'Could really use the elevator now.'

'What's the story with that, Greg?'

'Ran into a few issues. Guy I hired to draw up the plans got the specs wrong.'

Will doesn't comment – he can detect bullshit when he hears it. Lower and lower they go, the bag's strap slicing into his shoulder. Greg's face is scarlet and he's out of breath by the time they reach level eight.

'You okay, Greg?'

'Sure I am.' He grins and shoulders the door open. 'Remember this area, Will? Wasn't like this last time you were down here, was it?'

Will nods in feigned appreciation as he breathes in the

odours of damp and chicken shit and eyes the storeroom's hastily constructed cheap metal shelves and the walk-in freezer that he can see is second-hand.

Greg gestures at a serrated plastic sheet covering one of the doorways leading off from the main area. 'Through there's the hydroponics. Got some chicks as well.'

Will peers through the plastic ribbons, taking in the half-completed hydroponic beds, his eyes watering under the glare of the lights. The chickens are shoved into factory-farming-style cages and cluck at him mournfully. Greg hasn't mentioned any other staff living down here, but someone must be doing the upkeep. Unless . . .

'You been living here, Greg?'

Greg shrugs ruefully. 'Yup.'

'Must be lonely.'

'I come and go.'

'It's quite a drive to South Paris.'

Greg sighs. 'May as well come clean. Fact is, had to sell my place, Will. The Sanctum . . . it ate into my cash more than I thought it would. You know, things go wrong, foul-ups, people not doing their jobs. Like the elevator. Couldn't even make the payment on the cabin for that. I need this place to work, Will. Need to sell the last of the units to break even.'

Will doesn't know what to say. Right from the get-go he's thought of The Sanctum as nothing more than a rich man's folly, and he's never understood how Greg could expect to get a return on it. Sure, the state-of-the-art hatch and the tungsten condo doors were old stock from Greg's security business, but he saw the costings for the water filtration system, those fancy LCD window panels, the redundancies and the perimeter fence – which Greg insisted was necessary – which ran into seven figures. 'Sorry to hear that, Greg,' is all he can manage.

'I'll get through it. And besides, with all that's going on out there, building The Sanctum's the best thing I could've done. This place is gonna save our lives. C'mon, let's get these weapons stored away.'

The safe, a closet-sized affair discreetly set into a recess next to the freezer, is clearly top of the range. 'Not bad.'

'Got it custom made.'

Greg taps in the combination, and it cranks open to reveal a rack of rifles, several semi-automatics, boxes and boxes of ammo, and on a top shelf, what looks to be a detonator. 'That what I think it is, Greg?'

'Yup. Left over from the construction. Couldn't leave it lying around. Now listen up. I'm gonna tell you the combination, Will, just in case things go bad and I need you to back me up.'

'Hope it won't come to that.'

'Doubt it will, but think it's for the best. Trusting you'll keep it to yourself.'

'Sure.'

'Okay, so it's easy. One, nine, eight, four.'

'Nineteen eighty-four?'

'Yup.'

'Like the book?'

'Huh? Oh, I gotcha. But no. It was the year I joined the Marines. You think you'll remember that?'

'Got it.'

'Now, let's get these weapons squared away and we can go meet the rest of the folks.'

*

A small crowd – including the Guthrie men, Gina and the Maddoxes – is already gathered around the TV screen when Greg and Will enter the rec room for the briefing. Greg turns down the TV's volume, then gives his 'right-hand man' spiel. Vicki and James Maddox – who appear to have left the dog behind – greet Will like old friends, and a nervy Asian man jumps to his feet, his hand outstretched. 'It's an honour to meet you. I'm Yoo-jin Park. You can call me Eugene.'

'Isn't that a white person's name?' Brett Guthrie mutters.

'Now, Brett,' Cam Guthrie says. 'We've all got to get on around here.' He smiles at Yoo-jin, but it doesn't meet his eyes.

To Yoo-jin's credit he doesn't look flummoxed by Brett's rudeness. 'And this is my wife, Stella, and son, Jae.' Stella – a tall, overweight blonde – smiles broadly at him. The son, who has inherited his father's looks and his mother's height, looks up from his laptop and gives Will an ironic salute and a 'Hey, dude.'

'Are you here by yourself, Will?' Stella Park asks.

'Yes.' He decides not to mention Lana. He's had about all the pity he can take in the last few months.

Greg rubs his hands. 'Folks, let me congratulate you again for having the foresight to buy into The Sanctum. As you know, our motto is always be—'

Greg breaks off when a guy in his late forties, accompanied by an attractive redhead holding the hand of a small child, enters the rec room.

'Glad you could join us, Tyson,' Greg says. He waves at the little girl. 'Hey there, Sarita, how d'you like your bedroom?'

The little girl, who has dusky skin and the blackest eyes Will's ever seen – nothing like either the man or the woman she's with – buries her head in the woman's thigh. This group doesn't seem to fit together; the woman is on edge, acts like she can't bear to even look at the older guy. As Greg introduces them, Will's almost certain the guy blanches when he catches sight of the Maddoxes.

'You'll all have plenty of time to get to know each other,' Greg says. 'How about we get this place locked down?'

'Um . . . shouldn't we say something before we get shut in? A prayer?' This from Gina Guthrie. The Asian boy looks up from his laptop; Will is expecting him to smirk, but instead he smiles at her. She blushes and looks away.

Greg nods. 'That sounds like a fine idea, Gina.'

'Is this really necessary?' Vicki asks. 'Shouldn't we get straight to it? It's about time you locked us in, Greg.'

Greg's smile doesn't waver. 'That's correct, Vicki. But even without the hatch engaged, the inner door is double-skinned and—'

'Have you actually *seen* how this is escalating?' She points at the TV. On screen, a Fox reporter wearing a white face-mask is gesticulating into shot. Behind her, men and women in army fatigues are hefting bales of body bags out of trucks. The banner reads: 'West Coast Prepares for Mass Death Toll'. 'It's going to be chaos out there.'

Without looking up from his laptop, Jae mutters, 'We're in the middle of nowhere.'

Vicki glowers at him, then rounds on Greg again. 'You think people don't know about this place? What about all the people who must have worked on The Sanctum? What about the neighbouring townspeople? Where's the first place they're going to come if this situation gets any worse?'

Greg sighs. 'Mrs Maddox—'

'It's *Ms*.'

'Ms Maddox, Vicki, let me just put your mind at ease. No

one, except those of you who have had the foresight to buy into The Sanctum, knows its exact location or GPS coordinates.' Vicki opens her mouth to interrupt, but Greg holds up a hand to forestall her. 'The guys who worked on this place were migrant labourers, and most of them have gone back to their home countries or have moved to the cities to find other employment. The key staff, like Will here, are people who I trust with my life. We're a good thirty miles away from the nearest population hub, and we'll know well in advance if anyone is approaching the perimeter. Rest assured, we most certainly have time for a short prayer.'

Vicki twitches, looks as if she's going to let loose again, then shrugs. 'Fine.'

Everyone gets to their feet with varying degrees of reluctance. Will finds himself drawn into the circle, doesn't miss that the Guthrie girl has slid to the Asian boy's side and is studiously ignoring her father's black looks.

The redhead hefts the child onto her hip and takes Will's left hand. Her palm is dry but she's trembling.

'Cam,' Greg says to Guthrie, 'could I ask you to do the honours?'

Guthrie rips his eyes from his daughter and bows his head. 'We thank you, our Lord Jesus Christ, for providing us with this haven and trust that in His wisdom God in His mercy will keep us safe. Amen.'

'Amen.'

'Appreciate that, Cam,' Greg says. 'Anyone who wants to can come up with me while I seal the hatch.'

Guthrie eyes his daughter again. 'Gina, go back to your momma.'

'But, Daddy, can't I—'

'Do what I say.'

She colours, but scurries off to the stairwell. Stella Park also begs off, as does her husband. James Maddox hesitates, says something in his wife's ear and slinks back to the couch.

Greg shepherds the rest through to the control room. 'I reset the hatch code every day,' he says. 'It'll get sent to your room screens. The Sanctum takes everyone's security seriously. Now—'

'Greg!' Jae calls. He's staring intently at one of the security screens. 'There are people out there.'

Will peers at the screen, sees a Range Rover skewed outside the main gate at the foot of the rise. A small group of people is gathered around it: an elderly man wearing an old-fashioned fedora, and a thin woman, who appears to be propping up a far larger elderly woman. The man ducks into the car, returns with what looks like a crowbar.

'That's the Dannhausers,' Greg says. 'They made it.' He frowns. 'Not sure why the motion detectors at the first perimeter didn't alert me.'

Jae taps the mouse and zooms in. The old man's digging at the gap between the gate and the fence post. The image is clear – like watching a black-and-white silent movie.

'He won't break the seal with that,' Greg says. 'It's tungsten.'

The man pauses and looks straight into the camera, almost as if he can sense they're all watching. The older woman doubles over, as if she's coughing or struggling to breathe, while the younger woman grips her around the side and bears her weight.

Greg opens the door to the control panel and starts tapping in a code.

'Wait.' Vicki Maddox grabs his arm. 'What are you doing?'

'Deactivating the gate lock.'

'You can't. That woman, she's coughing – she could be sick, she could have—'

'I can't just leave them out there. They got a right to be here.'

'Lady's got a point, Greg,' Cam Guthrie chimes in, and Vicki darts a grateful look at him. 'That old lady looks sick. She may have infected the other two. We got our own to think about.'

'How Christian of you,' Jae murmurs, earning himself a look of pure venom from Brett.

Greg runs his hands through his hair. 'Those folks need help. I can't just leave them—'

'You can't go out there,' Vicki interrupts. 'I refuse to allow it. I paid a fortune for this place.'

'I'll go,' Will finds himself saying. Vicki snaps her mouth shut, and for several seconds all he can hear is the whir of the air-con. 'When I get out there, if it looks like they're sick, then I'll decide what to do.'

'What do you mean, *decide*? This is madness!'

'Oh, shit,' Jae breathes. Will turns back to the screen.

The skinny woman is now staggering under the weight of the old woman. She loses her grip and the elderly woman goes down, hitting her head on the Range Rover's hood.

6
TRUDI

'About time,' Trudi mutters as the gate finally crawls open. Her mother is slumped in the passenger seat, her left leg half slouched out the door, wheezing and clutching at the gash on her forehead. Thankfully it's not too bad and although Caroline's cheeks are that disconcerting mixture of ashen and florid, Trudi's seen her mother far worse.

'Leo,' Caroline murmurs. 'Leo, I want to go home.' She sounds like a child.

Trudi squats down by the car door and grips her mother's hands. 'Shh, Mom. We're going to get help for you.' It's not right, an old woman with dried blood on her cheeks, but she can't bring herself to look away from her mother.

'Get in,' Leo orders Trudi. He's already started the engine. He probably blames her for Caroline's fall, but he should have known she didn't have the strength to hold her up. Then again, when has her father ever needed a special excuse for his curtness? Ever since this started, he's shown nothing but his usual grim and angry determination, and she has to admit to herself that it's comforting in these circumstances. Trudi's always thought of Leo's bunker as some weird, paranoid affectation, but now that there's a reason to come here, she's relieved not to have to face whatever will happen in the city. Trudi climbs into the back seat next to her mother, who's started hacking away as if there's something caught in her throat. They'll need to get her onto the oxygen as soon as they're inside.

When the gates are wide enough, Leo guns the engine and accelerates through. Trudi's forced to grab on to the seat in front of her as he brakes almost immediately, narrowly avoiding slamming into a green pickup that skids to a stop inches in front of their car. Her stomach lurches as the driver jumps out. His face is hidden behind a gas mask, the plastic eye holes giving him a sinister, insectile appearance.

'Who is this, Dad?' Trudi says. 'Why is he wearing that mask? He can't think we're . . .'

Ignoring her, Leo throws open his door, but the man signals him to stay where he is. 'Mr Dannhauser?'

'Yes.'

'My name is Will Boucher. I'm Greg Fuller's, uh, project manager.' The respirator gives a robotic edge to his voice, as if he's some sort of alien creature. He moves around the car, stares at Trudi with his bug eyes and nods at her. 'I'm sorry about this, sir, but we need to take precautions. How long has the lady been sick?'

The man's looking at Trudi but talking to Leo and it annoys her. 'She's not infected with the virus,' she snaps. 'She has emphysema. She's suffered with it for three years.' Three long years.

'And she's just injured herself,' Leo adds. 'She needs immediate medical attention.' *Injured herself.* Trudi notes the choice of words. Caroline's misfortune is always her own fault, isn't it?

Will Boucher nods. 'I understand. But there are concerns that you . . . that your party may be infected. I need to assure the other residents.'

Now Leo's studied, neutral tone cracks. 'That's absurd! Look at my wife. She's injured, she collapsed!'

'I know, sir. We saw it happen.'

'And still you let us wait outside the gate?'

Will sighs, which through the mask comes out as a metallic hiss. 'Not all of us were—'

'We need to get her inside,' Trudi says, before her father's temper is allowed to escalate. 'We need to clean the wound and give her oxygen. Will you help us, Mr Boucher, or shall we turn around and go home?'

Will hesitates for a few seconds then comes to a decision. 'Of course. Follow me, please.' He climbs back into the pick-up, executes a swift three-point turn and drives up a grassy rise towards a low concrete building at the top.

Leo gets into the driver's seat but makes no move to follow. He's gripping the wheel and muttering under his breath.

'Dad,' Trudi says, knowing the right tone to take. 'Shall we follow him?'

Leo puts the car into drive and lets it creep forwards. Trudi reaches over and takes her mother's hand. Caroline doesn't respond, and her fingers are cold. Trudi has to choke down her worry at least until she's shepherded Leo and Caroline to where they're going.

Her father follows the pickup, parks next to it. The second the engine dies, Trudi flicks open the car door and hurries around to her mother's side. 'Help me, Dad.'

Leo comes to her side, but there's not enough space for both of them to manoeuvre Caroline out of the seat, and Trudi ends up taking the bulk of her mother's weight again.

'Let me help you,' Will Boucher says, but as he moves to Caroline's side she recoils.

'What's happening? What's happening?' she wails, whipping her head back and forth, her eyes cloudy with confusion.

'Quiet,' Leo murmurs, stepping in and taking over from Trudi. 'You are safe. This man is here to help.'

Caroline slumps, and Will and Leo half carry her towards an open gunmetal hatch, which reminds Trudi of a giant version of the door on her father's safe. As they approach, three large men, all gas-masked and with guns at their hips, emerge through it. Trudi scans their faces, but she can read nothing.

Leo peers at the tallest of them. 'Greg? Greg, is that you? How can you make us wait like this?'

'I'm sorry about this, Leo,' the man says. 'Truly I am. But you gotta understand we need to be cautious.'

'We are not infected!'

'Let's just get you and your family inside and then we can talk.' Greg turns to the larger of the two men flanking him. 'Cam, how about you and Brett help the Dannhausers with their luggage?'

'You heard the man, Brett,' the man says, the mask dampening the drawl in his voice. Despite his build, Trudi realizes Brett can't be much older than a teenager. Cam must be his father – they're dressed almost identically in camouflage pants and high-topped boots.

'Cam? Cam Guthrie?' Leo says. 'We met at The Sanctum's sales weekend.'

'I remember,' Cam says tonelessly.

'Is this your son?'

'Yep.'

Leo's ingratiating tone is jarring, but he's been in business all his life. Trudi knows he's working the stakeholders, already manoeuvring to forge a connection with this man and diffuse the tension. If there's one thing she knows about her father, it's that Leo knows where the power lies and how to exploit it.

But Cam isn't playing along. Brett grabs their cases from the back of the car and throws them into the dark space inside. Cam hangs back as Greg marshals everyone else in, his hand resting on the knife at his hip as if he thinks they're dangerous fugitives. Before she can even think, Trudi and her parents are squashed into a featureless hallway.

Caroline's body weakens and slumps heavily as she starts that gasping cough. Leo stumbles and Will grunts as he takes the strain. 'We have to hurry,' Trudi says.

'It's all under control, ma'am. Stand back everyone, please.' Greg squeezes past Trudi and taps a code into a numbered panel next to the hatch. There's a click, the hiss of hydraulics being engaged and the heavy metal door crumps shut. Trudi shudders.

'You good with those bags, son?' Greg says to Brett.

'Course I am, sir,' Brett says, but Trudi can see him struggling. He's carrying a lot of baggage for one kid, however strong he looks. She reaches over to relieve him of a sling bag but he jerks away, angrily perhaps, but she can't see his face through the mask.

'We must take my wife to the medical suite right now,' Leo says.

'We'll take good care of her, folks,' Greg says in his robotic voice and Leo picks up his evasion.

'The Sanctum has a fully stocked medical suite and a doctor on the staff, doesn't it?' he demands. 'That's what you promised, correct?'

Greg doesn't respond further.

A second door in front of them is opened and they're

corralled down a narrow metal staircase. Caroline's moans increase in pitch as Will and Leo help her along. Trudi feels a hand, or something harder, in her back. Her chest tightens, she's certain she's going to stumble and whoever it is pushing her from behind will trip over her. 'Hang on . . . wait,' she tries.

'Keep moving.' It's Cam – his voice a low, threatening drawl. Finally they emerge into a spacious room – some kind of lounge area by the looks of it. The bright artificial light makes her feel dizzy. A projected waterfall scene whispers on one wall, out of place and fake, like an elaborate stage backdrop. She glances behind her to check on Caroline. She's stopped coughing, but her breathing is laboured. Brett's masked eyes are staring at her with distrust and almost in some perverse desire to confirm his suspicions, Trudi feels a tickle in her throat. She fights it as long as she can, but her eyes start to water and her throat threatens to close, so she has to hack it out. The boy takes a step backwards.

Greg's nudging them towards another stairwell. Leo's face is sweaty. He's strong, and a good head taller than Will, but he's decades older and her mother's weight is taking its toll. 'Can't we take the elevator to the medical suite?' he huffs.

'Not much further now, Leo,' Greg replies.

They're press-ganged three more floors down, Will and Leo grunting as they ease Caroline down every step. Greg holds open the stairwell door, lights blink on, and they're ushered into a dark-carpeted corridor.

'This isn't the medical bay,' Leo says.

'Leo. I'm gonna need you to cooperate here.' Greg presses his thumb to a panel next to another door. There's a click, and he shoves it open with his shoulder, revealing the interior of a starkly modern, taupe-walled apartment.

'Step back, Will,' Greg says.

'I can help them inside.'

'Step back,' Cam Guthrie repeats. Will does so reluctantly and Trudi hurries to help her father. Her mother leans into her and she stumbles before taking up the weight.

Cam takes a step forward, hand resting on the handle of the knife on his belt. 'Get in.'

'Do it, Leo,' Greg says.

Leo sets his face, knowing that they're outmuscled for now, and they shuffle Caroline into the apartment. Brett chucks their bags inside the room and slams the door, which locks in its frame with a muted magnetic thunk. Leo and Trudi help Caroline to a bedroom and as soon as she's down, Leo's off, hammering on the door with his fist. 'Hey! Hey! Open the door!'

Caroline's coughing has slowed, but she's grappling with the covers, struggling for breath. Trudi props her up against some pillows and rushes to the luggage in the hallway and finds the oxygen kit. She only incidentally notices her father shouting, the way the German accent he's so successfully stifled in all his dealings with America is dredged up whenever he loses his composure. It's only when the tubes are strapped into position and Caroline's finally breathing with some comfort that Trudi can excavate a flannel and some disinfectant from the suitcases and see to her mother's head wound. It's not too deep, but it might need stitches and will probably bruise badly.

'Mom, how are you feeling?' Trudi soothes as she cleans the cut, concerned when her mother doesn't even flinch as she dabs the disinfectant into the wound. 'We're fine now.'

Caroline doesn't respond and, all the while, Leo's hammering against the door. She wishes he would stop. After so many years living with these two old people, with only a soup of memory around her, Trudi finds it all too easy to slip away from the present moment. She watches her mother's breathing slow now, her face go greyer, the purple blooms in her cheeks diminish. She listens to the shouting outside this room as if she's witnessing it from a disembodied distance, looking at fish in an aquarium. Better still, floating serene inside a huge amniotic tank while outside the world shuffles and flurries on without her.

Slam! Slam! Slam!

'We need a doctor. Right now! Let us out! You can't keep us here!'

Slam! Slam! Slam!

Caroline's entire body jerks and hitches once, then stills.

'Mom?' Trudi picks up her arm. It feels limp. She scrambles to find a pulse and, thank God, there it is, fluttering faintly in her wrist. 'Mom?' Should she be allowed to sleep?

The slamming outside stops. The sound of locks clicking and then that man's voice. Greg Fuller, the big man in charge, warm, like some congenial snake oil salesman.

'Stand back, please, Leo,' he says.

'I'm not—'

'Stand back, sir!'

When Leo doesn't respond, Trudi stands and peers into the sitting room. Brett and Cam are blocking the door, still wearing those respirator masks. They make her think of those gas attacks on the Tokyo underground. How long ago was that?

'How dare you!' Leo's saying. 'We paid a lot of money for this *service* and you can't treat us like this.'

'Hold on a minute, Mr Dannhauser,' Greg Fuller is saying.

'You'll get whatever help we can give you. We've asked Dr Park to come and see you.'

'Who the hell's Dr Park?'

The farmer and his son step aside to reveal a large woman in a garishly patterned cardigan, incongruous with the respirator mask shielding her face. 'This is Dr Park,' Fuller says.

'I'm so sorry about all this,' the doctor says. 'But to be frank, I'm not really sure I can help.' Trudi immediately feels a stab of relief. The woman's voice is kind.

'Fix her, Lady Doctor,' the teenager says, and gives a humourless laugh, like a big, slow dog barking.

The woman rounds on him, but before she can retort, Cam says: 'Can it, Brett,' then slams the door closed again.

Dr Park mutters what could be a curse under her breath, then asks to be taken to see the patient. She follows Leo to where Caroline is lying, still on the bed. The room feels very full.

Leo sits down beside Caroline, places a hand to her brow. The doctor makes no move to attend to her. 'What do you think is wrong with her?' she asks.

Leo glares at her. 'You tell me, Doctor.' Leo's silver hair is hanging lopsidedly down the side of his head.

'Mr Dann . . .'

'. . . hauser. Dannhauser.'

'Mr Dannhauser, I'll do my best, but I think you should know. I'm actually a dentist.'

Leo presses two fingers into his brow. After a moment of struggle, he calms his voice and says, 'Well then, you're right. You can't help. Please leave.'

For a second, Trudi thinks she's going to do just that, then she approaches Caroline.

'For God's sake, Dad, you could be a little helpful,' Trudi

steps in. 'She suffers from chronic emphysema, Doctor. She doesn't travel well any more.'

Dr Park glances up at her. 'Please, call me Stella.'

'We were promised that there would be a doctor on the staff,' Leo barks.

'Dad, please,' Trudi says and it's suddenly clear, in these circumstances, what she's been doing for the past six years of her life: *babysitting*. She's been babysitting this petulant old man, protecting her soft mother from his tantrums and his lack of empathy instead of living her goddamned life. She draws herself in and takes a deep breath, prepared as always to behave like the rational adult. 'We're mostly concerned about this wound. She fell and hit her head when we were coming in. She wasn't in a good way already and now she's particularly bad. Do you think it's concussion?'

'What would she know?' Leo says.

'Well, I do have general medical training – and common sense,' she says. 'We'll work it out. Did she lose consciousness at all after the fall?'

'I don't think so, no,' Trudi says.

'Any vomiting? Disorientation?'

'No vomiting. But, yes, she was disorientated.'

'What is her first name?'

'Caroline.'

Stella takes Caroline's hand gently, moves her fingers to her wrist and checks her watch. 'Hello, Caroline. Can you hear me?' She looks up at Leo. 'Her pulse is weak but steady. Is she on any medication?'

'She takes aspirin for her circulation. And she goes on oxygen when she's in respiratory distress. We brought one spare bottle. We assumed there would be more in the medical bay down here.'

'What medication did she take today, do you know?'

Leo looks to Trudi. 'I'm not sure,' Trudi says. 'We left so suddenly . . . Wait.' Caroline's handbag is lying discarded by the door, and she riffles through it, searching for the bottle of Ecotrin. She shakes it – there's a single aspirin inside it. 'She's running low.'

Caroline's eyelids flutter. 'Where am I?' She starts sobbing and cringes away from Stella. 'Trudi, who is this?'

'Mom, I'm here,' Trudi says. 'The doctor is going to take care of you.'

Stella sighs. 'Now I don't want to worry you, but she may have had a minor stroke. It may have caused her to fall, but it appears to have done no serious damage. There's no speech impairment, which is a good sign, and I can't see any signs of concussion, although these may only appear later.'

Trudi runs to the bathroom for a glass of water. Caroline's still darting confused glances at Stella, but her breathing is steadying, and Trudi manages to get her to swallow the tablet.

'So what now?' Leo asks.

'If it is a small stroke, aspirin should help. I'll make sure you get more. Keep a close eye on her.' She stands. 'You're not alone. I'll be available if you need me.'

Leo grunts his thanks and sees her to the door, where Cam Guthrie is waiting to escort her away and lock up again. Caroline's fists unclench, and she shudders. Trudi strokes her brow, and finally her eyes close.

Leo walks back into the room. She has never seen him looking so old.

'Why don't we just leave, Dad?'

Their bags are still slumped in the hallway. If they unpack them, it means that they accept their imprisonment.

'We can't leave,' Leo says. 'If this is a militarized biological agent, we're better off here, despite . . .'

'But Mom . . .'

'I know,' he says. End of discussion. He goes to the couch and puts on the TV. His coldness makes her afraid. If she's honest, that fear is a major reason why she came home when her life broke, when her career ended. Now she's a childless, washed-up ex-prima ballerina of forty-two whose only purpose in life is protecting her ailing mother from Leo, because she doesn't fully trust him. Or maybe she's just always been a mommy's girl. It kills her to watch her mother disappearing in front of her while her father skulks around in a puerile rage.

But at the same time she knows she's lying to herself, that hiding away from her disappointment was her choice. Six years ago, she swapped a rich life for this pathetic babysitting job. And the truth is, it suited her – at first, before Caroline got sick. And then when she did, there was no way Trudi could leave her with that secretive, uncaring man. Her therapist keeps telling her to move on, that dancing wasn't all she is, that there are seasons to a person's life and that every one bears fruit. But her life stopped years ago and she doesn't know how to start it again.

Maybe it won't matter anyway. Leo's probably right: the hospitals will be overloaded, and teeming with the virus. She's safer here for now.

'She didn't want to come,' she says to the back of his head.

She doesn't expect him to respond, but he turns to face her, stung by the accusation. 'You didn't want me to just leave her there, did you?'

Trudi shrugs, remembers the look on her mother's face when they saw the news this morning. Caroline was sitting awkwardly next to Leo on the edge of the sofa, all pink-and-cream damask roses and whatever you call those coy ribbons embroidered into the upholstery, as if it wasn't her sofa, hadn't been her sofa for most of her long married life. She looked up at Trudi and something odd crossed her face, a look of appeal. Trudi tried to connect with her mother's eyes, but then noticed that she was looking behind her, over her shoulder.

Trudi turned. The vast, flat screen against the wall was showing the same footage they'd shown all night, body bags in rows, Asian officials in dark outfits and stark white masks. It's the same material they'd had on constant rotation since yesterday.

'What is it, Mom?' Trudi asked. 'This is nothing n—'

'Look,' she said.

Trudi turned back to the screen. The crawl read: 'Breaking News: First East Coast Death Confirmed'. The newscaster was talking about the possible suspension of public transport.

Trudi went over to the bank of windows. There was smoke rising from the park. She slid open the window, letting in a rhythm thumping on the cool, stiff wind. She leaned out, almost hoping she'd be whirled out into the air like weightless jetsam. Right below her, thirty-seven floors down, the staff of the Ritz-Carlton, white sleeves standing out from their black uniforms like a caterpillar's stripes, stood in a phalanx outside the door. That was the first time Trudi felt afraid, but she told herself not to overreact. The smoke might be from anywhere, a simple bonfire, and the Ritz-Carlton was probably just putting on a show of readiness for its guests.

'I told you,' Leo said. 'We should have gone already.'

'Just leave me here,' Caroline said. 'I'm too tired. I'm too old.'

'This is not for discussion.'

'Now this thing has happened, the thing you always wished would happen, you should be happy. Just leave me. You don't need me any more to . . .' Trudi glanced at her mother, voicing what Trudi secretly suspected but wouldn't dare to say: that somehow her father wanted this. He was so keen to believe the apocalypse was upon them because it would prove him right, prove how foresightful and prepared he was. But surely that wasn't fair. Surely, even if he lived in fear that something like this would happen, he would never want it. But what would she know? She knew almost nothing about her father. Caroline probably knew a lot more about him than she did.

'Nonsense,' was all he said.

Trudi gathered up the book she was reading – a worn copy of *Kavalier and Clay* – stuffed it in her tote bag and went to the window, staring back down at the waiters lining the street.

'It's not fair that it should just be people like us,' she said, more to herself than to Caroline or Leo, 'rich people, who get the chance to be safe from this. But I guess we're lucky. Dad's hard work has made us lucky, so we should use that luck.'

As if to punctuate her point, a pair of fighter jets scrambling low over the city sheared the mist-marbled sky.

'Bring your bag and let's go, okay?'

*

Trudi gets up from the bed, her back muscles protesting. She's been sitting still for too long – scared to move in case she wakes Caroline – and creeps out into the lounge. The clock on the kitchen wall reads 9:10.

Leo is standing near the front door, fiddling with a kitchen knife against the wall. The muted TV's playing the same round of footage. He turns to Trudi. 'How is she?'

'Still the same. Sleeping. What are you doing?'

The doorbell goes, making Trudi jump. The door opens, revealing Will Boucher, still wearing that mask. 'Leo,' he says. 'I'm sorry about this.'

Leo stiffens. 'Save your apologies. You can see we are not sick.'

Will nods. 'Greg says folks have a right to protect themselves, and I got to go with the majority consensus.' But he's clearly uncomfortable; Trudi can hear the embarrassment in his voice.

'What do you want?'

Will hands him a plastic bag. 'Some aspirin for Mrs Dannhauser.' He proffers the bag over the threshold then closes and locks the door again.

Leo puts the medicine down on the hall table and returns to fiddling with the lock. 'It's typical,' he mutters to himself.

Trudi wishes he'd speak to her like she's a real live person in the room. 'What is?'

'Excuse me?'

'What's typical?'

'This whole place. Shoddy. I'm not surprised that the medical suite isn't completed yet. Fuller's cut corners on everything. Look at the cheap, outdated locking system here. Probably bought them at a military sell-off.'

Trudi chooses not to stoke his indignation, so changes

tack. 'So if they know what's wrong with Mom, we shouldn't have to stay locked in, should we? Will you talk to Mr Fuller next time he comes?'

'They won't listen.' He clips the cover in place and steps back. 'But we're not locked in. Not any more.'

7
JAE

Jae logs out and shuts his laptop. Writing in his journal is supposed to be therapeutic or some shit, but it hasn't helped with this situation. He's itching to lose himself in a game, but there's no way he can leave his dad alone right now. He's never seen him so twitchy – he's been obsessively wiping down the kitchen counters and glancing at the door every five seconds. Jae flicks through the channels, settling on an old *30 Rock* episode. They need some kind of a distraction that isn't the looping shots of body bags and traffic jams that are currently dominating the news stations.

His mom has been gone for nearly an hour now, refusing to let Jae or his dad accompany her. And you don't contradict her when she's adamant about something. Dad's been busying himself chopping ingredients for supper, cleaning the kitchen cupboards and mumbling about the shoddy workmanship in the condo. Most of the kids at his school come from divorced families where both parents work, and Jae's simultaneously proud of his parents' enduring relationship and secretly ashamed of his father's lack of ambition. For as long as he can remember, it's been Moms who's gone out to work. His dad has nothing but an unfinished PhD and his prepping hobby to define him. Jae knows he shouldn't judge – his social science teacher is always going on about 'the empty construct of societal gender roles' – but occasionally Jae wishes his dad would do more with his life.

'Dad, it'll be okay.'

He attempts a smile, but it's dismal.

'If Mom's not back soon I'll go—'

The door opens and his mom enters the kitchen. There's something slung over her shoulder. *No way.* 'Is that a gas mask?'

'Yes.'

'Jesus.'

'Jae!' his mom berates him automatically. She drops the gas mask – more a respirator, really – onto the kitchen counter, and Dad puts his arms around her. She hugs him back, but her body language is stiff. 'Well?' Jae asks when they break apart.

His mom peels off her surgical gloves. 'I suspect the older woman has had a minor stroke. I'm going to insist that we call an ambulance.'

'We can't do that,' Dad says. 'You have seen what's going on outside. We must wait out the incubation period.'

Moms snorts. 'Who is this "we", Yoo-jin? What if she dies?'

'Greg and the others are doing the right thing. The only thing we *can* do right now, Stella.' Dad never calls Moms by her first name. It's always 'Honey' or 'My Love'.

Moms turns away from him. 'When I agreed that you could buy this place, I didn't sign up for this.'

'You think I am happy about the situation, Stella?'

Moms flinches and something slithers greasily in Jae's belly. He's only seen his parents fight once before – and never about anything important.

'We are just being careful.' Dad softens his voice. 'Is the woman in immediate danger?'

'I can't be sure. I can't even move her to the medical bay.' Another flash of resentment. 'There's not even a bed in there. You assured me there would be a fully stocked medical bay, Yoo-jin.' Moms chucks the gloves in the plastics bin, slamming the lid. 'This goddamned place.'

Yoo-jin catches Jae's eye. 'Jae. Your mother and I need to talk. Please go to your room.'

'Can I go to the rec room instead?'

Dad nods.

Jae gathers his stuff together and slips into the hallway. *Fuck*. He can't shake the feeling that this situation isn't going to get better anytime soon, which isn't helped by the knowledge that they're locked in now. He mentally shakes himself. He's being stupid. This isn't a prison. They can leave anytime they want. Everyone here has chosen to be here – including the people he'd seen on the video monitor. He can hear the grumble of voices coming from the floor below. It sounds like it might be Greg and Will. Jae hates himself for not having the balls to go down there and see what the hell's going on with his own eyes.

Instead, he pads up the stairs to the rec room. Scruffy will probably be asleep but there's bound to be someone from his guild online who'll be up for a PvP. Yeah. He'll play a few games, get his head right. And who knows? Maybe he'll run into Gina again. He's been thinking about her quite a bit since they last met, almost mentioned her to Scruffy (aware that part of him was doing this to see if he could make Scruffy jealous). There's something about Gina that tugs at him. She's nothing like the girls at his school, who are all confident, glossy-haired, quick with a put-down or a disparaging look. But there's no chance of anything happening between them. There's the religion thing for a start, not to mention the fact her brother is some kind of racist nut job.

He thinks the rec room's empty at first, then sees that there's someone sitting on one of the couches next to the TV. It's the woman with the deep red hair who he's mentally dubbed Jessica, after the vampire in *True Blood*. Slender, tall (taller than Jae in fact), early twenties or so, but Jae's never been good at judging age. He sneaked glances at her during that dumb prayer circle, and he wasn't the only one – Psycho Brett's tongue was practically lolling out of his big dumb head. The guy she's with is way older than she is, but Jae doesn't get the impression she's a trophy wife: no make-up, jeans, Converse and a hoodie.

She's staring straight ahead, her legs curled up under her, her hands wrapped around a mug. Earphone cords snake from under her hair – no wonder she didn't hear him entering the room. He waits for her to notice him; he doesn't want to make her jump.

Say something, noob.

He's about to open his mouth to speak when she spots him and removes the earphones. He catches the tinny sound of a rap beat. 'Oh. Hey.'

'Hey.'

'You know what's going on with those people? Tyson says they've been put in quarantine in case they're sick.'

He likes her accent, the way the vowels seem to roll. He doesn't think she's British, like that scary blonde woman who was giving Greg a hard time. 'My mom says the old woman might have had a stroke.'

She bites her lip. 'Shit. She going to be all right? Your mom's a doctor, right?'

'A dentist.'

'A dentist?' She laughs humourlessly. 'This place . . .'

She and Moms would get on. 'Where are you from?'

'South Africa. Johannesburg.'

'Oh, cool.' Jae scratches his mind for what he knows about the country. Not much. Nelson Mandela, Charlize Theron. A bit about apartheid. That's it. It strikes him that he doesn't even know her name. 'I'm Jae.'

'Cait.'

A few awkward seconds pass. She stares into the distance again. He's not used to taking the lead in a conversation. 'Um . . . is your husband looking after your daughter?'

She shakes her head. 'Tyson isn't my husband. He's my boss. I'm the au pair. I look after Sarita.'

'Where's her mom?'

'She died.'

'What, like in a car accident or something?' *Nice, Jae. Way to be super-sensitive.*

'I don't know how she died.' She's gripping the mug so tightly her knuckles are white. 'This place . . . I didn't even know we were coming here. I can't even tell my mom where we are because I don't know exactly where here *is*.'

'We're in Maine.'

She smiles and rolls her eyes. 'That narrows it down.' She gestures at his laptop. 'You a gamer? You were glued to that thing earlier.'

'I could be writing a novel on it or something.' He feels a spurt of confidence – that was a cool line.

'I recognize the signs. I had an ex who was married to his Xbox. It wasn't all bad. I got addicted to *Black Ops* and *Skyrim* for a while.'

'*Skyrim*'s okay. I'm more of an MMO player.'

'MMO?'

'I play online.'

'What, like *Second Life, World of Warcraft*, that kind of thing?'

He's impressed. '*WoW* all the way. I've gone full-geek.'

She laughs. 'Nothing wrong with being a geek. Hey, why don't you set it up? I need something to take my mind off everything.'

'Really?'

'Really.'

'I can hook it up to the TV screen if you like.' He sounds like an eager kid. *Play it cool.*

'Why not?'

He plugs the laptop into the screen and logs in. 'You want me to show you how to create a character? Or you can have a go on my mount if you like?'

'On your *what*?'

Dumbass. His face is burning. 'Sorry. A mount is like a creature you can ride on to fly through the portals.'

'Mount it is.'

His hand is shaking slightly as he clicks on the mouse, calls up the character menu and logs his warlock and mount.

'Is that a dragon?'

'It's a frostbrood vanquisher,' Jae says, slightly defensively.

She rolls her eyes again. 'Of course.'

He portals through to Outland – he digs the graphics on this level – and shows Cait how to make the mount move with the mouse. She gets it immediately, laughing as she propels it through a chasm. 'This is so cool.'

Something's missing – they need a soundtrack. 'Hey . . . what kind of music do you like?'

'You choose.'

He uploads a Blue Stahli track – a tune he tends to pick when he's doing some high-octane raiding – and cranks up the volume.

Cait nods her head. 'Schaweet.'

'What?'

'Sorry. It means cool. Sweet.'

They share a smile.

'Next I'll show you how to create your own character.'

Cait looks up. 'Oh, hey.'

Jae follows her gaze. Gina's standing a few feet away, twisting her hands. Jae's hit with a stab of guilt – where did that come from? It's not as if he and Gina are an item or anything.

'Hi.' He turns the volume down.

Cait smiles at her. 'We're on the same floor.'

Gina blushes. 'I know. That little girl you're with is cute.'

'Sarita. Ja, she's lovely.'

'My dad says you're from Australia.'

Cait grins. 'I'm South African.'

'Oh.' Gina looks momentarily confused. 'Your . . . your hair is so pretty.'

'Thanks. It was really ginger when I was younger. You should have heard the names I was called at school.'

'I like it. Um . . .' Gina glances at Jae. 'Um. I just came to get a Coke.'

'Why don't you join us?' Cait says. 'Jae's inducting me into the secret world of *World of Warcraft*.'

'I shouldn't . . .' She glances at the mount on the screen, which is hovering over a chasm, flapping its wings every so often. 'Is it like *Harry Potter*?'

'It's nothing like *Harry Potter*.'

Indecision flashes over her face. 'Okay. Um . . . can I just watch?'

'Sure.'

She sits on the other side of Jae, her thigh almost touching his. She smells of strawberries. Jae wishes that Mufftown – a guild member who was always teasing him about Scruffy and boasting about his sexual prowess – could see him now. 'So this zone is—'

The door slams. 'Gina!' a voice gasps from behind them. Gina jumps. A woman with long scraggly black hair and a moon face strides towards them. Her eyes are fixed on the screen.

Gina grasps Jae's arm, then leaps to her feet. 'Momma!'

Cait shoots Jae a questioning look.

'Gina. What are you doing?' the woman says.

'I'm . . . I'm not doing anything, Momma.'

'Get away from them, girl. If Daddy sees you . . .'

'Momma, I wasn't—'

'Come away. Now!'

'Hi,' Cait says, getting to her feet. 'We haven't met.'

The woman ignores her. 'Gina. Go back to the condo.'

'Momma, I wasn't playing the game, I promise.' Gina's eyes are filling and she's frantically picking at her jeans.

'You have to stay with me,' she says to Gina, almost whispering, as if she's afraid. 'You can't be up here, playing with . . .' Now she finally passes her eyes over Jae's face. 'You just can't.'

Jae feels like he should say something. 'It's fine.' He can't bring himself to say *ma'am* but feels he probably should. 'You can tell him it's my fault. I asked her.'

But the woman ignores him, distracted by her own nervous thoughts. 'We'll pray on it, girl. That's right. Maybe that will help us.'

'Mrs Guthrie,' Cait says. 'That's not what is going on here. Gina wasn't actually playing the game.' Like Jae, she clearly thinks this reaction is some radical fundamentalist response to the demons inside video games. It's the only sense they can make of it.

'We'll pray on it,' the woman repeats. 'That's right. The Lord will keep us safe in His arms.' She grabs Gina's arm.

'I'm sorry,' Gina's saying to them over her shoulder. 'I shouldn't have.'

'Jesus,' Cait murmurs under her breath as Gina is dragged from the room.

The door slams behind them and he and Cait exchange glances. This is the part where they're supposed to laugh nervously and say, 'WTF was that?' But she looks just as shell-shocked as he feels.

8

GINA

I can sense the Devil sitting in the corner of the room, watching me.

I should have been more careful. How long has Momma trained me to be vigilant, to look after myself in the face of danger, but I slipped at the first smile from a boy. Although I don't think Jae himself is evil, that's how the Devil works, that is his power. That's what Pastor Barnard says at church. Those games and those books and those movies are the Devil's portal. He talks about how it is on the streets of America: the damned shuffling along in greed and vice, lechery and sloth, all because they have been drugged by their entertainment. Just look at the state of the world now. I knew that I should pray for the deliverance of my eternal soul. The words came to me from above. After Daddy yelled at me for leaving the unit, I prayed for guidance until my knees ached so bad, I had to quit.

I woke up in my bed, and the comfort of it reminded me just how much Momma and Daddy love me, how much they've given up to keep me safe.

Now I see his bright eyes, the Devil in my room. I invited him here, but I won't let him any closer. I squeeze my eyes shut and clamp my hands together over my heart and pray to the Lord with such fervour that I can feel His light surround me and protect me. The Devil will not pass.

The Sanctum's air-recycling system grinds and sighs, and I try to shake off the feeling that we're all locked inside Satan's body.

'Get thee behind me,' I whisper.

Then, screaming.

At first, I think it's the horses dying, but the noise becomes something real, a wild keening from outside my head. The room is no longer pitch dark. The red numbers on the electronic clock are shining 6:03. Those fake windows are now pushing dawn light through the drapes.

'Are these windows the Devil's work?' I asked Momma yesterday – before I was caught looking at that game. Even before we were pulled out of school there were teachers there who said computers and games and anything electronic was a path to the Devil. The pastor says it nearly every Sunday, picking all the kids out of the congregation. Brett used to laugh after the service, calling it Pastor Barney's Playtime, but not after whatever happened that spring with Bessie Carver. The last two years he's just sat in the pew, never looking up, or over at me, just fighting to hold himself in until the service was over. I never saw that movie about the polterghost, but I saw the movie poster in Dan Heisenberg's den – the little kid staring into the TV where the demons came from. We had a lousy little TV in the trailer, but here there's *two* big flat-screen TVs in the condo, and these electronic walls. They made me afraid, so I asked Momma if the teachers were right.

She looked at me, a flicker of doubt crossing her face. I

wanted her to have the answers for once. I needed her not to doubt.

She thought about it, then she came to a decision. 'The windows are fine, Gina. I guess they show the glory of the Lord's creation.' She shrugged. 'They're pretty, don't you think?'

So when I prayed last night, I got to know that forest and that mountain and that beach pretty well, until they faded off, long before I was done. I know what Pastor Barnard would say if I told him there were ghosts in my dreams. He'd say it means the Devil's trying to find a way in. But I feel like the Devil's already inside me.

Finally I recognize the noise. It's a siren, like a fire alarm. I check Brett's bed. It's rumpled and empty. I kick the blankets off and run to the door. I touch the handle, but then I stop. Daddy told me to stay in my room. I hear him and Brett talking from the living area.

'Daddy! Daddy!' I call. 'Can I come out of my room?'

A moment later, Daddy's voice on the other side of the door: 'Stay right there, Gina.'

'But, Daddy. What if there's a fire? You can't . . .'

His voice back in the living area.

'Daddy?'

The front door slams.

'Daddy!'

Still the siren is screaming.

I knock on the inside of the door. 'Momma?'

Nothing.

I don't think they'd leave me here if there was a fire.

Over the noise of the siren, I hear the front door slamming shut again.

'Is everything okay?'

No answer.

'Brett? Daddy?'

If Daddy saw me leaving the room, he'd be mad at me. He'd probably lock me in here till I'm twenty-one. But if the alarm's still on, it means the danger's still present. Maybe I just imagined the second slam – maybe Daddy, Brett and Momma are all assembled upstairs in a safe place.

I twist the door handle and peek my head through the smallest crack. I stifle a gasp. Momma's rushing past my door towards her bedroom, gasping and crying as if she's terrified of something.

I chase after her, not caring if I'll be in trouble.

She's sitting at the end of her bed, clutching her head in her hands, rocking back and forth like a frightened little girl, jabbering something I can't hear. There's the faint odour of sour smoke in the air.

'Momma!' I shout over the siren's din.

She doesn't take any notice.

'We've got to go, Momma. There's a fire . . . or something.'

Now she looks up. 'I've made a big mistake, hon. I was doing it for you, to protect you.'

I don't know what she's talking about. I wait, but she says nothing else. I'm not sure whether to go and find Daddy and get in trouble with him, or stay here with Momma.

I go to the front door, crack it open and sniff the air for smoke. I can hear a little girl crying, then the apartment next door opens and Cait comes out, holding the little one, stroking her hair. The little girl is calming down now. I can hear someone talking in the stairwell, the loud foreign voice of that lady with the dog, then the dog starts yapping. Cait hears it too; she turns and sees me. I know I should go back inside – I don't know what Momma would do if she saw me out here – but I give her a half-smile that I know looks embarrassed. She gives me a sad but kind look back and comes nearer.

'We have to assemble upstairs,' Cait says. 'I'm just waiting for Tyson.'

'I, I . . .' I stutter. 'My Momma's inside. She won't come out.'

Behind her, the man – Tyson – is closing their front door. 'Let's go, Cait!' he bellows over the noise, and heads to the stairwell.

Cait nods at me. 'Maybe it's nothing. If there's a problem, I'll come down for you, okay?'

'Sure. Thanks.' I duck back in and close the front door, heart hammering.

I look in on Momma again. She's still sitting where she was, but she's stopped rocking, at least. Her face is grey. I sit down next to her and wait.

A moment later, the whole world clicks off. The alarm stops, and even the noise of the air-conditioning is gone, and for a moment I think I've died: total dark, total silence. For that moment I shame myself by thinking that God has forgotten me. If I die, I expected light and joy, to be taken up into Heaven, into His warm embrace, but there's nothing, and the suddenness of it halts my breathing.

But it's only a matter of seconds before everything starts up again with a grind. I'm shivering, trying to remember myself. I can't rub away the imprint of that dead void from my heart.

I still haven't moved, just staring numb at the door, when I hear Daddy and Brett come back. It's only now I realize that Momma's hand is clasped between mine – she hasn't moved all this time. The click of a lock and Brett comes in and leans against the door frame.

Momma's out of it, and I have to face him alone. There's a clot in my throat and I can't bring myself to say anything to him.

'You don't want to know what that was about?' he says to me.

'Uh. Sure.'

'There was a small fire in the control room. The sprinklers came on, and Mr Fuller was in there fast. Everything got wet – some equipment shorted out. You shouldn't put water on electrical fires. Mr Fuller had to reset the main supply. He says most of the systems are fine, but he and that other guy have to check everything over now.'

Daddy passes the door, that respirator mask of his slung around his neck. He glares at Momma. 'What did you do?'

She looks up slowly. 'It was a mistake, Cam.'

'What were you even doing up there, for the love of God?'

'I . . . I . . .'

And then I realize it. I guess she was trying to protect me from Jae's game after all. She knows as little as me about how it works, but we all know the internet signal must come from somewhere. Maybe she was just trying to switch it off.

Now Brett advances into the room. 'Yeah, Momma. What were you doing up there?'

How dare he talk to her like that? And the way she looks at him – afraid! – makes me even madder with him. 'Get out, Brett!' I scream, ignoring my heart beginning to burst. Because I know if Momma had to say the reason, she'll have to tell them I was sitting with Jae. 'You can't talk to Momma like that. It's none of your business!' I grab Momma around the shoulders.

Thankfully, my outburst takes them by surprise enough so that Brett backs off.

Daddy glances between us. 'I've gotta go downstairs and apprise the Dannhauser family. Gina, you do your chores and make us breakfast. Then when you're done, you get back in your bedroom.'

'But—'

'You do your chores and get back in your bedroom!' he repeats. 'Brett, you keep to yourself, you hear.'

'Sure thing, Daddy,' he says, good as gold. He waits for Daddy to leave the condo, then he says with a smirk, 'I'm hungry, sis. Where's breakfast?' He's enjoying this all too much.

I've convinced Momma to take a shower and have put her clothes in the washer with extra powder. Now she's in her room, reading from her study Bible at the dresser. Daddy and Brett are in the sitting room, watching the news on TV – looks like they're already working on an antidote to the virus. They seem to have forgotten about me.

But as I pass, Momma calls out to me. 'Gina, hon?'

I backtrack and stand by her door. 'Yes, Momma?'

'Come sit with me. Close the door.'

I do as she says and perch on the bed behind her. She turns to me. 'You're a big girl now, Gina. Sometimes I forget how big, and that's my fault.'

I nod, not sure that I want to have this conversation, but I don't really have any option, do I?

'I realize that you're growing up. That a lot has changed in you since we moved to the lot. You haven't really had the chance to be with kids your own age. You haven't had the chance to socialize.'

I just about push down my laugh – it's not Momma I'm feeling bitter towards. Besides, bitterness is not healthy.

'It's natural that you want to be with people more your own age,' she goes on. 'And I want to explain why that's not a good idea down here. This isn't a natural environment and there's all sorts of temptation. While we're here, we need to watch out for each other.' She pauses. 'Are you listening, hon?'

'Yeah, Momma,' I say.

'I know you've heard this a thousand times before.' She lowers her voice. 'Your Daddy's sure drummed the preparation aspect of our lives into you kids since, well . . . And I'm with him. I need to be with him on this.'

'We're all in it together, Momma,' I recite.

I shift, as if I'm about to leave, but she turns around completely on her stool. 'But there's one more thing, and it's something Daddy can never understand. It's about women, about why we must follow the Lord's teachings on this, why we must keep our purity.' Her face is flushing and I'm feeling awkward in return. I don't want to hear this from her. I don't want to be the cause of her shame. 'You can't let them . . . There are too many men who would . . . You need to—'

Thank the Lord, the doorbell goes just then and I have an excuse to bound to the door like a coiled spring. I sneak back into the bedroom Brett and I share as Daddy goes to open the door. 'What now?'

'You mind if we come in, Cam?' It's Mr Fuller and Will Boucher, I can see as I stand in the doorway and peep into the hallway.

'I can talk just fine from here, Greg.'

'We'd rather come in if you don't mind.'

'Fine.' The door closes. The men gather around the kitchen counter. None of them sits. Brett stays where he is on the couch. 'What is it?'

'It looks like the fire in the control room might have been set deliberately,' Mr Fuller says. His voice doesn't sound as calm as it usually is.

'That so?'

'We're convening a general meeting at nine a.m. and we'll discuss the details then. But before that, I'd like to give you the opportunity to tell me if you have any idea who might have been involved. If you know any reason someone would . . .'

'What exactly are you saying, Greg?'

'Well, Cam, I'm not pointing any fingers, but I've been told of an altercation last night. Apparently Mrs Guthrie was very angry when she saw your daughter playing a computer game.'

Oh no. He can't know. Daddy can't know. For an instant I'm certain I'm going to vomit, then Daddy speaks again: 'Who told you that?'

'The girl who works for Tyson Gill and the—'

Will cuts him off. 'Cam, you know we can't tell you that.'

Brett's up now and strides towards the men. 'It was that Chink as well, wasn't it?'

'Now, Brett,' Daddy warns.

'You're going to believe the word of that Chink? They're the reason we're down here in the first place! If anyone—'

'Enough, Brett!' Daddy barks. 'Go to your room.'

'But—'

'I said go.' He turns to point the way for Brett so quickly that he catches me spying on them. 'What is it with you kids?'

Brett's face is burning as he scrapes into our bedroom. He lies on his bed, face to the wall.

'You mind if we ask Mrs Guthrie and Gina if they saw something?' Greg says.

'Bonnie's sleeping, but you can ask Gina if you must. We got nothing to hide.'

I'm still standing there – to hide away now would seem even more dishonest – and Daddy catches my eye. He trusts me.

Mr Fuller turns around and comes to my bedroom doorway. 'Did you hear what we've been talking about, Gina?'

'Yes, sir.'

'Did you see anything, hear anything that might help us?'

I don't give it a moment's thought. 'No, sir.'

He trains his worry-creased eyes on mine for a long moment. 'Alright, Gina. That's okay.'

9
JAMES

James tips his head back, opens his mouth and lets the tepid water run over his tongue. Showering or bathing usually calms him when he's feeling stressed, but it's doing nothing to soothe him this morning. He's over-tired, jumpy, keeps thinking he can hear that alarm ringing in his ears. After Greg reassured them that the fire was under control, he and Vicki spent the next couple of hours downing decaf and watching CNN: 'WHO Gives Go-Ahead for AOBA Vaccine Trials,' reads the ticker. He supposes he should be feeling smug – they're miles away from any of the 'hot zones' – but the idea of this supposed sanctuary on fire . . . that was something that never came to mind before. He winces as he's hit with an image of himself crawling through The Sanctum's stairwell on his hands and knees, blinded by smoke, vomiting strings of mucus and feeling his skin crisping as he's engulfed in greedy flames.

Jesus. He towels off and throws on a pair of shorts and a Ralph Lauren sports shirt. He doesn't bother shaving, brushing his teeth or moisturizing, although the recycled air down here must be playing havoc with his skin.

'James! Hurry up,' Vicki calls.

'Coming!' He glances at the bug-out bag where he's stashed his menthols. Why the hell not? He might get a chance to sneak a cigarette after the tenants' meeting, and God knows he needs one. He slides his lighter and a pack into his pocket, then ties a sweatshirt around his waist to hide the bulge.

He's greeted by a familiar vile odour as he enters the kitchen. Wonderful. The dog is busy 'doing its business' (another of Vicki's nauseating euphemisms) on one of its disposable doggy pads. Even its shit looks genetically engineered.

Vicki looks up from her laptop and assesses him with faint distaste. No doubt she thinks he should have made more of an effort. She's fully made-up, dressed in a designer sweatsuit and pumps. How can she look so fresh and put together? Has she been at the tranks? He doesn't think so, her eyes are clear. She raps her nails on the counter. 'There's still no internet. It's just not good enough. Greg had better have an explanation for what happened.'

James eyes the coffee machine, decides another cup isn't a good idea. 'Didn't he say it was an electrical fire?'

'I'm certain I smelled petrol in the control room.'

'Petrol?'

'Gas. Or paraffin, something like that. Didn't you?'

'Nope.' He only smelled smoke and the noxious fumes of melting plastic.

She sighs as if he's disappointed her. It wouldn't be the first time. 'We'd better get going.' Vicki gathers Claudette into her arms.

'You're bringing the dog?'

'Of course. Until we know for sure this place really is safe, I'm not letting her out of my sight.'

The Guthrie kid is standing to attention outside the Dannhausers' door, knife at his hip. James still hasn't handed his Glock over to Greg for storage, and he's damned if he's going to. He wouldn't describe himself as a gun nut, but knowing it's there reassures him. And he always gets a kick out of bending the rules. 'Morning, sir, ma'am,' the kid barks, and James almost expects him to salute. Like his father, he looks like he's been outfitted at Preppers R Us. James hasn't met the mother yet – he isn't sure he wants to. Christ knows what it must be like living in the shadow of so much testosterone. The daughter acted cowed enough when he saw her.

'How are the Dannhausers doing?' Vicki only sounds mildly interested, although she was one of the instigators of the family's lockdown. James is hit with a twinge of shame: he didn't even give the Dannhausers a thought when the alarm sounded.

The kid shrugs. 'Dunno. That lady doctor came to see them, but didn't say.'

James tries to catch Vicki's eye – sure that she'll have something biting to say about the 'lady doctor' comment. But for some reason she's chosen to ignore it.

'Aren't you coming to the meeting?' she asks.

'No, ma'am. Orders are to stay here.'

Orders. Jesus. The kid's future as an army grunt is written all over him. James has no trouble picturing him charging through a war zone and casually boasting about the number of towelheads he's waterboarded.

A small group is gathered around the TV screen when they get upstairs to the rec room. James is relieved that there's no sign of Tyson, but his daughter and the redhead – Cait, that's it – are perched on the couch next to the Asian kid and his parents. Not for the first time, James wonders if Tyson is fucking his au pair. And who could blame him? She's by far the most attractive person in this place – what the guys in his old frat would have called 'eminently doable'.

After the Dannhausers arrived, Vicki interrogated Greg about where Tyson's wife was but Greg was too distracted to tell them much. James knows that Vicki won't be able to resist digging for the gory details as soon as things settle down. Curiously, Guthrie senior and the women of his redneck clan are also absent. James would have thought Cam would be the type who'd want to be right in the heart of the action. Maybe he's joined his son for a spot of guard duty.

The little girl whispers something into Cait's ear. She catches James's eye. 'Sarita wants to know if she can stroke the dog.'

'Better not,' James says. Claudette has been known to snap at strangers; the last thing they need with all this going on is a lawsuit. He smiles at Cait to take the sting out of his words and Vicki looks at him sharply. He knows that look. Fuck. Just what he needs right now.

'Morning, everyone,' Greg calls as he emerges from the control room, shutting the door behind him. His cheeks are fusty with grey stubble, but he's doing his best to radiate his usual good cheer. 'I hope you all managed to get some sleep after the incident.'

'Of course we didn't,' Vicki snaps. 'Do you know what caused the fire yet?'

Greg's eyes dart around the room. 'Rest assured, we'll get to the bottom of it soon.'

Stella Park (who Vicki nastily dubbed 'the Biggest Loser' after their first group meeting) looks up. 'Are we safe here?'

'I can assure you we're perfectly safe here, Stella.' Greg gestures at the screen, which is showing footage of hazmat-suited military personnel swarming around a hospital parking lot. 'Safer than those folks out there, that's for sure.'

'How do we know it won't happen again?'

'Stella, you have my word that you've got nothing to worry about on that score. The Sanctum is one hundred and ten per cent geared towards protecting your safety. The second that smoke was detected, the sprinklers kicked in and controlled the situation with a minimum of damage.'

James is well schooled in the art of detecting bullshit, and it's clear by the way Greg's hands keep going to his mouth that he's hiding something from them.

Vicki shakes her head. 'And what about the internet? I have several urgent emails I need to send. Really, this isn't—'

'When are you going to let the Dannhausers out of their apartment?' Stella interrupts.

Greg nods. 'I understand that you are—'

'You can't keep them locked in there. What you're doing, it's . . . it's barbaric!' She's really working herself up, her jowls are wobbling. Her husband tries to take her hand, but she snatches it away from him.

'So you'd rather risk us all getting infected?' Vicki glares at her.

To her credit, Stella doesn't back down. 'I'd rather we acted like human beings. Showed some compassion.'

Vicki snorts. 'I'd like to see how much compassion you'll have if those people *are* infected and you or your son gets sick.'

'They're not infected. They have no symptoms whatsoever,' Stella says.

'And you're some kind of expert on viruses, are you? Just what kind of doctor are you, anyway?'

Stella colours. 'I'm an orthodontist. A specialist. I . . .'

Vicki throws her head back and laughs. Stella's husband is staring down at his lap, but the son has gone very still and is glaring at Vicki.

Greg holds up his hands. 'Calm down, everyone. We're all tired and concerned. Stella, rest assured we're doing all we can to make the Dannhausers comfortable. And if we can't fix the modem and router today, then Will and I will head into town tomorrow for replacements.'

'You're going to go out there?' Vicki asks. 'Are you insane?'

'We'll take precautions. We've got the biohazard suits and we'll make sure you are all secured in here if we do have to take this step.'

James bites his lip as he imagines Greg and Will galumphing through Walmart in their oversized breathing apparatus and white overalls.

'Like the stores will even be open,' Jae Park mumbles. He's stopped shooting daggers at Vicki and now his left knee is jiggling up and down.

Greg ignores him. 'What I'm saying is that Will and I have everything under control. And until we're back online, there's lots to keep you busy. There's the gym and the pool, of course, and I'm gonna need volunteers to help harvest the vegetables and collect the eggs.'

'Where is Will?' Vicki asks. 'Shouldn't he be here?'

'He's back in his condo, dealing with some personal business. I appreciate you all being patient while we handle this situation.'

Vicki rolls her eyes. 'Great. So that's it, then?'

'That's it for now. I'm here if you have any more questions.' As Greg turns back towards the control room, James gets a glimpse of the raw exhaustion underneath his jocular veneer. The Park family get to their feet. Stella lumbers ahead of her husband, resolutely ignoring James and Vicki. The kid mumbles 'Laters' to Cait and slumps after his parents.

James reckons he'll go insane if he watches any more of

the virus footage. Perhaps a workout will help calm him down – at the very least it'll give him an excuse to slip away and find a quiet corner to sneak a smoke.

'Bye, doggy.' Sarita waves as she and Cait make their way to the stairwell.

'Put your eyes back in your head, James,' Vicki says to him, loud enough for the redhead to hear. 'Could you be any more obvious?'

His gut clenches. *Shit.* 'I don't know what you mean.'

'I saw the way you were looking at her.'

'I really wasn't, Vicki.' *Try to keep it light.* He attempts a boyish smile. 'You know I only go for blondes.'

He's hoping against hope that this will do the trick. That it won't be one of *those* times. She's unpredictable. She made a joke out of him checking out Will when he helped them change the tyre, but he can tell by her expression and body language that this time she's gearing up for a big freeze. Jesus. She can't do this to him now. They need to stick together. She stalks towards the stairwell and he hurries after her.

'Come on, babe. You're being—'

She whirls around. 'What? Irrational? Is that it?' She taps her head. 'Don't think I don't know what goes through your head, James. I can read you like a fucking book.' Her voice is getting increasingly strident; he hopes to Christ no one else can hear, though it's probably echoing through every level of this place. 'Tell you what, why don't you take Claudette for a walk, see if you can run into your *girlfriend* again.'

She pushes the dog into his arms and James almost drops it as it squirms in his arms. If she's leaving him with the dog, he knows for sure he's in for a marathon sulking session. 'Babe!'

She hares down the stairs before he can stop her. He knows that not following her straight away will only make it worse for him, but he's sick of this shit. He's lost count of the number of times she's flounced out of restaurants after accusing him of checking out the staff, and her coldness after one of these incidents can last for days. Thank God everyone at the Boston Prepper Society was buttfuck ugly or over the hill, otherwise that brief hiatus would have been ruined.

No. He's not going to follow her like a gutless wonder. Let her stew. Now would be the perfect time to sneak a smoke. And he thinks he knows where to go.

He plonks Claudette on the stairs – no way is he carrying the fucking thing – and the dog looks up at him accusingly. 'You got legs. Use them,' he snaps at her. It's slow going – Claudette's legs are too short to match his stride, and he's forced to stop and wait for her every few steps. He slips past his floor and yanks the dog down to level six, where the unfinished condos are situated.

The dog lets out one of its whuffling barks as James pushes open the stairwell door, revealing a desolate passage, lit only by emergency strip lights. Where the condos' front entrances would be are two empty door frames, draped with clear tarps.

He chooses the one on the right, the unfinished medical bay. Claudette is whining now, sniffing at the floor and acting like a real dog for once. The yellow light from the passageway only illuminates two or three yards of the condo's interior. The rest of the space is pitch black – no way is he going that far in; just the thought of being surrounded by such pure darkness makes the hairs on his arms stand up. There's also a faint feral odour in the air, along with the new-paint smell that's been giving him a headache ever since he and

Vicki arrived at The Sanctum. He fires up his Zippo and waves it around. The place is basically a shell. Wires and air-conditioning pipes sag from the roof, and paint cans and empty water bottles litter the floor. Over to one side, there's a gurney sheathed in plastic, a drip stand, and the beginnings of a bank of closets. He shudders. At least there won't be any smoke detectors. He lights up and inhales, his head swimming as the nicotine hits his bloodstream. Claudette whines again and tugs on the lead. He decides not to let the dog off her leash. Vicki will have a conniption if Claudette ends up getting paint in her fur.

He hears a tinging sound and starts. What the fuck was that? He's almost certain it came from the condo's gloomy depths.

'Hello?'

Silence. He takes a step forward, and shines the lighter around again. Nothing. Claudette is snuffling at something on the floor and he bends to take a closer look. Rat droppings. That would explain the sound and why the dog is acting up. He'll need to have a word with Greg about that – it's a fucking health hazard. This goddamned place is getting ridiculous. What's the point of a luxury survival condo that bursts into flames and is overrun with rats? He's beginning to think he and Vicki should insist on a refund and take their chances back in the city. He takes a last drag, then kills the cigarette, chucking the butt into the condo's shadows. Dammit – he should have bought some breath mints. Why didn't he think of that?

'Let's go, Claudette.'

The dog is still standing to attention, and refuses to move when he tugs the lead. He's forced to yank it hard, making her yelp, a sound that slices through the still air. Tough. Why should he be the only one who has to suffer? But as he heads into the stairwell, he relents, like he knew he would. He lifts her into his arms as he trudges up the stairs to face the music.

10

CAIT

Sarita's eyelids flutter and her breathing steadies. I gently remove the photo album from under her arm and place it on the side table. I lie with her for a while, listening to my music, watching the static birds disappear and the sky darken on the fake window screens, until I know she's fast asleep.

I've tried to keep her busy – and not just for her sake. She's been whiny all day, unsettled by the break in routine and crotchety from being woken by the fire alarm. I needed the distraction as much as she did. I made her bedroom into a playroom, making cereal boxes and milk cartons and bowls and jars into building blocks and houses for her, Simba and Strawb, erecting a fort with spare blankets and bedspreads and stools. I took her down to the pool in the afternoon, then let her watch some TV in the main bedroom. Although I can feel the weight of dark, cold earth pressing in on us from all sides, I remind myself that this space is big enough for Sarita, and that's what's important.

Anyway, this place probably feels quite familiar to Sarita. The Sanctum's off-the-shelf luxury and total lack of personality is a lot like Tyson's house. It's weird, because in some of Sarita's photos of Rani in their house, there are bright hangings on the walls, colourful throws, arty ornaments on the cabinets, but since I've been there the house has felt stripped and drained, nothing on the walls, the odd toy or kids' book adrift in a bland expanse of dove-grey. It's as if Tyson erased all trace of Rani immediately after she died.

But what do I know? All I've seen of Rani is in the little photo album Sarita carries everywhere. A handful of pictures of Sarita's mom looking pretty and happy, a couple at their wedding, some shots from a skiing holiday. There aren't any of Tyson. Was he always behind the camera?

I pull Sarita's door closed behind me and pad out to the living room. Tyson's still slouched on the couch with the condo's robe over his suit trousers and button shirt, staring at a news channel, his laptop open on his knees. Since he got back from the meeting, he's been here all day, only moving to pour more coffee, instead of using the opportunity to spend some time with his daughter. Arsehole.

I start toasting some frozen bread and opening a can of beans without asking him if he wants anything. 'When do you think they'll get the internet working again?' I say. 'I'm really worried about my mother.'

'Why? What's wrong?'

I glare at the back of his head. 'She'll be trying to get hold of me, Tyson. She'll be watching the news and wondering if I'm okay.'

'Oh. Yeah. I don't know. Greg said he was working on it.'

Like that gives me confidence. Greg strikes me more as a thick-handed artisan than a techie. 'Tyson. I'm serious. I need to get out of here. Aren't you worried? After what happened last night?'

He shrugs.

Jesus. 'What if the fire was set deliberately? What if someone's trying to cut us off on purpose?'

'Well, it looks like they're downgrading the threat

102

anyhow,' he says, gesturing at the TV. 'The modified H1N1 vaccine seems to be working in Asia. Cases are tailing off. In a couple more days you could be home and I can go back to work.'

'And what will happen with Sarita?'

'Huh?'

'When you're back at work and I'm back in South Africa.' He finally turns to me and his opaque look riles me. I chuck my spoon into my bowl with a clatter. 'You act like she doesn't even exist, Tyson.'

'What?'

'Jesus, Tyson. You've got a daughter who's bereaved. She needs you to love her, to be with her. You know, I can act like her mommy for now, but that's just papering over the cracks. I'm not going to be here forever.'

I know I've gone too far and I'm bracing for his outrage, like I've heard him occasionally let loose on his PA over the phone. But all he says is, 'Yeah, I know. I'm sorry.' He stands up and comes to the kitchen counter. 'I've never had to be a hands-on parent. Rani always took care of that. I guess I didn't want to get in the way.'

I'm caught off guard and a flush of shame passes through me. It's the first time I've heard him mention his wife so directly and it reminds me that he's also in mourning. 'Well, it's great news that the situation out there isn't so bad. So why don't you use this time till it's clear as a vacation, some time to spend with her? She'll really enjoy getting to know you.'

'Sure. Okay.' But he looks unconvinced.

'Maybe it will help if you take her around the complex, show her the chickens, spend some time with some of the other families. That might take the pressure off, make it less intense for you. You guys could play some games in the rec room. There are some nice people in here.' Utter bullshit. Apart from Jae, I haven't met anyone I'd remotely want to spend time with in real life. Jae and I tried to laugh off that scene last night with Gina Guthrie's mother, but it rattled me more than I really want to admit. What if she is responsible for the fire? How safe is everyone with someone like that unhinged woman down here?

Tyson snorts. 'This place is full of lunatics.'

His candour makes me laugh. 'I know, right? You've met some of them before, haven't you? You seemed to know Cam Guthrie and that rich couple – the cougar and that guy.'

'James and Vicki Maddox. Yeah. We've met.'

'When was that? Do you know them from work?' I'm being nosy, but so what? His guard is down and now might be my only chance to get some answers. I push my plate aside. That nausea has lodged itself inside me now.

'Goodness, no. Greg Fuller invited all the interested buyers to an open sales weekend in April.' He's measuring his words, glancing at me as he speaks.

'Here? Did you stay in here?'

'No. The complex wasn't finished yet, but he gave us a site tour to show us the progress.' He pauses. 'We all stayed at a lodge over at Lake Auburn. It was cold.'

'Oh, so you've met them all?'

'No. James and Vicki were there. Cameron Guthrie and the old guy, Leo – from the sick family – came alone. I guess the others who were there decided not to buy.'

'Was this when Rani was . . . ?' I know I'm probing too much, but he's still telling me more than he's ever volunteered before.

He rubs his hand over his brow. 'Yes. Yes, of course.'

'Did she come with you? On the open weekend?'

'No'. He stares at my plate of congealing beans for a moment, stands up and goes back to the couch.

'I'm sorry', I say. 'It's not my business'.

He doesn't reply.

But it *is* my business. As long as I'm looking after their daughter. I want to know more about the parents I'm replacing – both of them. When I applied for the job, my friends teased me about the widowed American millionaire I was going to work for, imagining a heartbroken George Clooney type. But the guy doesn't date, he doesn't seem to have any interest in women. It's just work and more work. I haven't felt the slightest bit of sexual tension from him. And that, at least, is something I like about him.

It's later than I expected, past eleven, but I'm still feeling wired. I consider going back up to the rec room, but with the internet down, Jae's probably not going to be there, and the last thing I want is to run into any of the others.

Tyson barely acknowledges my 'good night' as I head to my room. Maybe Murakami will take my mind off everything – stop me stressing about Mom.

A bang.

My book falls to the floor as I sit up too suddenly. I must've dozed off.

I turn to look at the bedside clock: 3:24. Suicide hour. The darkest part of the night. But it's always dark down here, until you turn the lights on.

Then it hits. That sound – it was the click and bang of the front door closing.

I spring out of bed and run to Sarita's room.

It's empty.

Damn. I just assumed that Tyson would arm the door lock, just as he activates the alarm at home every night before he goes to bed, but we didn't discuss it. I try to comfort myself with the thought that Sarita can't actually go anywhere. It's not like she's going to stroll out the front door and wander off into the woods.

But it's no comfort. The Sanctum is still big. Big enough for a little girl to get lost and scared in. I pull on some jeans under the baggy sweatshirt I've been sleeping in and hurry out to the front door. Yes, the green LED's burning quietly, the door ready for anyone to open it. The lights flick on as I go out into the corridor. She's not here, so I race to the stairwell door, the phosphorescent 'Level 3' shining out of the darkness. Up or down? Perhaps she's gone downstairs to the pool – thank Christ she can swim – or she might as easily have gone up to the rec room.

I stare into the darkness, not stepping onto the landing so that I don't trigger the lights on this level. After a minute, my eyes adjust and I notice a glow coming from upstairs. There we go; she must have gone to the rec room. I jog up one flight, then the next, the lights tripping on as I go. Past level two, and around, when I run straight into Brett Guthrie.

My heart lurches. I'm aware of the floor's rough texture under my feet, the tang of singe in the air. 'Uh, hi,' I say. I move to step around him, but he blocks my way. He's a couple of inches shorter than me, but he's very broad and if he doesn't move I'll be forced to brush against him. 'Please get out of my—'

His red face is suddenly too close to mine and I smell his greasy hair and his cheap deodorant and his foul breath, like he's never brushed his teeth, like he's been cleaning them with sticks all his life. It smells like something's died in his throat.

I wince, knowing that I shouldn't show weakness, I shouldn't show aversion. I shouldn't make him feel bad or loathsome or powerful in any way. I shouldn't make him feel like he's having any effect on me, but I'm failing miserably. I know my skin is betraying me. By the cold sweat on my brow, I know it's gone pale white. I know my eyes are too big.

'You and that Chink told Mr Fuller my momma broke the computers.' He puts his hand on my shoulder and pushes me into the wall. 'You're a lying whore.'

I'm aware of pride and rage protesting somewhere in my brain, but it doesn't spread to my body or to my tongue. 'I . . . I didn't.'

Now he puts his other hand on my shoulder, pinning me into the crook of the wall. 'Don't lie to me,' he barks. He moves his left hand to my neck and stuffs his right hand onto my crotch, grabbing me like he's trying to lift me up, like he's done this before.

Then I know we've passed some point and the floodgate opens and my rage moves my body. I knee him in the balls and scratch at his face. 'Don't you fucking dare, you arsehole,' I say. 'Touch me again and I will fucking kill you.' I say it like I'm someone else, like it's a line from a movie.

He steps back like he's been bitten, clutching at his face.

The adrenalin is speeding through me. 'I swear, arsehole. Don't try your luck.'

'Brett? Brett,' someone's calling from downstairs. Arsehole Senior. 'You got the—' He pulls up when he sees me there, immediately assesses the situation. He looks me up and down once and turns away. 'Let's go, boy.' He takes his son by the arm and leads him back downstairs.

My knees cave in and I sit down on the stairs, waiting for the shaking to stop. I hear the Guthries' door slamming on the floor below. The lights go out on me, but I know I can't sit around for too long. When I can stand again, I head up to the rec room, but it's deserted. Sarita must be at the pool.

I'm trying not to think. I'm trying to breathe normally so that Sarita won't know anything's happened.

Back on our level, I poke my head into the corridor in case Sarita's waiting outside the door, but she's not, so down I go.

Level four, level five, nothing.

Level six. There's a flickering white light coming from somewhere. I step into the corridor and wave my arms to activate the motion sensors, but they don't come on. Only the sick yellow stubs of fluorescent emergency lights dot this floor. The apartment doors are draped with thick plastic.

The gap for the elevator doors seems tightly boarded up. I scan over them, sick at the thought there would be a large enough space for Sarita to slip through and fall. I'm trying to push away an image of her little body crumpled at the bottom of the shaft when I hear it – a curdling scream that freezes my blood. It's come from behind me, in that plastic-covered room. 'Sarita! Sarita?'

I'm swatting at the plastic sheeting, it's twisting my arms up as I try to shove through. 'Sarita!'

I manage to push through, then I hear her somewhere in the darkness. 'Caity.' I wheel towards her voice, my heart forgetting to beat again. Now she's framed by a flickering strobe coming from deep in the apartment, but as my eyes get used to the light I can see dark smears on her pyjamas.

I run to her, squat down and hug her. 'Oh God, Sarita. I was so worried. Why did you . . .' I stop talking when I smell what's on her clothes.

'I found something in there.' She turns her body and points into the gaping front of a suite, the strobe making shadows jump across the gap.

'Show me,' I say. I try the switches on the wall, but they're not working. In the flashing light I can make out a space of the same size and layout as our own, but the bare concrete floor makes it feel bigger. A clutter of medical equipment – a stripped gurney, a couple of drip stands and a stainless steel trolley are shoved into one corner. White cabinets without tops – carcasses they call them – a row of sinks with no plumbing. Sarita's leading me past two rooms and into the last one – two steel gurneys and a glass-fronted cabinet on wheels – and all the way back into the en suite bathroom. This is where the flickering is coming from.

I see it first, the halogen flashlight on the floor, its lens spider-webbed. I pick it up, shake it. The beam goes out for a second, then comes back on, steadily now.

Now I look at what the light reveals and I push Sarita behind me. My thinking mind has switched off.

Greg Fuller is lying on the floor. A red smear spreads off the lip of the bathtub, a jagged shard of copper piping lies in the pool of blood. Now I train the flashlight further, back out of the bathroom. Footprints, larger than Sarita's, are painted in blood across the bare floor, back the way we came.

11
WILL

The Maddoxes are the last to arrive in the rec room. James Maddox, puffy-eyed and dressed in silk pyjamas; Vicki Maddox in a skimpy kimono wrap and full make-up, the dog wriggling in her arms.

'There had better be a good reason why we've been woken at this hour,' James whines.

'I hope you're going to tell us you've fixed the internet,' Vicki adds. 'You have no idea what an inconvenience it is.'

'I'd appreciate it if you'd all settle down,' Will says. A huge part of him wants to get the hell out of here and drive back to Lana, leave this mess for someone else to clear up. He's fighting a powerful sense of unreality, which isn't helped by the fact that he's still more than a little drunk. He'd been making headway into the J & B when he heard the knock on the door, found Cait shivering outside it, Sarita clinging to her. He reminds himself that it's not the first time he's had to deal with a bad situation – three years ago one of his workers had an arm ripped clean off after a front loader lost its brakes, and he's lost more than a couple of employees to alcohol-related fights and meth overdoses over the years. But this is different.

And he guesses he owes it to Greg to take charge. The Sanctum was the man's life.

'Out with it, Will,' Cam grumbles. Unlike the Maddoxes and the Parks, who are dressed in their nightwear, he and his son are in full combat gear, knives at their hips. Will's grateful that the heavy-duty weapons are locked in the safe. The Parks are huddled together on one of the couches, their kid staring straight ahead, avoiding the black looks Brett Guthrie keeps shooting his way. Will suggested to Cait that it would be best if she, Tyson and Sarita stayed in the condo while he broke the news to the rest of them – that little girl has been through enough.

'Hey . . . Where's Greg?' James asks.

There's no other way to say it. 'Greg's dead.'

'*What?*'

'Greg's dead.'

There's a second of pure, shocked silence. Everyone – including the Guthries, Will notes – looks genuinely thrown. He scans their faces carefully, but can't pick up anything other than shock. Wary of panicking everyone, he's asked Cait to keep the existence of the footprints to herself. The cops can deal with that later. Right now, he needs to keep everyone calm.

'How?' Stella Park is the first to find her voice.

'He was found in one of the unfinished condos.'

'What do you mean "found"?' Vicki Maddox asks. 'Did he have some sort of accident?'

'I'm not sure.'

'What do you mean you're not sure? How can you not be sure?'

'I'm not a doctor, ma'am. But I gotta tell you, we need to call the cops.'

Will's been steeling himself for at least a couple of them – most likely the Guthries – to immediately rage against this, insist that it's too much of a risk to bring outsiders into The Sanctum, but no one speaks up.

'You think the cops will even show up?' Vicki says. 'It's hell out there.'

'The least they can do is advise us what to do.'

Vicki narrows her eyes. 'What are you not telling us, Will?'

'Ms Maddox – Vicki – I'm gonna be honest. I'm way out of my depth here.'

'Do you think . . . are you implying . . . that there's something suspicious about Greg's death?'

'I don't know that for sure.' Will's fairly certain that Greg's neck was broken, and he lost an awful lot of blood from the contusion on his head. If it wasn't for the other evidence, Will would have immediately assumed he'd tripped and fallen. But those footprints change everything. They're definitely adult, left by a woman or a small man as far as he can make out. Could someone have stumbled on the body and got spooked? Again he scans everyone's faces; can't detect even a glimmer of guilt. In fact, Cam Guthrie looks more shocked than the rest of them – something he wouldn't have expected from such a hardass.

'Are they related? The fire and Greg's death?' Vicki asks.

Will senses Cam and Brett stiffening beside him. 'Vicki – again, I can't give you any answers.' After Cait told him what Sarita had discovered and he'd raced down to see it for himself, Will had considered asking Stella Park to take a look at the body, but couldn't see the point. The woman's a dentist, not a medical examiner.

'So what now?' James Maddox asks.

'As you know, we got no internet access. Anyone here got a satellite phone?'

He's met with blank looks. Then Jae speaks up. 'Greg had one.'

'Yup. But it wasn't with him. Reckon it must be in his condo.'

'So go and get it,' Vicki snaps.

'First thing I thought of. Can't get in there. The biometric lock will only open with Greg's thumbprint. Just like I can't get into your condo unless you let me in.'

'There must be *some* way of calling for help.'

'The fire destroyed the modem and the emergency short-wave radio. Reckon we can fix it, but it's gonna take a while. To get a cell signal means a twenty-mile drive – anyone have a radio in their truck? Mine has limited wavelength.'

Cam Guthrie grunts, 'I do.'

'Cam, I reckon the best thing is—'

'I'm not staying here a second longer,' Vicki blurts. 'James, go and pack up. I'll take my chances out there, thank you very much.'

'Where are we going to go?' her husband whines.

'Anywhere but this fucking place. It's been nothing but chaos since we arrived. And I'll tell you something else, I will be suing.'

'Good luck suing a dead guy,' Jae mutters. His mother gives him a warning look.

'That's your decision. Listen up. I'll go with Cam and radio for help, and someone needs to check on the Dann-hausers, tell them what's happening.' Will eyes Stella. 'They're past the incubation period now, right?'

Vicki huffs. 'What would she know? She's a bloody dentist. Unless the Dannhausers need their teeth bleached, she's useless.'

Stella keeps her voice measured. 'I told you – they

don't have the virus. I vote that they be allowed out of their condo.'

Then it hits him. Goddammit. How in the hell is he going to get the Dannhausers' door open? Their exterior lock is also set to open with Greg's thumbprint. He'll get the cops involved, then he'll cross that bridge. Exhaustion washes over him. Why the hell didn't he listen to his gut and get out after the internet went down? Greg had begged him to help calm everyone down, reassure them that the fire in the control room was nothing to worry about, promising an additional bonus. He'd used Greg's satellite phone to call the house, managed to have a few words with Lana, but she'd sounded slurry from the morphine. He should be with her.

'Do what you like,' Vicki is saying. 'I'm leaving.'

'If it's murder, shouldn't we keep everyone here?' Jae says, eyes flicking to the Guthries.

'I would like to see someone trying to stop me,' Vicki snorts.

'I can't tell you folks what to do,' Will says. 'I can't make you leave – or stay – if you don't want to. Cam? How about that radio?'

Cam wipes a hand over his face. 'Brett, you go with Will, I'll go back and wait with Gina and your momma.'

Brett nods. His colour is high, his eyes shining.

The last thing Will wants to do is spend time alone with the kid, but it doesn't look like he's got a choice. 'Let's go.'

Trailed by Brett, Will heads into the control room. The air-con hasn't done much to dispel the reek of melting plastic and soot, and his feet squish over the carpets soaked by the sprinklers. He supposes they got lucky – if anything about this situation can be termed lucky. Most of the wiring is embedded in the Kevlar- and rebar-enforced walls, so at least the security system wasn't compromised by the fire. He checks his phone, retrieves the hatch code, slots his thumb into the hatch panel screen and taps in the numbers. His hands are trembling from delayed shock or last night's binge. The panel's screen beeps then displays the word: **<incorrect>**

Goddammit. He tries again: 4, 7, 9, 3, 1.

<incorrect>

Did Greg change it? It's supposed to be changed every day and sent to everyone's room screens, but Will assumed he hadn't done so after the fire. He double-checks the numbers. He can't be certain, but he thinks he recalls Greg mentioning that the system shuts down after three attempts. Should he try one more time? His fingers are still shaking, so it's entirely possible that he messed up the sequence the first two times. He takes a deep breath and tries again, slowly this time: 4, 7, 9, 3, 1.

There's a high-pitched beep, and the lights die on the control panel: **<security override engaged>**

Shit. Three strikes, you're out.

Brett, who's been eyeing the melted electronics, looks over. 'What's that mean?'

'Not sure,' Will lies. 'Probably just a glitch.'

Now what? Should he try rebooting the whole system? Only . . . the manual override is linked to the main computer, and the hard drive, as far as Will can make out, is well and truly poked.

'Let's go up to the top, open the hatch manually.'

Will hurries up the passageway, Brett close on his heels. Sweat is creeping down his sides, there's a poisonous ball in his gut. This is a long shot. The hatch is state-of-the-art, with code-three security and a mortise lock. They needed a crane just to heft the thing into place – it took over five men just to move it into position – and it's sealed in with six feet of Kevlar-reinforced concrete. Will supervised the job himself. Even if the hatch lock has, by some miracle, disengaged, they'd need the strength of a hundred men to heave it open. But first, they have to get through the inner airlock door at the top of the staircase that leads to the goddamned hatch. He prays that it's not connected to the same system. That green door's not as impenetrable as the hatch, but with its bullet-proof coating and rebated sides it may as well be. Even the door frames are galvanized. The control panel next to the door is flashing red, the words: <security override enabled> flashing over and over. Will knows it's futile, but he tries shifting the handle just the same. 'Help me here, Brett.'

The kid bounds up next to him and grasps the handle. 'One, two, three, push.'

It doesn't budge.

'Again.'

Something pops in Will's back, but he keeps trying.

Nothing. Sick to his stomach, Will drops his hands.

'Mr Boucher?' Gone is the kid's usual swagger. He looks like a scared seventeen-year-old boy. 'We can get out, can't we?'

Will doesn't speak, knows he doesn't have to; the answer must be written all over his face. The answer is no. They're locked in.

12
TRUDI

They're shuffling and grunting on the other side of the door, heaving something heavy. Trudi can hear that boy swearing. Next to her, Leo's standing still and quiet, a deep frown of concentration on his forehead.

'Why don't you just open it, Dad?' Trudi says.

He shakes his head, puts his finger on his lips at her like she's a little girl.

'Come on,' she says, not bothering to keep her voice down. 'You know it's just going to make them madder when they find out.'

He takes her arm, pulls her away from the door and drags her down the hall to the sitting room. She wriggles free and glares at him.

'We can't let them know that we've overridden the lock,' he whispers. 'If Greg wants to come in, then he can. His thumbprint gives him access. But there's no way I'm letting those . . . those two into our apartment.'

Now she talks softly like him. 'But what if they're barricading us in or something? Being able to unlock the door's not going to help us then.'

'It didn't sound like that to me, but if you just let me listen, Trudi, then I'll figure out what they're doing.'

Trudi follows Leo back towards the door, sparing a glance at her mother's bedroom.

Outside, the muffled bumping continues – it sounds covert, nothing like when they were hammering to get inside yesterday – then pauses. *Yeah, that's it*, she hears. *Yeah, got it. Got it. Keep it like that, son*. It's the father, Cam Guthrie, no doubt about it.

Trudi cranes closer to the door, her head almost touching Leo's. Now there's no sound for a minute. A hushed whisper of something she can't make out. *Goddammit*, uttered, not shouted, as if in concentration. *Hold it still, Brett*. Silence. Two, three, four seconds.

Beep.

The panel of the door lock flicks from red to green and the magnetic lock clicks open, the door easing in the frame.

Trudi steps behind her father, who grabs the door handle and pulls. Greg Fuller's standing there at the gap, but there's something wrong. His face is grey, his hair and skin matted with dry blood, his eyes half closed and sunken into his skull. He's—

Trudi bites back a scream.

'What have—' Leo's saying.

Cam Guthrie pushes into the gap and says, 'Okay, Brett. Let him down now.' Behind him, red-faced and sweating, the boy twirls the body – the dead body of Greg Fuller – around in a gruesome pirouette and lets it slump against the opposite wall, leaving a dirty smear down the paintwork. And only then does Trudi turn away and stumble back towards the sitting room.

She waits for her father to question the men again, but he remains silent. Now it's Will's voice behind them. 'Leo, don't let this door close all the way. We can't reset the lock and we don't want to have to do this again.' And then Trudi understands. Somehow, Greg has died and they've brought his body here to unlock the door, using his thumbprint. She doesn't know whether to laugh or cry. She looks to her father, knowing that they can't allow her mother to witness this farce.

'Unless you like being in jail,' the red-faced boy drawls. 'Maybe it's where you belong.'

'Shut up, Brett,' Cam says.

'Would you mind waiting outside, Cam?' Will says.

'Yeah, Will, I would. We haven't decided what we're going to do with these people yet.'

Will turns to him, a terrier against a bull. '*These people* are condo owners just like the rest of you.'

'But they could be carrying the virus.'

'No. The incubation period is past, and we've established that Mrs Dannhauser has emphysema. There's nothing more to it. No reason to keep them quarantined. And now with . . . especially with circumstances changing, we need their help.'

'We haven't put any of these decisions of yours to a vote, Will,' Cam says, advancing.

'Stop bickering, for God's sake,' Trudi shouts, her voice too shrill. 'What the hell happened to Greg? And how the . . . how can you just be . . .'

'Let's sit down,' Will says. 'Trudi, Leo, may I sit?'

Leo nods, eyeing Will and Cameron Guthrie. He sits down on the sofa opposite Will, and Trudi shifts till there's some room between them, looking back towards the doorway. The brief glance Trudi got of that broken head is going to burn in her mind forever.

'We're all reasonable people here, Cam, and I'm sure we

can all agree that there's no reason, or justification, to keep Mr Dannhauser and his family locked up any longer. They are struggling enough as it is.' Cam stares back, but his lack of response signals assent. 'And you can also understand that it's essential that we get Greg's, uh, Greg, down to the cold storage, uh . . . make some space down there as soon as possible. You understand that, right?'

Trudi glances over at Cam, worried that Will's pushing the patronizing tone too far.

'You and Brett are the men for the job,' Will continues. 'Let me tell the Dannhausers what's happened.'

Cam backs down. 'Yeah, but this isn't over. Nobody's put you in charge and we're gonna decide who's who around here.'

'First things first. Okay?'

Without acknowledging him, Cam pushes past Trudi into the corridor and makes to slam the door behind him.

'Don't let the door close!' Trudi calls, jumping up and grabbing a book from the hall table as she goes. She swoops down and shoves the book in the jamb as the heavy door slams into her knuckles. She makes sure the book is tightly wedged – Leo overrode the lock, but who knows if it was damaged? The thought of that dead man's thumb pressing on the glass panel has made her wary of taking any chances.

She wrings her hand and goes to the little fridge to check the freezer for ice. The depth of her relief at keeping the door open indicates just how these past two days of imprisonment have affected her. She would have thought that after six years back in her parents' apartment, she would have been used to it, but no. When she sits down again next to Leo, she notices that he's waiting for her, as if she's a part of this, important to him. He turns his palms up and says, 'So, Mr Boucher, what in God's name is happening? What happened to Mr Fuller?'

'Sarita and Cait found him early this morning . . .' He notices the looks on their faces. 'Oh yeah, of course, you didn't meet them. You were just rushed in here the other day, and I have to say how sorry I am for that, but Greg – and the others – were concerned and I guess we've got to understand that too.'

'Sure, sure,' Leo gruffs and Trudi knows he's storing that battle for later; he's most definitely not over it. 'Go on.'

'Anyway, Sarita's a little girl and Cait Sanford is her nanny. They're with her father, Tyson Gill, in Unit 3B.' He looks up at the ceiling. 'Right upstairs from here.' Trudi would like to think she could hear a little girl – playing, laughing, crying, living – in an upstairs apartment, but she guesses the floors are thicker here, everything made to withstand . . . any circumstance. She's heard nothing but their own noises and the constant hum of the air system tamped down by the thick walls. She doesn't want to think of the thick layer of earth that covers them, far more than six feet deep.

'They found Greg in the medical suite down on level six. It looks like he fell badly, hit his head on some loose piping, broke his neck . . .' Will looks down, then sideways. If Trudi has noticed Will's evasion, she knows Leo will have too. Her father hasn't built a corporation from nothing by letting bullshit go uncalled or weakness go unpunished, especially from people rungs below him. An urge to defend Will comes over Trudi. He's obviously working bravely to manage all the egos down here. There's also some sadness about his soft brown eyes that she recognizes. It's pure fancy, but she feels a connection to Will, a melancholy person forced into an untenable situation – just like her. And she refuses to let Leo bully him. Before Leo can open his mouth, she changes the subject, 'Dr Park told us last night that some equipment was damaged in a fire.'

'Stella Park told you?' Will says. 'You mean Greg didn't even come down to fill you in?' He scrapes his hand across his cheeks, closes his eyes. The muscles in his jaws tense.

When the fire alarm went off yesterday morning, Leo listened at the door and poked his head out when it was quiet to confirm that there was no smoke. Half an hour later he heard the couple with the dog from next door trooping back to their apartment, both of them complaining like rich city brats, and he knew that the situation was over. Leo had sat on the armchair in front of the TV, that terrifying, smouldering look in his eyes. 'They didn't come for us,' he muttered. 'They would have let us roast in here like rats!' He wasn't going to let this go.

He'd bypassed the door lock.

And now Greg Fuller is dead.

Trudi glances at her father and she's not sure what he's capable of. She knows nothing about him. She never has.

'So, uh,' Will says when neither of them replies. 'You folks have probably noticed that there's no wi-fi.'

Trudi hasn't noticed. She used to live on her BlackBerry, whirling with Armand and the one per cent, as if their privilege was a birthright, but now she keeps her smartphone off and stashed in her handbag most of the time. With everything that's happened, and with her mother unwell, she hasn't given it a second thought.

'But the TV's working,' she says, before she really knows why. She's not an idiot, but it's another indication of the strange, protective urge she's feeling for this man. She's doing what she can to make him feel less out of his depth.

It works. Will visibly inflates, extending his spine and sitting straighter, as he explains something to her that he thinks she doesn't know. 'Well, ma'am, the, uh, TV is cabled into every condo. The internet was wireless. Unfortunately the wi-fi router was destroyed in the fire. This is one of the things we need your help with, Mr Dannhauser. Of course, everyone knows about Danntech, and we were wondering, maybe, if you had some practical experience with the actual gadgets.'

'Of course,' he says. 'When I started working, a man didn't come into a business with a case full of money and sit behind a desk shuffling papers around. I learned my trade on the factory floor. I know the products I sell.'

Will sighs and manages a smile. 'Then I think we've got you a job, sir. First, the power in the control room's shorted out and the computer that manages the control system's offline. That's why we can't reset your lock for now. The shortwave radio system was also, uh, damaged in the fire . . . but not burnt up like the router. If we can wire it up again, we can get it working.'

'What do you mean damaged but not burnt? Did someone break it deliberately?'

Will leans forward. 'Look, you'll get the picture up in the control room, sir. Would you come up with me?'

Trudi stands. 'I'll check on Mom meantime.'

Caroline is lying still, breathing smoothly, a thin sheen of sweat covering her face, but her colour does look better and it appears that she's really resting. Trudi straightens the blanket over her.

She's checking that the oxygen is flowing through the mask when Caroline stops her hand and flips the mask away from her mouth. 'You shouldn't have come home, Trudi.'

She's so surprised to hear Caroline talking so lucidly that she wants to ask her to repeat herself, but she doesn't need to – the words were clear enough. Her mother emits a slow, grating wheeze. 'You didn't have to come home to take care of us.'

'Shh, Mom. You know that's not what happened. My career and marriage were over. I had nowhere else to go. You took me in and I'll always be grateful.' Just saying words like *always* gives Trudi a sick feeling. She doesn't want to be talking to her mother like this. Caroline will get better, the threat will pass over, and they'll all go home.

'But you stayed too long. You're a young woman. You have a life to live.'

Trudi won't admit that the reason she stayed so long was to defend Caroline from Leo's rages. While she stayed there, they seemed to get worse and worse – she was worried about what he might do to her.

But Caroline knows the truth anyway. She gasps in another breath. 'I love him, you know. I trust him.'

'How, Mom? When he's . . .'

'He was my only love. I knew him before all the pressures. He was softer, gentler then.' A long drag of oxygen. 'But he's still the same man.'

Trudi scans her memory for any evidence of kindness or softness from Leo, but if they exist, they're deeply buried. It was always Caroline entertaining and nurturing Trudi, with Leo a dark cloud – often distant, away at work – or threatening to let loose with fury when he was at home. Shouting from behind the closed door of his study.

It was an easy decision to come back home after she was dropped by the company, and by Armand. She knew it from the start – it didn't even come as a surprise when her life crashed in – ballet is a young girl's game. You can't go back into the chorus and peter out quietly. The career ends suddenly, with a finality like death. You can teach, that's all, really, and Trudi never had the patience to teach. Men like Armand are part of that young person's lifestyle. Even in her prime, he was looking at the other girls, sizing them up to see who would replace her. She knew he wouldn't stay when she stopped dancing and she honestly wasn't surprised. She was just going to come home for a little while until she found her feet again.

Caroline had welcomed her back too warmly, as if she was the missing piece in her life. She made things too comfortable for Trudi, didn't encourage her – like normal parents should do – to live her own life. She must have been delighted when her star waned, when her independence faltered.

But maybe she's been wrong all this time. Trudi wonders if 'the pressures' Leo's been suffering are the pressures of having a daughter rather than the pressures of work. So when she returned, perhaps Leo was outraged by nothing other than Trudi's presence. If she had just left after a month or two . . . Maybe it was she who drove a wedge between them when all she was doing was trying to help.

Armand never wanted children. He was brutally impatient with youngsters who seemed to misunderstand or obstruct his rarefied pleasures of fine music and fine art and fine food. Of course it shouldn't come as any surprise, after years of therapy, that Armand was exactly like Leo. When Armand left her, Trudi scurried back into the arms of the first man she had loved. It shouldn't come as a surprise, but the realization mortifies her.

'Mom, I—'

'Trudi?' Leo's in the doorway. 'I'm going up now.'

Trudi follows him to the door, where Will is waiting in the corridor. He gives her a sweet, lopsided smile.

'How is your mother, ma'am?'

'Better, I think. And please call me Trudi, Will.'

'Yes, ma'am,' he smiles again, and she feels a little warm, for the first time in a long while.

Leo joins him in the corridor, giving the book that's jamming the door open a concerned glance. She's stayed in the Millennium Place apartment for days on end so often that she's lost count. There's no physical difference between these past two days of enforced imprisonment in this comfortable apartment and her six years of voluntary imprisonment in that one, but her mind has started to rebel down here.

She closes the door as far as it will go and glances over at the TV screen. It looks like the threat is coming under control. But this misadventure has been good in a way, a real wake-up call. Trudi promises herself that she's going to make a change when she gets home; she's no longer going to live in a trap.

She checks in on Caroline, who's fallen asleep comfortably. Trudi should stay here with her, but she needs to get out of the condo and get a sense of the layout of this place. She wants to go down to the suite where Greg's body was found. She's probably read too many books and watched too many movies in the last few years, but she knows it will set her mind at ease if she just has a look around. She won't be long.

The regular vacations she's taken with her parents to Cape Cod and Key West don't really count – Trudi realizes that this trip right here is the biggest adventure she's been on since she stopped dancing.

Scanning the corridor, she sneaks out of the condo. Her eyes are drawn to a yellow and black chevron across the boarded-up gap where elevator doors should be. It will be difficult for Mom to get up the stairs when she's better, she thinks as she quickly glances away. To the red-brown smear on the wall opposite.

She stares at the blood, willing the return of some physical repulsion, but she's over it; it's simple set-dressing now. Too rationally, she wonders if she could really suspect her father. It's true that there are parts of him she never looks at and she knows there are a lot of shadows in the dark corners of his past. But that was all supposed to be long ago, before he came to America. Yet if it came to protecting his family, avenging his injured pride, just how far would he go? A cold vein of his blood pulses through her and fortifies her when she should feel shocked and horrified at the thought. *We are better than them. They've pushed us down for generations, but we always rise to the top.* She hears that blood whispering in her father's voice. She sees the view from their penthouse, the American city prone at their calloused eastern European feet. She pushes through the stairwell door, and the disembodied light on the landing flicks on. The stale, cold air swirls a pungent smell of egg and bacon grease circulating from someone's breakfast. She heads down towards level six then, before she can think too hard, pushes through the thick plastic sealing the gaping mouth of Unit 6A. Now she's found a use for her new smartphone: its torch function shines a sharp circle of light through the apartment.

As Trudi's drawn deeper through the suite, her thin frame magnetically pulled into its recesses, the shadows of metal stands and trolleys follow her light and bend and tug, reflecting against the glass fronts of vacant cabinets. And here, in the rear bathroom of the suite, is where it happened.

Trudi scans her light over the space, her picture of the room building up in layers as she sweeps the circle over the bathtub and shower and the bare, cold floor. On which another semi-opaque tarpaulin is the only marker of Greg Fuller's death.

Squatting down, fully inhabiting the fictional detective of her fantasies, her heart thumping at the thrill of this un-accustomed adventure, Trudi tries to penetrate the plastic with the light. There are dark patterns beneath the tarp, but she can't see them clearly enough. She shuffles to one side, grabs a corner of the sheet and, ignoring her nerves, folds it back.

It's a large pool of blood, dried to dark brown and stain-ing the crisp grey of the floor, streaked and dragged like modern art, spatters and swirls where Will and the Guthries blundered about dragging the body over onto another length of sheeting. But between the boot smudges and the drag tracks are footprints. Bare footprints, making off from the central corona. Three of them are clearly marked – a right foot. They are counterpointed by four left footprints half stamped on the floor. The trail goes on for a few yards before the blood wiped off the person's feet, and what follows are less defined blotches trailing their way towards the exit.

And as Trudi follows the line of the barefooted flight, a man's shape comes around the bend in the passage and a flashlight blinds her. She drops the phone, face down, and is left in darkness.

'Ma'am?'

She knows that voice.

'Hello, ma'am. What are you doing down here?'

'Oh God, Will. You nearly gave me a heart attack. You have to see this.'

'What is it?'

She gets her balance back and picks up the glaring phone again.

'Come look.' He approaches, his yellow flashlight tracking through the room. 'Footprints . . . Someone was here. Greg didn't die by accident.' And as she says it, she can't shake the feeling that she's an actor in one of the art noir movies she loves to watch.

'Yup,' is all he says.

Trudi stands. 'What do you mean *yup*? Did you know about this?'

'Yes, ma'am.'

'For the love of God, call me Trudi, Will.'

'I knew about it. Cait and I thought it better not to tell anyone. We're the only ones who know.'

'Who's Cait?'

'Tyson Gill's nanny.'

'Oh, yes. You said so. Okay. But why don't you want to tell anyone? You don't think people would like to know there's a murderer in here with us?'

'Not a good idea.' And Trudi can see that it's not. What good would starting a panic do? 'We need to get to the bottom of this quietly. Before whoever these footprints belong to figures out we're on to them.'

'We?'

'Well, Cait and me. And now you. Will you help? I know you didn't do it.' He looks down at her ballet-tortured feet, a flattened, contorted size eight, the joints and gnarls jutting out of her sandals. If he's disgusted by them, fuck him. As far as she's concerned, these feet are her only badge of honour.

'How do you know I didn't?'

'Well, we guessed the prints are around a seven, about your size, maybe a little smaller. But you were locked in your apartment when it happened.'

'Oh, right.' But they weren't, were they? 'Okay. Sure,' she says, conscious of the fact that Leo wears a dainty size seven, which he blames on his meagre East German diet while he was growing up. 'So we'll make quiet enquiries. Is that the plan?'

Will smiles that lopsided smile of his again. He's not stupid, this man – he understands her subtle ironies, and the thought warms her surprisingly. 'Yes,' he says. 'We'll investigate.' He bends down and covers up the blood stains, rolling the tarpaulin carefully over the prints again, and turns towards the exit. Trudi follows the tail he makes with his flashlight.

Once they're out of the suite, Will says, 'You must be very worried about your mother.'

'Yes. Do you have family?' She's rusty at making small talk. Hasn't needed that skill for the last six years.

'My folks passed on a few years ago.'

'I'm sorry.' She glances at his left hand, angry at herself for the slight disappointment she feels when she sees the simple gold band. 'And your wife?'

His eyes cloud. 'She's at home. South Paris.'

'You didn't want to bring her here?' She's aware that she's probing, but she can't stop. 'To get her away from the threat of the virus, I mean.'

'She's already sick.'

'I'm sorry.'

'Cancer. I wasn't supposed to be staying here. I was meant to do some final checks and then, well . . . I shouldn't be here.

I got myself locked in here. And Lana's out there and I have no idea whether anyone's still taking care of her.'

Trudi wants to reach for him, but she doesn't know this man. 'I'm sorry,' is all she can think to say.

13
CAIT

'Tell them to stop, Mommy!'

I don't correct Sarita, just hug her closer to my chest and try to cover her ears as the shouting goes on. She nuzzles her face into me, wet and hot. I breathe in the scent from her hair and look at everyone's feet.

'Why don't you just take her back down to the apartment?' Tyson says next to me.

'Because I want to know what's happening, that's why. Because my vote was as important as anyone else's.'

'She's tired. She had a rough night.'

'You don't have to tell me about her rough night, Tyson. I'm the one who—'

'Okay, okay. I'm sorry. I'm just saying she looks like she could do with a rest.'

He's right, but I snap, 'We'll go when we're done here.'

He shakes his head – the help getting uppity again – and looks back stonily at the fighting. I feel removed from it, as if this is some spectacle put on for our amusement, as if we're in the front row of a boxing match. All I'm thinking about is my mom and how long it's going to be until I can go home and leave these strangers to their self-destruction. But there's still Sarita, always Sarita, and I simply do not want to leave her to this messed-up man.

Some of the Sanctumites are perched, like Tyson and me, in a laager of bar stools and easy chairs; others are standing, jostling around in the scraps of the lunchtime status meeting. In the centre of it all, Vicki Maddox is standing firm on her power heels, squaring up to Cam Guthrie, hurling profanities at him that seem to rock him back as much as if he'd been hit. Even during the thick of the fight, I notice Tyson shooting hostile glances at James. There's clearly some bad blood between them, and I can only imagine it has something to do with Vicki, who's still holding her own against Cameron Guthrie's brawn. She's a tough woman, no doubt used to fighting hard to become as successful as she has in the corporate world. But her world, where respect can be earned, is a different universe from the Guthries'. No matter how well Vicki can argue, how deftly she can out-talk and out-think her enemies in the courtroom, to Cam Guthrie she's just a woman who doesn't know her place. He's much larger than her, has bigger, blunter fists, and down here – in the Guthries' element – I'm beginning to realize that's all that matters.

But maybe Tyson's right. We've cast our votes and made Will our interim chair, so maybe I should get Sarita away from here now. I look around me, checking for a straight route to the stairwell door, and my gaze slams into Brett's dull stare. My face heats up and I fight my blush for all I'm worth. I stare back into his eyes, feeling a fist of pain and fear – of rage – grabbing at my guts, but I don't look away. He's like a million men who've hurt a million women. I want to grab those dead fucking eyes out of his head and stuff them down his throat.

At last he looks away from me.

'It's okay, sweetie,' I tell Sarita. But it's not, really.

Will Boucher is struggling to be heard. 'We've taken a vote, Cam, and this is the decision we've come to. We'll keep consulting, of course. But this is a majority decision.'

'We're still in the United States, last I looked.' The voice of James Maddox. 'It's a democracy.'

'In our democracy,' Cam says, 'foreigners don't get a vote, for one thing. Kids don't get a vote, criminals don't get a vote.'

'That's fucking rich coming from you, Guthrie,' Vicki spits and glares past him to Bonnie. 'What with your crazy, fire-starting loon of a wife—'

'Enough, for God's sake!' It's Stella Park, sitting on the opposite side of the circle with her docile husband. She strikes me as someone who doesn't lose control – she held her own with Vicki Maddox the last time I saw her – and the screeched words shock everyone into silence for a moment.

'We've made our decision for now,' Will says.

'This is not over,' Cameron's saying. 'Gina, Brett, come here!' The stairwell door slams.

The meeting's clearly finished, though. I'm bending down to check around our seats to see if Sarita's dropped anything when I hear a woman's voice say, 'We're holding a prayer and devotion circle. Will you and the little girl join us?' I look up and see Bonnie Guthrie standing over me.

I'm surprised she hasn't scuttled off with the rest of her family. It seems that Vicki's insult hasn't even registered with her; maybe she's used to parrying verbal abuse. She offers me a nervous smile, probably still embarrassed after her freak-out at Gina the other day. 'You're very welcome.'

'Uh, no thanks.'

'Why don't you and Sarita join in?' Tyson says to me.

'It's really not my thing,' I say. Why would he even suggest it? It might be that he's trying to suck up to the Guthries, or perhaps he just wants us out of his hair so that he can trawl, guilt-free, through his stock portfolios or whatever it is he stares at obsessively on his laptop all day. The lack of wi-fi hasn't stopped him tapping away at it.

Tyson turns to his daughter. 'You want to join the lady's group, Sarita?'

Sarita looks at her father, then at Bonnie. 'I want to go with Caity.'

'It might be good for you,' he tells her.

I'm about to open my mouth, but Sarita beats me to it. 'No!' she yells and folds her arms. She looks like she's about to start crying, and that's enough to make Tyson back off. He murmurs something about heading back to the condo and disappears. Bonnie doesn't seem fazed by Sarita's reaction. She drifts across the rec room and starts arranging chairs into a circle. Nobody else here seems very religious, so I'm not sure who she expects to entice into the group. 'Well played,' I whisper in Sarita's ear. She giggles and leads me downstairs.

Sarita's watching a kids' show with a bowl of canned peaches in her bedroom and I've been replaying what's happened over and over in my head. Will and I are the only people who know about the footprints in Greg's blood and, though we've agreed not to say anything, they make it pretty clear that we're stuck in here with a murderer.

Brett Guthrie would have been the ideal suspect. He's a fucking psycho, and he was wandering around in the middle of the night, but his feet are too big, unless he's hiding size sevens in those massive boots of his. Because the prints were medium-sized – about a six or a seven. The prints could belong to any of the women – perhaps Yoo-jin or Will also. It's ridiculous, though – I wear size sevens myself and that's no good reason to become a murder suspect.

Sarita doesn't know what the footprints mean, and I've built a story for her, that Greg fell and had a bad accident and died. That's all. Nobody's fault, just an awful accident. I wish that was true, that I could tell myself the same story, but his injuries looked too serious to have come from a simple fall. We laid out the tarp – deliberately over the wettest, most recognizable of the footprints – and placed Greg's body on it, agreeing not to tell anyone what we'd seen. 'No good causing a panic,' Will said, and I had to agree.

I feel like I should be more worried knowing all this, but maybe something about living in Johannesburg has taught me to rationalize my fear, shove it into some recess in my mind. But still, I feel pretty safe while we're locked into the flat, and they wouldn't try anything in a group meeting, so the trick is just not to go anywhere alone. That's manageable. Maybe whoever it was had their own reasons, and it's over now. Maybe.

It still pisses me off though. I come all the way across the world to be imprisoned by fear again. Maybe you can never leave your fear behind.

Tyson emerges from his room, creased from a nap. I check my watch. It's only been two hours since the meeting. It feels longer. He sits on a stool at the counter and yawns. 'Is there any coffee?'

He could have spent his naptime playing with his daughter and I'm irritated that he can't see that I could do with a rest too. I nod at the counter. 'Machine's there. You think you can figure out how to use it?' He jerks as if I've slapped him. Good.

'Is Sarita alright?'

'Yeah, she's fine. Watching *Tiny Toons* in her room.' Not that you care, I almost add, then bite it back. He looks like crap, maybe I should tone it down a bit. 'You know what this reminds me of?'

'Hmm?' he says, disturbed from deep inside his own thoughts.

'That meeting,' I repeat. 'You know what it reminded me of?'

'What?'

'This is like *Survivor*, don't you think? Everyone jostling into factions. Everyone knows exactly what to do in a disaster.'

Something in this piques Tyson's interest. 'Did you know the producer's English?' he says. 'He created *Survivor*, *The Amazing Race*, all that other stuff.'

'English? Really? I assumed he was American.'

'Nope. He's worth over $400 million.' Of course the business story would grab his attention. I have to smile. Tyson's actually straightforward, if you concentrate, and I'm glad we're having something like a regular discussion.

'Huh,' I say, coming around the counter. 'So there's an English guy teaching Americans how to react in an apocalypse.' I try to stuff the word back in, but it's too late. The fact is, this isn't a TV show. This is actually happening. Even though this isn't the end of the world like half of the people in here hoped, thousands and thousands of people are dying.

I plonk myself onto the couch and Tyson joins me in staring at the TV. The same lines scroll along the bottom of the screen. Early signs of success in West Coast vaccination programme. No decision yet on East Coast local transport.

'It's looking promising, at least,' I say.

'I miss the stock tickers,' he says. 'They keep changing, you know. You feel there's something you can do about them. I can make a buy or sell order and maybe nudge a number up or down a sixteenth. There's nothing I can do about this. About that damned hatch being broken.'

I glance over at him. I've never seen him like this. Vulnerable – he's almost like a human being. 'You wish we weren't here,' I say.

'Of course,' he says. 'You think anyone wants this?'

'No, I mean you. You'd rather have taken your chances out there, wouldn't you?'

I'm grappling with this sense I'm getting from him that this is all a mistake. Not coming to an emergency shelter in itself, but there's something personal.

'It's frustrating that we're stuck in here because of that Greg Fuller's sloppy work. I know it's not right to speak ill of the dead, but I never liked him. He was a two-bit hustler. I should never have trusted him.' I look across at him. 'A project like this takes trust, and tact.'

I'm not sure what to make of that last word, but it tallies with this sense that there's some underlying atmosphere between some of the residents here. Secrets, a lack of discretion. For one thing, there's that weird vibe between Tyson and the Maddoxes.

But of course I couldn't ask him about that outright, no matter how oddly forthcoming he's being. Not wanting to press him back into his shell, I change tack and start babbling to keep him at ease. 'In South Africa, we had this treasure hunt show where the studio contestants would direct a sporty woman on a helicopter to the treasure. This was before GPS, so there was . . .'

But I've lost him now. He's not listening. I wouldn't listen to me either.

Later, I take Sarita back up to the rec room. The prayer circle's empty and somebody's set up an urn of juice on the bar top and laid out some highball glasses and stubby little tumblers that might be more appropriate for Sarita. I wonder if Will was behind this. He seems a more empathetic sort of person than Greg, conscious of the lived details rather than the abstractions of The Sanctum as a business scheme he isn't quite pulling off.

Wasn't.

Greg's dead.

The smell of blood – I haven't ever smelled so much blood in one place. It's not something I want to smell again. The thick air. And perhaps I'm just imagining a tinge of old cigarette smoke, my imagination running away with me, turning it into a scene from some detective movie.

'Caity! Come look!' Sarita's voice rescues me from my thoughts.

She's found a shelf full of games, all new in their boxes, old-fashioned games I haven't played since I was a kid: Monopoly, Scrabble, Risk, Clinical Anatomy. My mom always dusts off her Scrabble set when the family gets together for Christmas. I'll be back home for Christmas, I promise myself.

Sarita shuffles through the boxes and finds a jigsaw. Two thousand pieces, a vase of Van Gogh's sunflowers. 'Can we make this, Caity?'

'Uh, it looks like a hard one. Let's see if there's anything else.'

'Please. It's so pretty.'

If she's happy for the moment, I'm happy, and I know she'll lose interest soon anyway. 'Okay, sure. Go to that coffee table. You can start by turning all the pieces the right way up and sorting them into colours. Then try to find the straight edges.'

The rec room's growing on me. It's the most spacious room in The Sanctum. The nature window displays are pretty calming if you let them be and it's soothing in here – when there's no meeting. Sitting down opposite Sarita I stare into an electronic evening seascape and try not to think about anything. Sarita's chatter washes over me and I answer with thoughtless *uh-huh*s.

I must drift for a second because I'm startled when someone comes up behind me and says 'Hi, Cait.' It's Brett's face that's first in my mind, but that friendly voice isn't his. I turn and see Will, with Trudi Dannhauser by his side. I can't place her age. She's emaciated and her pale skin is plastered over with foundation, but moods seem to sweep across her face like it's a landscape. A brief smile makes her seem young, then a dark cloud billows from those intense eyes and ages her. She's a bit scary.

'Hi,' I say.

Will scans through the rec room then glances down at Sarita. 'You think we can talk? About . . .'

Sarita's sorting through jigsaw pieces, humming a tune, oblivious. 'Yeah,' I say, but move a few paces away from the girl anyway, then frown at Trudi.

'Uh, Trudi knows what we know. She found the prints this morning, so she's helping canvass everyone, you know.'

Trudi smiles again, but again it's instantly chased by a dark expression. The woman's face doesn't stay still for a second. 'We just wanted to ask,' she says, 'whether you're sure Tyson was in your apartment the whole of last night. You're sure he was there when you went out after her . . .'

I want to tell Trudi that her name is Sarita, but that might jolt Sarita out of her trance, so I just nod. 'Yeah, he was definitely there when I went out around three-thirty. I checked in his room first to see if she was there. But I can't be sure about the rest of the night. I guess I fell asleep about midnight, half-past.' There's something intimate about the mirrored glances that shoot between Will and Trudi. 'But it wasn't him down there, anyway,' I add.

'How so?' Trudi says.

'He wears size twelves.'

'Ah. Alright. We can check him off, I guess.'

'Let us know if you remember anything else, okay?' Will says and both Trudi and I laugh because he delivers the line just like a cop on *Law and Order*.

As they turn, Trudi sneaks a look at my feet.

'Size seven,' I say, and hold her gaze for a long few seconds until I feel like I'm going to be skewered by those dark eyes. I have to look away first.

14
GINA

'We must be on our guard, son,' Daddy's saying to Brett as he smoothes his blade over the whetstone, with a softer hand than he ever used on any human. I'm peering at them through the crack in the door. 'This is how it starts, if you know your history. *The people*' – he drips the word sarcastically like he always does when he's talking politics, usually to his friends at the range – 'choose the weakest leader, the one they know will just let them do what they want, then they go ahead. Do what they want. There's an immediate onslaught on moral values.' He hands over the whetstone to Brett, who scrapes boredly at his own bowie knife before setting it aside.

I can do this, Daddy. You taught the both of us. You know I'm a better shot than Brett. I'd protect us better than Brett, I want to yell. It's Brett we've got to be afraid of. But of course I don't. I don't even know if he'd hear me, I'm so invisible to him.

'That's what Hitler did, Mao, those North Koreans, Saddam, Putin, Obama – swoop in when a weak leadership wasn't vigilant, when all the people needed was some moral direction. And see where it got us.' He lifts another knife out of its grey foam compartment in the aluminium case where they sleep in a row. Mr Miller down by the gun store made the weapons cases real neat. The rifle cases Mr Fuller made

UNDER GROUND

Daddy empty have a perfect-sized hole for every part, the sights, the magazines, the oil, the tweezers, the brushes for maintenance. I love unpacking everything and putting them back in their beds; since we've been home-schooled, Daddy's taught us to strip and reassemble every new weapon like he learned in the military. He taught us both and I can do it better than Brett.

There must be a reason he's excluding me. Daddy loves me and there's always a good reason for what he does, even when it seems harsh. Maybe it's about roles when we're in an emergency. We all have our parts to play. And mine is keeping our environment clean, uncluttered, prepared. Momma's seemed a bit out of it since we've been here, so my role is also helping make sure Brett and Daddy are fed, strong in mind and body, ready. The last few days, Momma's turned even more inward – maybe upward – like her relationship with God is the only one that matters to her.

I get to thinking about Mr Fuller. He's dead now. I've seen one dead person before – Gramps, at his funeral, but he was so painted over, he didn't look at all like himself. Mr Fuller was a kind man, always friendly to everyone. Daddy says Mr Boucher told him Greg slipped and fell, but he's been nervy ever since we found out – the case of knives came out straight as he heard, and I swear he suspects something.

'Why're you snooping there, girl?' I jump. It's as if just thinking about her has called her up. 'The Devil makes work for idle hands.'

'Sorry, Momma. I was just wondering if . . .'

Daddy looks up from his bed where he's sitting, with the case open at his feet. That same warning look in his eyes since the fire, and he says, 'You should be thinking about supper, shouldn't you? It's close on five-thirty.'

'Yes, Daddy,' I say and head to the kitchen, making sure, since they're all watching me now, to walk like I haven't got an attitude problem. I stuff down my resentment.

Truth be told, though, I like working in this kitchen. It feels somehow professional, like a doctor doing an operation, everything so clean and sharp, so many new implements to cut and poke with, not the blunt objects in the cluttered, tiny kitchen back in the trailer. I think I'll make a beef stew. There are onion flakes and oil in the cabinet, tins of tomatoes and peas. But when I stoop to the little fridge Mr Fuller helped us stock, I see we're out of meat, apart from a single package of bacon. Brett and Daddy sure haven't struggled for appetite; Momma's barely touched a thing and I haven't been all that hungry. I have this pain in my gut that's replaced any appetite. I still wonder why Momma set that fire. When she saw me looking at that game – or was it because I was sitting next to Jae? – I saw a fear and panic in her eyes that I never saw before. I still wonder if I should tell Mr Boucher the truth. Not to tell him what I know is the same as lying. I've scoured my conscience back and forth, asking the Lord what's the right thing to do and he's been silent. My only answer has been from Daddy, not the Lord. I see it in his face whenever he looks at me – he wants me to know that he'll punish me if I ever say anything to anyone.

Family comes second only to God. That's a truth to hang on to, even if it doesn't make this ache in my belly any better. Maybe Daddy's pushing me away because he's telling me my job's to be with Momma, while his job is to bring Brett back into the fold. Maybe our time down here is our chance to become a family again.

So when I look over at Momma on the armchair, watching an old rerun of Hal Lindsey on the TV, she looks lonely, and I feel guilty for preferring Daddy over her. She never did anything wrong to me. And I feel a little bit bad for her as no one wanted to join the prayer group she tried to set up.

'Momma, would you like to . . . could you help me go get some supplies downstairs?'

'You can manage, Gina.' She doesn't look away from the screen. I can't help feeling a little hurt that she'd rather watch TV than help me, even though I was just asking out of duty. But I feel a little glad anyway because Momma's looking a lot stronger than she was yesterday. She's got colour back in her face. That's something, at least.

I flip through Mr Fuller's Welcome to The Sanctum brochure on the kitchen counter to where it tells about the downstairs storage area. Apart from the 'hydroponic' fresh produce and the chicken coop, the brochure says there are enough non-perishables and water in a reservoir to keep The Sanctum going, fully occupied, for over a year. Maybe six months in Brett and Daddy's case, I smile to myself, even though it's not really funny. Each condo is assigned its own dry storage and freezer shelves in the store down on level eight. I write our shelf numbers on my hand: *shelves 3 & 4*.

'So I'll be going down to the stores now, Daddy,' I call. 'Get some meat.'

'Bring up some of that hash and beans while you're down there,' Daddy says.

'And some of that Kool-Aid, right,' Brett says.

It would probably be less creepy down here if the lights weren't so clear and bright, if they were flickering like in that episode of *Lordsville* where Jimmy and Samantha go to their school gym to make out and the lights splutter and the Devil gets inside them. Satan came in the form of spiders and rats scuttling in the shadows and then they grouped together and turned into this faceless person and when Jimmy and Samantha looked into its face, they saw themselves, but a corrupted version of themselves, all spotted with sores and blight from the fornication that lay at the end of the route they were going to head on to. So Jimmy and Samantha repented and came back out into the light and went home. Maybe they got married later, I'm not sure.

Down here, though, level eight, there are no shadows. The lights show all the corners and there are no rats and spiders. Behind the loud whine from the machine room, where the air and water pumps are, there's an irregular *thup-thup-thup* sound from somewhere behind the walls. The freezer seems to vibrate in the glare, but there's nothing alive down here, nothing at all. The air is dry, smells of concrete dust and plastic and electricity. I miss the birds on the lot, the horses most of all, but hand to heart I don't think I'd mind if I saw a rat or spider – it would feel like we're still living on earth, not in this lifeless, dust-coated . . .

Thup-thup. Thup.

I peer through the crack in the plastic covering the doorway at the raised pit where hot lights glow under awnings. There aren't many vegetables growing there: some chard, a few withered tomatoes and tiny strawberries. I wonder if some fresh fruit would improve Momma's appetite. She always preferred a salad to too much meat. I think of fetching some for her, but I'm wary. Maybe she'll say it's unnatural, growing in Hell. I don't want to set her off again.

Instead, I back away from the hydroponics room and slide a case of canned hash and beans and two cartons of cereal off the dry goods shelf marked *Unit 3A* then step across to the freezer.

The muffled banging sound is louder here and I can trace it to above me, through the ceiling. It must be coming from the floor above.

Thup . . . thup-thup. Then a scream. An anguished, bellowing scream.

Oh, that's what it is! It's Brett playing ball. The gym's upstairs. He must have come down straight after me. I guess he's playing by himself since he hasn't really made friends with any of the other people here. I can't imagine Jae coming down there again after how Brett treated him. But I hold on to that thought of Jae for a little, shutting out all the judgement from Momma and Daddy and Brett. I hold on to that picture of his smile for a minute, nice and warm, but not too pretty. I know it's wrong, but this is a thought for me alone.

Then I let him out with a sigh and open the freezer, which is so big, you can walk into it. It's kinda fun, this sudden change of temperature, like I've been transported to winter in the hills, Brett and me sliding on flat cartons. That must have been a few winters ago, before Brett stopped playing with me. It's like between fifteen and seventeen, I think as I find the right packages of meat, Brett suddenly became like Daddy. I don't know if they want me to become like Momma, but we're not the same like Daddy and Brett.

There's a bang behind me. I wheel around, dropping the hard, cold, plastic-wrapped slabs of meat. But there's nobody there, just the door swinging closed.

I squat down to pick up the meat. The sausages are leaning against a tarp rolled up under the rack of shelves. As I move the package away, my fingers rub against something gooey on the tarp. I turn my hand over and bring it closer to my face, rub my thumb over the sticky substance. It's blood. Must be a drip from the shelves above. But everything's frozen solid, isn't it?

I feel around the tacky patch. It's not just a rolled tarp – there's something solid under it. I press down. Solid, but also giving a bit. Half-frozen, like the blood.

I pull my hand away from what I've been kneading. I don't want to see what's under there. I want to pick up my things and go. The icy air is hurting my lungs. But my fingers freeze to the surface and the plastic sheet comes away as I wrench my hand free.

His eyes staring at me, all clouded. And the purple skin of his face. A congealed gash at the side of his neck.

I scream and run to the door, pushing. But it doesn't open.

15

JAMES

James hesitates outside the unfinished suites on level six – the floor where Greg died. He was planning to go straight down to level eight and sneak a smoke before hitting the gym, but instead he finds himself walking towards the black mouth of the doorway closest to him. The other one is sealed with plastic, so this has to be the one where Greg met his end – the medical bay. It's the last thing he should be doing – he's shaky enough as it is, his guts churning with that sick feeling he gets whenever Vicki slips into one of her funks. It's been a long time since he's seen her quite so vitriolic. She went at Cam Guthrie like a viper at a pit bull during that meeting; the man didn't know how to react. But this is Vicki all over. Stress causes her to lash out. He's the opposite, tends to bury his head in the sand and block out the things that worry him. He has no intention of allowing himself to dwell on the fact that Greg's taken the hatch code with him into whatever circle of hell is reserved for ex-security experts and property developers. Besides, there's no need to panic. The place is self-sustaining – they're not going to go hungry – and worst-case scenario, even if no one picks up the emergency radio signal, before much longer someone outside will realize they're missing and haven't been in touch. With the exception of the Guthries, the others are all well-heeled and must have family or friends outside The Sanctum who'll miss them. Unfortunately, this isn't true in their case. As Vicki has pointed out endlessly, none of their contacts know where they are. Their PA, Benedict, will probably assume they're holed up in their cottage in Martha's Vineyard.

He uses his iPhone to light his way, taking in the dust and bags of creosote piled on the floor. His mouth is dry from the Xanax, and for once he doesn't feel like smoking. He lights up a menthol anyway – mainly to hide the slight whiff of spoiled meat, which he's certain he isn't imagining. Must be blood, Greg's blood. He shuffles deeper into the gloom, catching his breath when the light picks out a dark stain on the floor. He shines it upwards, and makes out the ceramic lip of the bath, which is still shrouded in plastic, waiting to be installed, and peppered with dark brown matter. He shudders. Will implied that Greg tripped and fell, bashing his head on the edge of the tub and breaking his neck, but James isn't convinced. Tripped on what exactly? The floor around the bath is free of debris. Holding his hand over his mouth, he nudges closer to the stain, sees a trail of smudged footprints leading away from it, disappearing into the dark space where presumably one of the condo's bedrooms must be located. He places his feet next to them. They're too large to be from the little girl who stumbled on the body. He supposes they could belong to Cait, Tyson's hot au pair. Tyson . . . another issue he'll have to deal with eventually. He hadn't missed the glances Vicki was shooting Tyson's way during the meeting, along with the barbed looks she fired in Cait's direction.

Enough.

He kills the cigarette and chucks the butt into the shadows. Shit – he probably shouldn't have done that. No doubt the cops will be all over this place when they finally get out, especially if Greg's death is deemed suspicious. Time to get the hell out of here. He leaves and pads down the stairs to the gym. There's a thumping sound coming from inside it, like an erratic heartbeat. Someone's knocking a ball about in there. It's probably the Guthrie kid. No way is he going to hit the treadmill with that seething mass of hormones and acne hanging around. No. He'll do what he initially planned, and grab another cigarette in the hydroponics area, where he knows for sure he won't set off the smoke alarm. He's used it as a secret smoking spot a few times now. He scurries down the last flight, pushes through the door and breathes in the scent of plastic and dried apples. At least this area is fairly well organized, the packets of pasta, generic tomato sauce, pickles and canned tuna and ham all neatly placed on shelves labelled with each condo number. A fully stocked larder was part of the deal, but he doubts much of what's been assigned to them will ever be consumed. Vicki would rather starve than put corned beef hash in her mouth. There's even an 'emergency supply' store in the corner, stocked with freeze-dried vegetables and sinister foil packets of dehydrated meals, none of which are labelled (he suspects Greg bought them as a job-lot from a bankrupt supplier). He's noticed that Greg cut corners here and there and—

A muffled yell makes him jump. He freezes, his senses on high alert. Now there's a clumping sound, and it appears to be emanating from the freezer. Jesus. He approaches it cautiously. 'Hello?'

'Help me!'

Gingerly, he opens the door, stumbling back as the Guthrie girl flies into his arms. 'What the *hell*?'

She presses herself against him, her body trembling. He

disentangles himself and steps away from her. Her face is red and streaked with snot and tears.

'I . . . I thought I'd be locked in there forever,' she sobs, wiping her nose with the back of her hand.

'What were you doing in the freezer?'

'Getting some food. Some meat. And then . . . and then . . . I saw him.'

'Who?'

'Greg.'

'*Greg's* in there?'

Well where else were they going to store him? Curious, he peers inside the space, sees a tarp covering what is most definitely a body, a packet of rib-eye steaks sitting neatly on top of it. Gina must have dropped them. Thankfully he can't see much of the actual corpse, just a shock of hair crusted with ice diamonds. He checks the back of the door. 'Look, Gina, there's a handle on the inside. You weren't really trapped.'

'Uh-uh, I don't want to see it.' She shakes her head and wipes at her face again, leaving a snail trail of glistening mucus across her cheek. He pats his pockets on the off-chance he has a tissue, but comes up empty. He grabs a toilet roll from the mountain next to the bank of fridges and hands it to her. 'Come on. I'll take you back to your condo.'

'No! I mean, I can't let Momma see me like this.'

James doesn't blame her. He hasn't actually spoken to Bonnie Guthrie, but the little he's seen of her is enough to creep him out. 'You want to go to the rec room then?'

'I . . . I guess. I need to clean up first.'

'Come on. You can do that in my condo.'

She brightens. 'Really? Thank you, Mr Maddox.'

'James. My name's James.'

A flicker of a smile. 'I know.'

Vicki won't be thrilled, but fuck it. God knows how long they're going to be stuck down here, and they should at least attempt to be neighbourly.

They head up the stairs without speaking. The thumping sound has ceased from the gym, presumably Brett or whoever was in there has moved on.

He presses his thumb to the door pad and waves Gina inside.

'James?' Vicki calls. 'James? That you?' She emerges from the bedroom, tying the belt of her silk kimono around her waist. She blinks when she sees Gina standing behind him.

'We have a visitor,' he says before she can start in on him. Vicki's pupils are dilated. She's clearly been dallying with Prince Valium again. Good. It will take the edge off her mood. James has often considered sprinkling it over her macrobiotic breakfast cereal every morning.

'Oh, how lovely,' she says, her face saying the opposite.

'Gina's had a bit of a shock.'

'What kind of shock?'

'She got trapped in the freezer. With Greg's body.'

There's a long, almost comic moment while Vicki digests this, then: 'They put Greg's body in the freezer?'

'Yes.'

'With the food?' James almost laughs at the moue of disgust on his wife's face. *A body next to the veal? Good Lord, it's just not done.*

'Where else were they going to put it?'

James nudges his head in Gina's direction and Vicki slaps on her 'we have company' face. 'I'm sorry, Gina,' she says in her formal voice. 'That must have been horrible for you. Can I get you some sweet tea? It's supposed to be good for shock.'

'Yes please, ma'am,' Gina says. James ushers her towards the lounge. She looks around, and strokes her fingers over the back of the couch. 'It's nice in here. I like the colours you've chosen.'

James gives her a non-committal smile. Vicki griped for hours that the colour scheme wasn't the one they'd chosen in the plans, whinging on that the chairs were upholstered in pleather rather than calf leather. Gina sits primly, folding her hands in her lap as if she's in church. Claudette snuffles up to her, sniffs at her feet, and thankfully allows Gina to pet her without taking off any of her fingers. 'Shall I put the TV on for you, Gina?'

'Yes please.'

He flicks on the display, hands her the remote and reluctantly slides back to the kitchen area where Vicki is slamming her way through the cupboards.

'What the hell were you thinking bringing her here?' Vicki hisses. 'You know I'm not feeling well.'

'She was in shock.' He pours himself a glass of apple juice and chugs it down.

'What were you doing down there anyway? I thought you were going to the gym.'

James guiltily fingers the box of cigarettes in his pocket. 'I was. But I thought while I was down there that I'd check on the supplies, see how long it will be before we have to resort to lentils and those survival packs.'

'It won't come to that, James,' she sniffs. 'The vaccine looks like it's going to work. It was all over the news this morning. It's dying out.'

'The virus?'

'Yes, the virus, what else would I bloody well mean?'

'Yeah, but Vicki . . . We're locked in here, remember.'

'Don't be ridiculous. There must be a way to bypass the hatch. It's not as if we're going to be stuck in here for weeks, is it?'

'I'm sure you're right.'

'I'm always right, James,' she says with a hint of a smile. 'Get me a mug, will you?' He digs in the cupboard, but nearly all of their crockery is piled in the sink, waiting to be loaded into the dishwasher. It's been a while since they had to do anything as plebeian as clean up after themselves. That's a thought – perhaps Maribel, their housekeeper, will report them missing. He meant to send her an email to let her know they'd left the city.

'I can wash up for you if you like.' Gina's sneaked up on them.

'It's fine, thank you,' Vicki says frostily. 'We can use the dishwasher.'

'I'd be happy to do it, ma'am. I do all the cleaning at home.'

'All of it?'

'Yes. And the cooking.'

'Doesn't your brother help?'

'No.'

Vicki's face softens, but before she can respond, Claudette yips and runs to the door.

'What is it, my baby?' Vicki coos.

James can hear the sound of raised voices in the corridor outside. Male voices. Now what?

'That sounds like my dad,' Gina says. 'He . . . he might get mad if he sees I'm not looking after Momma.'

Vicki bristles. 'Well there's no reason he has to know you're here. Go and see what's going on, James.'

James cranks the door open, and sees Brett, Cam and

Will arguing on the stairs. Brett's yelling: '. . . should have done it when we took him up to the Dannhausers'.'

'Well, we didn't, and I regret that now,' Will fires back.

'Well?' he hears Vicki saying from behind him.

'It's nothing. You stay with Gina. I'll deal with this.' Before she can argue, he steps out into the hallway, shutting the door behind him. The last thing he needs is Vicki starting in on Cam Guthrie again.

James joins the men in the stairwell. 'Is there a problem?'

Brett and Cam turn towards him, red-faced. 'Nothing we can't handle,' Cam gruffs.

'Let's ask him, Dad,' Brett says, nodding at James. 'See what he thinks.'

'See what I think about what?'

'Will says we have to fetch Greg's body and haul him all the way up to his condo so we can unlock his door and get the satellite phone.'

Will sighs and scrubs his hands over his face. His eyes are sunken back into his skull.

'So what's the problem?' James is already formulating excuses in his head as to why he won't be able to help with this particular errand – a bad back, an old sporting injury perhaps. He has absolutely no intention of helping them drag a half-frozen corpse up eight flights of stairs.

Brett pulls a serrated knife out of the holster at his hip. 'I'm saying that there's an easier way.'

James tries – and fails – to hide his disgust. 'You want to cut off his thumb?'

'Boy's right, Will,' Cam says, ignoring James. 'Greg's dead. He won't know no different.'

'We can't tamper with the body, Cam,' Will says. 'It's not right.'

'Then you can carry him up by your own self,' Brett huffs. 'See how far you get. Greg must weigh over 250 pounds.' Brett looks James up and down, a sneer on his face. 'You could get this guy to help you.'

That's not going to happen. James needs to think fast. 'Will . . . thinking about it, it makes no sense to drag Greg all the way up there. Besides, by now rigor will have set in, which will make it almost impossible to manoeuvre the body.' James has no clue if this is true or not.

'Man has a point there, Will,' Cam says. He gives James a respectful nod, and James loathes himself for the small thrill this gives him.

Will shakes his head, but it's clear that he doesn't have the energy to fight any longer. 'Come on then. Let's get this over and done with. But you're the ones who are going to have to explain this to the cops.'

'I have no problem with that,' Cam says. 'We're in a tight situation here. They'll understand.'

James really doesn't want to join them, but Cam and Brett stand back and gesture for him to walk ahead of them. Cam claps him on the shoulder as he passes and even Brett gives him a nod of approval. James tries to catch Will's eye, but Will avoids his gaze. Great – in one fell swoop he's managed to alienate the only guy who seems to have any sense in this fucking place and join the cast of *Deliverance*.

When they reach the storeroom, Brett pushes past him and heads straight for the freezer. He yanks the door open and props it ajar with a catering-size tin of Italian tomatoes. 'Here goes nothing,' he says with one of his shit-eating grins. Will turns his back and it takes all of James's willpower not to do the same. But for some reason he feels compelled to show the Guthries that just because he spends his time in an office instead of wrestling gators or whatever macho shit they get up to, he's just as much of a man as they are.

Brett rips back the tarp, and James can't stop himself from flinching when he sees the matted, semi-frozen blood coating Greg's head and face. Knife in his hand, Brett drops to his haunches next to the body.

James turns his head at the last minute, hears the snick of the knife, a crunch, and Brett's triumphant yell. His eyes swim, his chest tightens, and then his hastily consumed apple juice surges up in a bitter flood.

16
JAE

Jae follows his mom down the stairs, trying not to lose his grip on the mountain of Tupperware containers stacked in his arms. Delivering veal lasagne, cabbage kimchi (his folks brought along enough of that to feed an army) and strawberry cheesecake to the Dannhausers is pretty much the last thing he feels like doing right now. He was hijacked into the errand when he left the control room to use the bathroom, and his mom wouldn't take no for an answer. He didn't question why his dad didn't offer to come along. Jae recognized that rabbit-caught-in-the-headlights look in his eyes. The look he used to get when he and Moms had to leave the apartment for a social or school function. It took an apocalypse to prise his dad out of his comfort zone, but really, he's just swapped one set of four walls for another.

'Do I seriously have to come, Mom? I've got sh– stuff to do in the control room.' Yeah, right. All he's been doing for the last two hours is play Pyramid on his laptop and vent in his journal.

His mom stops on the stairs, and presses a hand to the wall as if to steady herself. Just two flights and she's out of breath.

'Moms? You okay?'

She bends slightly, places her free hand on her stomach. 'Yes. Yes. Just a touch of colitis. I'm fine.'

'You sure?'

'I'm sure.' She looks over her shoulder and gives him a brave smile. 'It won't take long. You can go back to the control room afterwards. I thought you liked Mr Dannhauser?'

'I do. Kind of.' To be honest, Jae isn't sure quite what to make of the old dude. Leo didn't say much to him when they were in the control room together; he basically just got on with the job at hand, which suited Jae fine. And sure, Leo knows his shit – it had taken him less than five minutes to reroute the radio signal, which was fairly impressive – but there's also something intimidating and more than a little creepy about him. He reminds Jae of the actor who played Magneto in those old *X-Men* movies. Another fun fact he can't share with Scruffy. *Hey Scruff, so I'm holed up down here with a bunch of rednecks, a dead Expendable and Charles Xavier's nemesis.* Ha de fucking ha.

The Dannhausers' door is ajar – a tattered copy of *Flowers in the Attic* shoved in the jamb. It must belong to Trudi. Jae hasn't said much to her, although earlier she was hanging out with Will and came to their unit to speak to Moms about something.

His mom knocks on the door anyway, and seconds later, Trudi opens it wide enough to peer out at them.

'I've come to see how Caroline is doing, Trudi.' His mom smiles. 'Is that okay? We can always come back later.'

'Oh. No. Now is fine. Please, come in.'

The Dannhausers' condo stinks of soup – a smell Jae always associates with old people. He carefully places the Tupperware containers on the kitchen counter. Trudi looks at them blankly.

'We thought you might not feel like cooking,' Jae's mom says, tapping one of the boxes. 'This is kimchi. My husband's speciality.'

Her face relaxes. 'Oh. How very kind.' Jae can't stop staring at her arms. He can make out every vein under her skin. She's seriously thin. Cancer-patient thin.

Leo emerges from one of the bedrooms. 'Good of you to come, Stella,' he says, acknowledging Jae with a small nod.

'How is Caroline?' Moms asks.

'I'm still worried. Please, come through.'

Jae's mom follows Leo into the bedroom, leaving him alone with Trudi. Time to make his exit. 'Cool. So I'll just go and—'

'I'm a terrible cook,' she blurts, gesturing at a pot hissing on the stove. 'Just awful. Everything I make tastes like shit.'

He laughs – he would never have expected someone like her to curse. 'I can't cook either. My dad's tried to teach me, but I can't get into it.'

'It's really kind of your parents to think of us.' She blinks, and he realizes that her eyes are filling with tears.

'Oh, hey . . . I'm sorry.'

She wipes angrily at her eyes and gives him a little smile. 'No, I'm sorry. Don't know where that came from. I guess . . . I guess I'm just worried about my mother.'

'Yeah. I know what that's like.'

And then, out of nowhere, he finds himself telling her about his folks. About his mom's poor health. About his dad's weird shut-in behaviour.

Trudi is a good listener, and he gets the impression she understands exactly what he's talking about. 'It's not easy,' she says. 'Caroline – my mother – needs almost constant care at the moment. She doesn't like being alone. It can get a bit wearing. This place is claustrophobic enough as it is. I left her alone this morning to . . . Well, I went out, and I felt so guilty about it afterwards.'

'I could come up here and help you if you like,' Jae says without thinking it through. 'Maybe I could sit with her or something. Read to her.'

'You'd do that?'

'Sure. I have a ton of stuff downloaded.' Mostly Joe Abercrombie, but, hey, maybe the old woman is into epic fantasy.

'She likes romances.'

He'll have to borrow his mom's Kobo. She has a load of stuff like that on it. 'No problem.'

'Thank you, Jae. That's really kind of you.'

He feels his face growing hot. 'No problem, really.'

Trudi opens her mouth to speak when there's a knock on the door and he hears Will calling: 'Okay to come in?'

'Of course.' Trudi touches her neck and a small smile dances around her lips.

Jae's shocked at Will's appearance. He looks like crap, like he's sick or something.

'Is Leo here, Trudi?'

'He's with Caroline and Dr Park. He's busy. Can I help?' She's looking at Will like she could eat him up. Play it cool, Jae wants to say. Jae doesn't know much about Will, but Cait's told him that he's married and his wife is sick. 'I'd rather not disturb him.'

Will's eyes land on Jae. 'You think you could help us?'

'I guess. What with?'

'We're going to check out Greg's condo. See if we can find his satellite phone. Maybe get into his laptop and see if he's got some kind of override for the hatch on the system. You're the best person equipped to help with that.'

Jae almost laughs. With the possible exception of Leo and his folks, everyone seems to think he's some kind of hacker instead of what he actually is – just a kid who's into gaming. To be honest, he's been playing up to this, especially to Gina and Cait. But why not go with Will? He doesn't have any other plans. 'Okay.'

'I'm coming too,' Trudi says.

Will looks at her for a second, then nods. 'Good. Thanks.'

Trudi calls: 'Dad? I'm going out,' and then she and Jae follow Will into the corridor. Great. Psycho Boy and his dad are standing to attention there, along with James Maddox, who looks pale and sweaty and keeps wiping his mouth with his hand.

'I thought you were fetching Leo?' Cam grunts, barely glancing at Trudi.

'He's with his wife. I asked Trudi and Jae to come instead.'

'Awesome,' Brett says under his breath.

Jae ignores him and turns to Will. 'I thought Greg's condo was sealed?'

Brett grins. 'Yeah, but we've found the key. Hey, Jae-Jae . . . catch!'

Brett throws a small object at him and Jae automatically snatches it out of the air. He stares down at what's lying on his palm and feels the air leaving his lungs. The thumb is grey-blue, the severed end black with clotted blood and yellow gristle; the section below the knuckle covered in fine dark hair. Greg's thumb – he's holding Greg's fucking thumb. He hears himself make a lame yipping sound, and drops it onto the floor. Trudi gasps.

'Pussy,' Brett mouths, bending to retrieve it.

'You're disgusting,' Trudi says and Brett, like his dad, ignores her.

'Enough, Brett,' Will snaps. 'We don't have time to fuck around.' This is a new side to Will – grim, determined, daring to stand up to the Guthries. Nothing like the calm collected man he'd been at the meeting. Brett colours. *Cool.*

Jae hangs back as the others jog up the stairs, wiping his hands on his jeans and trying not to think about the cold rubbery feel of that thumb against his skin.

'Let's give it a go,' Will says to Brett when they reach Greg's condo.

Brett smirks at Jae and presses the thumb to the door screen. Nothing happens.

'Try again. Maybe . . .' Trudi shudders. 'Try warming it up.'

'Oh, for the love of Christ,' James says, looking away.

Brett cups a fist around the thumb and then breathes on it. Jae looks away; isn't sure if he wants to laugh, cry or throw up.

Brett presses harder – the top of the thumb now bent back at a sickening angle – and finally there's a click as the lock disengages.

Will grabs Brett's arm just as he's about to walk in. 'We'll take it from here. You and Cam go get some food.'

Brett shrugs his arm free. 'You trying to get rid of us? You wouldn't have got in if it wasn't for me and my dad.'

Will nods. 'I know that, Brett. And I appreciate what you and Cam have done to help, but it won't take more than four of us to search the condo.'

Cam is watching Will carefully; something definitely went down between these two earlier. 'Fine. C'mon, Brett.'

'But, Dad!' Brett whines. 'How come the Chink gets to stay and I don't?'

'Nice,' Jae says, just as James murmurs: 'Unfuckingbelievable.'

'C'mon, Brett,' Cam says. 'Let's go eat. You'll let us know if you find something, won't you, Will?' Somehow he makes this sound like a threat.

'Yup.'

The four of them wait until Cam and Brett have disappeared down the stairs before entering the condo.

'Jesus,' James whistles. 'What a dump.'

The air is stale and smells like dirty socks. The sitting-room and kitchen areas are sparsely furnished, the carpet tracked with mud, the sink heaving with unwashed dishes. And the place is unfinished; pencil lines score the walls where the eye-level cabinets should be. Jae wouldn't have expected this kind of mess from Greg. He assumed he was one of those anal military types.

James heads straight to the sink, turns the water on, and drinks straight from the faucet. Will and Trudi are already digging through the junk on the couch. 'Jae,' Will says, 'can you go and check Greg's bedroom, see if you can find the satellite phone or a long-wave radio? James, can you check the kitchen?'

James burps. 'Sure.'

Jae picks his way over a couple of bin bags leaking yellowing documents and steps through into the bedroom. There's no bed or wardrobe, just a mattress on the floor, a bunch of clothes and a stack of printouts and papers scattered around it. Jae picks through the clothes, most of which stink of BO. Jesus. Greg really was a total slob. He unearths a rusty hunting knife, a copy of *Guns 'N' Ammo* from 2007 and a *Playboy* from around the same era. He heads back into the kitchen. James is rooting through the few cupboards around the sink. There's a half-empty bottle of Old Granddad on the floor next to him.

Will glances up from where he's checking under the couch cushions. 'Any sign of it, Jae?'

'Nope. Sorry.'

'Dammit.' He waves at the monitor set up on the counter. 'How about you fire up the computer?'

'Sure thing.' He clears a roll of crumpled floor plans off a bar stool, sits down and boots it up.

'Hey, Will,' James calls. 'Can I ask you something?'

'Sure.'

'You really think what happened to Greg was an accident?'

'Why do you say that?'

'I went into that condo. The one where Greg bought it. There were bloody footprints in there.'

This is news to Jae. He turns in his seat to check out Will's reaction. Trudi's reaction as well.

Will rubs a hand over his face and exchanges glances with Trudi. 'Yeah. I saw them. Trudi did, too.'

'Are they Cait's?'

'I don't know.'

'They were pretty small.' He hiccups. 'Seemed as if they were heading away from the body. I guess I'm asking—'

'You think someone killed him?' Jae jumps in.

Will sighs. 'More than likely he just tripped and fell. It would've been dark in there.'

'You think?' James says. 'I couldn't see what he might have tripped on. Floor was clear in that area.'

Jae wishes he could discuss this with Scruffy. She'd love this kind of intrigue. 'Who would want to kill Greg?'

'Exactly,' Will says. 'We all needed him. He runs – ran – this place.' James opens his mouth to speak, but Will holds up his hand. 'We can talk about this later. And once we get out the cops can handle it. How's that computer looking, Jae?'

Jae looks down at the screen. 'It's password protected.'

'Can you hack into it?'

'You mean like they do in the movies?' A montage of him typing very very fast while a camera pans around him pops into his head.

'Can you?' Will presses.

How would I know? 'Um . . . Did Greg have a wife?'

'Why?' James slurs. The level in the whisky bottle has dropped considerably, but Jae hasn't seen James necking it. He must have Ninja drinking skills.

'He might have used her name as the password.'

'No wife,' Will says.

'Girlfriend?'

'Not as far as I know. For the last four or five years this place was his life.'

'Okaaay. Let's try the obvious then.' He types in 'TheSanctum'. No go. Next he types in: 'Sanctum'. Zip.

'Keep trying.'

'When was his birthday?' Trudi asks.

Will thinks for a moment. 'It's in April. April 1st. He was always joking about that.'

'What year?'

'Um . . . try 1965, around there.'

'Nope. We might get locked out. Other ideas?'

Will sighs. 'James, can you look around, see if Greg wrote the password down on something?'

'Like what?'

For a second, Jae is convinced Will is going to lose it. 'Christ. I don't know. A notebook, maybe.'

'Okay, okay,' James mutters, and makes his way unsteadily

into the sitting-room area, the whisky bottle under one arm. He starts desultorily flicking through the papers spilling out of the plastic bags on the floor.

'Wait. Try 1984.'

'Why?' Trudi asks.

'Just do it.'

Jae does so. 'Nada.'

'Okay. Leave it for now. Help James. Trudi and I'll check the rest of the condo.' Will hurries off to the bedroom, Trudi close behind him. 'Hey, Jae,' James says. 'You think those two have the hots for each other?'

'Trudi and Will?'

'Yeah. Make quite the team, don't they? The Lone Ranger and Sherlock Bones.' James snickers.

'They're okay.'

'Sure they are.'

Embarrassed, Jae turns back to the keyboard and, on a whim, types in 'Sanctum1984'.

'Holy shit,' Jae breathes. He's in! A desktop with a background pic of a stag looking over a valley appears, littered with folder icons. Several are labelled with the surnames of the people staying in The Sanctum – including his. Curious, he clicks onto the Guthrie file and scrolls through it. There are scores of sub-folders labelled, 'birth certificates', 'bank statements' – even 'school reports'. He clicks on one labelled 'Brett', feeling a twinge of satisfaction when he reads that Brett's Junior High GPA sits at 1.2 per cent. He knew he was a dumbass. There're also folders containing pics – an aerial photo of a trailer on the back lot of a farm, a shot of the Guthries leaving a church that resembles a shopping mall. Gina's smiling in this one; her hair is longer and draped over her shoulder. Cute. He should really alert Will, let him know that he's in, but he can't resist snooping for a little longer. He jumps to the folder marked 'Park'. Jesus. It's just as comprehensive. He tentatively clicks onto the sub-folder labelled 'Jae-lin' and scans through his own – more impressive – school records. They go all the way back to third grade. He feels the blood rushing to his face when he unearths a document headed 'psychological assessment'. That was years ago. He couldn't have been more than eleven. Trouble adjusting or some shit.

James appears at his shoulder. 'Hey . . . you got in!'

Jae jumps and kills the pages before James has time to read the content. 'Yeah. Figured it out a second ago.'

'Found anything interesting?'

Jae hesitates, then says, 'Greg's got files on all of us.'

'Huh?'

'Like really detailed stuff. Bank details, school reports, that kind of thing.'

'Really?' James grabs a bar stool and scoots next to him, bringing a waft of booze with him. 'Me too?'

'Yep.' Jae clicks on the folder labelled 'Maddox', and James flinches when he sees the sub-folders labelled 'business details', 'tax records' and 'personal'.

James leans across him and clicks onto the 'personal' folder. A slew of thumbnail pictures appears on screen. Jae doesn't have time to take many of them in before James kills the page, but a couple definitely showed James canoodling with a glamorous blonde woman who doesn't resemble Vicki. 'Jesus Christ,' James breathes. 'How the fuck did he get access to all this?'

'Beats me.'

'Hey. Try Dannhauser. See what the creepy old fuck is hiding.'

'You think he's hiding something?'

James gives him a look. 'I haven't seen much of him, but I'd say so, wouldn't you?'

Jae shrugs, and clicks on the file. Most seem to be military records, written in German as far as he can tell. A grainy picture comes up of a much younger Dannhauser, dressed in a military uniform.

'You get anything, Jae?' Will calls from the bedroom.

Jae exchanges glances with James, who nods. 'Yeah! I got in.'

Will and Trudi hurtle through to join them, Will clapping Jae on the back. 'Well done.'

'Did you know Greg has files on all of us, Will?' James says stiffly.

'What sort of files?'

'Like NSA or Homeland Security-style files. The stuff he's got on us . . . it's like he was doing surveillance on us or something.'

'Hey . . .' Trudi gasps. 'That's my father.' She bends close to the screen, leaning over Jae so that he can feel her breath on his cheek.

'Looks like dear old Dad has some kind of shady military history,' James burps.

Trudi flinches. 'I . . . I didn't know about this.'

'That's enough, Jae,' Will says. 'There any sign of that reset password?'

Jae flips back to the desktop and reads through the directory. 'There are no folders which say . . . oh, wait. There's one here called "log".'

'Try it.'

Trudi backs up and turns away as Jae clicks on it. It appears to be some kind of time sheet. It takes him several seconds to make sense of the data. 'Looks like a list showing what time the locking system on each condo door was disengaged.'

'And the hatch?'

'Not that I can see. But there's tons of data to work through.' He types 'security hatch' into the search function, but comes up blank.

'Hey, Jae,' James says. 'See who opened their door around the time Greg died.'

'We haven't got time for that, James,' Will says. 'We need to find the password for the goddamned hatch.'

'Yeah? Well I need to know if we're locked in here with a fucking murderer.' Will glares at James, but it's clear that he isn't going to back down. 'Do it, Jae.'

'Um . . . what time am I looking for?'

'What time did the kid find Greg?'

Will sighs. 'Three a.m. or thereabouts.'

'Try anywhere from two till four a.m.'

Jae's getting a handle on the way the document is formatted, and he manages to call up the relevant details after the third try. 'The condos aren't listed by name, only by floor number.'

'We can figure it out.'

'Okay . . . so the door of Unit 2A was opened at 2:15 a.m.' Shit. That's his condo.

'Must be Greg,' James says.

'And there's lots of movement on level three. Both condos. 3A at 2:35 a.m., and 3B at 3:20 a.m., 3:25 and 3:45. Level three is the Guthries and Tyson and Cait, isn't it?'

'Well, if the kid found Greg at 3:30, then 3:20 must be when she left. Christ knows what the Guthries were doing out and about at that time. Anything else?'

Jae leans forward. 'Yeah. Level four. Lock disengaged at 2:30 a.m. Then again at 2:45. There's an error report, so I can't tell which condo it is.'

'That's my floor,' James says, blanching slightly. 'But Vicki and I didn't go anywhere.'

'You sure about that?' Will asks.

'Of course I'm fucking sure. I couldn't sleep, spent most of the night watching reruns of *How I Met Your Mother*.'

'Well, the Dannhausers are the only other folks on that level. You were locked in, right, Trudi?'

Trudi nods and stares at the floor.

'Did Greg maybe come to see you that evening?' Jae asks.

James scoffs. 'At 2:30 a.m.?'

'He didn't,' Trudi snaps, appearing to have regained some of her composure. 'I should know. I was there.'

'Well, one of us is a liar,' James fires back. 'And I know it's not me. For all I know your father managed to bypass the locking mechanism.'

Score, Jae thinks. James isn't as stupid as he looks. The truth is written all over Trudi's face.

'Trudi?' Will asks gently.

'He was doing something with the door – I don't know if he managed to unlock it or not.'

'I knew it!' James crows. 'He's some kind of ex-military guy, and I noticed his dainty feet when I was looking at his bespoke brogues, so those prints could easily be his. That bastard sneaked out and killed Greg.'

'My father didn't kill Greg!'

'You sure about that, Trudi?' James asks. 'You'd be willing to bet your life on it, would you?'

They wait for her to answer. She doesn't.

17
CAIT

It's after eleven and Sarita's finally asleep. This place is screwing with our circadian rhythms; Sarita's getting far less physical activity than normal and it made her tetchy and restless tonight. I'm sure coming across a dead body hasn't helped her sleeping much either, but I think she's alright. It's not quite real for her, like something scary she saw in a movie and is forgetting about.

I'm feeling cramped-up and lumpen. It's this recycled air, the lack of sunlight. I could go to bed now, but I don't feel at all tired. Just like Sarita, I'll feel better if I get some exercise. I'll head down to the pool and swim a few laps. I haven't swum for ages, maybe since our trip to Manchester Pond – far too long.

I go to my room and dig through my big suitcase – everything I own, everything I wanted to take back home with me. Yesterday? No, a few days ago. It worries me that I can't immediately remember how long we've been down here, even though it can't be more than two or three days. Squatting over my disembowelled suitcase, I force myself to count back, remember how many sleeps and how many meals we've had down here, try to punctuate the stretch of artificial gloom with an idea of sunrise, of authentic sunset.

Get it together, Cait.

That's it. Tonight will only be our third night here.

Finally, rolled up inside a boot, I find my swimsuit. Unfurling it, I get a whiff of sweaty boot leather, but beyond that, sunscreen lotion, chlorine from the pool at the lodge at the Pond – the smells of summer. I close my eyes and draw in a deep breath; a burst of sunlight and greenery and birds, of blue sky and Sarita laughing all smack into me and clog my chest. It's fucking ridiculous, but I start crying. It seems so far away, so long ago. And it reminds me of summers back home with my mom and my sister Megan and before Dad died . . . him standing at the braai. The last time we were all together. The last time we were all happy. I'm on the other side of the world from Mom and Megan, buried underground like Dad, but the whole planet between us.

I don't want to think it, but the thought squeezes between the tears: will I ever get back home?

I wipe my eyes roughly, angry with myself. I can't swim in this costume down here. Maybe it's okay for fun in the sunlight, but down here, in the dark, with people like Brett and Cameron watching . . . no. I remember how they looked at me when we arrived, how I felt half naked.

Opting for a pair of board shorts and a T-shirt instead, I get changed and unpack a large swimming towel. For a second I wonder whether I should even risk going down to the pool, but I pull myself together. There's no bloody way I'm going to let them imprison me any further than Tyson already has. Besides, at this hour, the Guthries should all be asleep like the moral citizens they are.

On my way out, I pass by Tyson, sleeping deeply on the couch, like I'd so often find him in the morning back at his house. He'd fall asleep watching TV and not bother going to bed. I took it for the behaviour of a man in mourning. His cold bed would only remind him of his dead wife. But now I wonder: what if he was used to sleeping on the couch? What if his marriage wasn't so idyllic? My cooped-up mind makes the grinding connection to the weird vibe I noted at the meeting between Tyson and Vicki and James Maddox.

Then it finally hits me. Of course there was something familiar about that awkward evasiveness. I've seen it a dozen times in my circle of friends back at university . . . It happens when someone in the group is fucking around on someone else. The same self-conscious glances, the same way they avoid each other's eyes, as if they're trying and failing to act normal. It's so clear to people looking from the outside – that deliberate disconnection becomes a glaring spotlight screaming *Look at me! Look at us! We're deliberately not acknowledging each other!*

That same morning-after shame I've seen after countless parties.

That *must* be it: Tyson and Vicki must have had an affair. Maybe at that Sanctum sales meeting in April. That was before Rani died.

What if it's the *reason* she died?

I pull myself up. I know nothing about Rani and what happened to her, and while it's fun, I suppose, to make up stories and it's Tyson's own fault for not telling me anything, I want to keep the facts from the bullshit. More than ever – down here – that seems important. And, replaying all those uncomfortable glances and stiff exchanges between Tyson and Vicki and James, I'm certain that Tyson and Vicki had an affair – and that James knows about it. But, beyond that, any more guesses would just be indulging in fantasies.

I look in on Sarita before I leave. She's in that deep, four-year-old's sleep and I know she won't shift for the next few hours. She'll be fine with Tyson. He is her father, after all, I remind myself as I sling my towel over my shoulder and close the front door behind me. The strip lights along this section of corridor come on as I move to the middle of the carpet. I glance at the Guthries' front door down the passage, and before I lose my nerve, I hurry to the stairwell door and push through.

The light on the landing doesn't come on immediately, but there's a light on a few levels down. Someone must have been moving there. I stand still, listening in the thrumming silence. No sound stands out from the constant whir of The Sanctum. The light downstairs flicks off. In the pitch dark I listen for the sound of a door closing, or opening, or breathing . . . anything.

Come on, Cait. It's not unusual for other people in an apartment building to move around.

I've noticed that the motion sensor on this landing is a little dull, needs more coaxing than the others to activate. It starts up when I wave my arms, then I hurry, with big, obvious movements down to level seven, not acknowledging the landing between levels four and five where Brett pinned me last night, not thinking too hard about what Sarita and I found, as I pass the door to level six. Not thinking about Greg's lifeless body, the blood coming from his head, the gash in his neck. Not thinking about footsteps in the blood. Not thinking about them at all as the motion lights down here flash on in seamless sequence, the way they're supposed to.

What the fuck am I doing?

I'm going for a swim, okay? I'm going for a fucking swim. There are no ghosts or murderers after me. I am an adult, and I will not be caged by irrational fears.

I realize I'm not breathing when I push through the door to level seven and then into the pool room. The sight of the tropical blue tiling around the water, the fake palm tree, the yellow and red mural and little fake-stone water feature starts up my lungs again. It's warm in here, and bright.

That's not so bad, is it? I breathe in the tang of the salinated water, imagining myself by the sea, filling myself to the brim with the happy thoughts it brings, trying to ignore the acrid smell of burnt-out fuel that underlies it.

Dipping a toe in over the shallow step, I feel that the water's heated, so I plunge straight in and stay under as long as I can, enjoying how it envelops and shields me. I open my eyes and see the dark shape of the palm tree through the surface, rippling against the blue and red and yellow patterns from the wall.

Finally coming up for a breath, I float on my back, my eyes closed, trying to teleport myself back home. Megan and I used to have this theory, that if you were feeling the exact same thing as someone else and you were both thinking of each other at the same time, then you could teleport to where that person was. The reason teleportation didn't often work was that you had to match every detail of that feeling correctly, something that was complex and difficult to do. The number of times we lay on our beds, trying to get inside the mind and emotions of some boy . . . If he was feeling the same longing and desire at just the same time, he would magically appear. But of course he wasn't, we'd comfort ourselves after an hour of intense feeling; he was probably watching rugby or wanking over some movie star in a magazine.

But it's probably a crisp, sunny spring morning in Johannesburg. Maybe Megan's swimming some laps before she heads to work, worrying about me, missing me. If I try hard enough, I could just—

A shadow passes over my eyes, something blocking out the ceiling lights for a moment. Shunting my feet down to standing, I wipe my eyes and have to blink them a few times to get them clear.

I look around. Nothing.

I stand still, trying to hear a sound over the receding ripples.

I don't want to say it, but I do. 'Hello? Is anyone there?'

The fear of last night comes back to me, but more than that, the fear of every time I've had to walk somewhere alone at night. I've never had the luxury of being scared of ghost stories, of being worried about monsters. It's never some titillating fiction that stalks women at night, it's always men. Real men.

So my mood's been spoiled now. I'm pissed off with this whole situation. I get out of the pool, bend down and flick my hair back into the towel. I should have brought another one, of course, for—

There's someone behind me.

I don't want to turn, but I do, and I know who it will be. Know he wouldn't let it go.

Instinctively, I cross my arms over my chest, my hands curled into fists, and stare him down. The towel slips off my head and flumps down behind me.

'Hey, Cait,' Brett says.

His tone is placatory, but I'm not going to be disarmed. Any further than I am already, standing in front of him, barefooted, dripping wet in shorts and a T-shirt. But at the same time, I do want to avoid a confrontation. 'Yeah, hi.' Not taking my eyes off him, I step backwards, over the towel, lift it up and drape it over my shoulders and around me, like a cape. Like it makes me a fucking superhero.

He's been standing in the gloom against the dark grey far wall, near a pair of storeroom doors. 'I just wanna apopo . . . apologize. For last night.' He smiles at me and I can think of all the high school girls who'd dream about being smiled at by this dickhead. 'I was mad, and I shouldna.'

'I'm going now,' I say, wanting to turn but also not wanting to take my eyes off him. The result is that I look at him over my shoulder, appearing hesitant. He seems to take it as a cue.

'Hang on, hang on,' he says, approaching me – too fast. 'Now that we're friends again, can't we just . . . you know. It's lonely down here. We could . . . you know, just hang out.'

There's no time even to process what I'm hearing, the sheer, bewildering . . . The leering grin on his face is no disguise. I have to get away. Now.

Judging the distance to the stairwell door, I grip my towel, take a slow step towards him to get him off balance, then turn and run.

I'm almost up one flight of stairs before he can react, but I misjudge his pace and he's caught me by the time we're on the landing of level six.

The unctuous smile is gone now. He grabs at my shoulders, catching my hair in his right hand as he twists me around and pushes through the stairwell door. 'You're going to play nice, aren't you?' And for a moment I hear his father's voice coming out of his mouth, feel his father grabbing me, his godawful stink in my face. I'm thinking I should have just kept talking as we walked calmly up the stairs, not run. Why did I run? Why didn't I just keep calm? Why didn't I why didn't why didn't . . .

Stop it, Cait, for Christ's sakes! Fight!

And I find room for my hands and scratch at his face, going for his eyes but they're squinted shut in folds of fat and muscle and rage. And I think I'm screaming, raking at his shins with my feet but my bare toes get no traction. And I try to turn so that I can knee him but he's twisting me round and he's dragging me away from the dull yellow light of the bare concrete corridor and slapping through that thick tarp and into the half-finished medical suite I never wanted to see again, and now he's pushing me back against the sharp edge of a wooden carcass and he's scrabbling at the waist-band of my shorts and my knee is at the right angle I just need to . . .

And there's a shadow racing somewhere to my right and a hard, hollow sound and he jerks me upwards and there's another hard hollow sound and now Brett has let me go. He stumbles back, clutching his head and bellowing.

There's a short man, a man I haven't seen before, bobbing like a boxer in the darkness, hefting a length of metal pipe like a baseball bat in his hands. He looks at me, juts his chin. 'Go.'

18
WILL

Sleep deprivation is taking its toll on him. Lights seem too bright, noises too loud, and the layer that keeps his emotions in check is eroding. Whenever he closes his eyes, he sees Lana lying helpless and alone on the cot he set up for her in the parlour after she came home from the hospice, the tubes connecting her to life tangled around her limbs. The image is clear, sharp, so detailed that he can almost hear the suck and hiss of the oxygen tank, smell the medicinal tang that permeates the room. He sees her reaching for a glass of water, straining for it, crashing off the bed, calling out for him.

He can't give into it. She's fine. She has to be fine. Only . . . he should have been home more than two days ago. She would have told the nurse where he was or found the strength to call one of their neighbours – she's been to The Sanctum, knows its location. But no one has come. He's praying this is because the authorities are overwhelmed, coping with the virus, and not because she . . . because she's . . .

Stop.

He has no one to blame but himself. The last time he Skyped the nurse, he told her she could leave if he wasn't back when her last shift was over. He didn't think it would be an issue, assumed he'd be home well before then, maybe a couple of hours over if Greg made it worth his while. Money. It all came down to money. The agency charges triple-rates for overtime, and he reckoned it wouldn't matter if Lana was on her own for an extra hour or so. *Please, God, don't let her be alone with no one to help her.* He should have moved her to Portland months ago. Been within easy reach of the few family members who still checked in on them now and again. Lana's been ill for so long now, most of their friends have drifted away. He doesn't resent them for this. Sometimes he wishes he could do the same.

His mind is also buzzing from the hours spent trawling through the data on Greg's computer. Most of it is incomprehensible, but he's almost certain the hatch code isn't hidden in the reams of files and folders on the hard drive. He came across several photos of Greg proudly standing outside the concrete entrance of the original bunker, beaming into shot. Others show the progress of the building – the construction of the wind turbine, the day the hatch was hauled into place. That goddamned hatch . . . He's pored over the building's original plans that Trudi dug out of the bags of paper strewn around the floor of Greg's condo. It was built to last. Built to keep the occupants safe and protected from the spectre of nuclear fallout.

He can't give up.

No. There has to be a way out of here. And Leo Dannhauser could well be the key. The man has skills, specialist knowledge. Will's motive for begging James not to spread the news that Leo had bypassed his condo's locking mechanism was purely selfish. It took more than twenty minutes of dedicated and exhausting effort to convince him to keep quiet. Trudi had surprised him. She hadn't defended her father, had merely said: 'Tell them if you want to.' James was adamant that the others should know, and more than once Will almost lost it with him. But James came round in the end, buying Will's excuse that the last thing they needed was more tension. He was drunk and on the verge of passing out when they left Greg's condo – Will and Jae had to help him back to his unit – but Will knows it's only a matter of time before he spills the beans to the rest of them. James isn't someone who can keep his own counsel for long.

Will rubs his temples, closes his eyes again.

She's dead, and she died waiting for you, your name on her lips, she's lying there on the cold hardwood floor, and—

Thump. Thump, thump, thump.

The door – someone's knocking at the door.

He slings his legs off the bed, feels the floor dip as he stands. He's been drinking too much again; the bottle next to the bed is empty. He doesn't remember finishing it. And to his shame, earlier he stole the only hard tack left behind the bar – a quart of gin and a bottle of Wild Turkey.

Thump, thump.

He staggers through to the living room and disengages the lock.

It's Trudi. Dishevelled, barefoot, dressed in a pair of over-sized men's PJs, the shirt buttoned up incorrectly.

She doesn't wait to be invited in, pushes past him in a haze of musky scent. 'You got something to drink?'

Wordlessly, he hands her the gin and a tumbler.

She pours a slug, takes a sip and gags. 'Sorry for barging in like this. I couldn't sleep.'

He nods, trying to remember the last time he's been alone with a woman who isn't Lana. As she bends forward to refill her glass, her shirt gapes, and he catches a glimpse of her small breasts. He clears his throat, looks away. He's no saint, his marriage isn't perfect. Sometimes he wonders if he and Lana would even have stayed together if she hadn't gotten sick. Over the years, occasionally he's indulged himself with a night of flirtation with one or another of the bar regulars, lonely desperate people for the most part. But since the illness he hasn't strayed once. He's betrayed her enough coming here. He should never have done it.

Trudi's voice snaps him out of his thoughts. 'My father. What James said about him . . . you think it might be true? That he's a murderer. That he killed Greg.'

'I don't know. Have you asked him?'

Trudi downs her drink, coughs. 'No. Of course not. What would I say? "Hey, Dad, just wondering, are you a murderer by any chance?"' She gives a hollow laugh and drains the glass.

'Slow down.'

'I can handle it.' She looks straight into his eyes. 'You know how everyone wonders if they're capable of murder?'

He nods.

'Well, where my father's concerned, I'm almost sure—'

There's a bang on the door and she jumps.

Goddammit, what now? Another bang, and then a woman's voice: 'Will! Will!' *Thump.* 'Will!'

Cait comes flying into the room the second he opens the door. She's shivering, barefoot, her hair clinging to her cheeks in damp strands. 'You've got to stop him, Will!'

'Stop who?'

'Brett. Brett Guthrie. He tried to . . .' A flash of anger. 'That *fucker*. If that guy hadn't shown up when he did . . . you have to stop him!'

A spectre of a headache throbs behind his eyes as he

fights through the fog to make sense of what she's saying. 'Cait . . . calm down. I have no idea what you're—'

'Brett! You have to stop him! He's beating the shit out of that guy down there.'

Then Trudi is there at his side. 'What guy?'

'I don't know who the fuck he is! But hurry! They're on level six.'

'Okay, okay. I'll go check it out. You go back to your unit and—'

'I will, now go!' She practically shoves him out the door. 'Hurry!'

'Trudi – can you take Cait and—'

'Yes, yes, just go!'

Will jogs down the stairs to level six, rubbing at his eyes to clear them. He slows as he reaches the landing. Brett is standing in the doorway of the empty condo, his back to him, heaving as if he's out of breath. There's a metal pipe hanging loosely in his left hand. 'Brett?'

The boy drops the pipe, which hits the floor with a hollow clang, and turns around slowly. He flexes his fingers, winces, and says: 'He asked for it.' He stares defiantly at Will, as if daring him to contradict him. 'He attacked me first.'

Will pushes past him. A few feet from the entrance, half obscured in the gloom, a man lies curled in a foetal position on the concrete floor. His face is hidden, his arms wrapped around his head as if to protect it, but Will sees instantly that it's not someone from The Sanctum. The guy's too small to be James or Jae, his hair too long to be Yoo-jin.

He turns back to Brett. 'Who is it?'

'Don't know.'

Will drops to his haunches next to the man, touches his shoulder. The guy flinches. 'I'm not going to hurt you.'

The man moans and slowly removes his arms from his face. Will recoils. His face is a bloom of blood and bruises, one eyelid swollen shut. But there's something familiar about him. He knows this guy. He thinks back, searching for a name. Raymond . . . no, Reuben. A quiet man, reserved. He'd been part of the core labouring crew. Greg had set up a small compound for the migrant workers at the edge of the property, little more than a corral of trailers and prefab buildings, and it was a hotbed of drink and drug-fuelled fights. Far as Will remembers, Reuben had never been part of that.

'Reuben? Can you hear me, Reuben?'

Reuben inclines his head slowly.

Brett gasps. 'You *know* him?'

'He was part of the construction crew. One of the labourers. What did you do to him, Brett?'

The boy puffs out his chest. 'He attacked me. Didn't have no choice but to defend myself.'

Will thinks back to what Cait had said. 'Cait implied that you—'

Brett sniffs. 'Me and her, we were just having some fun, then this guy came at us. I prob'ly saved her life.' He fingers the knife on his hip. 'He's lucky I held back.'

Reuben shakes his head. 'No.'

Brett takes a step towards him. 'Shut your mouth.'

Will gets to his feet. 'Go and get Dr Park.'

'What for?'

'Reuben needs medical treatment.'

'He don't deserve that! He should be locked up for what he did. What's he doing here, anyway?'

Will feels the thin veneer holding his fury inside begin to crack. 'Do it. Or so help me, I'll—'

'You'll what?' But the bluster is gone from Brett's voice.

'You don't want to know. Now, *go*.'

Brett hesitates, then stalks off.

Will drops back to his haunches next to Reuben. 'Can you stand?'

Reuben coughs and spits out blood flecked with white shards of broken tooth. 'Uh. I do not know.'

Will helps him into a sitting position. Reuben hangs his head forward and spits out another glob of blood.

'What are you doing here, Reuben?'

The man takes in a raggedy breath, flinches and wraps an arm around his chest. 'I need a place to stay.'

'How long have you been here?' A surge of hope. Is it possible Reuben knows a way out of this place?

'Not long. From when I first hear about the virus. I think it will be safe here.'

'How did you get in?'

'Greg was coming and going many times. He leaves the hatch open. When Greg laid us off two month ago, I have no place to go, so I live for a while in one of the old trailers. It was no good. Cold. Then, here.'

'And you've been hiding out in this unit?' The condo where Greg died. Reuben's slight – barely taller than Yoo-jin. Those bloody footprints could well be his.

'Yes.' Another grimace of pain, another globule of blood-drenched spit. 'Also the machine room.' Reuben grabs Will's wrist. 'The boy. He was going to hurt the girl. I stop him. You believe me?'

'Will!' Jae appears at the doorway, momentarily blocking out the light, Stella close behind him. Will is relieved – but not surprised – to see that Brett isn't with them. Jae steps further into the unit and stares down at Reuben in disbelief. 'Who the fu– Who is that?'

'Reuben Montoya. One of Greg's construction workers. He's been hiding out in here.'

'Since we've been here?'

'Yeah.'

'Seriously? But . . . how? Wouldn't we have known?'

'Seems not.'

'What's wrong with his face?'

'Brett.'

'All he said to us was that someone was hurt down here.'

'Figures. Can you help him, Stella?' Will's relieved to see that she's brought a medical kit with her. He's surprised Yoo-jin isn't with them. If a thug like Brett had shown up at his door, Will would never have let Lana go off without him. He supposes that makes him old-fashioned, out-of-date. She's looking paler than usual, but that could be the poor light.

'Of course. Can we bring him into the light?'

Will helps Reuben to his feet. He moans, stumbles, and Will is forced to catch him around his waist to prevent him from collapsing. They shuffle into the hallway.

Stella silently assesses Reuben's injuries for a couple of minutes. 'Where arc you feeling the most pain?'

Reuben touches his sides. 'Here.'

Stella gently lifts his shirt, sucking her teeth as she takes in the blaze of bruising colouring Reuben's sides and back. 'I'm going to examine you. I'll be gentle, but it may hurt.'

Reuben nods, closing his eyes as Stella runs her hands over his ribs. She digs in the medical box, takes out a stethoscope and listens to Reuben's chest. 'Does it hurt to breathe?'

'*Si*. Yes.'

'He could have a pneumothorax,' Stella says to Will.

'A collapsed lung caused by a broken rib. His breathing is laboured.'

'What can we do for him?'

She briefly shuts her eyes and grimaces. 'There isn't much we can do. I'm hoping it's not a tension pneumothorax, which could be extremely serious. I'll give him something for the pain, strap him up, and clean the wounds on his face. Brett Guthrie did this?'

'Yeah.'

Stella's face clouds with anger. 'Brutal.' She grimaces again, and then Will realizes this isn't just a visceral reaction to the violence. She's not well.

'Hey,' Jae says. He bends down and picks something off the floor lying close to the doorway – a small tubular piece of metal.

'What is it?' Will asks.

'Wait.' Jae steps back into the condo, using his cell phone light to illuminate the floor. He disappears out of sight, then shouts, 'It's Greg's satellite phone.'

'What?'

Jae reappears and hands it to Will. The antennae is snapped off and the screen is smashed, but Will can still read the Iridium label. 'You know anything about this, Reuben?'

Reuben avoids his gaze. 'No.'

Jae and Will exchange glances. The implications of this are obvious, but Reuben isn't in any state to be interrogated right now. Will hands it back to Jae. 'You think Leo might be able to fix it?'

Jae shrugs. 'It's possible, I guess.'

Reuben groans again.

'C'mon. Let's get him out of here.'

'Where to?' Stella asks.

With the medical room little more than an empty shell, there isn't much choice. 'My condo's closest. You reckon you can help me get him up the stairs?'

'I can walk,' Reuben says, leaning forward and spitting out more blood.

'Let us help you,' Stella says. 'Put your arms around our shoulders.'

'I'll do it, Moms,' Jae says, clearly concerned about his mom's health.

It's slow going. Reuben may be small, but the stairwell isn't wide enough for three people, and Will is forced to take the bulk of Reuben's weight. His shoulder muscles are screaming and Reuben's face is slick with sweat when they finally reach the top.

Stella takes Will's place at Reuben's side so that he can open the door. 'Let's take him through to the—'

'Hey!'

Will turns to see Cam Guthrie thumping towards them. *Goddammit*. Exactly what they don't need.

'This the wetback who attacked Brett?'

Will steps in front of Reuben. 'Go back to your condo, Cam.'

Cam places a hand on the knife on his belt. 'You can't give me orders.'

Will's veneer cracks a little more. 'I just did. What you gonna do, stab me?' For a second, Will almost wants him to. It would mean an end to the spiralling thoughts about Lana. And maybe Cam can read this on his face, because he turns his ire on Stella and Jae. 'Why are you helping him? He's not one of us. He's an illegal. He tried to kill my son!'

Stella keeps her face blank. 'Calm down, Cam. That attitude isn't helping anyone.'

'Take Reuben inside, Stella,' Will says before Cam can lash out again.

'Now hold on,' Cam says. 'You can't just—'

'We'll talk about this in the morning, Cam.'

'You taking sides against me, Will?' His tone is almost jocular.

'No one's taking sides.'

'Not what it looks like to me.'

'Sorry you think that, Cam.'

Several tense seconds follow, then Cam relaxes his grip on the knife. 'You're going to regret this, Will.'

'Maybe so.'

Cam shakes his head in disgust, then disappears back up the stairs.

Will stands over the sink and forces himself to finish the can of cold beans. All he's been putting into his stomach lately is booze and coffee, and he needs the fuel. He'll have to call another meeting in a few hours, let everyone else know about the stowaway, and that's going to be a shit-fest. And soon enough he'll have to question Reuben about Greg. The guy's hiding something, he just knows he is. And what if he did kill Greg? What then? Will rubs at his forehead with the heel of his hand: *why me? Why's it fallen to me to deal with this?*

Thank God for Stella and Jae, who he reckons he can count on if things get nasty, which they invariably will. Yoo-jin he's not so sure about. And Trudi will have his back. He's asked her to stay with Cait, who was clearly deeply shaken, and she agreed without hesitating. Cam Guthrie and that dangerously unstable son of his will be gunning for him soon. He'll need all the backup he can get.

But for now, he has to try to grab a few hours' rest. Stella said she'd come back to check on Reuben in the morning, when the pain medication has worn off, and there's no point moving him out of the bedroom until then. Will chucks the can into the sink, and creeps through to the bedroom to grab a blanket.

Reuben stirs as he enters the room.

'Thank you, Mr Boucher,' he whispers.

'You need to sleep.'

'Wait.' Reuben leans over and shakily takes a sip of water. The bruised flesh above and below the bandages strapping his ribs is already turning a sickly yellow. Brett didn't hold back; he must have booted him dozens of times. 'The phone. You must know. I took it.'

Will slumps down on the corner of the bed, not sure he's ready to hear this. 'Did you kill Greg?'

Reuben looks down at his hands, the fingernails grimed with dirt and dried blood. 'No. But I found him. I come back from the storeroom – I'm hungry – and I see that he is lying there. I check if he is dead. I was afraid.'

'That we'd find you?'

'Yes. So I hide again.'

Will doesn't know the man well enough to be sure if he's telling the truth or not. 'You didn't see anyone else there? Someone leaving in a hurry maybe?'

'No.'

'Why did you take the phone?'

Reuben shrugs, which causes him to grimace in pain again.

'And it got smashed in the fight?'

'*Si.* Yes.'

'Reuben . . . you do know we're locked in here, don't you?'

He nods. 'Yes. This is what this place is for.'

'No. I mean there's a problem with the exit hatch. Greg changed the code before he died. We can't unlock it. We're trapped in here.'

'Why do you want to get outside?'

'The virus isn't as serious as everyone thought. And . . . my wife. She's sick. I need to . . .' The heaviness shifts in his chest, and he's hit with a flood of bitter emotion. He fights it, but knows it must be written all over his face.

Reuben glances down at his hands again. 'I am sorry for that, Mr Boucher. Why don't you use the radio for help?'

'It's broken. So's the wi-fi.' He gets shakily to his feet. 'We can finish this tomorrow. I'll be on the couch if you need anything.'

He's at the doorway when Reuben speaks again. 'There maybe is another way out.'

'What now?' Vicki says, the second she enters the rec room. James trails in after her, red-eyed, hair mussed, white flecks at the corner of his lips.

Will decides he may as well get started. Tyson and Cait have opted to stay in the condo with Sarita – no doubt to avoid Cam and Brett; the Guthrie women are absent as usual, and Jae is slumped on the L-shaped couch next to his parents. Yoo-jin has the air of a man who'd rather be anywhere else in the world – his left knee is dancing up and down – and Stella looks as exhausted as Will feels. Earlier he thought he could count on her, now he's not so sure. Brett and Cam are lurking over by the bar, and Leo and Trudi have chosen to sit opposite the Parks.

Will takes a deep breath, and drops the bombshell about

their uninvited guest. Vicki is the first to break the shocked silence. 'A *stranger* has been living here? Down here, with us?'

'The man's name is Reuben Montoya. He was part of the construction crew.'

'Greg assured us the casual labour had all left long ago.'

'He was wrong.'

'Okay,' James says, holding his hands up. 'I am now fucking officially sick of this place. First we get locked in, next there's some homeless dude hiding out in—'

'How did you discover him?' Vicki talks over her husband. James shrugs and smiles sardonically.

'I found him, ma'am,' Brett says. 'He was in that empty condo on level six. He tried to attack me.'

'*What?*'

'Yup.' Brett shows off his bandaged knuckles. 'Had to fight for my life, the guy was—'

'Cait might disagree with you on that, Brett.' Will jumps in, before Brett can continue. The last thing he needs right now is a lynch mob.

The boy colours. 'I didn't do nothing. She asked me to go with her.'

Vicki purses her lips. 'Can someone please explain what the hell he's talking about?'

Without taking his eyes from Brett's, Will says: 'Brett was with Cait when they discovered where Reuben was hiding out in the medical bay.'

'*Cait* was there?' Jae says.

'Yeah,' Brett smirks. 'Said she wanted to spend some time alone with me.'

Will suppresses the urge to stride over to the kid and punch him in the mouth. 'That's enough, Brett.'

'I don't understand,' Vicki continues. 'How could this man have been living here without anyone knowing?'

'If he knew the place well, it would be possible, I think,' Leo says.

James laughs. 'Yeah. You'd know all about sneaking around, wouldn't you, Leo?'

Will raises his hands. 'Calm down, everyone. There's something else I—'

'Where is the man now?' Vicki asks.

'In my condo. We're going to move him to a vacant unit soon.'

'He a big guy, Will?' James asks.

Will hesitates before answering. 'No.'

Vicki stares at her husband in confusion. 'Why are you asking that, James?'

'Because there were bloody footprints next to where Greg's body was found. Leading away from the body. Small-ish footprints.'

'So?'

'It's obvious. Greg must have run into the stowaway, and Reuben killed him so that he wouldn't blow the whistle on him.'

Everyone starts talking at once. 'Quiet!' Will roars. 'We don't know what happened to Greg. We may never know. But what's important right now is that we keep our heads. Now listen up: as far as getting out of here, we now have a couple of options.'

Even Vicki pays attention to this. 'What options?'

'We've found Greg's satellite phone. It's broken, but we're hoping you can fix it, Leo.'

Leo shrugs. 'I'll try, of course.'

'Hang on, back up,' James says. 'Where did you find it?'

'On the floor of the condo.'

'The stowaway had it?'

'It looks that way, yes.'

'So he did kill Greg then!'

'We don't know that for sure.'

This time it's Leo who shouts for silence. 'Listen to what Will has to say.'

Will nods his gratitude. 'And there might be another route out of here.' Thankfully, no one tries to interrupt him this time. 'Apparently the exterior wall of the elevator shaft isn't as reinforced as the rest of the structure. It's possible that if we get through it, we can get into the service conduit and from there it won't be too far to tunnel up to the surface.'

'Who told you this? The Mexican?' Brett sneers.

'And how do you propose getting through the wall?' Vicki asks. 'Do you have the equipment?'

'Most of the tools are in the equipment shed up top, but we have enough to make a start. The hard part will be constructing the scaffolding across the top of the shaft.'

'Sounds dangerous,' Cam says. 'And we're safe here. We got supplies to last us months. Maybe not as long as a year like Greg promised, but long enough. I vote we just hang tight until help comes.'

'What help?' Stella asks. Everyone turns to look at her. 'We haven't been able to contact the outside world for over two days now. How many people know about this place?' She fixes her eyes on Vicki. 'Did you give anyone the coordinates? Tell them about your luxury survival condo?'

Vicki examines her nails. 'No. Of course not. Greg advised against it.'

'No. Nor did we.' She laughs bitterly. 'Against my better

judgement' – Yoo-jin squirms as his wife speaks – 'I told my partners we were planning to head to Vancouver to visit family for a while and not to worry if we weren't in touch. That's the whole point of this place, isn't it?'

'What about you, Leo?' Will asks.

'No one knows we are here.'

'The lawyers?' Trudi asks.

'No.'

'Christ,' James mutters. 'But maybe Cam's right. We're safe down here for now. Even if they have got some kind of vaccine for the virus, it'll take weeks, even months, for them to get things back on track.'

'James,' Will says quietly but firmly. 'I can't wait. I need to get out.'

'I'm sorry about your wife, Will, but that's not my problem.'

Will waits for the anger to burst through, but it's gone, leaving a numbness in its place.

Trudi stands. 'I'm with you, Will.'

'Oh, there's a surprise,' James murmurs.

Trudi ignores him. 'We must do something. My mother needs to get to a hospital.'

'What are we going to do about the wetback?' Cam asks.

'Don't use that language,' Trudi hisses.

'Well, what about him? He's a murderer. Got to make sure he's locked up.'

'I agree,' Vicki pipes in. 'There are children here.'

Guthrie looks momentarily surprised – then gratified – to see a Maddox backing him up.

'He isn't going anywhere,' Will says. 'Brett saw to that. He's no danger to anyone.'

'Yeah, tell that to Mr Fuller, why don't you,' Brett mutters.

'We need to watch that he doesn't get out, murder us all while we're sleeping.'

'You can all do what you have to do,' Will says. 'But I'm sure as hell not going to sit around doing nothing.' He turns to Trudi. 'You ready to get started?'

'Yes.'

'I'll help too, Will,' Jae says.

No one else speaks up to offer their support but, for the first time since Greg died, Will feels a small stirring of hope.

19
CAIT

'What more do you want from me, Cait?'

I push away from the kitchen counter, knocking over the stool with a clatter. 'Forget it.' I don't know what I expected from him, actually – something approximating a human response would have been a start. I hurry down towards the bathroom, but he stops me.

'Please, Cait. I'm trying to understand. I'm trying to do the right thing, but I just don't know what that is.'

I wheel around on him. 'The right thing? The right fucking thing? I tell you someone tried to rape me and you say "At least you're not hurt." Is there a single authentic human emotion drifting around somewhere in there?'

He just gapes his mouth like a fish, and I realize he's telling the truth. He honestly doesn't know how to react, what to do. 'Listen, Cait,' he starts, in the rational tone I can imagine him using in a financial presentation, 'I checked that you were okay.' Now he's even counting the items off on his fingers. 'I offered to go and talk to Cam Guthrie. I offered to talk to Will. You said no on both counts. I'm not sure what else I can—'

'Just forget it, okay,' I say, then go into the bathroom and slam the door closed.

What *did* I expect from Tyson? A murderous outburst of

rage? For him to go next door with a butcher's knife and chop Brett Guthrie's cock and hands off? That would have helped, yes. For a moment. More than his cold response.

Maybe a hug?

Maybe not. The thought of anyone touching me right now makes me sick.

And the truth is, nothing will make me feel better. Sure, I could imagine all sorts of violence towards Brett Guthrie, but how would that help?

It would make sure he didn't ever do it again.

Right. That.

I pull off my shirt and look at myself in the mirror. My skin is red from all the scrubbing, but still I can feel his putrid saliva burning into me. I start the shower up again, make sure the bathroom door is locked, then take my clothes off.

When I feel cleaner, I tell Sarita that I'm going out for a walk.

She's been lying on the couch, still drowsy from the broken night, but now she jumps up. 'Can I come?'

Damn it. It's been hard enough for me to gather my nerve to leave the condo. I can't have her dragging along. I'm spent. 'No, you'd better stay here.'

'But—' she starts to whine.

'Please, Sarita, just this time. I'm not feeling great – a little grumpy – so you'll have more fun here. Do me a favour.'

She shrugs and slumps back into the cushions and stares at the TV again. I wasn't expecting her to give up that easily, and it makes me guilty. She must be feeling really lousy. I go over and kiss her on the head. 'I'll be back soon, okay. And *Charlie and Lola*'s on – you don't want to miss that, right?'

She shrugs again and I let myself out of the condo before I lose my nerve, slamming through the stairwell door and running down the stairs like a kid being chased by ghosts in a dark house. When I push out of the doorway to level five, my gut clenches. For a moment I think it's Brett, but it's Cam Guthrie standing at ease, like a soldier, next to the door of Unit 5B, his hand on the hilt of a gigantic hunting knife at his belt. I have to remind myself that Brett's undoubtedly lied to him about what happened, and in confirmation, he gives me a half-leer, half-smile. 'Morning, ma'am.' I'm not sure whether the *ma'am* is sarcastic or not. I shouldn't underestimate this man's wit just because of the image he projects. That would be a mistake.

Although my entire body is fighting against coming anywhere near him, I force myself to approach and open my mouth. My voice comes out as a croak and I have to clear my throat and try again. 'Hello. I want to see him.'

'Who?'

You know damn well who. 'The man in there.'

'Why? Man's a murderer. Can't let you do that.'

'And who has he murdered?'

'Greg. Found Greg's phone in the medical bay. All busted up.'

No one's mentioned this to me. Trudi's been kind, but she clearly hasn't given me all of the details. 'That doesn't prove anything. And I owe him.'

'Owe him what?'

'He saved me. He saved me from your son.' The anger is quick and hot and before I can stop myself I say, 'Your son is a monster.' I take two steps backwards, instinctively cross my arms, girding myself for his retaliation.

But to my surprise, Cam just looks down, almost sad. 'Brett didn't do nothing.'

His vulnerability provokes me, though, and I'm about to shout at him – *Your son tried to rape me*, but I'm halted by a clanging sound from the stairwell. Will and Jae round the landing, hefting a plank they must have sourced from the hydroponics room. Trudi says that Will's planning to break through the wall in the lift shaft. I hope he makes it, I really do.

I turn back to Cam. 'Let me pass.'

'I can't stop you.' Both of us know this isn't true. Seconds pass, then he nods. *Women, right? Go figure.* 'He ain't in any condition to threaten you, but just holler if you need me.'

I push past Cam Guthrie and glance through the half-lit condo until I find him. He's in the last bedroom, lying face up on a stripped-down mattress. Someone's bandaged his torso, but the rest of his clothes are blood-stained and stinking. He doesn't even have a blanket. I search around the room for something to cover him with – as much for him as for me. A voice in my head is saying I caused this, didn't I, but I shut it down. There's a small backpack and a jiffy bag shoved into a corner, its contents strewn over the carpet.

It's only now that I look at his face. I thought he was sleeping, but now I see that his eyes are so badly swollen that he can barely see out of them. But he's awake and I can see the narrowest flicker of his pupils watching me. He looks afraid.

They've left him a bowl of soup and a glass of water on the bed stand, but it doesn't look like he's capable of sitting up to drink it. I take the glass to the bathroom, rinse it out and run some fresh water into it, then bring it back.

Then I hesitate. Who is this man, after all? What is he

doing down here? Is Cam right – is he the one who killed Greg? But he's looking at me and at the water glass and I sit down next to him and, ignoring my body's protests, push my arms under his shoulders and easily lift his light weight up to a slump against the headboard. When I put the glass to his lips, he slurps thirstily, then coughs. I feed him some more water then stand up again.

'Thank you,' he says, his voice raspy and high-pitched.

'I must thank you,' I say. 'That's why I'm here. For stopping him . . . But I'm so sorry for what he did to you.'

He says nothing.

'They think that you . . . that you killed Greg Fuller. Do you even know him? Why are you here?'

'I didn't do it,' he says. 'I just hide here. For a place to stay. I work here for Mr Fuller when we build the place.'

'You saw him, though, didn't you? When he was dead.' I look at his feet, dirty and small for a man's. I know the answer already.

He nods.

'You walked through the blood, didn't you?'

He nods again. 'A mistake.' A rueful grimace.

'It's okay,' I hear myself saying, as if I get to say what's okay. As if I can make this whole bloody situation better with my liberal magnanimity. When he reaches for the glass with his left hand, he winces as he twists his torso and I come closer again, put the glass to his bruised mouth.

'Why did you help me last night?' I ask when he's done.

'I was in the next apartment, taking food. There are cans there. I hear you. I know there is trouble so I come in. I see him. I don't think.'

'Maybe if you thought, you wouldn't have done it,' I say. 'Look at you now.'

He shakes his head as vehemently as he can manage. 'I am happy I did it.'

I watch him ease himself back down to lying. 'It's not right,' I say. 'Someone will have to stop him.'

20

GINA

I haven't told Momma or Daddy about what happened in the freezer, and just thinking about it, I have to take a deep breath, steady myself against the wall. It was just a few minutes that I was stuck in there and I never want to be closed in again. Never. The things that went through my mind . . . If I was really faithful, I would have stayed steadfast and calm in the face of death, looking forward to reunion with God. But I had no faith. I was filled with panic – I knew the Devil was inside me.

It was a test from the Lord and I failed. If I'd died inside that freezer with my soul in that state, I'd never have found my home with the Lord.

But I need to get out of our unit. I heard someone say that walls can close in on you. That's what it feels like. Back home on the lot, I never used to sneak around, but it's all I seem to do here. In the condo, I tiptoe about, trying to be invisible, in case Momma catches me doing something I don't even know I'm doing wrong and explodes like she did the other day. But since the fire, she spends more and more time in her room and it's easier to slip out.

Daddy and Brett are on guard duty on level five, so now I creep up the stairs to the rec room, where Will is working on getting through the wall in the elevator shaft. Trudi is standing at the hole where the wooden boards used to be, a bandanna tied over her head. She smiles at me as I approach. Daddy and Brett haven't done much to help – they think Will's plan is dumb and impractical. I don't know what to think. If we get out, we'll have to go back to the trailer.

I peer into the gap, the dark hole that falls all the way to the basement making me feel light-headed. Will's brave – I wouldn't want to be doing what he's doing, balancing on a narrow plank stretched across this empty space, thumping away at a wall.

'Is it working?' I ask.

Trudi shakes her head. 'No. And no one else will help.' She says this bitterly, meaning Daddy and Brett. This makes me mad, because they have a proper job to do –they have to guard the Mexican who murdered Greg. Thank Heaven Brett found him when he did.

I turn, just as Will slams the hammer into the concrete again. *Thunk.* I can almost feel the jolt through my own arms and into my shoulders. It's muscle memory: I've done more than my share of wood-chopping and stone-crushing at home.

I slink across to the control-room door. I'll just say hi to Jae, which is the real reason I came up here, then I'll go back to the unit. I think of knocking, but I hear voices so I stop. They all have their backs to the door – Mr Dannhauser furthest away, bending over the worktop. Cait is sitting next to Jae, who's in front of the computer screen, his head turned to her. There's still the smell of wet ash and melted plastic and there's rock music playing softly from where they sit. Cait's beautiful flame hair is looped into a plait. I feel like a troll, my thick legs planted into the floor. I could just say hi, act normal, but I don't want them to see me. If Momma came up now . . .

Not a troll, a demon. I'm disgusting inside and out.

But then Cait says, 'I don't know where to go. I feel so trapped. Whenever I leave the flat I'm afraid I'll run into him. And I don't want to be afraid. I have to try and be positive for Sarita, but she's noticed already. Christ, do you know how shitty it feels when a scared little four-year-old is trying to cheer you up?'

'He won't try anything again,' Jae says. 'I'll make sure of it.'

'Yeah, what're you going to do?'

I see Jae's shoulders shrug.

'I don't want to be mean, but you know how he is. He's big and stupid, just like his Daddy.' She sneers out that last word in a bad accent and I know who she's talking about. 'Down here, he'll do whatever he wants to.'

I can rail against Brett's behaviour all I want but to hear some outsider badmouthing my brother makes me clench with anger. I try to swallow it – I know it's not my place, that Brett can look after himself – but I can't. I feel like Cilla in *Lordsville*, the bad cousin from New York City who's always starting fights. I take three steps towards them. 'What exactly do you think he wants to do?' I say to Cait. 'With you?' Maybe there's less Cilla in my voice and more Momma.

Jae and Cait both turn around to look at me and I instantly regret my tone. Not only because Jae's frowning at me, but because Cait's face looks so terrible. Her skin is pale and waxy with blotches of high colour on her cheeks. There are dark rings around her swollen eyes. I can tell she's really in trouble.

She startles when she sees me, those red eyes quickly moving from fear to anger. 'Never mind,' she says, and starts to get up. Meanwhile old Mr Dannhauser has looked up from the wires he's been soldering, recording us all with his sharp blue eyes. I can see why Daddy says he shouldn't be trusted.

'I'm sorry, Cait. I didn't mean . . . Did Brett do something to you?'

She just stalks past me to the door. 'Don't want your *momma*' – again that tone – 'freaking out, talking to the unbelievers. To the fucking infidels.'

'Tell her, Cait,' Jae says from his seat, swivelling from side to side with his long legs planted in front of him. 'She should know about it. She's . . .' He doesn't finish saying what he thinks I am.

'Just drop it, Jae. There's no reason she should care. She *should* damn well take her brother's side.'

'Side? In what? What did he do?' I ask. Mr Dannhauser is watching quietly all the while, with a little smile on his thin lips, like he's enjoying this.

'Brett tried to rape Cait last night,' Jae spits out. 'This guy came to stop him and Brett beat him unconscious. Is your brother still such a hero?'

Thun-clank thun-clank. Thun-clank.

'He what? Please wait.' But Cait just slips out the door.

Jae and Mr Dannhauser look at me for a few seconds, and then I run, too.

It's all starting to fall into place, all starting to make sense. This picture is starting to build up in my mind about the last few years and it's a picture I don't want to see. We were fifteen, Brett and me, the spring just before ninth-grade finals. We had visitors to the house, a whole stream of them, more than we ever normally got. Mr Goetsch, the school principal, Dr Kripke, the head of the school board, other men in suits

I didn't know. And Bessie Carver's daddy – Bessie Carver who lived across the street and who Brett liked but she preferred Art Jonas, the Junior team's wide receiver.

Momma was in tears a lot that month, but that wasn't too unusual – Grampa had died back in January after all. I just figured she was sad and I didn't really bother to make sense of what was happening. Nobody told me anything, but also I wasn't paying attention, my head filled with whatever was important to me back then.

But next thing Daddy had moved us to the trailer on Mr Harber's farm, pulled us out of school before we could even write finals. Book learning ain't gonna help you in the real world, he said. You need to learn to survive and I have to teach you myself. As long as I could remember, Daddy was always big on weapons, always wanted to learn to farm for himself, was always into prepping. He always told us that one day, the world order would collapse, and that US citizens would be under attack from the inside and out – we'd have to live in a country without laws, without money. I think he wished he could make us ready for anything, and it's as if what Brett did that spring gave him the excuse he needed.

I'm not even thinking right as I go downstairs, I'm crying. Bessie Carver. All I see in my mind is the face of Bessie Carver as we drove off that evening. Her face was pale and waxy with blotches of high colour, just like Cait. She stared at Brett from dark-ringed eyes and he bore straight back into her. She dropped her gaze as we passed and only then did I see the bruises on the side of her face.

I thought then maybe Brett just hit Bessie – that would have been bad enough – but I was young and stupid. I don't want to think of my twin brother as the sort of person who could rape someone, but I know he is. I know that all this time, the last two years and four months, Daddy's been protecting the world from Brett. Including me and Momma – that's why he's been keeping us apart. It isn't because he hates me, but because his love for me is so deep.

I stop short when I hear the rumble of Daddy and Brett's voices from where they're guarding the murderer. I pause, listening.

'We should move into this unit,' Brett's saying. 'It's much bigger. We should lock him up in our little condo and come down here. Dad, can we?'

'Quiet, Brett,' Daddy snaps.

But Brett whines, 'One spic murderer taking up all this lush space. It's just not f—'

I step through the door.

Brett whirls around, fists at the ready. 'Oh. It's just you.' Brett smirks and relaxes, lifting up the bottom of his T-shirt to wipe the sweat off his face, the way I've seen him do in the mirror here. We didn't have much of a mirror in the trailer. I guess if we were still at school and he was on the team he'd pose like that for the cheerleading squad. But we're not and he can't. Here there're no cheerleaders to see his abs.

'What did you do to Cait, Brett?'

'Huh?'

'Gina . . .' Daddy warns.

Brett's face darkens. I know that look. I know what it means. 'I saved her. I saved all of us. You know that.'

'Go upstairs, Gina,' Daddy bellows. 'Right now!'

I think I understand now. That Daddy's only treating me like this because he wants to protect me. I should just listen to him and leave – immediately – but everything that's happened in the last few days boils over and I don't just button my lip and go. Instead I wail, like a stupid little girl, 'Tell me why you're cutting me out, Daddy,' I say. 'Why're you choosing him?'

Maybe it's because I'm crying and I haven't cried for years that he doesn't smack me right then. 'Do you know what he did, Daddy? Do you know what he did last night?'

Now Brett comes right up to me, leans his face and his chest into me, pushing me backwards into the closet door. 'What? What did I do?' he says.

'Brett! Gina!' Daddy barks, but neither of us take any notice.

'You've done it before, haven't you? That girl at school, Bessie Carver.' I search Brett's face for any acknowledgement but there's nothing behind his eyes. I shove him with my shoulder and twist away. I realize that nobody else in this place would dare to touch Brett, but I've wrestled him down a thousand times. 'That's why we sold the house and went to the trailer, isn't it? Not because Momma and Daddy forced us to, but because of you. Because you couldn't . . .' I want to say *keep your dick in your pants*. I don't even know where I've heard that phrase. But I bite my tongue. We're not kids roughhousing at home any more – I don't know him any more, I don't know what he'd do to me if I pushed him too far. We used to be best friends but now the last two years sit between us like a brick wall. And the sad weight of that shuts my mouth at last, way too late.

'You don't know what you're talking about,' Brett says, but he backs off.

'It's true, isn't it, Daddy?'

I'm still expecting him to hit me or something, not accept this disobedience, but he's quiet instead. Then he says, softly, almost to himself, 'I did what I did for the good of this family. You know how important it is to be prepared. The world's going to hell. There are people out there who want to kill us, who want to destroy America and the values we stand for . . .' I open my mouth to ask another question but finally Daddy reminds me who and where I am. 'Just be quiet, Gina. Go and see to your mother.'

I used to go out into the woods or up onto the hills every day back home, just to be by myself. Nobody called it sneaking around up there, so why should they stop me from going where I want down here? But I still feel wrong going downstairs to get away from them all – Momma, Daddy and Brett – and the further down I go, the stronger the pull of guilt from upstairs.

I want to go down and have a look at the chickens in the coop – maybe it will do me good to see something innocent and natural. Maybe I can put my fingers in the soil of the vegetable trays and remind myself that the world isn't made of concrete and electricity, that we're still blessed, that we're still alive. The lights flick on as I round each landing and go off above me. I look up into the deepening dark above me and hurry on downward.

'Gina! Sss.'

It's just as well that Jae opens the door to level six and shows himself immediately or I don't know what I would've done. Either had a heart attack thinking the voice was coming from inside me or punched out at whoever was lurking behind that door. Probably the last – Jae's lucky he's not lying on the floor with a busted nose.

'What are you doing?' I whisper, checking up the stairs behind me. Still dark – nobody else is on the stairs.

'Come here,' he says and I follow him into the corridor.

UNDER GROUND

'I want to show you something.' I shouldn't be on this floor
– I don't want to be here, but I trail him as he passes the
unfinished sickbay where Greg was found, and pushes
through the thick plastic covering the doorway of 6A.

I hesitate outside. 'What is it, Jae? What do you want to
show me?'

There's no answer, but I see a blurred yellow glow sput-
tering through the see-through plastic.

'You shouldn't be in there, Jae.'

No answer.

'I'm going downstairs now, okay.'

Now I see his silhouette coming towards me and he sticks
out his arm and grabs my hand. His palm is warm and dry.
I should pull away but he says, 'Please. Come and see. I made
it for you.'

I push aside the tarp and follow him. The unit's the same
shape as ours, the same three-piece lounge set as in our unit
sits in its regular cluster in front of the kitchenette, but it's
still wrapped in plastic. There's no carpet on the concrete
floor and no lights on, but Jae's lit a collection of tea lights on
top of an up-ended paint can.

'It might be a nice place to hang out. Just us, you know.
There's no power, but the candles are fine, right?'

'It's nice, Jae.'

He unsticks one end of the plastic covering on the couch
and I help him pull it back, lifting the end of the couch while
he yanks the sheeting off.

'All we need are some tunes,' he says, and goes to his computer which is sitting in one of the topless kitchen cabinets.

I remember the music he was playing upstairs, how it
made me feel, and I say, 'No, don't. I don't mind the quiet.'

'Sure. Okay,' he says.

Sitting down on the far side of the sofa, he looks disappointed so I think I should say something, something that will make him feel good to answer. 'Uh, how's it going with the computers? I mean, in the control room.'

He shrugs. 'I'm no expert. I think everything's as it was. Internal control systems fine and wi-fi fubar. Leo fixed the radio and has apparently set up a distress signal.'

'Daddy says he's a spy. That he worked for Hitler. Do you think that's true?'

'Uh, no. He's seventy-something now. He was a baby when Hitler was running Germany. Unless Hitler used baby spies. You think?' he says. I start to blush. I don't know anything about anything and I'm embarrassed – Jae is so smart – but when I look at him, he's smiling kindly.

'I guess,' I say.

'But who knows? He is German, after all. In the sixties, seventies . . . There was lots of work for spies then too. You know, it wouldn't surprise me. You want to go up and ask him?'

'No!' I say, before I realize he's joking again.

A silence drops on us, and I can tell that we're both thinking of the other person in the control room this morning.

'Do you think Cait hates me?' I say.

'What?'

'She was so nice to me . . . before. She blames me for what Brett did.' I know I'm being disloyal to speak like this. I shouldn't discuss it, or at least I should deny everything, defend Brett. But, down here, just between Jae and me, I know he had it in him. I know he did what she said he did.

'She's just angry. That asshole she works for doesn't even back her. You know, sometimes I just think the world would be a better place without certain people. But I'm sure she doesn't blame you,' he says.

'I just want to go home,' I say. I don't want to let myself cry but I can feel my face getting hot. Down here, in our private little space, I feel far away from the judging eyes of my family. 'I'm so scared.'

Jae shifts closer to me on the sofa, slowly reaches his fingers out to my hands where they're clasped in my lap. I let him touch me, then turn my hand over and take his fingers. 'I won't let anything happen to you, Gina.'

I look into his face, wanting to tell him he's just a kid like me, with no control over what's happening either inside or outside The Sanctum, but his eyes are so clear and still that I believe him.

When he raises his hand to my cheek and wipes away some of the tears, I worry that my skin is greasy and he's going to feel all my spots, and I worry about how I smell and how I look and that he's going to be disgusted at me, but when he leans in and I can smell salt and mint and he puts his lips on mine, I forget everything and all I can feel is his tongue on my lips and then his teeth and the sweat at the back of his head as I push myself into him.

21
JAE

Jae barely recognizes his dad's voice. It's strident, a pitch higher than usual: 'I don't want you going out there, Stella.'

'We've been through this, Yoo-jin. Reuben Montoya needs help. So does Caroline Dannhauser.'

'It could be dangerous, Stella. That man killed Greg!'

'I'm not going to just sit here and do nothing, Yoo-jin.'

Offer to go with her, Dad, Jae silently begs. *Do something apart from ghosting around the condo, wiping up imaginary dust.* But Jae knows his dad won't. Listening to the alien sounds of them arguing makes him feel unmoored. He flumps back on his bed, tries to block out the raised voices. He's been daydreaming all morning about Gina, replaying what happened between them over and over in his mind. He's desperate to see her again, but they'll have to be careful. If Cam or Brett or Mad Ma Guthrie get an inkling of their relationship, he'll end up like Reuben, beaten to a pulp. Jae's thinking about asking Cait if she'll act as a go-between, maybe get a message to Gina for him. Cait's cool, she'll probably do it. She's still messed up about what happened with Brett, but she might like the idea of doing something that would really piss him off.

'. . . least you could do is help Will and Trudi,' his mom is saying. His dad responds that Will's excavations are a pointless exercise, and Jae sort of agrees. He's done his bit, helping to lug the wood and piping up to the rec room so that Will could build his scaffolding, but as far as he's concerned, the whole thing is an accident waiting to happen. The scaffolding is basically just a plank tied to the rusty old ladder on the far side of the shaft wall. Will and Trudi have secured it with bolts, and Trudi has made Will tie a rope around his waist for safety, but Jae can see it's mission impossible. There's only room for one person on the plank, and he doubts Will is going to get very far smashing through the brickwork with the small hammer he managed to unearth from the supply room. There aren't any other tools.

'There's no reason to leave this place,' his dad is saying. 'We're safe here.'

'Ha! Safe! After what that boy did to . . .' his mom's voice dissolves into a coughing fit. Shit. Now desperate to relieve the tension, Jae jumps up and hurries into the kitchen. His mom is doubled over, Dad flapping around her.

'I'll come with you, Moms. I told Trudi I'd read to Caroline anyway.'

She looks up. 'At least one of you has some backbone,' Moms spits, fighting to catch her breath.

'Maybe Dad's right, Moms. Maybe you should stay. You don't look good.'

'Not you too, Jae. I'm fine.'

His dad turns away and mutters something about preparing something fresh to eat for supper. Good luck with that, Jae thinks. Jae's taken his turn to feed the chickens – which stink, no one's prepared to clear up their mess – and either they've given up laying or someone has been sneaking in and stealing the eggs. The vegetables in the hydroponics room aren't doing much better, and no one wants to eat the meat in the freezer, not with Greg's body on the floor in there. They've been surviving on Dad's soups and whatever he can cobble together out of the canned goods.

Jae grabs his backpack, shoves his mom's Kobo inside it, and follows her into the hallway. The faint twocking sound of Will slamming the hammer into the concrete greets them as they reach the stairwell.

It takes Moms longer than usual to navigate the two flights down to the Dannhausers' place, but Jae decides not to bring up his worries about her health again. There's no point; they're here now. The door is ajar – it can no longer be shut all the way unless they want to use Greg's thumb key. Jae shudders and follows Moms inside it.

'Hello?' Moms calls. No one comes to greet them. Leo must be up in the control room, fiddling with the satellite phone, and Trudi will be helping Will. There's a pause, and then the old woman calls out to them weakly. She's lying half off the bed – her nightdress rucked up her thighs.

'I'm trying to get to the bathroom,' she gasps.

Moms tuts and hurries over to her. He looks away while Moms adjusts the old lady's nightdress, then helps steady her to the bathroom. The flesh on her arms squishes through his fingers. He can't imagine ever being so old and helpless. 'I can manage now,' Caroline says when they reach the basin.

He and Moms sit side by side on the bed while they wait for Caroline to finish. Jae clears his throat. 'Moms . . . about Dad. Are you two okay?'

Moms gives him one of her brave smiles. 'Of course. We're just . . . we're not seeing eye to eye on a few things at the moment, that's all.'

No shit. Jae searches for something to say next. He wants to ask: *Aren't you fucking furious at him for not helping us with Reuben? Or, how could you let him bring us to this fuck-ing place?* but he's not sure he wants to hear the answers to those questions.

His mom sighs. 'I thought buying this place might snap him out of it.' Jae fidgets; it's as if his mom has just read his mind. 'I thought that knowing we had a safe haven might put his . . . anxieties to rest. But coming here . . . When we're at home, his behaviour' – she lets out a short humourless laugh – 'or lack of behaviour is easier to ignore. I guess I was wrong to let him have his way on this.'

'It'll be okay, Moms.' It's all he can think of to say. Pathetic. He's feeling light-headed again. However messed up it is, his parents' relationship is the one constant in his life.

The toilet flushes and his mom gets up to help Caroline back to the bed. 'I'll go down and check on Reuben,' she says once Caroline is settled.

'Should I come with you?' Suddenly, he doesn't want to be alone with the old woman. She seems nice, but her help-lessness is bringing him down. She reminds him of Dad.

'No, you stay and read to Caroline.' Moms smoothes down Caroline's duvet, then leaves.

Squirming with self-consciousness, Jae digs out the Kobo. 'What sort of books do you like, Mrs Dannhauser?'

'If we're going to be friends then you must call me Caro-line. And I like a good story. A good mystery or a love story.' She smiles at him. 'I might not stay awake. I'm sleeping a lot lately.'

'That's okay.'

She pats his hand. 'You're a good boy.'

He scrolls through his mom's list and picks out a Jodi Picoult novel. It's awkward at first, but then he feels himself getting into it, losing himself in the words, lulled by his own voice. Moms used to read to him when he was a kid. Did Dad ever do that? He must have. When he reaches page twenty, Caroline is snoring softly.

'Thank you,' a voice says behind him. He turns to see Trudi.

'How's the work going?'

'It's not. Will says the brickwork in the shaft is also reinforced. We just don't have the tools to get through it.' She sits down on the bed and pulls a face. 'And Will is working himself into exhaustion.' Something rises in her face when she says his name and Jae wonders if he looks like that when he thinks about Gina. Maybe.

'I'll come back later and read to her again.'

She nods distractedly. 'Thank you.'

He sees himself out, making sure to use the dog-eared paperback to keep the door from closing. What now? He should really go and see if his mom is still with Reuben. He walks slowly down the stairs, preparing himself to run into Brett guarding the vacant unit but Cam's there instead. He's better than Brett, but still as intimidating as hell.

'Is my mom still in there?' Jae asks.

Cam's chewing on a toothpick, like he thinks he's Stallone. 'Yup. Can't see why she'd want to help a murderer.'

Jae can't help himself. 'It's the Christian thing to do.'

Cam narrows his eyes, but doesn't take the bait. Probably can't figure out if Jae is serious or not. Jae looks away as Cam uses the thumb key – now wrapped in a piece of plastic – and opens the door.

The condo is silent. It smells fusty, as if it's uninhabited. Jae feels a flicker of anxiety. What if Dad and Cam are right? What if Reuben *is* a murderer? An image of his mom lying on the floor in a pool of black blood jumps into his head. *Shit.* The bedroom door is ajar, and he lunges for it.

'Moms!'

She's sitting on the bed, next to where Reuben is sleeping, his breath coming in wheezy gasps. She looks up with a tear-streaked face. He's never seen her cry before.

22
JAMES

Slap, slap, slap. Someone's batting at his chest. 'James! James! Get up, get the hell up!' He opens his eyes, sees Vicki staring down at him. He sits up too quickly, the room spins and he almost vomits as someone jabs a kitchen knife into his head and twists the handle. He breathes in deeply, swallows bitter spittle. And, Christ, his neck is killing him from sleeping on the couch again. He thinks back to last night's intake: two Valium and half a bottle of Stoli. No wonder he feels like shit.

Vicki digs her nails into his shoulder. 'James! Snap out of it.' Claudette's dancing around Vicki's heels, her frantic yips spiking into the core of his brain.

He blinks to clear his vision, scrubs a hand over his face, and takes a good look at his wife. She's naked, yesterday's make-up smeared around her eyes. 'What's . . . why aren't you dressed?'

'I can't believe you didn't hear it!'

'Hear what?'

'There was a booming sound from above us – like a cannon going off – and I could have sworn the place shook.'

'You mean like an earthquake?' A spurt of adrenalin helps clear his head.

'No. More like an explosion.'

'Jesus.'

'It can't be a gas main, can it? The whole place runs on electricity, doesn't it?'

'Maybe a water heater burst or something.' It hits him that the lights in the condo are dimmer than they usually are.

'You think?'

How the fuck would I know? 'It could be.' He gets up, staggers to the sink and turns on the faucet. God, he's thirsty. The pipes chunder and spit out brown residue. 'The water's off.'

'James . . . I'm scared. What are we going to do?'

He's not used to seeing her like this – unsure of herself, turning to him for support. 'You'd better get dressed.'

'Okay.' She hurries off to the bedroom, the dog scuttling behind her. He goes to the fridge, grabs a Miller Lite and chugs half the can. He belches, hides the can in one of the cupboards and then opens the door and peers out into the hallway. The timer light blinks on, but it shines at only a fraction of its usual wattage. He sniffs. He can't smell smoke, but detects the odour of melting plastic, and the air is hazy, as if a light fog has fallen. That can't be good. The Dannhausers' door opens and Leo steps out, dressed in a pair of pyjamas and running shoes, a heavy-duty flashlight in his left hand.

James waves at him. 'You know what's going on?'

'No. I'm going to look now.'

From the stairwell above he makes out the murmur of raised voices and a child crying – it must be Sarita.

'Vicki said it sounded like some kind of explosion.'

'Yes. You didn't hear it?'

Is the old bastard judging him? James shakes himself. He's just being paranoid. 'I sleep like the dead.'

'James?' Vicki creeps up behind him. 'We know what's happened?' Claudette slips out through the door and James

223

lunges to catch her, the sudden movement setting off another series of fireworks in his head. She wriggles, nips at his hands, and he pushes her roughly into Vicki's arms.

'. . . stay here with your mother,' Leo is saying to Trudi, who's now peering out of the door. 'I will not be long.'

James knows he should offer to go with him. The beer has helped stall the worst of the hangover, but he's not really in any state to do anything other than sleep. But still . . . as much as James doesn't trust the secretive old fuck, for some reason he can't bear the thought of looking like a coward in front of him. *Be a man.* Christ, where did that come from? 'I'll come with you, Leo,' he hears himself saying.

'If you like,' Leo shrugs, then heads for the stairwell.

Vicki grabs James's arm and hisses, 'Let the old man go,' but James shakes her off.

Before she can stop him, he jogs up the stairs to catch up with Leo.

Tyson, Cait, Sarita, Stella and Jae are gathered on the level three landing. The little girl has her thumb in her mouth and she's clinging to Cait's legs, and Stella looks like she's about to collapse. There's no sign of Yoo-jin or any of the Guthries. One of the wooden boards that covers the elevator shaft on this level is splintered and half-sheared away.

'I was just about to go down to get Will,' Jae is saying to Leo. James glances at Tyson, but he's clearly avoiding looking in his direction. 'Do you want me to come with you?'

'No. We don't know what we are dealing with yet. James and I can handle it.' Despite himself, James feels a flicker of pride at this. *The best men for the job are on it.* 'Why don't you check that everyone is accounted for?'

'We'll do that,' Jae says.

James follows Leo up to the next floor. The air is getting

hazier and he coughs as he inhales a lungful of dust. He pulls the collar of his sports shirt up to cover his mouth.

Leo hesitates. 'You are fine to continue?'

'Yes,' he says. 'Of course.' *Of course. What a man.*

The lights are out on the stairwell leading up to the rec room, and Leo clicks on the flashlight. The dust is thicker here, and he blinks as it stings his eyes. They shuffle towards the rec room entrance, which is also shrouded in darkness. Leo steps into the room, and shines the beam around the interior.

'Holy *fuck*,' James breathes, trying to piece together what he's seeing. The flashlight bounces off a blanket of glass shards – presumably all that remains of the plasma screen – and a mound of rubble, dirt, twisted rebar and broken furniture is concentrated in the area around the elevator shaft. Leo shines the beam into the shaft. Water spits through the wall on the far side and there's a strong stench of sewage. Metal mesh shines through the section Will was excavating, but most of the damage appears to be in the rec area itself.

'Could . . . did someone from the outside try to blast their way in here?'

'No. This comes from the inside,' Leo says. 'Explosions follow the route of least resistance. And as you can see, most of the damage originates from inside the shaft.'

On the other side of the room, a couple of sprinklers are spitting water. Simultaneously, they sputter, then die.

'Who goes there?' James hears Cam call from behind them. He turns, wincing as he's hit in the face with the beam of Cam's flashlight. 'What in the hell happened? Where's the . . .'

'Dad?' Brett looms behind his father.

There's the sound of a cough, and a figure stumbles out

from the darkened depths of the control room. 'That you, Will?' James calls. It has to be him. Thank fuck he isn't hamburger at the bottom of that shaft.

Will shuffles towards them. 'Can we get through?'

'What?'

'The wall. Can we get through the wall? Leo, shine your light into the shaft.'

Leo does so, and Will leans forward dangerously, gripping the edge of the doorway. 'Shit.' He steps back and slams his fist into the wall next to the shaft entrance. 'It didn't work.'

James feels an icy finger trail down his spine. 'What do you mean, Will? What didn't work?'

Will hesitates, his shoulders slumping, then says: 'There was no way I could break through that wall. Reuben was wrong, it was reinforced with rebar mesh and Kevlar. I had no choice.'

'What did you use, Will?' Leo asks quietly.

'C4.'

James isn't sure he's hearing correctly. 'Huh?'

'Plastic explosive,' Leo says.

It takes a moment for this to sink in. 'I know what the fuck it is, Leo. C4? You brought plastic explosive into a fucking underground bunker, Will?'

'It was already here. It was in the safe. The gun safe. Along with a detonator. Greg used it on the project—'

'What in the *fuck*?'

Brett shoves past him and lunges for Will. 'You dumb bastard!' Leo steps between them just in time, moving with more speed than James would have expected for such an old guy.

'Settle down,' Leo says quietly. 'It is done.'

'I'm sorry,' Will says.

'Sorry?' Brett shouts. 'You could've got us all killed!'

'Cam, get your son away from here,' Leo says. 'Now.'

For once Cam does as he's told. Murmuring threats, Brett allows himself to be led out of the room.

No one says anything for a couple of minutes. James runs his tongue over his teeth, which are now coated in fine grit, and listens to the distant whir of the air filters. Thank God they're still running.

'We need to assess the true extent of the damage,' Leo says, breaking the silence.

'We can see it just fine. Room is fucked.' Christ, he needs a cigarette. Really needs one. Suddenly, it's all he can think about. He wants to rip that carton out of the bug-out bag, and sit and smoke one after another until his lungs collapse.

'I am not speaking of what is in here. We must check the machine room for damage.' The accent that Leo usually hides so carefully leaks into his voice. *Ve hav vays off making you talk.* James burps a giggle, hides it with a cough.

'Leo is right,' Will says, his voice thick with regret. 'I'm worried about the electricity supply. Seems like we might have kicked over to emergency power.'

'But all the . . . machinery and stuff is in the basement, isn't it?'

'Yup. But the wiring and connectors are built into the wall cavity, they're part of the infrastructure.'

'Shit.' Those icy fingers trickle across his skin once more as he remembers that hollow sound the water pipes made.

With the rec room out of action, they're all squashed into his and Vicki's unit. James squeezes himself on the couch between Vicki and Stella Park. Stella's ample thigh squashes against his, but she doesn't attempt to budge up. She smells faintly of salt and soap – which isn't entirely unpleasant, but makes him think of tears. No sign of Yoo-jin again. Weird. Maybe she's eaten him.

'You okay, Stella?'

She doesn't acknowledge him, looks like she's lost in dreamland. Perhaps she's been helping herself to the Oxycontin. She closes her eyes and sighs as if she's in pain. He hopes she's not sick. He leans as far into Vicki as he can. The others are trickling in, taking up the few remaining chairs or leaning against the breakfast bar, the Guthries – including Ma Guthrie for once – seeming to take up most of the space. He senses someone staring at him, turns his head and, for a second, locks eyes with Tyson. Tyson rips his eyes away and stares down at his feet. He looks terrible – his cheeks grey with stubble, his pale pink shirt creased and stained.

James wonders if he should be the one to start, or if they should get right to it and lynch Will, which is pretty much what is written over everyone's faces. But it's Leo who speaks up first.

'We have lost connectivity from the grid, but the back-up generators arc working fine and we have a good store of diesel.' He pauses. 'Unfortunately we suspect that the water purification system and the pipes connecting us to the reservoir are compromised.'

'But you can fix them, right?' Jae asks. 'Will?'

Will, who's looking like he wants the earth to swallow him up, says: 'Not from in here, no.'

'And back-ups?' Vicki waves The Sanctum flier she's been twisting in her hands. She's been reading it obsessively since the explosion, which is pointless as far as James is concerned

– there's no real information in it, just PR bullshit speak. 'It says here that there are three back-ups for the water supply.'

'Greg took some shortcuts.' Will continues, 'We've got plenty of bottled water, but until we can figure a way out of this, we need to conserve it.'

Cam Guthrie shakes his head. 'We don't need any more of your advice, Will Boucher. You're not the leader any more.'

Christ. James can see exactly where this is going.

'There's always the water in the pool,' Jae says.

'It's salinated,' Will mumbles.

'So what are we going to do about showering?' Vicki asks.

'Never mind that,' Stella says. She must have snapped out of her funk without James noticing. 'Without water we won't be able to flush the toilets.'

Vicki shudders. 'Ugh. I didn't think of that.'

'Fortunately we still have the compost toilet down on level eight,' Will says. 'We can use that.'

'One bathroom for almost twenty people?'

'Yes, but—'

'Quiet, Will,' Cam growls. 'You don't get a say in this. It's because of you we're in this mess.'

Trudi pipes up. 'He was only trying to help.'

Vicki lets out a sardonic laugh.

Leo steps forward. 'What we must do is collate how much bottled water we have and distribute it equally to everyone. It'll be up to each unit how they ration it.'

'That murderer can't have none.' This from Brett. 'Will neither. They don't deserve it.'

'I don't think we should go that far,' Vicki says. 'But certainly Will should be held accountable for what he's done.'

'What do you suggest?' Trudi asks bitterly.

James knows his wife, suspects she wouldn't be satisfied

with anything less than a public flogging. 'I'm just saying he should be made accountable for what he did.'

'At least he was trying to do something,' Trudi says. 'What about you? All you seem to do is complain.'

James winces. He almost feels sorry for Trudi. She has no idea what is about to come her way. Vicki is not to be fucked with. Years spent as a lawyer – she narrowly missed taking silk in the UK – and navigating their business to its place as one of the top firms in Boston has honed her tongue to a deadly point.

Vicki composes her features, lets a couple of seconds pass, and then says, 'I think it would be best if you saved your energy for dealing with your eating disorder, Trudi. If you think I need advice from someone who clearly needs psychiatric help, then you're very much mistaken.'

'You can't talk to me like—'

'I can speak to you in any way I choose. I'm sorry that you have the poor taste to fall in love with an alcoholic handyman, but that's not my problem. What is my problem is how we proceed from here.'

'Silence!' Leo roars, his voice ripping around the room. Even Vicki shuts up. 'This is getting us nowhere. We need to ration out the water. Jae? Could you do that?'

'Nuh-uh,' Brett says. 'I don't trust a Chink with something like that.'

'You're disgusting,' Cait spits. He smirks at her.

'There's only one thing we can do now.' Ma Guthrie. 'We must pray. Prayer will save us.'

'Jesus Christ,' Vicki rolls her eyes. 'Not this again. Someone will come for us soon.'

'We must plan as if nobody will come,' Leo says. 'I will attempt to repair the equipment that is compromised, and we must ration out the water – fairly – including to Mr Montoya.' He speaks with an authority that even Vicki appears to find intimidating. 'James, perhaps you and Tyson could please start inventorying the bottled water. Does anyone have an objection to these two men doing this duty?'

James is about to object – he can see that Tyson is about to do the same – but perhaps now will be their chance to talk. They need to clear the air, get everything out in the open. 'Fine by me.' No one else objects.

'Then I suggest that after this, one member of each family meets in the storeroom to collect their share of the water, which they will keep in their unit,' Leo continues.

'Who made you the leader?' Brett gripes.

Leo ignores him. 'James, Tyson, perhaps you should get started.'

'Shall we?' James says to Tyson, who's refusing to look at him.

'Daddy?' Sarita asks. 'Are you angry at that man?'

'Not now, Sarita.'

'Daddy?'

'I said, not now.'

The child starts wailing. God, it's like a buzz saw going through his head. Cait attempts to comfort her, but she continues to screech.

'Someone shut that fucking kid up!' Vicki snaps.

'She can't help it! She's frightened,' Cait says, hauling the child up onto a hip and glaring at Vicki.

'Well, do your fucking job and look after her then.'

'Tyson. Come on,' James says before the argument can escalate.

'Look after Sarita,' Tyson barks at Cait before getting up and heading for the door.

Vicki gives James a sardonic half-smile as he gets up to leave – she doesn't know, he tells himself, she can't know – then follows Tyson into the hallway. Tyson's racing down the stairs, and James has to hustle to catch up with him. 'Tyson, wait!'

Again, James longs for a cigarette, but there was no time to slip away after the meeting. He wishes he'd thought to bring the Glock along. Sneaked it under his jacket, just in case. 'You hear me, Tyson?'

No response. As they reach the landing on level six, James grabs his arm. 'Hey . . . look, I know it's tough, but we've got to—'

Tyson whirls around, his eyes livid with hatred, and pushes him away. 'Don't touch me. Don't you fucking *dare*.'

James backs off. 'Hey. No problem.'

Speechless, James watches as Tyson thumps through the door to level seven, wincing as a door slams.

23
JAE

Moms heaves herself up on her elbows. The bedroom stinks of sweat and worse, and he knows she feels bad about this. The only way to flush the lavatory is to lug water up from the pool. There's the compost toilet on level eight, but his mom isn't strong enough to make it all the way down there. 'You need to rest, Moms. I'll go and see Reuben.'

'His bandages need changing.'

'I can do it.'

'Jae . . . ask your father to go with you. I don't want you going out there alone.'

'I will, Moms,' he says, although he can't see the point. Dad hasn't left the condo since the morning after the explosion.

'Thank you. Be careful.' She sinks back onto the pillows. She doesn't have the strength to argue. She hasn't been able to keep anything down since yesterday, and although she's trying to underplay it, he can see that the pain in her abdomen is getting worse.

Jae heads into the kitchen and grabs a can of Mountain Dew out of the cupboard. There are three six-packs in there, courtesy of his dad. As well as the Mountain Dew and some beer and Coke Lite, there's enough water for two weeks, working on approximately a gallon of water per person per day. Jae's done the calculations, but he refuses to allow himself to believe that they'll be stuck down here for that long. Someone will come for them.

He cracks the can and checks his laptop for the second time in an hour, hoping against hope that by some miracle the wi-fi has come back on. Stupid. Even Leo has given up attempting to fix it, although he's still doggedly trying to mend the satellite phone. And, along with the water, they've lost the cable connection. Losing the TV is no biggy compared to what else they're dealing with, but it was a distraction, a link to the outside world. Jae pictures his room back at home – set up just like he wants it. Thinks about heading out to get a burger, or to the mall, how he did that without even thinking about it. All the things he took for granted. Google. Reddit. Talking to Scruff. Running water. Toilets that didn't need flushing with a bucket. It's only been two days since Will fucked them all, but his skin itches from using the salinated pool water to wash.

'Jae?' His dad comes out of the bathroom, a bottle of bleach in his hand. 'Can you go down to the pool and get more water, please?'

You fucking do it. 'I'll do it later.'

'Fine.'

It's not fine. Jae wishes he knew where his dad's massive social anxiety stemmed from. It can't be from his childhood. Jae's grandparents died before he was born, but Dad has never said a bad word about them, and Moms knew them for a few years and said they were lovely. They emigrated to Canada when Dad was ten or so, scrimping and saving to open up a small grocery store specializing in Asian ingredients, and made sure Dad got a good education and went to university, where he hooked up with Moms. Jae's seen the pics of their university days – Dad seemed to be smiling and partying as hard as everyone else. It could be that this weird behaviour is an integral part of Dad's personality that he's allowed to grow, unchecked. Jae can't help wondering if his dad's paranoia has reached the levels it has because Moms let him get away with it for so many years . . . Facilitated it. No, that's not fair. And his dad isn't that bad. He could be a lot worse. He could be Cam Guthrie.

'Dad, Moms has asked me to go and check on Reuben. She wants you to come with me.'

'You are not to go and see that man, Jae. We've spoken about this.'

'I really don't think he's violent, Dad. Moms has been there loads of times and he's barely able to stand.'

His dad opens his mouth to reply, when there's a knock on the door. Jae can't help feel a stab of hope that it might be Gina.

'Who is it?' his dad calls through the door.

'Trudi.'

Dad reluctantly opens up, then excuses himself and disappears into the bedroom, leaving Jae to deal with Trudi. She's holding a stack of Tupperware in her arms. 'I thought I should bring these back.' He takes them from her and piles them on the counter. Dad will be able to spend hours arranging them later, he thinks bitterly.

'How's Caroline?'

'I think there's an improvement.'

'Cool. Should I go and read to her?' He's been putting it off all day. He kinda enjoyed reading to her the first time, but now being around her just makes him feel sad. She falls asleep almost the second he starts reading. He doesn't think she's improving; he thinks she's decided to give up.

'She's sleeping now, Jae. Thank you, though. Just so you know, Brett and Cam Guthrie and Tyson are working on getting through the inner airlock door that leads to the hatch.'

'With what? Isn't it made of steel?'

'Whatever they can find.'

Despite his doubts, he's really pleased to hear they're working on getting everyone out of this place; it gives him hope. It's the sort of grunt work he could actually trust Cam and Brett with, something useful for them to do. But Tyson? 'And *Tyson*'s with them?' Jae tries to imagine Cait's boss, as slick and urbane as James Maddox, getting his hands dirty. He wonders what Cait will say about him working so closely with the Guthries.

'Yes. But Will's not doing anything to help. You think . . . do you think your mom could talk to him?'

'My mom?'

'Yes. I know Will respects her.'

'She's sick.'

'Oh.' She frowns. He waits for her to ask how bad Moms is, but she doesn't.

'What about Leo? Can't he talk to Will?'

She glances away. 'My father is working around the clock attempting to fix the phone. The Guthries are probably doing the right thing. The only thing. Busting through that door and the hatch is the only way out of this place.'

'What about the building plans? There must be a weak spot somewhere.'

'I've checked. So did Will before . . . He tried the only clear weak spot and look how that turned out.'

Trudi makes her excuses and leaves, and Jae decides to slip out and see Reuben before his dad reappears. He fills one of the empty Tupperwares with the remains of the pasta they had last night, and heads down to level five. The Guthries won't be lurking in the hallway outside Reuben's place now that they're on their own mission. He tries the door handle, but the door is locked. Of course it is. There's no way to open it from the outside unless he uses Greg's thumb.

He knocks. Waits. Almost decides to get the hell out of there and head to the gym when a voice rasps: 'Who is it?'

'Jae.'

A pause, and then the door opens slowly. Jae can't tell if Reuben is glad to see him or not. His face is still a mass of bruised flesh, and his eyes are wary. 'Are they outside? The men?' His breath hisses with each word.

'Brett and Cam? No. They're trying to get through the hatch door. You know what's been going on, right?' Reuben nods, then stands back to let him in. The place doesn't smell as rank as it did last time and it looks like Reuben's made an effort to clean it up. A pack of battered playing cards are laid out on the floor in a solitaire pattern, and there's half a gallon of water on the counter, probably supplied by Leo. Jae puts the pasta on the counter. 'I brought you something to eat.'

'Thank you. Is your mother okay? I have not seen her for a long time. Your mother is very kind to me.'

'She's sick.'

'I am sorry. The last time she was here she looked bad.' Genuine concern or self-interest, Jae can't decide. Still, it's a more generous reaction than he got from Trudi.

'She says you need new bandages. I can do that for you if you like?'

Reuben shakes his head. 'It hurts me less if I do not have them on.'

'Oh. So is there—'

Reuben freezes and grabs Jae's arm. Jae tries to twist away, but Reuben's stronger than he looks. 'Let me go!'

'Listen. Outside.'

'Huh?'

'Outside the door. You hear?' He releases his grip. Jae backs away from him. But he's right – there are loud voices out in the hallway. They sound close.

'We should listen what they are saying,' Reuben says.

Jae nods, creeps to the door and opens it a crack. He's not the one who's under Sanctum arrest or whatever bullshit way Brett and Cam probably describe it, but he'd still rather the Guthries not know he's hanging out with Reuben un-supervised.

'. . . get those guns, Will,' Cam is saying. 'We can use them to get through the hatch.'

'The hatch is blast- and bullet-proof, Cam.' Will's voice is lower than the others, slurred as if he's been drinking, and Jae has to strain to make out his words. 'So's inner airlock door. Bullets will ric . . . ricochet.'

'It's worth a try, Will.' Tyson – hesitant, but trying to be authoritative.

'Nuh-uh. Too dangerous.'

'*Make* him open it, Dad.' This from Psycho Boy.

'No need to talk like that, son. I'm sure Will's gonna come to his senses soon,' Cam says.

Cam's ominous tone chills Jae as he comes back into the room and shuts the door softly. Will's smart to keep the guns locked away from the Guthries, but how long is he going to withstand their pressure? And what if they're right and the guns are their way into the airlock? 'Tell me, Reuben. Do you think we could shoot our way out of here? Through the door up top?'

'I don't know. Maybe.'

Jae searches for something else to say. Should he offer to play cards with Reuben? But really, isn't reading to Caroline enough of a good deed? He's done his duty. 'I'd better go. I'll make sure you get some more water.'

'Thank you.'

He double-checks to make sure the hallway is empty before leaving the unit. The Guthrie men and their new friend Tyson must have returned to the airlock. Should he take advantage of this and risk going to Gina's unit to see if she's around? If Bonnie answers the door he can always say he wants to join her prayer group. James said he saw her praying at the green door while the others tried to chisel through the latch. 'Not sure even JC can get through tungsten,' James said, which was pretty funny.

No. He'll go and see Cait instead, ask for her help contacting Gina.

He's seriously on edge, and feels like a noob going into his first match, his stomach churning, his fingers tingling with nervous excitement. He brushes his teeth for the third time, then rinses his mouth out with Listerine. It's taken him over an hour to clean up. The dust from the explosion still coats everything – it's grimed its way into his pores and he can feel it crunching between his teeth. He checks his hair in the mirror – the pool water is giving him dandruff, or maybe it's just salt crystals – and scrabbles his fingers through it. His T-shirt should be cool. They haven't been able to do any washing, but he's only worn it once.

Cait dropped the note off an hour ago. She'd come through for him after all. She said that she'd run into Gina in the storeroom when she was collecting some crackers for Sarita's supper. He reads it again: 'see you later tonight x'. He pockets his one and only condom (he's had it for years since they handed them out at school during 'Safer Sex' month), feeling it burn in his back pocket. He isn't going to push her, but it would be stupid not to be prepared.

He grabs his bag and slings it over his shoulder. His dad is sitting on the couch, staring into space. 'Dad, I'm going out.' No response. 'Dad?'

'I'm sorry, Jae. I should never have brought you here.' He gets up, strides over to Jae, wraps his arms around him and rests his head on Jae's shoulder. His parents are affectionate with each other, but his dad hasn't hugged him for years. Jae can't tell if he's trying to take comfort or give it. Gently, Jae disentangles himself.

'Dad . . .'

'I mean it. I'm sorry. I've been selfish bringing you here.'

'Dad, it's cool, really.' He's getting that dizzy feeling again. What will happen if his mom is sick and his dad loses it completely? But for now, Gina is waiting. 'Look after Moms. I won't be long.'

'I'll do better, Jae-lin. You'll see. I'll make sure we're okay here.'

'I know you will, Dad.'

It's only when he's in the hallway that he realizes his dad didn't even ask where he was going. Pushing the worry aside, he races down the stairs to level six. Jae isn't superstitious, but he tries not to look at the Death Unit's dark doorway as he hurries past it to 6A. Whenever he's down here he's hit with an image of Greg's cold, dead hands – the left one missing a thumb – curling around the door frame.

The second he's inside the unit, he sets up the speakers

for his iPhone and scrolls through to the Adele playlist he downloaded for his mom ages ago. It's not his thing, but it's the closest he's got to something romantic – his iTunes library is full of gaming music. He and Gina have never discussed their taste in music before – for all he knows she might be into thrash metal (although this is doubtful; he reckons it's more likely to be country or gospel or something). Next, he fishes the tea candles he's stolen from the storeroom out of his bag, and places them in a heart shape on the floor. He lights them, stands back and surveys the effect. Too much? He doesn't know.

Preparations over, he sits down on the couch and waits. Gina doesn't drink – neither does he, not really – but he wishes he had something to take the edge off. Instead he's brought along two cans of Mountain Dew. He cracks one open and takes a sip. The first track comes to an end, and a second later the door opens and Gina walks in.

She gasps when she takes in the candles, then smiles shyly at him. 'Hey.'

'Hey.' His mouth is suddenly dry.

'It's beautiful, Jae. Did you do this for me?'

He thinks about making a joke, maybe saying, 'Nah, but Rihanna couldn't make it,' or something, but it's a bit lame and she probably wouldn't get it. She approaches him slowly, tugging at her T-shirt and smoothing her hair, which is damp. 'How did you get away?'

'I told Momma I was going to feed the chicks. I haven't got long.' She tucks her hair behind her ears. 'I missed you,' she says, and even in the dim light cast by the candles, he can see the blood rushing to her cheeks.

'Me too.'

'Really?'

'Really. Come here.' She smiles and moves to sit next to him. He takes her hand – feels it trembling – and before he loses his nerve, he leans in and kisses her. She makes a little sound, and then she's kissing him back.

Jae never expected it to feel like this. He's been fully aware of the mechanics of sex for as long as he's had his own internet access. He's jerked off in several creative ways ever since he was eleven, but just the feel of someone else's warm hand on the back of his neck, her hot tongue over his lips and in his mouth and now her cold fingers sliding up under his shirt blows everything he's ever thought and ever felt out of his mind.

He's nothing now but sensation as he follows her body, cupping her smooth, warm flesh in his hands. He's going to overload as he tries to understand the smell of her skin, of her breath, of her saliva – it's like woods, like rain, like blood, like life. He feels himself being pulled into her and he thinks she's putting her hands into his pants but he's trying not to think about that because he's working out where her clothes end and her body begins and what that rough feeling is between his fingers.

Gina stiffens, and Jae is figuring out how to use his words again to ask her what the matter is when something whacks into his head, stunning him. For a second he can't make sense of what's happening, then he looks up, sees Brett looming over him, thinks, *how the fuck did he get in without us hearing him?* Then his face explodes as Brett slams his fist into his cheek. The pain is huge – Jae's never been punched before, why didn't anyone tell him how much it hurt? – and he instinctively curls himself into a ball. He can hear Gina screaming at Brett to stop, but he doesn't, another blow lands in Jae's kidneys. He feels his head being yanked back, burning needles digging into his scalp as Brett twists his fingers in his hair and hauls him off the couch.

Jae rolls onto his hands and knees to scuttle away, but Brett kicks his arms from under him, flips him onto his back, and then there's a crushing weight on his chest. Brett's staring down at him, his face just inches from his, his eyes dark holes in his skull – the fucker is straddling his chest. Jae tries to twist out from underneath him, kicks his legs up and flails with his arms, punching and slapping wildly at Brett's head, neck and arms. Brett barely seems to feel it – doesn't even flinch, and Jae can smell the full animal stink of him, days of old sweat and shit and something that reminds him of burning plastic.

'That's my sister, you Chink,' Brett hisses, spraying Jae with spittle. 'You were touching my sister!'

Jae can hear Gina sobbing and pleading in the background.

'Get off me!' he half begs, half yells, pushing with all his strength against Brett's chest.

Brett shifts his weight, bats Jae's arms away, and wraps his hands around his neck.

The pain is instant and all-consuming, and feels like his throat is being forced up into his mouth. *Oh shit, oh Jesus, he can't breathe and it hurts, it hurts, oh fuck.*

He writhes and bucks again, scratches at Brett's arms, digs his nails into the flesh, tries to reach for his eyes, but he's too heavy to shift and Jae can feel his strength leaking away. Dark spots bloom in front of his eyes, and he has a second to think, *that really happens, it's not some cliché* – and then the pressure lessens.

'Brett! No!' Gina screams again.

Jae sucks in a reedy breath, coughs, his throat as raw and

ragged as if it's been toasted on an open flame, then realizes that Gina has climbed onto Brett's back and is attempting to haul her brother off. He needs to help her, he has to help her, but all he can think about is sucking in the next breath. Keeping one hand wrapped around Jae's throat, Brett twists his upper body and elbows her in the side of the head. She drops.

The pressure is back around his neck again. 'You're dead. You're fucking *dead*.' There are tears streaming from Brett's eyes now, which scares Jae more than the rage.

Another wave of agony, and then he feels a peculiar coldness trickling through his limbs. *So this is what it's like*, he thinks, *this is what it feels like when you—*

And then he's released. The deadlock around his throat eases, the weight is gone from his chest. He sucks in air, but it won't come at first, he bats at his throat, begging it to work, begging it to let in oxygen. He curls into a ball, but still he can't seem to get the oxygen into his lungs. He's vaguely aware that Brett is howling, there's a thudding sound, *dunk*, *dunk*, *dunk*, and then the dark spots seem to join together to make one big mass and then, nothing.

24
TRUDI

Standing – like a ballerina after all this time, lifting herself from a cross-legged lotus pose without using her hands – Trudi imagines the grace of her body in the studio mirror. She takes five final deep breaths, willing the meditation, the calm to heal her, but she's not sure how well it's working down here. She feels frayed.

She peers through her mother's doorway, where Jae is reading to her from his e-reader. His face is puffed from the beating, his lips swollen, and occasionally he winces and touches his throat, but he insisted on coming. Caroline's resting with her eyes closed, but Trudi can see from the smile on her lips that she's awake and listening.

She pours a small bowl of warm water, folds a clean facecloth and brings them through to the TV room, where Leo is sitting wordlessly, as he has ever since he came back in after beating up the Guthrie boy yesterday. His face is reflected in the dead black screen.

'I've brought you a basin of water, Dad.'

He doesn't answer.

'Do you want a new shirt?'

Leo has always dressed neatly. Never opulently, never flashing his worth – he had the air of a respectable civil servant from a more elegant age – but always neatly pressed.

It's not only the smatters of blood on the rumpled cloth, but the sweat stains under his arms, the coating of bristly white over his sallow neck, that offend her.

'We can't allow bullies to get even a taste of control,' he says, without turning to her. 'You understand that, don't you?'

'Excuse me?' Trudi says. She's glad that he's talking.

At last he trains his eyes on her. 'You judge me, don't you?' he says. 'For what I did to that boy.'

'I don't even know what you did, Dad. I heard the basics . . .' He's never spoken to her like this. He's never in any way offered her a justification for anything he's done in his life. 'It's not my place to . . .' Her words swallow themselves again.

'I was there, you know,' he says, jutting his chin towards the TV.

Trudi glances at the screen, but there's nothing on, of course. 'Where, Dad?'

'Prague. August 1968. The Stasi was interested in the Soviet Union's reaction to the uprising there. They sent me to monitor their methods.'

'I didn't know you were ever in Prague,' she says, trying to ignore the fact that her father's seeing ghosts on a blank TV screen.

'I was all over Europe in the late sixties and the seventies.'

Trudi's not quite sure how to react. All her life, ever since she knew there was something secret in Leo's past, she's craved to know the truth. But now, just these few words, more than he ever told her before, seem cursed, as if he's opening a tomb. She's stuck immobile between competing urges to clap her hands over her ears and run and to ask him a thousand breathless questions. She's not sure what's brought his mood on, but she knows it will be broken any second. She says nothing, standing behind Leo and imagining grey people on the screen waving at their liberators or oppressors, whichever they might be, passing in columns through their city.

After a long moment, Leo looks up at her and says, 'Come and sit, Trudi.'

She rounds the couch and sits on the other cushion, a clear gap between them. She places the bowl of cooling water and the cloth as a barrier between them.

'It is my shame that you are afraid of me, Liebe,' he says and Trudi flushes from the chest upwards and looks away. To have her fear stated so clearly, the poison that's festered between them all these years, seems to be another secret that shouldn't be spoken.

'I am so worried about your mother,' Leo continues.

The awkward, heavy chips of conversation pierce into her until finally something dislodges from her. 'I realized something the other day, Dad. When I came back home, I was worried that you would harm Mom if I wasn't there to protect her.'

He looks at her, and the hurt in his face is shocking to Trudi. 'Harm your mother? How can you think that? She is my only love. I risked my entire life to leave Berlin and go back to her American home with her. How could you not know that? I would have done it again, even if we'd ended up living in the streets. Even if I'd been discovered and shot in the back. I would have died with her smile in my eyes.' His face darkens and his voice grows ominous. 'It makes me very sad that this, at least, you didn't see. That I love your mother beyond words.'

'I didn't finish, Dad. I finally realized that you were angry with me, that I was getting between you and Mom ever since

I came home. And what you've just said confirms it all.' Trudi's eyes are burning. 'I guess you never loved me as much as you love Mom.'

Leo shakes his head. 'I was a bad father, unprepared. I was constantly getting things wrong. Every time I got angry, you got scared and made me more anxious, and angrier – and you got more scared. I never found my way out of this cycle. The answer for me was to withdraw from you. We were strangers from each other since you were a little girl. And I have lived with that mistake all my life.'

Trudi's upset by this bald honesty, sure, but it's also affirming because he's being honest. She knows the truth of it, and she can move on. She knows that when they get home, she can leave them together and start her life again. There's already a kernel of excitement inside her, her mind's already flashing to looking for work and finding an apartment – and someone to share it with.

She leans over, the fear now fled, and takes her father's hands and wipes at his scored and bloodied knuckles. He looks at her, a frown gradually dissolving from his forehead. It's probably the only time in their lives that there's been a clear peace between them.

'I need to know a few things, Dad,' she says. He nods. 'What you've told me now has helped me piece most of it together, but I need to know for sure. Were you a spy, Dad?'

'*Spy* is a grand term for it. I was a soldier, Liebe. A soldier working in foreign countries. Everyone was a soldier in those days. And everywhere in Europe was a foreign country. Not like here.'

'So you worked for the Stasi?'

Her shrugs. 'Naturally. Who else? My home was in East Berlin. The victors picked me for that team.'

'And you learned skills?'

'Many, yes. Useful ones, skills that made our business here.'

'You've killed people?'

He looks over at Caroline's bedroom door and answers softly. 'Yes.'

Now she's come to the most immediate question, but she doesn't know how to ask it. She glances down at his feet. Finally, her need for the truth outweighs her fear of knowing it, so she blurts it out. 'Did you kill Greg Fuller?'

He frowns and then smiles. 'No.'

'I know how angry you were with him for the way they treated us when we arrived here, for locking us in. I'd never say anything,' she says, not sure if she would or not.

He looks into her eyes, the pale blue shooting her through with something powerful – pride? 'I have really got it wrong if you need to ask this question. It is my mistake. I left killing behind a long time ago.'

And Trudi believes him, at the same time as she understands how ridiculous the idea of Leo going anywhere in bare feet is. If he had been down there in that room in the middle of the night, he would have been wearing his slippers. Funny how this fact, more than anything he's said, settles the question for her. Leo is not The Sanctum Killer, after all.

She's barely seen Will since the explosion. Vicki's words at the meeting the morning after it had stung her. The woman is vicious and manipulative, and Trudi knows she shouldn't let it get to her. But she wants Will to know the truth about her father. Ever since they found those files on Greg's computer she knows Will has suspected him of Greg's murder. Hell, *she* suspected him.

Her heart is thumping in her chest as she stands outside his door. She knocks softly, telling herself that if he doesn't answer in ten seconds, she'll leave. But he does answer it, unshaven, the funk of alcohol surrounding him. For a moment, she's tempted to join the rest of the residents and shun this loser who's made such a fuck-up and caused them such trouble, but she looks at those uncalculating eyes, that country-firm body, and she can't hate him. Still swirling with loss and the heady sense of freedom that awaits her when they return home, and jealous of the invisible, perfect wife who's calling to Will from so far, drawing his attentions away from Trudi's grand adventure, she pushes past him through the doorway, heavy on the physical contact, and closes the door behind them. She raises up his arms and takes off his shirt and tongues his stomach, taut from heavy lifting, until his attention is entirely back in this room.

25
CAIT

Sarita is screaming into her comforter and I've given up trying to stop her. I slump down and sit against the wall of her bedroom and listen to the noise, pushing dark ooze off the slash on my arm. The rim of the wound – one of the many grazes and slices I didn't even notice getting when Brett attacked me – is a mouldy, dead white. None of the scabs are setting, nothing's drying out. My nails are packed with dark grime, but still I dig away at the sores.

With only a gallon of water a day, it's hard to keep clean, especially when I've been giving as much of my water as I can spare to Sarita. None of us realized just how bad the explosion was when it happened. Like sheep, we just sort of guessed that there'd be a back-up plan. But the blast blew away the main supply pipe to the reservoir and the sewer all at once, making a wonderful little shit lake at the bottom of the elevator shaft with all our potable water. And of course there's no back-up plan apart from a rackful of gallon bottles which have been portioned out to every unit, and which are disappearing fast. The Sanctum's brochure promises that people could live here for close on a year . . . I guess Greg Fuller couldn't have planned for Will's mistake, but still, what if there was an earthquake, a nuclear bomb? The Sanctum would never have held up in a real emergency. What the fuck was Tyson thinking buying into this place?

My clothes stink and I itch all over. Two days after the explosion, Sarita wet her bed so I thought I'd take her PJs and sheets down to the pool and at least use a bucketful of that water to rinse them. I took my chances, knowing that the Guthries would be on guard outside Reuben's door as usual. I had to get out of our condo, wanted to feel like I was doing something, back then when I thought I could still fabricate a veneer of normality for Sarita. But when I got down there, the water level was down a foot and there was a thick slick of scum lining the top of the water and the edges of the pool wall.

'Don't do it,' I heard behind me.

I turned. It was Trudi Dannhauser. She was kind to me immediately after Brett attacked me, but I haven't seen much of her since.

'I thought it would be a good idea,' she said, 'just to use some of the water to have a bucket bath. You know, like they do in Africa.'

'But it's highly salinated water,' I said.

'Yes, I didn't think of that.' And she lifted up her skirt to show me the peeling rash on the insides of her thighs. Thank you, Trudi. 'You don't want to know what they've been rinsing in there,' she said, as I left. Jesus.

Sarita's screaming has turned into exhausted, self-conscious sobs, her last-ditch effort to get me to respond. I feel awful for ignoring her, but I'm so tired and there's nothing I can do for her. I'd offer her some food – it usually improves her mood – but there's nothing she likes to eat here. Salty crackers with some artificial spread that will just make her feel thirsty. I'm saving water for lunchtime, so can't offer her a reconstituted soya-and-pasta meal yet, which she likes well enough. I could open a can of mixed fruit, I guess, but the sugar crash after that would be worse than this. Perhaps the hellish noise Sarita's making is an appropriate response to the situation. Why should I tell her to shut up, to cheer up? I feel like joining her, flopping down with my face in the musty, sweaty sheets and screaming, making myself so rigid that something will pop. But I don't have the energy, so I sit here. I never knew giving up could be quite so comforting.

But Tyson comes in and kneels down at Sarita's bedside. He's been hanging around with the Guthrie men – which I can't help but see as a betrayal – using whatever makeshift tools they can find to try and break through the door that leads to the hatch. I know what he's doing: aligning himself with who he thinks is the strongest. I listen at the door. But apart from a strangled 'Sarita', he doesn't say much else.

Sarita starts bellowing louder. I realize that she's afraid of him.

I remember who I am and why I'm here. Wiping my fingers on my jeans, I stand. I scoop Sarita up and she immediately quietens, snuffling into my shoulder. As much fun as five minutes' oblivious self-pity can be, I'm not going to let Sarita down. When we're out of here, her father will hopefully get his shit together, but for now I'm looking after her.

I'm closing the front door behind me when I hear Tyson. 'Where are you taking her?' I don't like the way he's looking at me. It's too direct, like Brett Guthrie's stare. As if Sarita and I are possessions, rather than people.

'Out. For a walk,' I say, turning to face him and lowering Sarita down and herding her behind my legs.

'I'm not letting her wander around when there's a murderer out there.'

'That's nonsense, Tyson!' I spit as firmly as I can. It is essential that Sarita doesn't listen to him, that she believes that Greg's death was just an accident. 'Don't be ridiculous.' I frown and nod my head towards Sarita, *Don't talk like that in front of your daughter, you idiot!*

But he doesn't take the hint. 'Cam says we should think about joining forces.'

'Against who?'

'We've got to make Will give us the combination to the safe, Cait. With the guns we might be able to—'

I don't wait to hear any more, just turn and drag Sarita out behind me, slamming the door.

'What was Daddy saying, Mommy?'

'Nothing, sweetie,' I squat down to her level. 'And I'm not your mommy, remember. I'm Cait. Remember your picture in your diary. That's your mom. Never forget her, Sarita.'

She shrugs this off. 'Is there a monster here? Is that who we saw with all the blood?'

'No, sweetie. That was a man called Greg Fuller. He had an accident.' I believe Reuben Montoya's story. I'm convinced that Greg had some sort of accident and Reuben might have been scrounging through the scene for anything that would help him get through his secret stay down here. I know he's not a murderer, and not just because he helped me get away from Brett. Nobody's been murdered and there's no monster apart from that sick boy and his messed-up parents.

I don't want to hang around the corridor for too long, in case Tyson comes after us, but I can't really imagine him chasing us . . . And what would he do when he caught up? He's not the chasing sort of type.

But now that we're out of the condo, where are we going to go? We could visit the scum-covered pool, or we could go down to level six and peer down into the elevator shaft into Shit Lake. Or we could head up to ground zero in the rec room. I know some of the residents have done what they can to tidy the dust and the shrapnel and clean the furniture, but when I last looked there were still shards of metal and chunks of concrete scattered around. It's not a safe place for a kid to play.

I decide we'll go to the one friendly place in this whole Sanctum, the one I've been avoiding since yesterday.

Yoo-jin lets us in and Jae looks up from the sofa, wincing as he tries to smile with his swollen lips. There's a red and grey ring around his neck like a smudge of dirt. I can hardly look at him. This is my fault. I thought it would be cute, Gina and Jae at least getting some joy down here in this cesspit, but if I had just thought a minute further than my own need to be the bloody hero, I should have known what would happen.

'You look sore,' Sarita says, and reaches out to touch Jae's eye. He flinches away but gives another of those painful, face-slipping smiles.

'You need a painkiller, Jae?' Yoo-jin asks.

I turn and look at him. There's something different about him. Harder. He's furious. You don't fuck with a parent.

'I'm fine, Dad.'

'I'm going to sit with your mother.'

Jae sighs. 'She still doesn't know how it happened,' he says. 'Not all the details, anyway. My moms . . . she's sick, but even if she wasn't . . . I'm scared what she'd do to Brett if she found out.'

Yoo-jin retreats to a bedroom and finally I can say it. 'Oh Jae, I'm so sorry.'

'For what? Did you put on an ugly-mask and hand me my ass?'

'No. But I might as well have. I put you in danger.'

'Bullshit. The person to blame for this is the person who did this to me. Some things in life aren't so clear, but that sure as hell is.' He's got a dark look on his face, or maybe it's just the bruises. He notices Sarita looking worried about the angry language and says, 'Come. Sit here. I'll set up some Snappy Croc for you.'

'I *love* Snappy Croc!' She flips herself over the back of the sofa and sits, ready to receive Jae's laptop. 'What version have you got?'

'Good question. I don't know. I didn't even know there was . . .' I have to laugh to see gamer Jae out-teched by a four-year-old.

I go around and sit on the armchair at his side while Sarita starts up the game. I look him up and down, trying to get the answer myself, but apart from the bruises on his face and his neck, I can't tell how badly he's injured. It's a dumb question, but I have to ask. 'How are you, Jae?'

He shrugs. 'You know, physically I feel like I've been hit by a truck, but I'll survive.'

'And otherwise?' I pat my hand on my chest, tap my head. 'Non-physically?'

'I'm fuc–' He remembers Sarita sitting next to him and lowers his voice. 'I'm mad. They can't let him get away with this sort of thing. To you, either.'

'I know,' I say.

'And I'm scared for Gina. I don't know what they might have done to her – be doing to her. Have you seen her?'

'No. But Tyson's been there a lot too and if something really bad was happening, I guess he'd say something . . . I hope he would.'

'Is he still hanging out with them?'

I don't want to say too much in front of Sarita. 'Yeah. Every chance he gets. It's like he's joined their clan. As if he's trying to ingratiate himself with them in case it all goes bad. And it's not just that. There's some history between Tyson and the others here. I can only imagine that something happened at that sales weekend in April because none of them knew each other before then. I have my suspicions about what that was and why Tyson's acting so weird down here,' I say, tilting my head towards Sarita again. 'But I don't have any evidence.'

'That's what I don't get about any of this,' Jae says. 'There was a sales weekend and all these people bought into this development even though it's a rat-hole. I don't understand why they would. I don't understand why my *dad* would.' He flicks an eye at the bedroom door. 'Okay, I sort of understand why he did, but . . .'

And suddenly Tyson's reasons for buying this condo become clear to me. 'It's just like a timeshare development, I guess. Tyson's got timeshares in Martha's Vineyard, the Hamptons, Cancun. He hasn't seen all of them – he buys them, often before they're built, and then sells them again.'

'But this is different, surely,' Jae says. 'This is for survival, not a vacation.'

'I'm not sure if Tyson believed in the whole apocalypse thing. I think this place was just another investment. He never expected something to happen, but when the virus hit, he had access to The Sanctum.'

'And it wasn't ready.'

'No, it wasn't ready.'

'And it wasn't anything like the promises at the sales weekend.'

'Normally you'd sue the developer,' I say. 'Tyson's got a whole team for suing developers.'

'But in this case the developer's dead and has left nothing behind.'

'Right.'

'And we're stuck in here with no water.'

For a moment I'd forgotten our predicament. I felt almost normal, just having a chat with a friend. But that stone I've been digesting around the whole time we've been here drops in my gut again.

Jae must notice the look on my face because he says, as cheerfully as he can manage, 'Someone will pick up the distress signal, don't worry. And in the meantime, there are things we can do to make the water last longer.' I nod, unconvinced, and Jae leans closer and says to me in a showy whisper, 'There might be a way we can get the answers you're looking for.'

'What is it?'

He stands. 'Come.'

'Are you good to walk?'

'As long as we don't bump into Junior, I'm good to go.'

'We won't,' I say, thinking that even if we do, the chicken-shit bully wouldn't try anything if we're together.

My God. Greg was keeping detailed records on all of the residents. Where did he even get all this information from? Jae thinks an NSA contact, but why the hell would the NSA have files on all of these people? Maybe one or two would be of interest, but from my glance at the directory, it looks like there's a file on all the residents here. Guthries, Maddoxes, folders on people called Carsten and Gupta – probably people who invested but didn't make it here this time around.

I skim through the surnames in the directory list. 'Hey, Jae, I can't find a folder on your family. Do you think you're off the hook?' I joke.

'He had one on everyone,' he says, coming to sit on a stool next to me. 'It must be here somewhere. But check this out. This is interesting.' He clicks open Leo Dannhauser's folder to an old-fashioned identity document. In the top-right corner's a black-and-white picture of Leo as a young man – tall, handsome, dark-haired, clean-shaven in a dark military dress uniform. He's unsmiling in the picture, something hard about the eyes and the set of the lips.

But it's the letterhead on the official form that makes me suck in my breath. I've read enough spy novels to know what the Stasi is.

Full name: Leopold Harald Dannhauser, rank, date of birth – he's seventy-three years old now and was working in East Germany as an operative in the depth of the Cold War.

I click through the rest of his file. There's a record from the US State Department. He defected to the US in 1974 and was valued for his extraordinary skills in Soviet bloc telecommunications systems. He had the technical knowledge and probably some US government support to start Danntech. *So what?* part of me thinks, there are millions of immigrants to the US who make a new start. But I can't be so naive. Leo is not a fool. He knows how to disable and enable electronics systems – and he knows how to kill.

But, I remind myself before I get carried away, Leo was locked in his condo on the night Greg Fuller died. In addition, he loathes the Guthries and that's reason enough to trust him.

I wonder what details Greg collected about me. I don't see a folder marked 'Sanford' anywhere, so I click open the 'Gill' folder with my bloody, broken fingernails, then I remember – he was expecting Rani, not me. Ignoring my dread at what I might find out, I skim through the documents. And now I hesitate. After hankering for the truth for all these months, I'm afraid of what I'll find out.

But I click in. Here she is, a radiant, beautiful woman, the image of a grown Sarita, smiling out at me. I skim through her file: birth date, the Newport maternity clinic she was born in, her social security number, addresses, her parents' names and identity numbers, her father's date of death (Rani's mother is still working as an occupational therapist in Providence). They've got her entire employment history, ever since a Saturday job at the Fudge Factory when she was fourteen through to her administrative position at the commerce faculty at URI, full transcripts of her high school and university results, scans of old passport pages, records of foreign travel, and pages of tables and codes I can't make sense of. None of it goes to answer the burning questions: why did she kill herself? And how did she do it? When these records were collected, apparently, she was still alive.

I'm about to click out of the folder when I see it, finally, a document misfiled in the temp folder – downloaded the evening we arrived, the death certificate. Rani Mariam Gill, nee Choudhury, died 7 May this year, age 34y 245d. Suicide: amitriptyline overdose.

Flushed with nausea, I turn to look at Sarita, sitting on the cluttered couch, still jumping over crocodiles on the laptop, smiling thoughtlessly as she does.

Why? Why would her mother have abandoned this little girl?

I realize that Jae's been hovering and has seen what I've read, but he doesn't say anything.

'Is there a printer on this thing?' I ask him. I want to print out the smiling photo for Sarita to keep. But he shakes his head, gloomy.

'I suppose I could just email it to myself,' I say, clicking the command over the picture.

'No wi-fi,' he says.

'Christ, of course.' If I could email this picture to my phone, I could email Mom and Megan, tell them where I am. We could email the bloody South Paris fire department and ask them to let us out of here. But there's no internet and we're trapped. Mom and Megan don't know where I am or if I'm alive.

My eyes well up and I will the tears not to start. I keep getting these flashes of normality, like my mind is fighting as hard as it can to avoid looking at the truth. My mind and my body do not want to admit the plain fact: I could die in here.

26
WILL

If only he could dream about Lana, that might help. If he could dream about her, perhaps he could say he was sorry. He's starting to forget her face and he didn't think to bring a photo with him.

Trudi shifts in the bed next to him. She's fallen asleep – usually she slips out immediately after they've conducted their business, but this evening she made no move to leave. Instead, she rested her head against his shoulder, her arm encircling his chest. He let her press her body against him. He didn't push her away, reject this intimacy; but he didn't encourage it either. That would have been a real betrayal. His and Trudi's frantic, often rough, couplings aren't a by-product of love. He's not sure if they're even driven by lust. He doesn't want to think too deeply about what compels them.

He should wake her. Tell her to leave. But he doesn't.

He sleeps. But still he doesn't dream.

When he wakes, Trudi is standing naked at the end of the bed, stretching her arms behind her back. Her ribs stand out beneath her fine, pale skin, which shows every blue vein. Her skinny, muscular thighs are patchworked with dry, reddish skin, casualties of the filthy pool water. He's getting used to the lack of hygiene; he can no longer detect the stink of his own body odour. He doesn't care that his nails are black with dust and grime, or that every pore is filled with dirt. He hasn't shaved for days now.

'Hey.' Trudi smiles. She looks happy. How could she be happy? Maybe she's lost it. Tipped over the edge. 'You sleep well?'

'Yeah. What time is it?'

'It's early.'

'Your father will wonder where you've been all night.'

'You think he doesn't know where I am?'

Leo knows. Of course he knows. Nothing gets past Leo. Sometimes Will wonders what he thinks about his only daughter sleeping with the man who has sealed all of their death warrants. 'Aren't you worried about your mother?'

'You trying to get rid of me?' Her smile falters.

'No . . . I'm just . . .' Just what? Truth is, he doesn't know if he wants her to stay or not. All he knows is that he doesn't want this conversation to stray away from the usual banalities they tend to stick to. They never talk about Lana. Trudi tried once to bring her up, but he shut her down. He doesn't want to encourage the hope he occasionally sees in her eyes. The hope that when they get out, that somehow they'll build on this – whatever this is – and maybe have some kind of future together. It's laughable really. That's not going to happen. They're not going to wander off into the sunset together. He probably has a dead wife to take care of and she has her own scars and issues to sort out.

Trudi stretches again. 'Jae's coming this morning to read to my mom, and she was sleeping when I left last night. Besides, I really think she might have turned a corner.'

'Good.'

'It is. You hungry?' she asks.

'No.'

'Can you get me some water from the pool?' she asks. 'I need to wash up.'

He knows she's only doing it to get him out of the condo. He's barely left the unit since the explosion. Once, he slipped out to restock his booze supply, hurrying furtively down to the storeroom, digging around until he unearthed a bottle of vermouth. He hasn't even gone next door to see Reuben. In the first few days he was furious at the man, wanted to blame him for what happened, for saying that the shaft wall wasn't reinforced, and he was wrong. But Will knows this is bullshit – he would have tried to blast through the wall even if he had known it was riddled with Kevlar.

'Will?' Trudi's looking at him quizzically. 'The water.'

'Fine.'

'I'll make us some tea.'

He grabs the bucket, then sneaks a quick pull of vermouth before he heads out into the hallway. Because there's another reason why he hasn't left the condo: cowardice. Until a couple of days ago, one of the Guthries was guaranteed to be standing in the hallway, Carn staring at him like he was a piece of shit; Junior ready with an insult. Biding their time until they decided to beat the combination for the safe out of him. And then, all bets will be off. He knows this is why Tyson's trying to align himself with them, never mind what Brett tried to do to his au pair. Tyson's a stockbroker, used to hedging his bets. He's chosen to go with the power. Will knows how it will go. If help doesn't arrive in the next couple of days, it will all blow up. He wonders if he'll be able to hold off telling them the combination if they threaten him again. If they torture him. He knows it will come to that eventually.

He steels himself in case they're back, but the corridor is empty. He hesitates, then walks slowly over to Reuben's unit. He knocks on the door. There's no answer. The lock hasn't been set, so when he tries the handle, it opens. 'Reuben?'

It's dark in here, the lights dimmed to little more than a brown glow. Will waits for his eyes to adjust, then makes out a shape slumped on the couch. 'Reuben?'

'*Si.*'

There's a mini avalanche of dried-food packages on the floor around Reuben, and the place stinks of old food and urine.

'Hey. How you doing?'

'Okay.' Reuben's voice is flat. Is he angry at Will for not backing him up? Will feels a jab of resentment. He doesn't owe Reuben anything. For all he knows Reuben is the one who killed Greg, but still . . . he and Reuben have a history. He could have done more. Uncomfortable, he glances around the room. God knows what Reuben's been doing all day. Sitting in that spot waiting for someone to bring him food, probably. His water ration sits on the kitchen counter in plain sight. If no one comes to dig them out soon, he's certain the Guthries will help themselves to it. For all he knows, they might have already been doing so. 'I'm sorry I haven't been to see you.'

'I understand.'

'I've heard they're no longer guarding you.'

A shrug.

'You getting enough to eat?' Christ, he's making himself cringe here. Too little, too late.

'Yes. Jae brings me food sometimes. He has been good to me. I can leave now but it is still like a prison.'

It's worse, Will thinks. At least in jail there's concrete hope that you'll get out one day.

An awkward silence stretches. 'Well, I'd better be going.' He edges towards the door. 'See you around.'

Reuben doesn't react.

Will realizes that he's sweating, his armpits damp. He resolves to make it up to Reuben. It's the decent thing to do, and nothing's been decent since he pressed that detonator and sent them all to hell.

He's about to head down to the gym, when he hears a shrill voice bouncing through the stairwell from the floor above. Vicki Maddox. Then, two male voices, lower in pitch. Again, he hesitates. *Not your business.* But curiosity wins over caution, and he finds himself creeping up the stairs as silently as he can.

'What we're asking is reasonable, Vicki.' Cam Guthrie's voice.

'Reasonable? You're asking me to kill my fucking dog.'

'Where's James? Maybe he'll have some sense about this.'

'He's sleeping, so why don't you go and—'

'You can't give the dog water, Vicki.' Will recognizes Tyson's voice. 'Not when there are people who might need it. It's immoral.'

Vicki laughs humourlessly. 'Immoral? Did you seriously just say that to me, Tyson? You're the last person who should be pointing fingers and preaching to me about morality.'

'What does she mean, Tyson?' Cam rumbles.

'Yeah, what *do* I mean, Tyson? Why don't you tell Cam what I'm talking about? I bet you haven't told him about your extra-curricular activities, have you? An upstanding, moral man like Cam won't—'

'Shut your filthy mouth!' Tyson yells.

'Oh, fuck off', Vicki snipes. 'Just fuck off, both of you.'

There's the sound of a door slamming.

Hating himself for his cowardice, Will slinks away before Cam has a chance to leave the hallway and catch sight of him.

The gym's kelpy smell hits him like a slap in the face. It's getting worse, and thanks to him, the waste pipes have also been damaged, so certain areas of The Sanctum reek like open sewage drains. He's bending to dip the bucket in the foul water, when he hears the smack of a basketball hitting a hard surface. He stands up slowly.

From his post on the basketball quad, Brett gives him an ironic salute. There's a nasty cut above the boy's left eye, and his bottom lip is swollen. Good. He deserved everything Leo gave him. 'Hey, Mr Boucher', he says with mock cheeriness.

'Hello, Brett.'

'How's it hanging?' *Smack*, goes the ball.

'Fine.' Bucket filled, Will stalks back towards the door.

'You gonna give us that combination, Mr Boucher?'

Will ignores him.

'Oh, Mr Boucher?' *Smack, smack.*

'What?'

'Is she a good fuck?'

'*What?*' Will turns slowly.

With calculated insouciance, Brett bounces the ball on the court, then spins and shoots it straight through the hoop.

'I *said*, is she a good fuck? That skinny bitch. I seen her sneaking in to your unit. I know what you're doing.' He smirks. 'Hey . . . Think she'll let me have a turn?'

The rage boils up, and Will almost takes the bait; almost throws the bucket of water down and charges at Brett. He catches himself just in time. It's what Brett wants. Instead, he takes his fury out on the door, hauling it open so that it crashes against the wall.

He races up the stairs, the water sloshing over the top of the bucket and soaking his jeans, hearing Brett's laughter echoing in his ears. He almost knocks Leo over as he slams through to his level. What's the old man doing here? Then Will gets a better look at him. Leo's face is as rumpled as old paper, and his eyes are red: 'I need Trudi.'

'What's happened?'

'Get Trudi.' It's an order.

Will unlocks the door and waves Leo inside. Trudi is standing at the kitchen counter dressed in one of Will's T-shirts and nothing else. 'Dad?'

'Trudi.'

Leo's chin wobbles, and then he's crying. 'It's Mutti – your mother.'

Trudi doesn't hesitate. She flies out of the unit, and Will stands in the kitchen stupidly, the bucket still in his hands. Leo covers his eyes with a hand. Will has absolutely no idea what to say to the man, deciding instead to go after Trudi. He runs up the stairs and straight into the Dannhausers' unit, wincing as the stench of shit hits his nostrils. He can hear Trudi saying: 'Mom, Mom, Mommy,' over and over again.

He walks slowly towards the master bedroom and peers inside. Caroline looks peaceful lying there on the bed, her hair spread around her, her face muscles relaxed. But for the woman sobbing next to her and the stench of body fluids, she could be sleeping.

Is this how Lana would have gone?

No. She wouldn't have gone so peacefully.

Lana wouldn't have had anyone to weep for her.

Something splits inside his head.

Trudi looks up at him. Her face is sodden with tears. 'Will?'

He backs away. He can't deal with this. He can't deal with someone else's pain right now. He has to get out of here.

'Will!'

He blocks out the sound of her voice and runs.

27

JAMES

They've run out of canned tuna and spaghetti sauce, so James has resorted to microwaving one of the ready-meals that are stacked in the storeroom. There's no indication what it is or how to cook it – the only label stamped on the foil package reads, 'Day 3 Meal 4' – but he reckons three minutes should do it. For once he doesn't have a hangover (not out of choice, they've run out of vodka), and his appetite has returned with a vengeance. He watches the packet gradually expand like a silver blowfish, then clips the top and upends it into a bowl. He pokes the sloppy brown mess with a fork; there are green bits in it that could be peas, and grey lumps which could be anything from tofu to Soylent Green. No thanks. He dumps it in the bin, which is overflowing. He'll take it down to the trash compactor later. That chore can wait.

'James?' Vicki calls from the bedroom. 'Is everything okay out there?'

'Yeah.'

'You sure? I thought I heard something.'

'We're cool.' Jesus. Her paranoia is growing to epic proportions since fucking Tyson and the Guthries ganged up on her about Claudette. She's now insisting that one of them stays in the apartment at all times, in case someone attempts to sneak in and steal their water ration. They've got their own secret stash of Evian, but that's not going to last long, even though there's one less person since old lady Dannhauser died. They're dropping like flies, he thinks.

Claudette slumps listlessly at his feet, head between her paws. She hasn't touched her food since yesterday. It's sitting in a crusty lump in her dish, adding a meaty edge to the condo's stale funk. Maybe Tyson's right. Maybe they should just ditch the dog. Vicki hasn't bothered cleaning up Claudette's mess for days – if he didn't do it they'd be up to their eyeballs in shit-stained doggy pads.

'Can you go get me some water?' Vicki calls. 'I want to wash my hair.'

'Yeah, okay.' Of course fetching the goddamned water from the goddamned pool is his job. But it's an excuse to nip out and top up his nicotine levels, and while he's there he may as well root around in the storeroom for anything edible. He hasn't bothered to wash or even brush his teeth for two days now. Neglecting his personal hygiene doesn't feel as odious as he thought it would; there's something liberating about not giving a crap about his appearance. To think he used to waste hours picking out the perfect suit, finding the perfect hairdresser (he would never have stooped so low as to visit a barber), not to mention the manicures, the massages, the facial scrubs, the shaving regime that ensured that he never suffered the indignity of an ingrown hair.

He grabs the buckets and heads out, breathing through his mouth. Damp and mould are the most pervasive odours on his floor, but each level is cultivating its own particular stink. Level five is by far the most nauseating – it reeks like a goddamned public convenience. Vicki refuses to use the compost toilet on level eight, choosing to flush their own lavatory with pool water. He's suggested she use Greg's bathroom on level two before someone else gets the idea, but she hasn't yet done so. The entire place is a health hazard – it's only a matter of time before someone gets sick. The last time he took Claudette out as an excuse for a clandestine smoke, the dog wouldn't stop yipping at the edge of the elevator shaft. He could hear something squeaking inside it. Rats. Goddamned rodents living in the soggy base of the elevator shaft. Big ones.

He passes the entrance to the gym, hears the thump, thump of a basketball being bounced around in there. Must be Brett Guthrie – or the Columbine Kid, as Vicki now calls him. James prays the psychotic bastard will be gone by the time he finishes his cigarette.

He lights up the second he's inside the storeroom. He's past giving a shit if he fills it with the stink of smoke. *So sue me.* The generators chug and growl reassuringly behind the machine-room door. He eyes the dried goods – mostly lentils and dried borlotti beans (God knows what they're supposed to do with them), and digs through the pile of mystery meals, hoping to find something that's labelled or doesn't feel like the slop he cooked earlier. On the other side of the room the walk-in freezer clunks and shudders. Inside it, Caroline Dannhauser is sharing the big sleep with Greg. He isn't sure what compels him to do it, but he's hit with a sudden urge to peek inside it. Before he can stop himself, he stalks up to it and cranks the door. The stench of putrefaction and rotting meat hits him before he's even opened it wide enough to take a look. 'Jesus.' He slams the door shut, bends double, and wills himself not to throw up. What the fuck was he thinking? The freezer must be malfunctioning like everything in this goddamned shithole. He takes a deep drag of his cigarette, screaming as he feels a tap on his shoulder.

He whirls, sees Reuben standing directly behind him.

James backs up until he's pressed against the freezer door. He should have brought the Glock with him. *Is this what he did to Greg?* 'What the hell are you doing, creeping up on people?'

'I am sorry. I was in the machine room. I'm thinking someone should check the generators.'

'Really?'

'Yes. Really. There is no one else.'

This is true. With Will and Leo now fully paid-up members of the Basket Case squad, God knows who'd think to top up the fuel tank or however the fuck those things work. And James has to admire Reuben – man has balls of steel. James doubts he would risk it if he was in Reuben's position. Not with Brett and Cam at large.

'You have a cigarette for me?'

'Huh?'

'A cigarette.'

James shakes himself out of it. Vicki's paranoia is becoming infectious. It's the first time he's been up close to Reuben, and he realizes how diminutive the guy is. Small-boned, almost delicate. Greg was the size of a grizzly; it's unlikely Reuben could have overpowered him. And the guy is hardly in any state to attack him. His skin is stretched tight on his bones and he appears to be continually out of breath. No. He should be worrying about the people who have proven themselves to be unhinged – the Guthries for example, with mad Preacher Ma, the Columbine Kid and trigger-happy Cam.

His fingers shake as he offers the packet to Reuben. 'They're menthol, I'm afraid.'

Reuben grins, showing off a gap where his left incisor should be (no doubt courtesy of Brett), and James relaxes.

Reuben lights up, inhales and closes his eyes. 'Ah.'

James searches for something to say. 'So . . . How are you feeling now, Reuben?'

'Better,' he says, belying this with a hacking cough. If his lungs are damaged he shouldn't be smoking, but James isn't about to point this out. 'It's bad. What's happening here.'

'That's the understatement of the year. You think we'll get out?'

Reuben shrugs. 'I don't know. Someone must come. You have people on the outside?'

'Not that know we're here. And you?'

'No.'

'No family?'

'No.'

'Not even in . . . ?' He doesn't even know where the guy is from. Mexico? Puerto Rico? Some third-world dive.

'No. My parents are dead.' A shrug. 'I am alone.'

James takes the last drag, stubs it out under his shoe, and hands Reuben the rest of the box. 'For later.'

'You are sure?'

'Yeah.' He's about to say that he has half a carton left, but decides against it. Paranoia again – he doesn't want to give the man a reason to come snuffling around their condo.

'Thank you, sir.'

'James.'

'Thank you, James.'

'No problem. Well, I'd better get on with it.' He taps one of the buckets with his foot. 'Got to get water from the pool.'

'You want me to help you? It is good to talk to someone. Jae comes sometimes. And the others . . .'

The others think you are a murderer. To be honest, murderer or not, he'd rather have Reuben with him than face Brett Guthrie alone, if the kid's still in the gym. 'Sure. Why not?'

James jumps again as the storeroom door flies open and Cait rushes in. Her hair is dishevelled and she's panting, out of breath. 'I'm . . . I'm just getting something nice for Sarita to eat.'

'Nice is the last thing you're going to find in here.' She doesn't seem to hear him, and barely acknowledges Reuben. He's not surprised: they're all on edge and Vicki has been nothing but a bitch to her since they arrived.

They make their way up to the next floor. James notes with relief that the thumping from the gym has ceased. The kid must have got bored. James prepares himself for the gym's odour – rotting kelp and wet carpet.

'So, Reuben, what made you come to—'

Reuben grabs James's arm. '*Puta madre.*'

'Huh? . . .' Then he sees it. There's a body in the pool, lying face down, blood tentacles blooming in the green water around it. James waits for his brain to catch up with what he's seeing. It's Brett – he doesn't need to see the boy's face to be sure of that. The back of the kid's head is a spongy mess, which must be the source of the blood.

Reuben shucks off his shoes, runs to the edge and jumps in, splashing towards the body. 'Help me!'

But James can't move. He watches as Reuben turns the boy onto his back, opens Brett's mouth, and starts breathing into his airway. A yard away from them, the basketball floats in the water. Reuben turns his head, spits out blood, then continues. Brett's bottom half sinks under the water, his shoes and jeans weighing him down. 'James!' Reuben shouts. 'Come!'

James jerks into action, drops the buckets, hurries to the side of the pool and slides into the water. The boy's eyes are open, and a bubble of blood pops in his nose. Dragging his eyes away from Brett's face, James lifts the boy's legs and torso so that he's lying flat once more. It's been years since he last did a CPR course, but some of it comes back to him. 'We should get him out, put him in the recovery position.'

'No time.' Reuben's face has turned a purplish colour; he's taking the strain, and James knows what's coming. 'You must do it. Give him air.'

Oh Jesus. 'I can't.'

They lock eyes. 'You must.'

Wheezing like an asthmatic, Reuben shuffles around to Brett's side. The boy's head falls back, and a fresh stream of blood blossoms around them. Water washes over Brett's open eyes, and it takes all of James's resolve not to jump out of the pool. James fumbles for the boy's pulse. Nothing. 'There's no point. He's dead.'

Reuben assesses him for a long second. 'You are sure?'

'Yes.'

Reuben crosses himself, and murmurs something in Spanish. 'A terrible accident. We must get him out.'

Together they inch Brett over to the side and Reuben holds him upright while James struggles out. James grabs Brett's arms and heaves, desperately avoiding looking at the gory mess at the back of his head. Reuben grabs Brett around the thighs and lifts, adding leverage, and slowly they manage to edge the body onto the side of the pool. James backs away from it, wiping his hands on his sodden pants. The boy's flesh was still slightly warm and . . . God, rubbery. The back of his heel strikes something, and he almost loses his balance. He looks down, sees one of the weights lying on the carpet.

Reuben drags himself out of the pool and lies on his back, fighting to catch his breath.

'Reuben?' James says. Reuben struggles onto his elbows and turns his head, his chest heaving up and down. 'This was no accident.'

'Oh God, oh God, oh God.' Somehow, although he doesn't remember touching the wound, Brett's blood has wormed its way under his nails and James scrubs and scrubs at them to get them clean. The Kleenex he's using (along with a bottle of Vicki's Clarins make-up remover) is piling up like bloody snow on the counter. He's dripping all over the floor, leaving rusty rivulets on the white tiles.

Vicki hurries back from the bathroom and hands him a towel. 'I still can't believe he's dead.' She was horrified when he burst into the apartment, soaked and half hysterical, but she didn't look that shocked when he told her whose body was floating in the pool. 'You sure Brett couldn't have fallen? Knocked his head on something?'

'Like Greg you mean? Like it's contagious?'

'Don't be flippant, James.'

He uses the last of the make-up remover, then wipes his hands on his sodden shirt. He reeks like a goddamned abattoir. He rips his T-shirt off, kicks his legs out of his jeans and bundles them into a garbage bag. Naked, he wraps the towel around his waist. That's better. Now all trace of Brett has gone, he's beginning to feel less shaky.

Vicki fusses around him. 'So someone definitely killed him?'

'Yes. One of the weights was lying at the side of the pool. Whoever did it must have used it to whack him on the head.'

'You think it was that Mexican? Reuben?'

'No. He was with me.'

'What do you mean he was with you?'

'I was . . .' He may as well come clean. 'Look, I was sneaking a smoke in the storeroom, okay?' He waits for her to snap at him, but she merely waves at him to continue.

'I know you've been doing that, James. I'm not an idiot.'

'Huh? How long have you known—'

'Does it matter?'

'No. I guess not. Reuben was checking on the generator and I was . . .' He decides not to mention looking in the freezer. 'We got talking – he's not a bad guy – and he offered to help me carry the water.'

'How sweet. And?'

It's only now that he sees that she's wearing a black T-shirt, jeans and running shoes. It's been days since she's worn anything but that goddamned kimono. 'Hey . . . you're dressed.'

She blinks, colours slightly. 'Yes. I thought it was about time I made an effort.' Is she lying? It's never easy to tell with Vicki. 'Carry on.'

'It must have happened while Reuben and I were there. I heard Brett in the gym just before then.'

'Oh my God. You could have been attacked as well!'

The thought jumps into his head before he can stop it: *Not if it was you.* Crazy. He can't think like that. No. It can't have been Vicki. She hasn't got it in her and she's not stupid – she knew he was down there getting water. And why would Vicki want to kill Brett? Scratch that, there isn't a person in this place who wouldn't want to see the Columbine Kid out of the way. Especially Cait. And Cait was down there just before they found Brett, wasn't she? He thinks about mentioning this to Vicki, decides against it. She's not in a terrible mood for once, and bringing up Cait could spark off a diatribe. Brett kicked the shit out of Jae (and Yoo-jin may be unfailingly polite and hides out in his condo 24/7, but who knows what's going on behind those eyes?); Will's officially lost it; and Leo's some sort of Cold War spy. Reuben and Vicki are pretty much the only people who couldn't have done it. 'I need a drink.'

'Me too.' She roots in the supply cupboard, shrugs, opens the magnum of champagne and slams a bottle of Cristal on the counter.

'Is that really appropriate?'

'It's all we've got.'

'Fuck it. Why not?' They share a brief smile. There are no champagne glasses of course – Greg wouldn't have bothered with that sort of detail – so Vicki grabs a couple of tumblers. She twists the cork, which explodes with a hollow pop, and froths warm champagne into the glasses. 'We can't trust anyone down here, James. And you know what the Guthries are like. When they find out about Brett, none of us will be safe.'

It's about time he tells her about the Glock in his bug-out bag. It'll put her mind at ease. 'Listen, Vicki, I—'

A knock at the door makes them both jump.

'Get down!' Vicki hisses. 'Be quiet!' Claudette lets out a half-hearted yip, and Vicki nudges her with her foot.

There's another knock, followed by: 'James? Vicki? Are you there?'

'It's Will,' James whispers.

'Don't let him in.'

'Wait. Let's see what he wants.'

Vicki frowns, but doesn't stop him approaching the door. He opens it a few inches. The last time James saw him, he looked like he was trying to drink himself to death. James reckons he's succeeding. 'Can I come in?'

James hesitates, then widens the gap enough so that Will can enter the room. He nods a greeting at Vicki, then says: 'Reuben says you were with him when you found the body. I just want to check that—'

A scream echoes down through the stairwell – a howl of pure pain. James slams the door, cutting it off. 'So they know.'

'Yeah. They know. Reuben told me, and I told them.'

'*You* told them?' James can only imagine how that went down.

'You think I wanted to? Who else is there?'

'How did they take it?' Stupid question. He can hear how they took it.

'Like you'd expect.'

'Listen, Will . . . you think they gave us all their guns? Me and Vicki . . . what I'm trying to say is that we're worried there might be a reprisal.'

'They gave us all their guns. You think we wouldn't know by now if they hadn't?'

'And they're locked in the safe?'

'Yup. Greg and I did it ourselves.'

'So you're the only one that has the combination?' Vicki slurs.

'Yup.' James knows exactly what Vicki's thinking: can Will be trusted? If help doesn't arrive before the water runs out, it's obvious what's going to happen. Survival of the fittest. *Fuck.*

'James, I need to know. You prepared to back Reuben up?'

'Huh?'

'If the Guthries accuse him of killing Brett. You'll back him up?'

He sighs. 'I'd prefer to keep out of it.'

James catches a flash of disgust in Will's eyes. *Fuck you*, James thinks. *You're one to talk. You've been doing nothing but boozing since you fucked us, so don't play Lone Ranger with me.* James burps, tasting the champagne. Will isn't the only one who's been hiding behind the booze. 'Yeah, for what it's worth I'll back him up. Why do you care, Will?'

'Guilt, I guess.'

'Huh?'

'After . . . after the explosion I didn't go and check in on him. Feel bad about that.'

James's eyes stray down Will's body. He's lost weight, which suits him, and there's something . . . alluring about the man's fragility and honesty. It's not something James has ever possessed. 'I see. *Someone* went after Brett.'

'Yeah.'

Will's eyes stray to the champagne bottle, but James can't read his expression. For a manic second he imagines saying: *Care to join us for a glass of champers, old boy, old fellow?*

'Any idea who it might be?' Vicki asks.

'No. But Brett had no shortage of enemies.'

'Well we have to find out who did it,' Vicki says. 'You have to do something.'

Will's eyes flash with irritation. 'Why me? I'm not a god-damned cop.'

Vicki blinks. 'I wasn't suggesting that—'

'I'd better get up there.' Without another word Will stalks

out of the condo, slamming the door behind him. Vicki stares after him.

'Stress,' James says, reaching for his glass. 'It's getting to all of us.'

'What's that?' Vicki asks, sliding down from her perch on the kitchen counter and weaving towards the door. She bends to pick something up, almost losing her balance. They've polished off two bottles of Cristal since Will left, and despite the situation, James is feeling that sense of euphoria he always gets with champagne: giggly, slightly unreal.

'What is it?'

'A note. Hang on.' She scans it, says: 'You're not going to believe this,' and hands it to him.

The message is written in neat block capitals: 'IN REMEM-BERENCE OF BRETT EPHRAIM CAMERON GUTHRIE. PLEASE JOIN US NOW FOR PRAYER AT THE PLACE WHERE JESUS TOOK HIM TO HIS HEART. ALL IS FORGIVEN UNDER GOD'S GRACE.'

'The Guthries are inviting us to Brett's funeral?'

Vicki huffs. 'Unbelievable.'

'It might be worth it. There might be snacks afterwards,' he says. There's a pause, and then they're both guffawing. It's not that funny, but he can't stop – the hilarity is so powerful that it seems to be ripping up from the depths of his stomach. They clutch at each other, Claudette yapping around their feet.

Barely able to breathe, James finally manages to get himself under control. He drains his glass and thinks about lighting up one of the menthols. He decides against it; Vicki knows he's been sneaking cigarettes and they're (ironically) getting on better than they have for months, but this might be a bridge too far. He tips the dregs of the second bottle into their glasses.

Vicki wipes at her eyes. 'Well, we can't go. It might be a trap.'

'What kind of a trap?'

'Y'know.' She waves her hand exaggeratedly. 'Get us all together and punish us all for Brett's death.'

'No guns. What they going to do? Preach us to death?'

'You're not seriously considering going, are you?'

Christ, is he? 'I did find him.'

'So?'

'And . . . if help doesn't arrive, things are only going to get worse down here. It might not be a bad thing to look like we're supportive.'

'What, you mean when we're all fighting each other tooth and nail for the remaining water, the fact that we showed up at his son's funeral will make Cam Guthrie think twice about slitting our throats in our sleep?'

'Yeah. Something like that.'

'Oh God. It won't come to that, will it, James?'

'No. But we could just show our faces.'

She thinks about this for a few seconds. 'God. Okay then.'

He looks down at his shorts and sports shirt. 'Should we get changed?'

Vicki snorts. 'No. Fuck it. The bastard doesn't deserve that.'

They make their way down the three flights to the gym, where Gina is standing at the door, dressed in a severe black dress that is several sizes too big for her. 'Thank you for coming,' she murmurs.

'I'm so sorry, Gina,' James says in a low, serious voice as if this is a normal funeral and not . . . whatever the fuck this is. He glances at Vicki, who grimaces and clutches his hand. He knows exactly what she's thinking: *you couldn't make this shit up*. Over by the pool, Will and Tyson are standing awkwardly next to Cam and Bonnie Guthrie, who are both dressed in their Sunday best. There's no sign of the Parks, Reuben or the Dannhausers, which is hardly surprising. And . . . oh Jesus. They've laid out Brett's body next to the weight bench – he's wrapped in a sheet, thank God, but James assumed he'd be in the freezer by now.

Vicki nudges him. 'Look,' she whispers. 'It's Wilson.' For a second, he has no clue what she's talking about, then he spots the basketball that's still bobbing in the rust-red swimming pool water.

The hilarity is just as immediate as before – an unstoppable volcano in his chest. He doubles over, trying to disguise it with a coughing fit, while Vicki thumps at his back.

'Are you okay, Mr Maddox?' Gina asks, which sets him off again.

'He's fine, Gina,' he hears Vicki saying. 'He's just upset.'

Oh God, oh God. Tears are streaming down his cheeks. He wipes at his eyes and straightens. Bonnie and Cam are ignoring him, but Tyson's staring at him and Vicki with sheer loathing.

'Let us join hands,' Bonnie says. Her voice rings clear and true, and James is unable to detect the slightest hint of grief in it. They all shuffle forward and form a rough circle. James has ended up next to Tyson, and there's an almost comic moment as Tyson grimaces, recoils, and looks as if he's about to refuse to take James's hand. On his other side, Vicki digs her nails into his palm.

Without any preamble, Bonnie starts reciting a long

prayer about repentance and eternal life, and James drifts off, the alcohol burbling acidly in his gut. The smell in the room is starting to get to him now. It's nowhere near as bad as the putrid waft that rolled out of the freezer, but there's definitely the iron tang of spilled blood in the air.

With no warning, Cam howls and breaks away from them.

'Daddy!' Gina calls after her father. He thumps through the door.

'What now?' Vicki mouths at him. He shrugs.

Bonnie looks to Tyson, who holds one hand up in the air, shuts his eyes and starts rambling on about justice and forgiveness and fuck knows what else. James tunes out, wonders what Bonnie would think if she'd seen Tyson that night – the night of the sales meeting – drunk as a coot, his pants round his ankles, hooting with laughter and begging—

The door slams open, making everyone jump.

'Oh fuck,' Vicki hisses.

Cam is lumbering into the room, pushing Reuben ahead of him, one hand clutching the man's hair, the other holding a knife to his throat. To Reuben's credit, his face is relatively serene for someone who's about to have his throat slit.

Will is the one who speaks first. 'Cam! Let him go, Cam.'

'Tell them what you did! Tell them what you did to my son!'

'Cam, he couldn't have done it. James was with him.' Will rounds on James. 'Tell him, James!'

But he can't. He can't find his voice. This isn't his problem. He shouldn't be here . . . Oh, thank God. Cam has taken the knife from Reuben's throat.

'No!' Will yells, too late, as Cam thrusts the knife into Reuben's side.

28
TRUDI

You'd think their souls would be thickening the air, but there's a dead void where they used to be. First her own sweet mother, then that monster, and it won't be long before Reuben will be joining that disgusting boy down in the freezer with the man who started it all. The corpses are piling up and it's impossible to feel that it's really happening. It could be a ballet – one of those modern restagings of *Hamlet* or *Titus Andronicus*, one of those orgies of violence where nobody gets out alive – all the dancers flouncing and prancing and then falling, stacked up in a pleasing array of paint-spattered tights and lean limbs. But there's nothing pleasing about a boy with his head bashed in, nothing aesthetic about an old woman shitting herself with her final breath.

Trudi lies flat on the floor and hugs her knees. Her back has been aching for the last few days and she's been resisting doing the exercises she used to do to keep herself limber. This one, though, comes naturally – trying to curl herself back into a foetal ball, even though it provokes an inflamed rip along her spine and she can feel the grit of the carpet coating her clothes and skin and hair even more. A gallon of water a day is not enough to cleanse her.

At least with everyone dying, the water's going to last

longer. She could take a fucking bath at this rate, some bitter part inside her cackles. Squeezing her knees in further, Trudi makes it hurt until she can bear it no more, and then stands. She should go and help Jae and Cait with Reuben, but her heart is desperate not to go down there, to avoid Will – the embarrassment and shame of being rejected by him, but she has to do this human thing, give Reuben some respect before he dies. She didn't get the chance to do that for her mother, and it may well be the last human thing she has the chance to do. It's not just Reuben who needs help. She should see if Stella needs anything. The woman had been kind to her mother, and now she's sick. The last time Trudi saw her, her skin was taking on a yellowish tinge. Jaundice.

And besides, fuck Will – she slept with him out of pity. In the real world she would never have looked twice at a yokel like him. But she can't convince herself. She misses his warmth, his soft touch. She's ashamed and embarrassed, sure – but she's also bereft.

She stands, momentarily distracted by the smell of coffee, the dregs of an espresso from last night on the kitchen counter. She's finally become an espresso drinker, thanks to the water rations. A pint of water a day on ten espressos, a glass of water when she brushes her teeth, a quart to wipe herself in all her folds, a hopeless act that only smears the stink and the festering microbes from one part of her body to another.

'Dad, I'm going out,' she says flatly, knowing he won't respond. He's still curled on top of the bed, but has stopped moaning at least, now lost in his dark, exclusive grief. Trudi reminds herself that he never had time for her, so she shouldn't be feeling his absence so keenly. She misses her mother, that's all it is, but that loss is so huge, it's numbed her.

It's hard to move her limbs, to convince her body that there's any point in going somewhere. She's found herself zoning out recently, and now she's hanging in the doorway thinking again – even though the memory has worn thin and metastasized by now – of the moment she knew that Caroline was gone. She can still smell that odour of shit and sweat and blood, the smell of her mother's emissions and she remembers where she is and the itch of her skin and the pain in her bones sets in again. 'Dad. Did you hear me? I'm going out.'

He murmurs something in German, but she catches her mother's name. 'She's gone, Dad.'

After Will left – abandoning her when she needed him most – she ran back to her parents' bedroom and the first thing she saw was not the leathery old man in a suit kneeling down at the side of the bed, his pomaded comb-over hanging in his face, or the ample woman with her long grey hair arranged over her shoulders, a look of peace on her face, but her own image in the wall mirror, a skeleton draped in a shroud. Three dead Dannhausers in a room, and her mother looked the most alive of all of them.

She felt a hole inside, so big, she didn't know how it fitted inside her. 'But she said she was feeling better,' she complained to Leo, as if he'd been mistaken. As if it were some error her father could fix.

But he didn't look like he's going to fix anything ever again, staring at Caroline's limp hand, crushed between his own.

'Dad,' she tries once more. She doesn't know when he last had anything to drink. Her mother's water ration, untouched.

'I should have been with her.'

They both should have been with her.

Now he looks almost as if he's going to cry and the prospect mortifies Trudi. She tries to ward off the embarrassment, tentatively stretching out her hand towards him, not quite reaching him before she stops, trying to rekindle some of that odd intimacy they shared the day before. 'It's not your fault, Dad.'

'I know it's not my fault!' he snaps. 'What do you think I am?' It isn't tears welling at the rims of his eyes after all, just because she imagined he'd be sad, but the redness of quiet rage which she's seen so often before and should have recognized.

'I'll be back soon.'

She opens the door to see Will waiting outside, leaning against the wall.

A flare of fury. He didn't even help them move her mother's body down to the freezer; Jae helped. Thank God for that boy. At least she knows that, thanks to Jae, her mother was happy until the end.

'Has Reuben . . . has Reuben gone?' Pathetic, she can't even say the word 'dead'.

'Not yet.'

'So why are you here?'

He doesn't say anything, just takes a step towards her, and before she can stop herself, she pushes into him and hides her face in his chest.

29

GINA

'Go get a glass of water for Mr Gill,' Momma tells me.

'But, Momma,' I say.

'Do it,' she says. She doesn't even have to turn to me. She's had that same look on her face ever since Brett passed, like a doll's face frozen between joy and pain. But the clouds that have sat in her gaze for the last two years have moved away and those eyes are razor-sharp now, piercing through that mask.

Just looking at the water as it goes into the smudged glass makes me feel the dry ache in my own throat. I decide to drink it myself before refilling it for Mr Gill. It's not yet ten, but I figure I'm saving on rinsing two glasses so I wonder if it'll be alright. I want to check with Daddy, ask his permission to drink my water early – three days ago he would have given me an answer one way or the other.

I set the water down for Mr Gill, who's sitting there while Momma reads her Scripture aloud, looking like he wishes he could be anywhere else.

When I go into his room, Daddy's still curled under the thin green blanket just where I left him three hours ago, his breakfast cereal untouched and bloated in the bowl on the nightstand. As my shadow passes, three fat roaches shoot out from under the bowl and streak down the wall.

When I sit at his feet, Daddy doesn't stir. He hasn't reacted to anything, really, since Brett. Well, since he stabbed that little man who killed Greg – but who we now know didn't kill Brett. He's cried a lot, yelled sometimes, but not at anything in particular. He's lying here, crying like a woman and not doing a darned thing to find out who killed Brett. Momma's no use either, only ever sitting and studying Scripture or praying at the hatch. How will that get justice for Brett? There's nobody in charge. I need Daddy back.

So I say, 'Momma wants me to wash the dishes again.'

He doesn't move.

'Did you hear me, Daddy? She wants me to waste Brett's drinking water just to show off for Mr Gill.'

Now, at last, there's some movement. But all he does is raise his hands to his ears and turn over. 'Go away, Gina,' he mutters. It's not much, but it's something to work with.

'She's making me pour him water out of our supply, Daddy, like it don't matter,' I press. When he says nothing, I start crying. 'That man's here all the time – he should bring his own water.' I want him to react, so I say, 'He's just here for our water. He should bring his own *goddamned* water.' But there's nothing.

Brett and I used to go exploring in the back yard together. He'd hold the branches up for me as we went into the growed-up patch. He used to collect special stones from the creek and keep them in there. Brett would always make sure there was one for me and one for him. 'Like twins,' Brett would say. 'We'll always be together.'

Something went wrong with Brett and Daddy couldn't save him.

'You can't let him drink Brett's water!' I yell.

'Go away, Gina,' he says again. But I shove my face into the covers and cry till I can't breathe any more.

'Gina.' Jae stares at me as if he can't quite believe I'm standing here, outside his door. The swelling has gone down, but even in the low light, I can see the bruises have spread and turned all sorts of deep colours, and the cuts aren't healing too good. I almost reach out to touch him.

'Do you want to come in?'

'Who is that, Jae?' Jae's dad comes to the door, flinching when he sees me. He's always been so quiet, the opposite to Daddy and Brett, but now I can't read him. 'I am sorry about your brother, Gina,' he says.

'Thank you, sir.' I know he must have hated him for what he did to Jae, but his words sound genuine. He glances at Jae, then drifts back into the room.

'You want to come in?' Jae asks again.

I don't want to go in there, not right now. 'Can we just go for a walk, Jae?' As if we're on the farm and can just go strolling through the woods.

'You won't get in shit?'

I shake my head. 'My daddy don't care.' For all the difference it'd make, I could have told him *I'm gonna go swap saliva with that Asian boy now*.

'Give me a minute.' Jae shuts the door on me and I listen to see if I can hear what he's saying to his parents. Then he reappears. 'Sorry. My folks don't like me leaving the place. Not after . . . But I convinced them it'd be okay.'

His shoulder brushes against mine as we head down the stairs. 'You were saying, about your dad.'

I shrug. 'I think he's given up. On everything. Including

me.' Jae looks down. 'And Momma doesn't try and stop me any more.' I feel like I'm going to start crying again and I'm tired of crying so I chew on the inside of my lip.

'Hey,' Jae says gently. He puts his arms around me.

A thought of Brett threatens to take over so I finally put my fingers on Jae's cheeks, trace the outline of his fading bruises, making a trail between the grazes and nicks. I don't want to think about Brett, so I kiss Jae. He starts getting excited, nudging into me – it's crazy that I can make him want to do that – but when he grabs my hand and starts pulling me through the stairwell door, I stop him.

'No?' he asks.

'Not yet,' I say. And I feel like there's a promise in that, from both of us. I feel like there will be a later, a time when we're both ready to do it again. Already, my feelings for him have changed. They're not as scared, they don't flitter off. They're solid. 'And not here. I don't want to go on that floor again. Let's go down and see the chickens.'

Jae rearranges the front of his pants. As we head down the stairs, he says, 'I think Reuben's dying. My moms went to see him, even though she can barely stand, and she says he doesn't have long.'

'That's too bad,' I say. But honestly, I'm too full of grief about Brett to let other people's issues in. When I hear people talking about old Mrs Dannhauser or Will's wife or Jae's mom or when Cait starts fretting about her family I just shut it out. I know if I start caring about their sadness, I'll just overflow – become drowned in the sadness like Daddy. 'I believe Cait. I don't think he killed Greg,' I say, even though I know nothing.

'Can you imagine what he felt like? Getting locked in here with all these crazy people?'

Crazy people like Momma and Daddy. That's what he means. 'Stop, please,' I say. 'Let's talk about something else.'

He stops and turns. 'No, but seriously, Gina. Isn't this the fucking problem with everyone in here? So caught up in paranoid hysteria that we're all willing to bury ourselves in the ground.'

Paranoid hysteria. I think I know enough about what that means. I straighten up and turn to him. 'You mean us, don't you? My family.'

'Christ, Gina. I mean *all* of us. We're all down here, aren't we, while the world's probably going on perfectly fine without us.'

I stare at my toes. They're filthy, and the nails are cracked.

'Well, our parents really,' he says. 'I didn't buy into this place. Nobody asked me. I'm sure they didn't ask you either.'

'Nope. My daddy didn't even ask my momma. When she found out he'd bought it, she went crazy. He blew her whole inheritance.'

Jae nods. I can see that he's been wondering how backwoods hicks like the Guthries managed to end up here, dying with the rich and famous. I think of all the times we've watched disasters on TV. Tornadoes, floods, bombings – they tend to make rich men poor and poor men heroes. Maybe the end of the world is the only time poor folks have any chance to come out winners. I'm starting to understand why Daddy was so keen on prepping. I'm starting to understand why Momma's beginning to take such comfort in Revelation.

I say nothing to Jae, but he takes my hand. Though we're so different, he makes me believe in a life after this, in a life where I'm not living in a trailer on someone else's farm. I squeeze his fingers and lean my head on his shoulder.

Jae leads me past the freezer – I try not to think of what's in there – through the hydroponics room, where all the plants have wilted and died from no water, and to the chicken coop. 'We'll get through this,' he says. 'Every day we wait in here increases our chances of being found. They're tightening the net, getting closer, it's only a matter of time before they come for us.'

'But we haven't got time. Maybe Momma's right and we should repent. We're going to die in here.'

'That's not true,' he says, but I know he doubts himself.

As we get to the chicken coop, there's a flurry of skittering and I see quick dark shapes darting and disappearing into the shadows. There's no real smell, no sound that you'd expect from the dumb old chickens. There, behind the empty water bowl, a last, brave, fat rat is gnawing through a red hen's guts, working its feathers apart with little claws.

I turn away, hearing my horses' death whinnies, and I know that it's all over.

When I get back up to our condo, there's nobody in the front room. Mr Gill has gone, and for that, at least, I'm glad. I find Daddy in my bedroom, standing by the closet door and holding out a T-shirt in front of him. It's the pale blue one Brett wore the day before he died.

'I got it all wrong,' Daddy says to me, as if he's continuing a conversation we weren't even having.

I can't get used to that weak voice. I don't like it. 'Where's Momma?' I say.

'I was trying to help you kids. Help you survive.' He drops the T-shirt and takes out Brett's red hoodie. 'I got it wrong.'

He puts the cloth to his face and breathes it in. I can't watch any more, so I turn and leave.

Momma's in the bathroom, leaning over the bath, gallon bottles of water piled next to her. Water spills off the ends of her hair as she leans over, the spatter carving dark rivers through the grey dust that's coating the wall tiles and the side of the tub. Murmuring a prayer, Momma uncaps one of the bottles. I'm moving too slowly to stop her. It's as if I'm pushing against some righteous force as I try to wade through the thick, slow air closer towards her.

By now, Momma has upended the bottle and it's gushing out. 'Stop, Momma! Stop! What are you doing?'

She shunts out her left arm towards me, still pouring the water out. I notice four empty bottles thrown beside her, and one last remaining full one beside her. 'It was his water. It was my son's water.'

Now Momma reaches for the last bottle. The last remaining bottle of Brett's water. She screws off the cap and finally I get myself to her. I half pin her against the wall with my body and grab at her hand as she tries to get the bottle open.

'Momma, you can't pour it away!' I'm bellowing. 'You can't!' I prise Momma's finger back, bending it back until she has to let go with one hand. But when she does, she smacks me across the jaw. I stumble back towards the door, clutching at my face.

Something dark and hot fires up inside me as I watch her turn back and drain the bottle.

30
JAMES

He can't ignore the ache in his bladder any longer. It's pushing through his Valium-and-booze-induced cocoon, letting the real world intrude. Christ knows how long he's been out this time, but it's easier this way.

James struggles to orientate himself, finally figures out that he's upside down on the bed, his head hanging over the edge, his feet on the pillows. He shifts his body around, drags himself across the covers and fumbles on the nightstand for the bottle of pills. Two left. He takes one, swigging it down with the dregs of a Miller Lite. The alcohol is all gone now – there's nothing left in the storeroom unless Will is keeping some back for himself – so it'll be cold turkey from here on in.

He rolls off the bed, waits until the floor stops moving beneath him, and shuffles into the bathroom, holding his hand over his mouth and nose to block out the stench. He pees into the shower, trying not to look at the brownish spatter trickling into the drain. Cigarette. He needs a cigarette, although he should really ration them. He's been chain-smoking since they'd returned from Brett's funeral. Vicki didn't say a word to him when he lit up in the condo the first time. There's no point. *Let's face it, babe, emphysema is the least of our concerns.*

He's about to slump back on the bed when it dawns on him that it's too quiet in the unit. It feels emptier somehow – too empty. 'Vicki?'

He almost trips over the dog's empty water bowl as he makes his way into the kitchen. He peers into the sunken lounge. No Vicki. And no Claudette.

'Vicki?' he tries once more.

It's not right. There's no way she would have left the condo. Since Brett's funeral her paranoia has reached pathological levels. *We're locked in with a murderer, James,* is all she seems to say, and the Guthrie kid's death has really shaken her up. Unless . . . Now it's coming back to him. A wispy recollection that she tried to get him up because she said she needed the bathroom – they could no longer use buckets of pool water to flush their own toilet as it had not-so-mysteriously blocked itself up – but he was drifting on the edge of a booze-and-diazepam induced precipice at the time. Yeah. Now he remembers. She snapped at him, shouted at him for falling apart when she needed him most, something like that. She must have gone to the compost toilet on level eight by herself. Taken the dog with her.

He digs in his pocket for the crumpled box of cigarettes and lights up, retching as the first pull of smoke hits his lungs. His mouth tastes like death, but he's not supposed to drink any water unless they're together. Fuck it. He rips open the fridge, grabs the last bottle of Evian and takes a sip. Just one. She'll never know. The water slides down his throat and then he can't help himself and he's gulping it down, letting it run over his chin. He stops himself before it's too late, before it's all finished.

He's drunk almost half the bottle.

Vicki will kill him when she finds out what he's done.

He paces, waiting for the Valium to waft in and take the edge off his guilt.

He should go and find her. Yes. That's the right thing to do. She'll appreciate that. He slips on a pair of Nikes and heads out.

Down he goes. He should really have a hangover by now, but a not entirely unpleasant numbness has taken him over – the last woolly embrace of the booze and drugs cocktail. He can't feel his feet, they're just blocks of meat propelling him along. *Meat feet for a meat head*. He giggles, which turns into a coughing fit. What happened to the cigarette? He doesn't remember stubbing it out anywhere. Maybe it's smouldering on the counter. Maybe the whole place will go up. Maybe they'll all die of smoke inhalation instead. At least then the waiting would be over.

Holding his hand over his mouth, he checks out the compost toilet in the basement, but it's empty. Perhaps she's decided to collect some water. He lurches into the gym. There's no sign of Vicki, but Jae is sitting over by the tread-mill, his arm around the Guthrie girl's shoulders. Even from here James can see she's upset and that he's interrupting something. His eyes stray to the place on the carpet where Brett's body lay. Was that just yesterday? Two days ago? A week ago? *No fucking idea, chief.*

'Hey,' he calls.

'Hey,' Jae says unenthusiastically.

'Have either of you seen Vicki?'

'Yeah. She was here earlier.'

'How much earlier?'

Jae shrugs, glances at Gina, who's wiping her face with the back of her sleeve. 'Hours ago, I guess.'

'What?'

'Three or four hours ago.'

Jesus. He really has lost time. But that doesn't make sense. Jae's saying something and James has to ask him to repeat himself.

'I said I saw her with Tyson.'

'Huh?'

'I said she was with Tyson.' Jae's speaking with the exaggerated care people use with the hard of hearing or drunk.

'Why would she be with Tyson?'

'How would I know?'

'Where? Where did you see her?'

'On level six. Outside the empty units.'

'Did you hear what they were saying?'

'Nope. Looked like they were really getting into it, though.'

Shit. Shit, shit, shit, shit.

'If you see her will you let her know I'm looking for her?'

Jae shrugs. 'Sure.'

He backs out of the gym and jogs up to level six. 'Vicki?' He pokes his head into the dark depths of his old smoking hideout. 'Vicki?' *I can explain, Vicki. I can explain.* 'Vicki? You in here?'

He's reluctant to go deeper inside, and in any case he can't see her hiding out in this shithole. And she doesn't trust anyone enough to hole up in one of the other units. He checks out the neighbouring condo just in case, but he can sense it's empty the second he steps through the door.

Could she have gone to Tyson's apartment with him? It's unlikely, but panic is beginning to gnaw at him now – it's worth a shot. He races up the stairs to level three, slams his fist on Tyson's door. 'Tyson! Open up!' He knocks again, harder this time. 'Tyson!'

'Who is it?' Cait's voice leaks through the door.

'James. Is Vicki in there?'

A pause. 'No. Why would she be here?'

'I need to talk to Tyson.'

The lock clicks and Cait opens the door, the kid wrapped around her legs. 'He's not here.'

'Caity, what's happening?' the child asks. She slips her thumb into her mouth.

'You really haven't seen Vicki?'

'No.'

'Where's Tyson?'

She sighs. 'He's gone to see the Guthries, of course. I think he's hoping they'll share out Brett's water. What's going on?'

He doesn't stop to answer, hares next door and slams his fist on the door.

Bonnie opens up, and he shoves his way past her. Cam is sitting on the couch, his head in his hands, Tyson next to him.

'Tyson!'

Tyson looks up, but Cam keeps his head lowered. James can hardly believe this stooped, broken man is the same gung-ho guy he and Vicki met on that first day.

'Where's Vicki, Tyson?'

'How the hell would I know?'

'Jae said he saw you talking to her. What did you tell her, Tyson? What did you say to her?'

'I told her she had to get rid of that dog. We need the water.'

'What else?'

'That's it.'

'You're lying, Tyson. What did you say to her?' He's yelling, and now Cam lifts his head. His eyes look smaller, sunken. James is aware that Bonnie is watching them carefully, twisting her hands together. '*Please*,' he tries once more.

Tyson glances at Cam, then at Bonnie and sighs. 'I wanted her to come clean.' He swallows. 'I wanted her to admit that she told Rani what happened at the sales weekend. I wanted to hear her say it.'

'Why would Vicki tell Rani anything?' She wouldn't. That wasn't her style. She didn't sneak around. She was upfront. If she'd found out she would have made him – not Rani – pay. The man was lying.

'Rani found out somehow. She knew, James. And she killed herself soon after that.'

'So where is Vicki now?'

'I don't know. But I do know that if she was responsible for Rani's death she should pay for what she did.'

'An eye for an eye,' Bonnie Guthrie murmurs and James has to fight not to scream at her to shut up.

'She's not responsible for anyone's death,' James spits. 'Your wife made her own decision, no one murdered her, no one—'

'What would you know?' Tyson roars, and James involuntarily steps back. 'Vicki's a vicious bitch. She's been at everyone's throat since she got here.'

'My son is dead,' Bonnie Guthrie breathes, apropos of nothing.

'Vicki hasn't done anything. Not like . . . Maybe you should ask your au pair what she was doing just before Brett was killed, Tyson. I saw her. Reuben and I saw her in the storeroom just before Brett was murdered.'

'What?'

Bonnie Guthrie has gone very still.

A mistake. He shouldn't have said it. He wanted to punish

Tyson, not Cait. James backs towards the door, desperate to get out of the toxic environment. He heads blindly back into the hallway.

We're locked in with a murderer, James.

She's fine. He can't go there.

We're locked in with a murderer, James.

No. *Think.* Greg's condo. Of course! She's gone up to use the bathroom in there. The hastily consumed water sloshing in his stomach, he races up the stairs. The door is propped open and he slams through it. He can sense immediately that the unit is empty, but he looks in every room just in case.

Don't panic. She could be in the rec room. He makes his way there, waits for his eyes to adjust to the gloom, then crunches his way over the broken glass that still litters the entrance. 'Vicki? Claudette?'

And then he hears it, a scuffling sound. There's something moving in the shadows next to the bar. He hurries over to it. 'Claudette!' The dog is whining and shaking, back hunched, tail between her legs, glass and grit woven into her fur. He picks her up and presses her to his chest. 'Where's Mommy?' he whispers. Vicki would never leave Claudette alone like this.

The adrenalin has now flushed away the Valium armour. Nausea swirls in his gut, and he's starting to sweat. He needs to calm down. She's just pissed at him. That's all. And . . . and she could easily have returned to the apartment while he's been looking for her. Yeah. That's it. He'll go back and he'll find her waiting for him, and he'll apologize, tell her it was all a mistake, he was drunk, he barely remembered it, it meant nothing.

We're locked in with a murderer, James.

No, no.

Claudette squeezed to his chest, he staggers back down to the unit, the nausea deepening now. Sweat is pouring down his face, and his legs are shuddering. Sick, he feels sick. Like he's getting flu. He doesn't manage to get the door open in time before the first spasm hits, doubling him over. He gags, but nothing comes up. He can't breathe, his heart is jumping in his chest. He retches again and this time a watery gruel spatters onto the floor at his feet. He's forced to drop the dog as knives stab his gut and he's hit with spasm after spasm.

Finally, the pain eases and he's aware that he's no longer alone. James turns his head, sees Trudi Dannhauser standing, watching him. 'Are you okay, James?'

Do I fucking look okay? 'Have you seen my wife, Trudi?'

'No.'

'I can't find her.'

'Come. Let me help you get inside.'

'Didn't you hear me? I need to find my wife.'

'I'll get Will. You're not well. Come on.'

James wants to say no, insist that he needs to look for Vicki, but instead he allows Trudi to nudge him into the condo – the *empty* condo because of course he knew it would be empty. It's easier to let other people take over. It's what he's done his whole life.

The butts are piling up in the coffee mug he's using as an ashtray. He counts them . . . nine, ten, eleven. Claudette lies limply on his lap. She hasn't touched the water he's slopped into her bowl – the last of the Evian.

'Mommy will be back soon,' he croons at her, running his

fingers through her matted fur. 'She's just hiding. Punishing Daddy for being naughty.'

The nausea has passed completely now, leaving a cruel clarity in its wake. He's been trying to imagine life without Vicki. He used to daydream about it; no more jealousy, no more watching what he says. No more . . . But instead of relief all he feels now is a sense that he's falling. Like the tether that's kept him from crashing to the ground all his life has snapped.

He jumps as someone knocks on the door.

Holding Claudette under one arm, James slips the Glock into the waistband at the back of his jeans and tugs his T-shirt over it. It's uncomfortable, but he's not going anywhere again without it. Then he opens the door. Will and Trudi are standing in the hallway. Will's face tells him all he needs to know.

'James. I'm sorry, but . . .' Will reaches out as if to touch him, but James jerks out of his reach.

The tether snaps, and for an instant, he's flying around the stairwell, out of control, wildly spinning. 'Take me to her,' he hears himself say.

'It is not a good idea, James,' Trudi says. 'It is best if you—'

'Take me to her!' It comes out as a scream. Claudette whines, and he clutches her tighter to his chest. 'Sorry, sorry, Claudette,' he whispers.

The Dannhausers' door opens and James hears Leo saying: 'What's happening?' James is distantly aware that Leo sounds like a confused old man. It's difficult to be sure as there's now a roaring in his ears.

They might be mistaken. They haven't said she's dead. She might just have fallen, she might be—

But he knows. He knows. 'Please, Will. I need to see.'

Will and Trudi share a glance. And then they're moving. He follows them up the stairs: one flight; two flights; three flights. Into the rec room, where he found Claudette.

Will stops outside the ragged hole in the wall that leads to the elevator shaft. 'James . . .'

'Show me.'

There's a flashlight attached to a rope lying on the floor, and Will drops it into the hole.

'I don't think you should see this, James.'

'Move.'

Holding the end of the rope, Will steps aside, and James shuffles to the edge and looks down, breathing in the stink of shit and damp brick. The flashlight illuminates a section of the water at the bottom. And something else . . . a lump. No. Not a lump. A body. Face down in the filth.

Vicki.

'We don't know if she fell or if she . . .' Will's voice trails away.

But James knows. They killed her. They killed Vicki. He should never have let her leave the unit without him. It's his fault. She told him, over and over again: *We're locked in here with a murderer, James.*

She was right.

He buries his face in Claudette's fur. They're speaking to him, but he drowns them out.

They killed her.

They killed Vicki.

For a second, he thinks about stepping off the edge, falling into the shallow murk at the bottom. Joining her. It would be so easy.

But no. They have to pay.

It's clear what he has to do. He has to survive. One of

them has to live. They're being picked off one by one. They took Vicki, but they won't take him. Holding Claudette so tightly to his chest he can feel the thrum of the dog's heartbeat, he pulls out the Glock, turns and points it at Will, feeling a savage thrill as he and Trudi recoil. 'James . . . please. Put the—'

'Let's go.'

'Go where?'

'To the safe, of course. I can't let you and the others get the guns. You know that, don't you? You can see that.'

Understanding dawns in Will's eyes.

'Take me to the storeroom, Will. Or I will shoot you right here.' His voice is calm and steady. And he knows, without a shadow of a doubt, that Vicki would be proud of him.

'James,' Trudi is saying. 'We're not the enemy. We're here to help you.' She has her hands up, and she's walking towards him slowly.

You can't hesitate in situations like these – it's the first thing he learned at the Boston Preppers Society. Hesitating can get you killed. He's a good shot. Vicki was better than he was, but he was still good. He disengages the safety, and fires.

31
CAIT

I jerk awake, sliding my knee across the sheet. Sarita's there next to me, snoring softly. Out of habit, I check the alarm clock, but since Sarita dropped it however many days ago, it just flashes *8:88, 8:88, 8:88*. Sarita started wailing when I unplugged it and made me promise to leave it on. 'It's not broken, Caity,' she said to me. 'Look – it's still working.'

'You're right, sweetie,' I said. 'It's not your fault.'

I've got used to the blinking red; I just shove a pillow over my face. And I've got used to the constant half-light she insists on. I need to help her get through this as intact as possible. Nothing else is important to me now. I've been trying to make every new fight, every new death, the stench and the filth all part of a great adventure story – one that will end sometime and we'll be able to go home.

Already the memory of the thump that woke me is dissipating. Something dropping perhaps. I lie back, wondering whether I should try to sleep some more, but I'm wide awake now, and thirsty. Getting up carefully to avoid disturbing Sarita, I check that our bedroom door is locked, unbolt the closet and check on our water, hidden in the top shelf behind a pile of blankets. Six gallon bottles, one of them a quarter gone. Most of the time I fool myself into believing that this is going to have a happy ending.

I pour two hundred millilitres into a glass, drink a third of it, transfer most into Sarita's sippy cup then splash the rest into the cereal bowl by the side of the bed which I've been using as a miniature basin for the most pressing of my hygiene. I squint at the tiny hands of my wristwatch – twenty to two. I'm not going to get back to sleep now. I haven't been properly tired since we got down here. Without fresh air or exercise, sleep is only something to break the boredom.

I'm wiping the yellow-edged gash on my arm with a damp cotton ball when I hear the shot. Another one? That may have been the sound that woke me in the first place. I freeze, judging the distance, calculating whether we're in immediate danger. It was loud but muffled, probably one or two levels away.

'Caity?'

'Go back to sleep, sweetie.'

'What are you doing?'

'Just, uhm, washing.'

'I heard a monster knocking on our door.'

I put the cotton ball down and turn to her. 'Just a bad dream.'

'No. She said they're coming for us.' Her eyes widen and her mouth starts to fold down.

'Who? Who said that?'

'The big monster. She didn't have a face. It was half made of blood.' She's trying not to cry but her chin is twisting and a fat drop of water runs down her cheek.

Jesus. No matter how hard I try to protect this little girl from what's been happening in here, she's absorbing it all. I shuffle across to her and hold her. 'It was just a bad dream, I promise.' And even as I say the words I hear a preternatural keening from upstairs, alongside distant doors slamming, banging, the low drone of men arguing. My gut clamps in instinctive terror that Brett Guthrie is barging his way here. But then I remember: Brett's dead. Thank God, at least Brett's dead.

'What's that noise?' Sarita asks.

'It's just the grown-ups playing a game.' She frowns at me; she knows that I'm lying. 'Drink some water and go back to sleep.'

She takes a half-hearted suck at her sippy cup, finding the tepid, stale, plastic-tasting water as unappealing as I do.

As I settle her back under the cover, arranging Strawb and Simba on the pillow next to her, I tell her, 'Dream of dolphins and rainbows. Dream of the sun and bees on flowers. There's a meadow with rabbits in it and a fresh, clean breeze. Smell it. Feel the warmth of the sun.' She closes her eyes. I almost tell her *Dream of your mother*, but I'm not sure if that will help. I notice, though, that she's clutching her little photo album under the covers.

I walk into the lounge and pace. Fuck, where is Tyson?

It *was* a gunshot that woke us, I'm sure of it. I know the sound of a gunshot. But the guns were supposed to be locked away.

Unable to settle, I stare at the blank TV screen. *We're trapped down here. Don't forget about us.*

The door bursts open and I jump up, swallowing a scream. It's Tyson.

'Where the hell have you been?'

'Daddy?'

I look around to see Sarita standing in the doorway of her bedroom. She walks towards us, Strawb clutched in one hand. I check my temper and lower my tone. 'Sarita didn't know where you were.'

'What have you done, Cait?'

'Done? What have *I* done? What are you . . .' He's looking at me with wide eyes, almost as if he's scared of me. He skirts around me and stands between me and Sarita. How dare he? I'm the only one in this place who's not a danger to her! The dam wall holding back my anger bursts and I want to hurt him, shame him, out all his filthy little secrets. 'I don't know what you're on about, Tyson, but while we're busy swapping accusations, I've figured out what *you've* been doing.' My voice is cold. He tries to interrupt, but I talk right over him. 'I know. I know about you and Vicki. I'm right, aren't I? You had an affair with Vicki Maddox at the sales weekend, and Rani found out about it. It's why Rani killed herself, isn't it?'

His whole body tightens and for a second I'm certain he's going to hit me. Then he seems to crumple.

'It wasn't with Vicki. It was with James Maddox.' He waits for me to respond, and when I don't – I can't, I honestly can't find the words – he continues. 'It was at The Sanctum sales weekend last April. I'd love to say it was the first time I'd cheated, but it wasn't. I think Vicki might have . . . I think she found out and told Rani about it.'

I look down at Sarita, who's groggily listening to him talk, thankfully not understanding what it all means. My mind's cycling through reactions. I'm shocked, despite myself. It doesn't really matter to me that the affair was with a man, but just how quickly I jumped to the wrong conclusion. That's the shocking part. What's burning in me most, though, is that Rani would choose to abandon her daughter because of it. Now I have to try very hard to keep my voice level. 'Rani

311

. . . because you had an affair? Because she found out you were gay? She left her daughter alone in the world because she was *embarrassed*?' With parents like this, the little girl has had no chance.

Tyson raises a hand and shakes his head. 'No, no, Cait. It was my fault. That isn't why she did it. I wanted to blame Vicki for it, but . . . Look, fact is, Rani was depressed for a long time. Since Sarita was born. I knew she was ill but I ignored it.' He straightens. 'She needed help and I didn't help her.'

We both jump as there's a rough thump at the door. 'Who's that?'

'They know, Cait. They know that you killed Brett. James told them.'

'Wait . . . that I *what*?'

Then, the crack of a gunshot, right outside the door. Sarita screams. 'How would they get a gun? Did Will give them the—'

Tyson looks from me to Sarita and back again and his face sets as if he's decided something. He grabs Sarita up and she wraps her arms around his neck. 'Remember that I always loved you, Sarita. I loved you and your Mommy. I wasn't a good man, but I tried my best and I loved you.' He thrusts her into my arms. 'Take Sarita and get into the bathroom,' Tyson says, his voice now low and urgent.

'But—'

'*Do it.*'

'Mommy!' Sarita screeches.

'The door's reinforced, isn't it?'

Tyson doesn't answer immediately. All I can hear is the blood thumping in my ears. And I realize – they don't need bullets to get in. Jae told me about Brett slicing off Greg's thumb. If they want to, they can get in that way.

'Please, Cait. Just do what I say!'

Tyson shoves us towards the bathroom, but before we can make it the front door slams open.

'Caity!' Sarita screams.

I turn my head, and see her, standing there: Bonnie Guthrie, a gun in her hand.

32
GINA

'Jae! Yoo-jin! Stella!' Will Boucher is at the front door, his voice muffled. 'Let me in!'

Yoo-jin looks to Jae, who nods, and then opens the door wide enough for us to see his face.

It's wet – has he been crying? – and as he shifts his position I can see there's something smeared down his shirt and jeans. Blood, it looks like blood. 'It's all gone to hell.'

'What's going on, Will?' Jae asks. We were all woken by the shots and the yelling. Since then we've been waiting in silence in the sitting room, Yoo-jin refusing to let Jae go anywhere near the door until now.

'Trudi . . .' Will sobs. 'Christ. Trudi's gone.'

'Gone where?'

'She . . . she died. James shot her. Vicki's dead. She was found at the bottom of the elevator shaft. James was upset, and he . . . Trudi got in the middle and she got shot.' He clenches his jaw and swallows something down and carries on. 'She's dead too. Now James has locked himself in his unit.'

Before any of us can react, Will continues: 'And there's another . . . uh, a situation.' His voice cracks, becomes thin and withered, like Daddy's. 'The Guthries. . . . uh . . .'

I push past Jae to get to the door. 'What's happened, Mr Boucher? Are my momma and daddy alright?'

Will glances at me as if he's wondering what I'm doing in the Parks' condo, but his eyes are quickly dulled again by the weight of whatever's been happening. If he asked what I'm doing here instead of down there, what could I tell him that would make sense? How could I tell him that my daddy's emptied out and my momma lost it? He clears his throat. 'Jae? Yoo-jin? Can you come?'

'I don't want to leave my wife,' Jae's dad says. 'She's not well.'

'What exactly is happening, Will?' Jae asks.

'James had a gun. She found it.'

'She?'

'Bonnie. She's broken into the Gills' place.'

'*Momma?*' I can't swallow. 'Why would she do that?'

'She's gone after Cait. She thinks she killed Brett.'

Cait killed Brett?

'No!' Jae yells. 'No! She didn't! Cait couldn't have. Why does Bonnie think that?'

'I don't know. Please, Yoo-jin. I can't do this by myself.'

'It is not our business,' Jae's dad says.

'Dad!' Jae cries. 'Dad, we have to help Cait!'

'I . . . I can't.'

'You have to go, Yoo-jin.' It's Stella. She's using the door frame to keep herself upright. 'There's a child in there.' In the spare bedroom, Reuben moans. Dr Park insisted that he was brought to their condo so that she could carry on looking after him, but his chances aren't good. *My daddy did that. If he dies, my daddy killed him.*

Yoo-jin turns to his wife and they share a long look. Momma and Daddy never looked at each other like that. Not that I can remember. It's as if they're speaking a silent language, part love, part anger and part pain. Then Yoo-jin nods and stands back to let Will enter the condo. 'You're right. Jae, Gina, you stay here.'

Jae shakes his head. 'No way. I'm not letting you go by yourself, Dad.'

'Bonnie Guthrie has a gun, Jae.'

And then, I can't listen to this any more. I can see what Jae is thinking, what all of them are thinking. *Those crazy Guthrie hillbillies.* I run for the door, and I'm through it before they can stop me.

I can hear Jae calling after me, but I'm fast, and I'm down the stairs and at Tyson's door in seconds. There's a single bullet hole like a round black eye next to the lock. I push it open, just as Jae, Will and Yoo-jin reach the top of the stairs. 'Momma? Daddy?'

But Daddy isn't here. Just Momma and Tyson. He has his back to the bathroom door, his hands up at chest level, blocking her way. I can't look at her – it physically hurts. She's living in her own fantasy world, her eyes sealed over by whatever it is she's seeing. The skin all over my body burns with shame; I can feel a trickle of sweat running down my back. 'Move, Tyson,' she says. 'I don't have no argument with you.'

I walk towards her. 'Momma. Momma, please don't do this.'

She whips her head and the look of hatred in her eyes stops me in my tracks.

'Where's Daddy, Momma?'

I hear Jae and the others entering the room. Momma doesn't flinch. Daddy trained her good. He trained all of us good. We don't panic in a combat situation.

'Listen . . . Bonnie,' Tyson says. 'It wasn't Cait. I did it. I killed Brett.'

'You're lying.'

'Bonnie, listen to me. It wasn't Cait. It was me.'

While he talks, there's this *squeak-squeak-squeak* sound, like someone's jiggling his foot or worrying a loose joint in his seat. *Squeak squeak squeak*. I look around the room but I can't see who's doing it. I wish they'd stop.

Squeak squeak squeak.

That *squeak squeak squeak* comes again, and now two rats scurry across the floor. Nobody even bothers to move their feet. That's how far we've gone.

33
WILL

Will almost wishes Bonnie would turn the gun on him. God, he's so tired. No, he's beyond tired. He's broken. His hands have been trembling for the last two days and his guts have been cramping non-stop. It's not water he needs, but something that will give him oblivion. His shoulder and back muscles ache from the effort of hefting Trudi's body down to the storage room. She was slight, a hundred and five pounds at the most, but she felt far heavier. He did it alone, his penance for not intervening in time. Leo shadowed him down every flight, stumbling on the stairs, face slack. He didn't say a word, only let out a moan when the towel he'd wrapped around Trudi's face slipped, revealing the shattered remains of her face: bloody bone and a snarl of ivory teeth. Will left him there, outside the freezer, alone.

Lana is probably dead, Trudi is dead. He slept with Trudi while his wife was dying. What sort of man is he? He left the gun where James dropped it. Irresponsible. Reprehensible.

The little girl's terrified sobbing cuts through the bathroom door. He's only got one last card to play. 'If you let Tyson go,' he says to Bonnie, 'I'll give you and Cam the combination to the gun safe. It's what you wanted, isn't it? You want to try shooting through the hatch? Let's do it.'

'This man must pay for what he's done to my son!'

'Then let's get out of here and let the authorities deal with it.'

'An eye for an eye,' Bonnie says with a chilling calmness. 'He murdered my son.'

'Cam was convinced that Reuben killed Brett. He was wrong. He killed an innocent man – or as good as – you also want that on your conscience?'

'Tyson confessed. You heard him.'

'Then keep Tyson locked in his condo. Bonnie . . . think about it . . . I don't believe Tyson even killed Brett. It makes no sense.'

'He confessed!'

'Stop this!' It's Yoo-jin coming in from behind. Even Bonnie snaps her head around to face him. It's almost funny. 'You have lost a son, but you still have a daughter.'

Bonnie wipes her forehead on her arm, keeping the gun on Tyson. 'My daughter is ruined.'

Gina gasps and buries her head in Jae's shoulder.

'How can you behave like this? This man has a child! Never mind what you think about Gina, what about the little girl in there?'

On cue, Sarita wails through the door, 'Daddy!'

'It is obvious that he is only saying he killed your son to protect Cait and his daughter.'

'Momma?' Gina tries again. 'Please, Momma.'

'Bonnie. You don't have to do this.'

'Who else is gonna protect the family?' she whispers, and now there are tears running down her cheeks. 'Who else is there? There's no family left.' Deflated, she lets her hand fall to her side.

Yoo-jin walks carefully towards her, his hand outstretched. 'Give me the gun.' She hands it to him limply. Yoo-jin looks at it in disgust and passes it straight to Will. Tyson sags against the door, his knees buckling.

Gina runs over to her mother, but she pushes her away. It's a vicious shove, full of pain and hatred. 'Momma,' Gina whispers.

'Get away, girl. You've made your choice. You're no daughter of mine.'

The freezer housing Greg, Brett, Caroline and Trudi chunders and clunks. He's alone down here. Leo is no longer outside the freezer door when he approaches the safe. Its surface is slightly pitted from where Brett and Cam attempted to break into it, but it opens smoothly when he keys in the code.

He slings one of the Guthries' bags over his shoulder and picks out one of Greg's shotguns and as many shells as he can carry. He knows it won't work, but there's a tiny part of him, a last tenacious flicker of hope, that refuses to die. The heavy bag tugs at his shoulder as he hauls it up flight after flight; he welcomes the discomfort. At the top of the stairs he opens the bag and takes his time choosing. There's no rush. He digs out a semi-auto. One of Brett's guns, he thinks. It's the kind of weapon the boy would have liked. Then he puts it back in favour of Greg's shotgun, a weapon he's more familiar with. He doesn't bother with earplugs or eye protection. He kneels on a step midway down the flight, the concrete biting into his knee, two boxes of shells next to him. His hands are steady. He loads the gun, breathes out through his mouth, aims, and fires at the green door. The noise in the confined space is immense, sears his eardrums, but he doesn't care. He fires and fires, reloading steadily, feeling the shotgun pummelling his shoulder, flecks of steel pocking into his skin, barely registering that he's screaming. When he stops, his arms are numb.

He's aware of a presence behind him. He turns, sees Jae and Gina. Wordlessly, Gina moves towards the bag, picks out the semi-automatic, checks the clip, and squishes in close to him. 'Let's go,' she says. Or he thinks it's what she says – he can no longer hear anything but a high whining sound. Together, they get to work.

They don't stop until Gina's clip is empty and dead shell casings litter the area around them – bright bronze spots in a grey landscape. It's Jae who steps past them to the airlock door. It reminds him of the signs near the hunting areas in Augusta, pockmarked and pitted. Gina's been concentrating on the area around the handle and the locking mechanism and Will sees with no surprise that her aim is true. Jae takes a deep breath and kicks at the door with his boot. It opens.

No one yells in triumph. Gina silently rummages in the bag for another clip.

Now for the hatch.

34
JAE

Jae rubs his eyes. He's been trying to compose a final message in his head, but he keeps losing his train of thought. Something along the lines of: *hey, rescuers of the future, you're too fucking late to save us, but don't get a shock when you look in the fridge.* What he should really do is list the series of catastrophic events that have led them to this point, but he can't face it. Fuck that. Whoever eventually discovers them can piece it all together. Let them think what they want. He pictures a swarm of CSI technicians dressed in hazmat suits picking over their corpses. *His* corpse.

Jesus.

Because it's going to happen now. This is actually it. And strangely, his thirst seems to have abated. For the last couple of hours it's his throbbing head that's been bothering him more than his parched throat.

Next to him, Gina stirs. She's been lying perfectly still on the couch for hours now, barely breathing. Her eyes have sunk further into her skull, her lips are almost bloodless. The last time they'd had anything to drink was yesterday – or maybe it was the day before, he can't remember – when they shared the syrup from a can of peaches. They've even drunk the mouthwash. There was a brief moment of hope when he and Dad tried to decontaminate the pool water, boiling it down to lessen the salty content and adding water purification tablets to it, but it didn't work. It made them all sick; Jae's gut still aches from the stomach cramps and dry-heaving, and his mouth is gummy and foul.

He looks at his silent laptop and considers starting it up for the first time in days and writing a final farewell message to Scruffy, along with a note asking whoever comes across their bodies to pass it on to her. She's the only one of his friends he's really missed while he's been down here. But what would he say? And, anyway, there's not much battery life left and the electricity supply has browned out so there's not enough current to charge it. When he powers it up again, it'll be for the last time.

He hears Sarita crying again from inside his room. Seconds later, Cait appears at the doorway. She and Tyson showed up a few hours ago, Sarita clinging to her dad like a baby monkey. With Reuben taking up the bed in the spare room, they'd moved into his room. Cait's hair pools around her shoulders like dried blood; the dim light accentuates the dark circles under her eyes. 'Where's Yoo-jin?' Her voice is raspy and she touches her throat as she speaks. Behind her he can hear the soft rumbling of Tyson's voice talking to his daughter.

'He's checking on Reuben,' Jae says.

'Sarita's vomiting again, but there's nothing left to bring up. Tyson was wondering if there's any of that rehydrate powder left we can give her.'

'No. I'm sorry.'

'Me too.' She gives him a small, sad smile, then disappears back into the room, shutting the door behind her.

Jae leans back and shuts his eyes. He's only aware he's dozed off when someone touches his shoulder. He looks up, sees his dad standing over him. Finally, he stepped up when he had to.

'Is it time?'

'Almost. Your mother wants to see you.'

Jae stands up slowly and follows his dad into the bedroom. The room smells of piss and sweat. He approaches the bed slowly. 'Moms?'

She's lying on her side, a hand cupping her face. She looks peaceful. Her breathing is shallow, and when he leans down to kiss her forehead, he can feel the heat blazing off her.

Her eyelids flicker. 'Jae? You're a good boy, Jae.' He flinches. That's what Caroline said to him the first time he read to her. He waits for the tears to come. But they don't. They never do.

'And you're a great mom.'

She doesn't respond.

'Goodbye, Moms.'

He turns away, and together, he and his dad return to the sitting room. Unsure what else to do, craving the comfort of the familiar more than anything else, Jae sits down next to Gina and picks up the laptop and presses the power button. It's always been his escape. There are fifty-three minutes of battery life left. About the same amount of time he has left.

They won't feel a thing. His dad will see to that. Moms and Sarita will get the last of the sleeping tablets and painkillers. The rest of them will get a bullet. Will made sure there were enough left after they'd exhausted most of the ammunition on the hatch door. They'd barely grazed its metal skin. Gina said they were lucky none of them were killed by a ricochet, even though Will had eventually made them set up a shield of tables and chairs. Jae's ears had rung for hours after they'd given up. A painful reminder that there really was no way out.

He jumps as a faint banging sound echoes from deep within The Sanctum. A gunshot? Yesterday, Will handed out weapons to everyone left, including James, Leo and the Guthries.

His dad moves over to the kitchen counter and starts mixing the crushed tablets into the remains of a can of Mountain Dew that's been saved for this purpose.

Jae tries to swallow, but his saliva has dried up. 'Will it work, Dad? What if they wake up and see all of us . . .'

'They won't.'

His dad will be the last, and Jae reckons this must be the loneliest feeling in the world. Moms will be first, then Sarita, then Reuben, then Gina, then Cait, then Tyson and then . . .

Gina stirs again, opens her eyes and looks up at him.

'Hey,' he says to her, stroking her hair.

'Is it time?'

'Nearly.'

'Jae . . . You think I'll be punished?'

'For what?'

'For . . . for going against Momma. For what we did.'

'No. Of course not. You didn't do anything wrong.'

It's the first time she's mentioned her parents since Bonnie's meltdown. There's no point discussing this right now. It's too late for recriminations. He's tried so hard to make it right, but he's failed.

'You think I'll go to hell, Jae?'

'No.'

'You think there really is a heaven?'

No. 'I guess. I mean, sure there is.'

'But—'

325

'Shh.' He can't talk about this now. He just can't.

His dad pours the mixture into a large syringe. Neither Moms nor Sarita will be able to drink it without help. Jae focuses on the laptop screen as intently as he used to when he was in the climax of a battle so that he doesn't have to watch his dad walking into the bedroom. He opens a document, names it 'End Game Message' and starts typing.

October 19 18:35

To whom it may concern.

My name is Jae-lin Park, and I am preparing to die. Our water is now gone.

You'll find a list of the names and details of all the people who are down here on the computer belonging to Greg Fuller, who built this place. Some of us have died already. There are others in the supply room, so don't

There's no point. Fuck it. He hasn't got the energy after all. He's about to shut it down when an unexpected icon at the corner of the screen catches his eye. He blinks, rubs at his eyes, clicks onto the icon, and reads the words: 'Wireless Network Available'.

It can't be. He clicks on the icon. It isn't The Sanctum's network, but – impossibly – another one. Zen-net7986.

It's there – it's really there.

He can't speak at first, but he has to find his voice, he has to.

'Dad! Dad! *Stop!*' And then he's screaming.

35
JAE

October 31

Nearly 2 weeks since we got out. Time for an update I guess.

Dad's been making me and Gina see this trauma counsellor and therapist called Dr Levene. She's OK. Mostly just listens and says 'uh-huh, how did that make you *feel*?' a lot. I told her I've been neglecting my journal and she asked if this was because writing triggers flashbacks of what happened down there. She says that I should only do it if I 'feel comfortable' and that writing it all out could help in the long term as it's a way for my 'brain to process everything' (blah blah, bullshit, bullshit).

I haven't been writing because I've been too busy catching up with Scruff and visiting Moms in hospital and hanging out with Gina and helping her deal with life in the real world. She still asks if it's OK every time she makes tea or grabs a snack from the fridge, and she always tells us when she's going to the bathroom like we're keeping score or something. The Guthries' home life must have been seriously fucked. When we first got home Dad had to keep telling her that she didn't have to cook and clean for us and that she could download and watch whatever the hell she wanted from Netflix. Dr Levene's put her on SSRIs now which seems to help although they make her sleep for like 14 hours a day. It's kind of unspoken that she'll be living with us for a while as Bonnie is stuck in a hospital for psychos in Portland and Cam's in custody for stabbing Reuben. Gina's doing OK physically but we've had to cool off on the relationship stuff as she's withdrawn and spacey all the time. Dad says I should try to stop her going on the internet or watching the news as there's so much shit going around about what went down in there.

So yeah. There's lots going on.

Lucky for me, Dr Levene's bullshit detector is crap, and as long as I stare off into the distance and let my lip wobble a bit, she says I'm making good progress. Her main concern at the moment is how Gina and I are coping now that we're celebs. I just checked, and the footage of the rescue crew blasting off the hatch has had over 8 mill hits on YouTube already. Everyone wants to know the gory details and we're the only normalish people to talk to. The Guthries are fucked, Cait's back in South Africa, Tyson is refusing to talk to the press, not allowing them a single shot of Sarita, Leo's vanished behind his corporate walls and Will has basically become a full-on alcoholic, so it's us they're focusing on. Scruff says we should get an agent and milk this for all its worth. Try and get a book or movie deal out of it. She says the British tabloids are also obsessed with the story and are calling it 'Paranoid Prepper Paradise Gone Bad' and stuff like that. Dad says we can't talk to any reporters until after the inquest otherwise we'll look callous. When we first got home they were everywhere and Dad said we might have to move, but we've kind of got used to them now. We just say 'no comment' if they hassle us when we leave the apartment.

What else? Oh yeah, the inquest has been delayed again while they wait for yet another expert to go over the findings and the DNA tests to be done. Gina's worried about it as Cam will have to be there and it'll be the first time she's seen him since we got out.

There's no official report yet, but so far they're saying:

UNDER GROUND

Greg Fuller: Accidental death or murdered by someone unknown

Caroline Dannhauser: Undetermined

Reuben Montoya: Death resulting from injuries inflicted on him by Cam Guthrie

Brett Guthrie: Murdered by person/s unknown

Victoria Maddox: Accidental death / murdered by person/s unknown

Trudi Dannhauser: Shot by James Maddox

James Maddox: Death by suicide. James gave the last of his water to Vicki's dog, another survivor.

TBH, the cops and FBI who BTW are nothing like the ones you see in movies, have been awesome. Thought they'd give us more of a hard time, but as our stories all matched up, they've been pretty sympathetic. So far, the feeling I'm getting is that they think Reuben is the prime suspect for the killings, although they haven't explained how he could have killed Vicki if she was pushed down the lift shaft and didn't fall.

Here's something weird. Don't feel like playing *WoW*, even though there's a new expansion. Thought it would be the first thing I'd do when I got out.

November 1

Just got back from visiting Moms in the hospital. She's looking way better now that she's had the operation and her gall bladder has been removed. We had a long talk about Dad. She says he's agreed to go and see someone about his issues (hopefully not Dr Levene) and she says that from now on she will stop neglecting her health. Then she tried to get me and Gina to talk about birth control which was seriously embarrassing.

For a while I thought about talking to Scruff about Gina and asking advice about how to get through to her, but that kind of feels disloyal. Gina's been cool so far about the fact that me and Scruff have reconnected and chat a lot. They even exchanged messages once or twice. Maybe after the inquest I will go and visit her in the UK and Gina can come too.

November 2

Kind of a boring day. It was raining so there were no reporters around to bug us when Gina and I went to see Dr Levene. More blah blah how are you feeling crap. She likes details, so I told her that the taste of Mountain Dew now makes me puke (it doesn't, but I had to say something) and she latched onto this and wanted to explore why.

UPDATE: Dad came home from visiting Moms looking stressed. Press were waiting outside the hospital, and he says *Inside Story* want to do a big feature on how paranoid you have to be to buy into something like The Sanctum. It's like everyone is blaming us for what happened to us, almost as if we asked for it. Now that it's over, people seem to have forgotten how freaked out and panicked they were about the virus. The roadblocks and deaths and the shit that went down in Asia. It's like it's been scrubbed from their brains. All of us down there were only doing what we thought would keep us safe. It's not our fault it all went wrong.

Anyway, Gina overheard me and Dad talking about The Sanctum and got really upset. I followed her into her room and she let me hug her and then we just lay down on the bed together until she fell asleep.

November 3

So this is cool. We went to get Moms from the hospital and although she's a bit weak and has lost a ton of weight, she's almost back to normal. I thought Dad might slide back into his old ways, but he's been pretty cool since we got back, doing the grocery shopping and fielding phone calls. It's like the whole situation snapped him out of it, and although he and Moms aren't as loved up as they used to be, there's hope. Gina's been with Moms all morning, making tea and fussing round her. Gina asked if she could stay home from therapy today, and Moms said yeah, but that I should go. Will report back.

Dr Levene wanted to talk about what it felt like to 'face one's own mortality'. I spent a lot of time gazing at the window blinds and sighing, so I think it went OK. I asked her if everything I said to her was confidential and she said yeah and 'is there something you want to tell me?' I was almost tempted to tell her the whole deal, but fuck that.

When I got home Moms was up and she and Gina were in the kitchen drinking tea and it looked like they'd both been crying. Gina gave me a smile when I came in which is an improvement and very cool. Go Moms. It looked like they needed their privacy so I holed up in my room to write this and see if I could get back in the game. Scruff is in a new guild and she messaged me to say they've agreed to let me join. Still don't really feel like it. It's like that was part of my old life. My pre-Sanctum life. Don't feel like downloading anything. Might read a book or something, I dunno.

UPDATE: Just got an email from Cait. She sounds upbeat about stuff. She Skypes Sarita every day and it looks like the kid and Tyson are doing OK. It seems fitting that they're the ones who adopted Vicki's dog. Cait says it follows Sarita everywhere. They're staying with Sarita's grandmother. The way I see it, Tyson did a Dad and came through in the end. Cait says he confessed to killing Brett when Bonnie was going apeshit because he couldn't bear the thought of Sarita losing another mother figure in her life. The South African press have been treating Cait like a hero and she says she's been offered a major book deal. She's supposed to fly back for the inquest, but her lawyer is trying to get the DA's office to let her testify remotely. It still freaks me out to think that our escape was all down to Cait's mom and that it took someone in South Africa to get our cops to start looking in the right place. She bugged the crap out of them, even got the FBI involved because she said Tyson must've kidnapped Cait. The cops eventually found the location of The Sanctum when they went through Tyson's office computer and when they matched the coordinates of The Sanctum with Danntech's independent investigations, the FBI got out to Maine quickly after that.

But it's also down to me. If I hadn't written that final message and seen the wi-fi signal Search and Rescue set up above ground to communicate with their base camp, we would have been toast. As soon as I connected to the signal, I Skyped 911. They patched me through to the search and rescue team, and they told us to stay together in the basement while they blasted the hatch. I often wonder how things would have been different if we'd made contact two days earlier, when Search and Rescue first arrived. But then I remind myself that we wouldn't have got out any sooner because they had to bring in special military equipment to open the hatch. It had just arrived when I got in touch. It wasn't my fault.

Whenever I think about those final hours it's like I can hear movie soundtrack music behind me. Even Moms tried to get out of bed. She was too weak, but thankfully Dad hadn't been able to face dosing her after all, so we didn't have to panic about that. Me and Dad went to tell the others. There was no answer from James's unit but Will, Sarita, Tyson, Cait, Leo and the Guthries were with us at the end, which was awkward as Bonnie kept trying to get us to pray together and Gina couldn't even look at her or Cam. Later we found out that Reuben died on his way to Portland General. They airlifted him, Sarita and Moms out as they were the ones who needed the most urgent medical treatment, but he didn't make it.

We only found out a day later that James had shot himself.

November 4

They've delayed the inquest again while they do more tests, but Greg's autopsy report has finally been released and HOLY CRAP. Looks like Reuben was telling the truth all along. Greg died from a brain aneurysm and must have hit his head when he collapsed. Caroline Dannhauser's death is still 'undetermined'. But what are they going to say? She was old and sick before she even came to The Sanctum.

Gina started trembling after Dad finished giving us the lowdown. It looks like the authorities are now leaning towards James as the Sanctum Killer. His marriage wasn't great, and although he was the one who found Brett's body along with Reuben, they're saying it's not unusual for killers to 'stumble upon' their victims. They're reaching, but hey – everyone wants a resolution, so why not blame it on a dead guy?

UPDATE: Got a call from Will. He wanted to talk to Moms, but couldn't as she'd gone with Dad to see Dad's counsellor. Will was drunk, slurring his words and crying and all kinds of shit. I told him we were sorry we didn't go to his wife's funeral, but I wasn't sure if he even heard me. She died from a cardiac arrest or something on the day the internet went down in The Sanctum, which you'd think would make him feel better as he was freaking out the whole time that she was alone and dying in their house. The authorities tried for a while to locate him, but at that stage they had their hands full with the virus and they let it slide. Then he asked me what I thought about the blame being put on James or Reuben for the murders.

I said it was possible, wasn't it?

He got really angry, said it was proven Reuben didn't kill Greg and he'd seen James's face after they found Vicki. No way had he killed her.

I hung up on him.

FUCK

Just need to keep calm.

November 5

FUCKFUCKFUCKFUCKFUCKFUCK

Got a Google alert today. Will has been talking to a reporter at the *New York Times*. Couldn't face reading the whole article but I got the gist. He's insisting that neither James nor Reuben could have killed Brett and Vicki and someone else is guilty.

Tried to talk to Dad about this, but now he's doing so well, I don't want to bring him down.

November 6

Shit day.

The inquest is being held next week even though Caroline Dannhauser's autopsy results are still sketchy.

Had the usual blah session with Dr Levene and then me and Gina sat on the couch and watched some dumb movie with Vince Vaughn in it.

UPDATE: It's past 3 a.m. Can't sleep. Going to see if anyone is up for a raid.

UPDATE: Shit. Stupid, stupid, stupid. I was still up when Dad came through to make Moms her morning coffee. I guess it was because I hadn't slept and wasn't thinking straight but when Dad asked me if I was OK instead of saying 'yeah' I asked him if he thought the FBI or the cops or whoever would ask us to take lie detector tests after what Will had said.

HOW COULD I BE SO STUPID????????

Dad didn't say anything for a long time, but then he told me not to worry.

November 7

Weird disconnected day. Dr Levene cancelled, so Gina and I stayed at home and I downloaded series 1 of *GoT* for her. She'd never seen it before cos of the whole Dragons are Evil and from the Devil thing. Kind of made me feel funny watching all the sex scenes with her, but she loved it and sat really close to me on the couch all the way through it. She asked me what me and Scruff talk about all the time and what I write about in my journal which was cool as it shows she's still interested in me and my life.

Could see Dad wanted to talk about something all day. Avoided him and pretended to sleep when he knocked on the door of my room. Couldn't face him. Couldn't even face messaging with Scruff.

November 8

Will's allegations have gone viral and Who is the Real Sanctum Serial Killer? Memes are popping up everywhere. So far Leo is the number 1 suspect cos of his dodgy past. Cait's also high on the list because of Brett trying to rape her.

I'm number 3.

Scruff thinks this is cool and keeps joking that she's never been in a guild with a murderer before.

The cops haven't said they're going to interview us again, but they might if this kind of shit continues.

November 9

OK.

HOLY FUCK

Dad snuck out early this morning and went on NPR today to say that he's 100% certain Leo was the Sanctum Serial Killer. He didn't tell any of us he was going on the show, not even Moms. It's so out of character for him to do this, Moms has got to know something's up. I downloaded it soon as I found out. Dad didn't come right out and say Will is delusional and an alcoholic, but he implied it.

November 10

A guy from the coroner's office came round to talk us through what we'd have to do at the inquest. He was very cool and implied that the DA wasn't taking Will's crap seriously and says we might never know who killed Brett and Vicki. Gina got upset and the guy promised that she wouldn't have to see Cam or her mom if she didn't want to. Moms tried to talk to her after he left, but she shut herself in her room and wouldn't come out for hours and refused to go and see Dr Levene again.

Also, I'm beginning to think maybe Dr Levene isn't as dumb as she looks. Today she picked up on the fact that I was on edge and kept asking me why this was. I spun some line about being worried about the inquest and Gina, but I could tell she didn't buy it. She wants me to do a 'personality test' but I told her I didn't believe in them.

I'll need to be more on my guard in the future.

3 days until the inquest.

November 11

Stayed in my room all day playing *WoW*. Fucked up the raid because I kept losing concentration. I'm going to give it up for good, move on to another MMO.

November 12

Been up all night. It's now 5 a.m.

I've been thinking about it, and the only one I regret is Caroline, although this doesn't make sense as I reckon she would have died anyway.

The idea that I should do it hit me when I was reading to Caroline. An impulse. I pretended to leave, and after Trudi snuck out to hang with Will, I slipped back in, went into Caroline's room, and just did it. I keep trying to figure out what I was feeling when I put the pillow over Caroline's face. But I don't remember feeling anything much, even though I should've been scared as Trudi or Leo could've walked in at any time.

It took longer than I thought it would.

Brett was a no-brainer. I was hanging out in the basement when he came into the gym. I knew it was him the second I heard the basketball thumping around in there. I was planning to hide until he left, but then he dropped the ball into the pool and it just seemed like the right thing to do. I snuck up on him as he was trying to reach it. Again, it wasn't planned. I just did it. Picked up one of the weights and *BAM*. I had to hit him twice to knock him out as the first hit just stunned him. The second one cracked his skull and I was lucky

I didn't get any blood on me. Rolling him into the pool wasn't easy. He was way heavier than I am. Dead weight.

Brett was fucked in the head. You could see it in his eyes. I was doing the world a favour. I knew Reuben and Will were right. If Cam and Brett had got hold of the guns, if they'd made Will give them the combination, they could have done anything. They could have gone after Moms or Dad or anyone. And with Brett gone I reckoned at least Gina would have more water, although that backfired because Bonnie lost it.

But still no one came to rescue us and still we couldn't find a way out. I had to think about Moms and Gina and Cait and Sarita. They were my priority.

TBH I hadn't planned who would be next. Cam would have been my Number 1 choice, maybe Reuben as he was dying anyway. Or Will, who you could see wanted to die. It was all down to the dog. Vicki had gone into Greg's condo to use his bathroom and I was in the rec room searching one last time for any soda that might be left behind the bar for Moms. The dog ran in and started barking at the elevator hole. Rats. Must have been. Vicki came in and it was kind of like what happened with Brett. She was trying to drag the dog away, and I snuck up on her and pushed. She'd been so vicious to Moms and Cait and Sarita and pretty much everyone in the whole place that I guess I rationalized she wouldn't be missed.

She didn't scream and I guess I got lucky with that as well.

After Vicki I didn't see the point of getting rid of anyone else. I guess I was resigned to the fact that no one was coming to save us by then.

Dr Levene is right. Writing about it has put it all in perspective. I'm not a serial killer or anything. I'm not Hannibal fucking Lecter or even

UNDER GROUND

Dexter or Jeffrey Dahmer. I didn't do this for fun. No one suffered. I did what I had to do to save Moms and Dad and Gina. There's a lot of crap about gamers being violent etc. etc. blah blah, and if this ever got out they'd blame it all on *WoW* like they did when they found out that the Norwegian guy who shot all those kids on that island was into the game, but this wasn't violence. This wasn't revenge for Brett kicking my ass because he found me fucking his sister. This was survival. Caroline was old, she'd had a stroke, she was going to die anyway. What was the point of giving her our supplies? And I was right, wasn't I? If I hadn't done it then we wouldn't have made it. The others were collateral damage.

People do this kind of shit all the time. It was war. You do what you have to do to survive.

36
GINA

I read Jae's words one more time and close his laptop gently. So much has happened, so much has changed in me. But some things, I realize, always stay the same. He grunts and gurgles behind me.

The twinkling lights of the city and the windows of the apartments opposite us look like a palace made of crystal. And I can't get enough of walking on the streets. There's people all over, pushing trolleys of boxes and racks of clothes, walking, smoking, reading newspapers, laughing, yelling, shoving. I've never lived anywhere this . . . full. And the smell of moving air, real light from the sky that I'll never do without again – I don't care if it's grey or blue. Maybe I've been locked away all my life. It's Sunday, and I haven't been to church. I don't think I'm gonna go again. I'm scared they'll see that the Devil got inside me and that I made peace with it and let it live here. I'd rather sit by this window and watch the real world go by, all the people living their lives without a thought for God or Heaven or Hell.

The warm, sticky trail has made its way across the floor to the chair where I sit and now runs between my bare toes. I lift my feet and fold them on the seat under me. I'll deal with the mess in a bit.

Jae never imagined a backwoods girl like me would get into his computer, but the password was so obvious. Twinki – the name of his elf-thing in that dumb game.

Is he calling to me for help from the couch? What does he expect me to do for him?

I pick up the handgun from beside me, Brett's M1911 that Daddy gave him for his fifteenth birthday, the one with the honeycomb grip. I tamp and polish, spray a bit of oil, ensure the mechanism's smooth, wipe it down clean after every use just like Daddy taught us. I put it to my face and breathe in that magic scent of singe and gun oil. I would never have thought Jae had it in him, smashing Brett's head in with a dumbbell. How does it make me feel? Everyone's asking me that lately.

Jae grunts again from behind me, and I turn. Listlessly, I watch the fluid pooled beneath him where he sits, snaking its way over the parquet floor. I'd better clean it up, though I really don't feel like it.

Daddy instilled that sense of duty in me. He taught me to be useful, to honour the home, to keep things orderly. Momma taught me a lot too; I guess one day I'll be a good wife because of what Momma and Daddy taught me.

I trace the pattern on the grip of the gun, then stand up and bring it to where Jae is sitting. Daddy always taught me to finish what I started.

Jae looks up at me. I'm standing between him and the window and his eyes take a moment to adjust. I try to keep the facts straight in my mind, but I've read so many new things I have to get used to. This man, right here, killed my brother. He says he did it to save his family . . . and me. But he killed that old lady too, and Vicki, and Lord knows if he's telling the truth about any of the rest.

He looks back at the screen and grunts again as the marine he's playing takes a beating from a living corpse.

'You knocked over your coffee again,' I say.

'Yeah, sorry,' he says, twisting his body as if he's actually in the fight on the TV.

Checking the safety and slipping the pistol into my waistband, I sink down to my haunches and kiss his cheek. There's a sudden movement at the corner of my eye. 'There's another one behind you!' I yell. 'Chop his head off!'

'Shit!' Jae's soldier has been clubbed to death by another zombie. Game over.

'Sorry,' I say. 'I distracted you.'

'Don't worry,' he says. 'I've got another life.'